KU-752-332

NOVEMBER OF THE HEART

By the same author

Bitter Sweet
Spring Fancy
Morning Glory
The Hellion
Vows
The Gamble
A Heart Speaks
Years
Separate Beds
Twice Loved
Hummingbird
The Endearment
The Fulfilment
Forgiving
Bygones

NOVEMBER
OF THE HEART

LaVyrle Spencer

HarperCollins*Publishers*

439729

MORAY DISTRICT COUNCIL
DEPARTMENT OF
LEISURE AND LIBRARIES

F

HarperCollins*Publishers*
77–85 Fulham Palace Road,
Hammersmith, London W6 8JB

Published by HarperCollins*Publishers* 1993
1 3 5 7 9 8 6 4 2

First published in the USA by
G.P. Putnam's Sons 1993

Copyright © LaVyrle Spencer 1993

The Author asserts the moral right to
be identified as the author of this work

A catalogue record for this book is
available from the British Library

ISBN 0 00 223974 4

Set in Janson

Printed in Great Britain by
HarperCollinsManufacturing Glasgow

All rights reserved. No part of this publication may be
reproduced, stored in a retrieval system, or transmitted,
in any form or by any means, electronic, mechanical,
photocopying, recording or otherwise, without the prior
permission of the publishers.

This book is sold subject to the condition that it shall not,
by way of trade or otherwise, be lent, re-sold, hired out or
otherwise circulated without the publisher's prior consent
in any form of binding or cover other than that in which it
is published and without a similar condition including this
condition being imposed on the subsequent purchaser.

A great big thank you to Skip and Marge Johnson of the Johnson Boatworks, White Bear Lake, for your invaluable help with the boatbuilding and sailing elements of this book. I couldn't have done it without you two.

Thanks, too, to Ted Glasrud, for giving me the book *Reflections,* which inspired this story, and for introducing me to Skip and Marge.

To my husband,
Dan . . .
after thirty-one years
still the best gift life ever gave me

Chapter
ONE

White Bear Lake, Minnesota
1895

THE dining room of Rose Point Cottage hummed with conversation. Eighteen people sat around its immense mahogany table in the glow of the gaslight chandelier, supping on a third course of asparagus ice surrounded by pickled nasturtium seeds, dinner rolls shaped like swans and butter chips molded into the image of water lily leaves. The table, spread with Irish linen bearing the Barnett family crest, was set with Tiffany silver flatware and Wedgwood Queen's ware. Its centerpiece held precisely fifty Bourbon Madame Isaac Pereire roses from the cottage's own gardens, their overpowering scent scarcely diluted by the nine P.M. breeze fluttering in the lakeside windows.

The walls of the room were decked in William Morris paper spreading grape clusters and acanthus leaves across a burgundy background. The woodwork, crafted of ruby-rich cherry wood, climbed to shoulder level and surrounded the nine-and-a-half-foot windows with wide, ornate moldings from which, at each corner, a hand-carved cherub grinned down upon the gathering.

At the head of the table presided Gideon Barnett, a thickset man with a graying walrus moustache and chins as stacked as thick, poured pudding; at the foot sat his wife, Levinia, overfed too, with large breasts carried as high as a full-bellied sail. She wore her hair to suit her station, like a diadem high upon her head, the sides rolled back in a perfect silver coil, secured by combs and one silk organza rose. The four Barnett children, ages twelve to eighteen, had been allowed at the table tonight, as well as the aunts, Agnes and Henrietta, Gideon's spinster sisters, who were permanent fixtures in the Barnett family. Also present were the elite coterie, members of the White Bear Yacht Club, friends of the Barnetts who—like they—had migrated from Saint Paul to their seasonal cottages here for the summer.

The supper was to have been a victory celebration: The Minnetonka Yacht Club, amid much hoopla and publicity for the burgeoning sport, had challenged the White Bear Yacht Club to a three-year series of regattas. The first had been run today. In a society where sailing had become an obsession and its participants nearly rabid in their zeal to excel, the afternoon's defeat had left as bitter an aftertaste as a lost lawsuit.

"Damn!" Commodore Gideon Barnett exploded, thumping a fist on the table. "It's unthinkable that one of us didn't win!" He was still wearing his white duck trousers and blue sweater with *WBYC* in big white letters across his breast. "The *Tartar*'s faster than the *Kite* and everyone knows it!" Barnett banged the table again and his goblets chimed together.

At the foot of the table Levinia lofted her left eyebrow and shot him a reproving glance: The stemware was Waterford, from a matched set of twenty-four.

"We should have changed sail plans!" Gideon continued.

"Changed sail plans?" replied his friend Nathan DuVal. "She already carries six hundred and seventy feet of sail. That's about all a seventeen-footer can handle, Gid, you know that."

"Then we should have made them out of silk and saved weight. Didn't I say all along we should have tried silk?"

Nathan went on with much more forbearance than Gideon. "The problem's not with the sail, Gid, it's with the drag. The *Tartar* seems bottom-heavy to me."

"Then we'll reduce the drag! By next year—mark my words!—we'll reduce the drag and win that second race!"

"The question is how."

"How?" Gideon Barnett threw up both hands. "I don't know how, but I for one refuse to lose ten thousand dollars to those damned Minnetonka sandbaggers, not when it was *they* who challenged *us* to these three years of races!"

Levinia said, "Nobody forced you to place so large a bet, Gideon. You could as easily have made it a hundred dollars." The betting, however, was as keenly enjoyed as the races themselves, and the members of the club cheerfully put up their collected ten thousand dollars.

A servant stepped to Gideon's right elbow and inquired quietly, "Are you through with your asparagus, sir?"

Gideon flapped a hand and barked, "Yes, take it away." To his wife, he railed, "Every man at this table has an equal stake in these regattas, Levinia, and none of us wants to lose, especially not to *that* bunch, with all the newspapers in America watching what happens, and Tim here photographing the event." He referred to Tim Iversen, a club member and a successful photographer, who had chronicled the formation of the yacht club itself from its beginnings. "The money aside, I'm the commodore of this yacht club, and I detest losing. So the question remains—how do we come up with a boat that'll beat theirs?"

Gideon's daughter Lorna had been biting her tongue long enough. From halfway down the table she spoke up. "We could hire the Herreshoff brothers to design and build one."

Every eye in the room swerved to the pretty eighteen-year-old who sat with her brown eyes fixed upon her father. Her auburn hair was combed in a "Gibson girl" pompadour, its intentional droop and neckline squiggles so much more alluring than her mother's braided crown. She had worn it so ever since the previous summer, when Mr. Charles Dana Gibson himself had been a guest at Rose Point Cottage, and had indulged her with long interludes of conversation about the personification of his "girls" and the message they conveyed: that women could have freedom and individuality while remaining feminine. In the wake of Gibson's visit, Lorna had not only changed her hairstyle, she had eschewed her elaborate silks and bustles for the more casual shirtwaist and skirt, which she wore tonight. As she faced her father, her brown eyes seemed to sparkle with challenge.

"Couldn't we, Papa?"

"The Herreshoff brothers?" her father repeated. "From Providence?"

"Why not? Certainly you can afford them."

"What do you know about the Herreshoff brothers?"

"I can read, Papa. Their names are in practically every issue of *Outing* magazine. Do you know of anyone better?"

Lorna Barnett knew full well her father disliked her interest in the unladylike sport of sailing, to say nothing of tennis. If he had his way she would sit through this entire meal biting her tongue, as a lady ought. Lorna regarded true ladies, however, as unmitigated bores. Furthermore, it salved her secret sense of retaliation to realize that her father blamed himself for her newfound attraction to sports, which Mr. Gibson had so encouraged. After all, it was her father who'd invited Gibson to Minnesota. No sooner had the young artist arrived, with his radical views on liberating American females, than Lorna had adopted the habits and dress of Gibson's "boy-girl." Gideon had blustered, "This is outrageous! A daughter of mine slapping around a tennis court with her ankles flashing! And coercing her friends to form a female contingent of the White Bear Yacht Club. Why, any fool knows a woman's place is in a drawing room!"

Now, at a dinner party before all his friends, Gideon's daughter had the temerity to suggest a solution to their woes.

"Do you know of anyone better?" she repeated when he continued glowering at her.

Support came, however, from young Taylor DuVal, who was seated next to Lorna.

"You'll have to admit, Gideon, she has something there."

Gideon drew his eyes from his daughter to Taylor, who at twenty-four already resembled his father in both appearance and business acumen, a dapper and bright young man who would surely go places. Around the table glances were exchanged among the men—Gideon, Taylor, Nathan, Percy Tufts, George Whiting and Joseph Armfield—the most powerful and persuasive cartel not only of the White

Bear Yacht Club, but of the Minnesota financial scene in general. They read like the *Who's Who* in Minnesota, their vast wealth earned in railroading, iron ore mining, flour milling and, in Gideon Barnett's case, lumbering. Lorna was right: They certainly could afford to hire the Herreshoff brothers to build them a winning sloop, and if their wives objected . . .

But the wives wouldn't object. Levinia's chiding meant little. She and all the other wives in her social circle enjoyed the notoriety brought about by their husbands' yachting. It was considered chic, privileged and newsworthy enough to get the women's photographs in the newspapers right along with the men's. Every wife present realized she was measured primarily by the length of her husband's shadow, and none would have voiced the slightest objection to the commissioning of a sailboat by the best-known boat designers in America.

"It could be done. We could commission them," Barnett said.

"Those New Englanders know how to build boats, always have."

"They'd know about the relative merits of silk sails, too."

"We could telegraph them immediately, tomorrow!"

"And have a scale drawing in hand by the end of the summer, and the boat itself by next May, in time for the yachting season."

The disgruntlement of earlier had been displaced by excitement as the men went on discussing possibilities with bright expressions on their faces.

Meanwhile, around the table the third-course dishes had been removed. A server approached Levinia's elbow and announced quietly, "Your main course, ma'am."

Levinia looked up, twin creases between her eyebrows, while the man simply stood there with a covered gold-rimmed plate in his hand. "Well, put it down, for heaven's sake!" she ordered in an undertone.

From three inches above the tabletop Jens Harken dropped the heated plate. The domed silver cover bounced to one side and rang out like a bell buoy.

Levinia looked up. She, like every other wife there, might be nothing more than her husband's shadow in most regards, but the one place she reigned was at the head of her own household staff.

Abashed that her prowess as a hostess should be compromised by that staff's incompetence, she inquired sharply, "Where is Chester?"

"Gone home, ma'am. His father is ill."

"And Glynnis?"

"Ill, ma'am, with a bad tooth."

"And who are you?"

"Jens Harken, ma'am, the kitchen odd-jobs man."

Levinia's face had turned scarlet. On the night of an important dinner party, the kitchen odd-jobs man! The housekeeper would hear about this! She scowled at the outsized young fellow, trying to recall if she'd ever seen him before, then ordered, "Remove the cover."

He whisked it away to reveal roasted teal in a surround of alternating Jerusalem artichokes and brussels sprouts. Around these an arabesque of oven-browned mashed potatoes formed a perfect oval frame.

Levinia examined the work of art, selected a fork, poked at the duck, nodded to Jens and said, "Proceed."

Jens went sedately through the swinging door. On the other side he broke into a run, carrying him the length of a ridiculously long hall, through a second swinging door and finally into the kitchen.

"Hell's afire, fourteen feet of passageway just to make sure smells don't drift into the dining room? Rich people are crazy!"

Hulduh Schmitt, the head cook, thrust two plates into his hands and ordered, "Go!"

Eight more times he ran the length of that passageway, careening to a halt just before reaching the dining room doorway, trying to hide his breathlessness as he entered and placed the dinner plates before the diners. On each trip he overheard bits of conversation about today's regatta and why Barnett's sloop, the *Tartar*, had lost, and how they could make sure one of their next year's entries would win, and whether it was the drag or the sails or the distribution of sandbag ballast or the hired skipper that had caused the afternoon's loss. Oh, they were a zealous lot, all right, bitten by the sailing bug so badly it had spread over them like a rash, this desire to best the Minnetonka club.

And Jens Harken was the one who knew how they could do it.

"Hulduh, find me a paper!" he ordered, bursting through the kitchen door with the last two silver plate covers.

Hulduh removed her mouth from the double-sided bombe mold into which she'd been blowing in an effort to free the ice cream. "A paper? What for?"

"Just find it, please, and a pencil, too. I'll work tomorrow, my day off, if you just find it fast and don't ask questions."

"Sure, and lose my job," remarked the German woman, giving one more puff into the mold, then guiding a perfect fluted cone of ice cream onto a waiting almond-flavored meringue nest. "What would you be wanting with a pencil and paper? Here, put this one in the ice cave," she ordered the second kitchen maid, who took the dessert and placed it, on its saucer, in a metal box full of crushed ice, then closed its lid.

Jens dropped the domed plate covers into the zinc sink and zipped across the hot kitchen to take the cook's two puffy red cheeks into his hands.

"Please, Mrs. Schmitt, where?"

"You're a nuisance, Jens Harken, and a big one at that," she scolded. "Can't you see I've got ten more ice creams to unmold here before the missus rings for dessert?"

"We'll help you, won't we? Here, everybody—" Jens motioned to the first and second kitchen maids, Ruby and Colleen. He picked up a bombe mold out of the ice chest. "How much should we blow?"

"Ach, here, you'll ruin it, and it'll mean my job!" Mrs. Schmitt snatched the copper mold from his hand and began unscrewing its stem base. "On the wall, the list for the housekeeper, you can use the tail end of that, but I don't see what's so important it needs writing in the middle of the most important dinner of the year."

"You're right! It could turn out to be the most important dinner of the year, especially for me, and if it does I promise you my eternal love and gratitude, my dear and lovely Mrs. Schmitt."

Hulduh Schmitt succumbed to his charm, as always, with a flap of the hand and a tinge of additional color in her cheeks. "Oh, go on with you," she said, then covered the screwhole with a small piece of muslin and continued her blowing.

Jens neatly ripped off the tail end of the paper and printed in well-formed letters: *I know why you lost the race. I can help you win next year.*

"Mrs. Schmitt, wait! Give me that plate." He snatched a dessert plate from her hands, placed the note on it and covered it with one of her fluffy, tan meringue nests, letting a corner of the note show. "There. Now put the ice cream on top."

"Of that paper? You're the one who's crazy. We'll both lose our jobs. What does it say?"

"Never mind what it says, just blow into that mold and get the ice cream on this."

Mrs. Schmitt got stubborn. "Nossir, Jens Harken, not on your life. I'm the cook. What goes out of this kitchen is my responsibility, and there ain't no desserts going out of here with notes underneath them."

He saw that unless he told her, she'd remain adamant. "All right, it's for Mr. Barnett. I told him I know how he can win that regatta next year."

"Ah, boats again. You and your boats."

"Well, I don't intend to be a kitchen handyman forever. One of these days someone will listen to me."

"Oh, sure, and I'm gonna marry the governor and become first lady."

"He could do worse, Mrs. Schmitt," Jens teased. "He could do worse." Mrs. Schmitt got that flat-chinned look he knew too well. When he saw he was getting nowhere, he promised, "If it backfires I'll take all the blame. I'll tell them I was the one who put the note in there even after you warned me not to."

In the end, Levinia Barnett herself decided the issue by yanking the satin bellpull in the dining room and tinkling the brass bell above the kitchen doorway. Mrs. Schmitt looked up at it and grew flustered. "See what you do! All this talk and I don't have the ice creams ready. Go, go! Take the first ones and hope I got enough hot breath to keep them coming steady to the end."

In the dining room, Levinia kept a hawk's eye upon the odd-jobs man, Harken, as he brought in the desserts. After his first faux pas he performed the remainder of the serving without mishap. The ice-cream molds still had sharp edges in spite of the summer heat, and each was delivered and placed on the table with the inconspicuous motions she expected from her help. The peach ice cream was covered with a thin layer of apricot ice and filled with sweetened strawberries. The meringues were crisp, appropriately tanned, and the plates beneath them chilled. Surely the ladies present could find no fault with the food.

As if divining her hostess's thoughts, Cecilia Tufts praised, "What an exquisite dessert, Levinia. Where *ever* did you find your cook?"

"She found me over fourteen years ago, when she very cleverly had some of her special tortes delivered to me by messenger. She's been with me ever since, but lately she's been making sounds about quitting—she's well over fifty already. But I don't know what I should do without her."

"I know what you mean. Anyone bright enough to know their elbow from a soup bone seems to be going into service as a governess these days, and one can scarcely find kitchen help capable of—"

"Levinia!" It was Gideon, interrupting from the opposite end of the table. His consonants snapped like sails taking wind. His mouth was as tight as a bowline knot. "May I speak to you a moment?"

At the tone of his voice, Levinia's heart gave a thump. She looked up across the low-sprawling roses to find Gideon telegraphing disapproval with every angle of his body. A mouthful of apricot ice seemed to slip down her throat of its own volition while she wondered frantically what could be amiss.

"Now, Gideon?"

"Yes, now!"

He pushed back his chair while Levinia's blood rushed up her neck and she touched a linen napkin to the corner of her mouth.

"Excuse me," she murmured, leaving the table and following her husband into the servants' passage. The servants' passage, of all places, while her closest lady friends looked on! The narrow, windowless hall was dimly lit by a single gas wall sconce and held the faint stench of boiled brussels sprouts, which, thankfully, had not escaped into the dining room before the vegetables themselves were served.

"Gideon, whatever—"

"What in the *deuce* is going on here, Levinia!"

"Keep your voice down, Gideon, I'm already dying of mortification at being summoned to the servants' passage by my own husband in the middle of a dinner party! We have a library and a morning room, either of which would—"

"I make enough money to keep you in silks and ice creams and two fancy houses! Must I oversee the kitchen staff as well?" Into her hands he thrust a note. It had a strawberry stain on its edge and stuck to his thumb when he tried to release it.

She pulled it from his skin and read it while he informed her acidly, "It was *in my dessert.*"

Her eyes shot up. "In your dessert? Surely not, Gideon."

"It was in my dessert, I tell you, obviously put there by someone in the kitchen. The kitchen is your domain, Levinia. Who's in charge of it?"

"I . . . why . . . w . . ." Levinia's mouth hung open. "Mrs. Lovik." Mrs. Lovik was the housekeeper, whose job it was to hire all the kitchen and cleaning staff.

"She goes!"

"But Gideon—"

"And so does the cook! What's her name?"

"Mrs. Schmitt, but Gideon—" He was storming down the passageway toward the kitchen, leaving her little choice but to follow.

"And whoever wrote this note also goes, if it's neither of them, and I can scarcely believe a cook or a housekeeper would have the temerity to suggest they know how to win a regatta that the entire White Bear Yacht Club couldn't win." He rammed open the kitchen door with Levinia at his heels and bellowed, *"Mrs. Schmitt! Who is Mrs. Schmitt?"*

There were four people in the room and only three were cowering. Gideon pinned his eyes on the one who wasn't, the dolt who had dropped Levinia's plate earlier. "I repeat! *Who is Mrs. Schmitt?"* he roared.

A woman shaped like her own bombe mold, with a face as red as the coals in her kitchen range, whispered, "I am, sir."

Gideon skewered her with his eyes. "Are you responsible for this?"

Her starched white cap trembled as she gripped one hand with the other upon the soiled paunch of her white floor-length apron.

Jens spoke up. "No, she's not, sir. I am."

Gideon snapped his attention to the offender. He let his disdain impart itself fully, for ten long seconds, before speaking. "Harken, is it?"

"Yes, sir."

The man neither trembled nor quailed but stood beside the zinc sink with his shoulders erect and his hands at his sides. His handsome face was shiny with sweat, a trickle of which ran from his left temple to his jaw. He had a direct gaze, blue eyes, fair hair and the shaved face Levinia demanded in all her male help.

"You're fired," Gideon declared. "Collect your things and leave immediately."

"Very well. But if you want to win that regatta, you'd better listen to me—"

"No, you're going to listen to me!" In a flash Gideon crossed the slate floor and thrust his index finger into Harken's chest, hard. "I own this house; you work in it! You don't speak to me unless spoken to. Neither do you embarrass my wife and myself by delivering missives in the dessert when we are entertaining half the residents of White Bear Lake! And you sure as hell don't give *me* advice on how to race boats! Is that understood?"

"Why?" Jens replied calmly. "You want to win, don't you?"

Gideon spun away with his fists clenched, forcing Levinia to leap aside. "Have him out of here within the hour, Schmitt, and yourself right behind him. Your week's pay will be sent to you."

Harken jumped after him and grabbed his arm. "It's got nothing to do with canvas sails or poor skippers or too much ballast. Mr. DuVal is right. It's got to do with drag. The sloops you've been racing have to cut *through* the water. What you need is a skimmer that'll sail *over* it. I can design it for you."

Barnett turned slowly, a superior expression on his face. "Oh, you're the one. I've heard about you."

Harken dropped Barnett's arm. "Yes, I imagine you have, sir."

"Every yacht club in Minnesota has turned you away."

"Yessir, and some on the east coast, too. But one of these days someone's going to listen, and when he does his boat is going to sail circles around the fastest sloop ever built anywhere in the world."

"Well, I'll say this for you, boy. You've got gall, offensive as it is. What I want to know is what you're doing working in *my* kitchen?"

"A man's got to eat."

"Well, eat somewhere else. I don't want to see you anywhere near this place ever again!"

Barnett stalked back into the passage with his wife plucking at his sleeve. The door swung closed. "Gideon, stop this instant!"

Her shout was heard clearly in the dining room, where Lorna watched her parents' guests exchange uncomfortable glances. Indeed, everything that followed could be heard clearly as the guests stopped eating and Lorna fixed her eyes on the passageway door.

"Gideon, I said stop!"

When he refused, Levinia grabbed his elbow and forced the issue. Gideon relented with an air of long-suffering.

"Levinia, our guests are waiting."

"Oh yes, this is a fine time for you to remember our guests, after you've turned me into an object of ridicule before them and the help! How dare you, Gideon Barnett, undermine me with my own staff! I will not have Mrs. Schmitt dismissed simply because you're offended by one of the kitchen staff. She's the best cook we've ever had!" She squeezed his sleeve so hard she inadvertently pinched him.

He winced and yelped, "Ouch! Levinia, we can't have the staff—"

"We can't have the staff witnessing you overriding my decisions. If they think I'm not in charge of my own domicile, their respect for me will vanish; then how shall I be expected to order my own kitchen staff? I insist on going back in there and telling Mrs. Schmitt she can stay, and if you don't like it—"

The argument had grown louder and louder until Lorna, now blushing herself, could sit by quietly no longer. Whatever were Mama and Papa thinking to strike up an argument in the kitchen passage in the middle of a dinner party!

"Excuse me," she said quietly, and rose from the table. "Please continue eating, everyone."

She hit the swinging door with both hands just as Gideon was shouting, "Levinia, I don't give a damn—"

"Mother! Father! What on earth is going on!" Lorna halted, scowling, as the door swung shut behind her. "All of your guests are staring at this door and shifting on their chairseats! Don't you realize they can hear every word that's being said? I can't believe you two are out here fighting over the kitchen staff! What's gotten into you?"

Gideon tugged at the waist of his sweater and resumed an air of dignity. "I'll be there in a moment. Go back in and suggest that they retire to the parlor, and play them something on the piano, will you, Lorna?"

She stared at the two of them as if they'd gone mad, then left the door swinging once again.

When she was gone Gideon said in a much quieter tone, "All right, Levinia, she can stay."

"And Mrs. Lovik, too. I'm not the least inclined to spend my summer training a new housekeeper."

"All right, all right . . ." He raised both palms in surrender. "They can both stay, but tell that . . . that"—he pointed a quivering finger at the kitchen—"upstart in there to get his hide out of my house within the hour or I'll have it upholstering one of the chairs, do you understand?"

With a sniff and a lift of her nose, Levinia swung away.

In the kitchen, everyone was speaking at once. When Levinia pushed open the door the babble ceased. The maids, washing dishes at the sink, let their wrists hang limp against it. Each bobbed her knees once. Harken and Mrs. Schmitt, near the ice chest, halted an argument and self-consciously closed their mouths. The room was a good ninety-five degrees, steamy and strong-smelling yet from the brussels sprouts. Levinia had the fleeting thought that she'd rather eat raw food than cook it here.

"My husband spoke precipitously, Mrs. Schmitt. I do hope you won't take offense. The food tonight was splendid, and I very much hope you'll stay."

Mrs. Schmitt sniffed once and shifted her weight to the opposite leg. With the skirt of her soiled apron she dried the sweat from beneath her nose. "Well, I don't know, ma'am. My mother's getting on toward eighty and all alone since my father died. I've been thinking it might be time I gave up this hard work and went to take care of her. I have a little money put by, and to tell the truth, I'm getting on myself."

"Why, nonsense. You're just as spry as the day I hired you. And look at the magnificent dinner you just prepared without the slightest hitch."

Mrs. Schmitt did something she'd never done before: She sat down in her mistress's presence. She plopped her heavy form onto a small stool and her spare flesh seemed to droop over its edge like a soufflé when the oven door is opened.

"I don't know," she said, shaking her head tiredly. "I get dizzy these days, blowing into those ice-cream molds. And all the hurrying . . . Some days my heart gets palpitations."

"Please, Mrs. Schmitt . . ." Levinia joined her hands together like an opera singer delivering an aria. "I just . . . Well, I don't know what I'd do without you, and now in the middle of the summer out here in the country, I cannot think where I'd find anyone to replace you."

Mrs. Schmitt's fleshy forearm in its rolled-up sleeve rested on the scarred wooden table in the center of the room while she studied her employer and considered.

Levinia's hands gripped each other tighter.

Mrs. Schmitt glanced at Ruby, at Colleen, still gaping, motionless, at the sink, and with a *flap-flap* of one hand and not so much as a word, sent them scuttling back to work.

Levinia said, "Perhaps an extra three dollars a week would convince you."

"Oh, that'd be nice, ma'am, it surely would, but it wouldn't ease the work none, especially with him going." The cook thumbed over her shoulder at Harken.

"I'd be willing to put on an extra kitchen maid."

"To tell the truth, ma'am, I don't want to train a new one any more than you do. I'll take the extra money, and I thank you, ma'am, but if I stay, he stays. He's a good worker, the best I've ever had in the kitchen, and he's willing. Like tonight, filling in when he wouldn't have had to. And he does the heavy work, lifting and carrying and washing vegetables, and pretty soon the canning starts, as you know. Those boilers get heavy."

Levinia's corset stays seemed to bond themselves to her ribs. She regarded Harken with her sternest expression and made a sudden decision. "Very well, but I want you to stay out of my husband's sight, and you must promise me, Harken, that you'll never—*never!*—again do anything like you did tonight."

"No ma'am, I won't."

"And you are to stay strictly to the kitchen and the vegetable gardens, is that understood?"

Harken gave a slight bow in answer.

"Then it's settled. And, Mrs. Schmitt, in the morning I'd like you to prepare the coddled eggs on spinach boats that Mr. Barnett loves so much."

"Coddled eggs it is, ma'am."

Without further word, Levinia left the kitchen. All the way along the length of the stuffy, ill-lit passageway she felt her heart thunder at the realization that she had defied Gideon's wishes. He'd be incensed when he found out, but the kitchen was her domain—hers! He had his politics, and his business, and his yachting and hunting, but what did she have besides the pretty compliments from her peers when perfect ice-cream molds and exotic vegetables came out of the kitchen?

At the door to the dining room she paused, adjusted her corset, patted her forehead, discovered it was beaded with sweat from that insufferable kitchen, found a handkerchief in a hidden pocket of her skirt, wiped it dry, patted her hair and went in to face her guests.

The dinner party was ruined, of course. Though the guests tried valiantly to pretend they'd heard nothing of what was said in the kitchen passage, they'd heard most of it. The women, ever competitive when it came to hostessing social gatherings, exchanged sly, silent, superior messages while treating Levinia as if she'd just heard her dressmaker had died.

At the piano, Lorna observed her mother's reentry, Levinia's forced calm while ordering Daphne and Theron up to bed. She was still rattled, Lorna could tell, and having trouble disguising it. Whatever had caused the set-to? Had the handsome blond server prompted it? Who was he, anyway? And who had been responsible for his serving in the dining room when he hadn't been trained to do so?

To draw attention away from her mother, Lorna said, "Come on, everybody, let's sing 'After the Ball.'"

Immediately Taylor DuVal moved up behind Lorna, rested his hands on her shoulders and began singing robustly. Taylor was a good sport, always willing to do whatever Lorna suggested. The others, however, barely peeped, so Lorna shut the key cover and left the hostessing to her mother, suggesting she and Taylor step out onto the veranda.

Immediately her sister Jenny jumped up and announced, "I'm coming, too!"

Lorna got disgusted. A sixteen-year-old sister could be such a pest. Only this summer Levinia had allowed Jenny to stay up later with the adults on occasions such as this, and she'd been hounding Taylor ever since. Not only did she make moon eyes at him every chance she got, she ran back and told Levinia everything that was talked about.

"Isn't it your bedtime?" Lorna asked pointedly.

"Mother said I could stay up until midnight."

Lorna checked with Taylor. Behind Jenny's back he shrugged and feigned helplessness.

Lorna hid a smile and said, "Oh, all right, then, you can come along."

The veranda crossed the entire front of the house and wrapped around two corners. Wicker chairs, tables and chaise longues were scattered upon it, splashed by the light from the parlor and morning room windows. It smelled of roses and must, from the climber on the south trellis and the cushions that had been in storage all winter.

The estate itself was situated on the eastern point of Manitou Island, with White Bear, the lake, spreading in a cloverleaf shape to the north, east and south around it, and White Bear, the village, spread along the northwesterly shore of Snyder's Bay, behind it. The house was set back seventy-five feet from the water, with the yard fanning out flat all around it, giving way to gardens, both formal and utilitarian, and a glasshouse, where a full gardening staff kept Levinia in flowers and the family in both summer and winter produce.

Now, on this warm summer evening, the fruits of their labors scented the night. It was June, with the gardens in full bloom and the imported Italian fountains gurgling background music. The moon had risen and lay golden as a trumpet across the water. In the distance the naphtha launch *Don Quixote* could be heard, *splut-splut-splutting* its way back toward the town dock with a load of concertgoers from the Ramaley Pavilion across the lake. Nearer lay the dim finger of Rose Point's own dock and, beside it, a mast, scarcely swaying in the soft lap of waves.

The romantic setting, however, was wasted tonight. Jenny gripped Lorna's arm the moment they reached the shadows. "Tell me what happened in the kitchen, Lorna! Did Papa go back there? What was it all about, anyway?"

"We mustn't discuss it in front of Taylor. Jenny, where are your manners?"

"Oh, never mind me," Taylor said. "I'm just an old family friend, remember?"

"Come on, Lorna, tell me."

"Well, I don't know everything, but I know this much—Papa wanted to fire the cook and Mama wouldn't let him."

"The cook? Why? Everybody loved the food tonight."

"I don't know. Papa's never been in the kitchen in his whole life, much less in the middle of a dinner party, and Mama was livid with him. They were shouting at each other fit to kill."

"I know. We could hear it in the dining room, couldn't we, Taylor?"

Lorna recounted what she'd heard, but the sisters could make no sense of any of it. Lorna found herself as baffled by the scene as Jenny was, but before they could discuss it further Tim Iversen wandered out to the veranda, interrupting their speculation. He lit his pipe as if he meant to stay awhile and the conversation shifted to the photographs he'd taken of the regatta that day and what newspapers might run them.

Soon others drifted out of the house to join them, and the two sisters found themselves with no further opportunity to discuss the altercation during dinner.

Lorna was still puzzling over it when the party broke up. She and Jenny went upstairs together, leaving Gideon and Levinia to wish their last guests good night.

"Has Mama said anything about that scene in the kitchen?" Jenny whispered as they climbed.

"No, nothing."

"So you still don't have any idea what it was about?"

"No, but I aim to find out." Upstairs, Lorna kissed her younger sister's cheek. " 'Night, Jen." They went to their separate rooms— Jenny into the one she shared with Daphne, and Lorna into her own. Inside, it was hot in spite of the high ceilings and ample windows. She removed her earrings and lay them on her dressing table, then her shoes, which she left beside a chair. Fully clothed, she sat down to wait for the sounds of activity to grow quiet in the hall. When she was sure Papa, Mama and Jenny had finished traipsing back and forth to the bathroom, she opened her door and listened a moment, then slipped out.

All was quiet. The hall lamps had been extinguished. The aunts had come up a little earlier and were undoubtedly asleep.

In the dark, she tiptoed past the main central staircase to the crooked servants' stairway at the very end of the hall. It led from their third-floor bedrooms directly to the kitchen, accessible from the second-floor hallway through a door that was always kept closed.

Lorna opened it now and turned up her nose at the stale smell of brussels sprouts. In spite of it, she descended.

When she opened the kitchen door and peeked inside she found four people still there: two maids, the cook—Mrs. Schmitt—and the fellow Harken, who had dropped Mama's plate tonight. The maids were putting away the last of the dishes. Mrs. Schmitt was slicing ham and Harken was sweeping the floor. Goodness, he was a treat for the eyes, she thought, watching him a moment before he knew she was there.

Finally, realizing how improper it was to admire the help, she said, "Hello," and everyone stopped dead still.

Mrs. Schmitt remembered her manners first. "Hello, miss."

Lorna stepped inside and closed the door softly behind her. "What time do they let you go to bed, anyway?"

"We're done now, miss, just finishing up."

On the wall hung a hexagonal clock the diameter of a dishpan. Lorna glanced at it.

"At twelve-forty?"

"Tomorrow's our day off, miss. Soon as breakfast is over we can leave to go to church ourselves. All we have to do is get the cold buffet foods ready for the other two meals first."

"Oh . . . yes, of course . . . Well . . ." Lorna flashed a smile. "I had no idea you worked such long hours."

"Only on party days, miss." The room fell silent. The two kitchen maids stood with their hands full of clean copper kettles. Harken had stopped sweeping and stood with his hands draped over the broom handle. Ten seconds of discomfort passed.

"Is there something I can get you, miss?" the cook finally asked.

"Um . . . oh . . . oh, no! I was just wondering what . . . well . . ." Lorna realized her mistake immediately. The question she'd come down to ask was beyond all impertinence, even to the kitchen help. How could she inquire of these tired, sweaty people what they had done wrong tonight to set her father off? "It's very warm upstairs. I wondered if you have any fruit juice down here."

"We haven't squeezed the juices for morning yet, but I believe there's a little judy left over, miss. Could I get you a cup of that?"

Judy contained champagne and rum; Lorna had never been allowed to drink it.

"It's mostly green tea and mint, miss," the cook added.

"Oh, well, in that case, yes . . . a cup would be grand."

The cook went off to get it. While she was gone, Harken spoke up. "If I may be so impertinent, miss, I imagine that you're wondering what all the commotion was about in the kitchen earlier."

For the first time she looked square into his eyes—they were as blue as the spots behind one's eyelids after watching a bolt of lightning.

Harken looked right back, for she was too pretty to deny himself the pleasure.

"It was me they were angry with," he admitted forthrightly. "I put a note in your father's ice cream."

"A note? In my father's ice cream?" Lorna's mouth dropped open in amazement while Jens resumed sweeping. "Did you really?"

He cast her a quarter glance, very brief. "Yes, ma'am."

"*You* put a note in *my* father's ice cream?" The corners of her mouth began to twitch. When she burst out laughing, the kitchen help began exchanging uncertain glances. She covered her mouth with both hands and filled the room with sound, finally managing, as her chortles subsided, "My father, Gideon Barnett?"

Harken had stopped sweeping to openly enjoy this very improper exchange with her. "That's right."

"What did it say?"

"That I know how he can win the regatta next year."

She controlled her grin but let her eyes grow mischievous. "And what did he say?"

"You're fired."

"Oh, my . . ." She sobered with an effort, realizing the poor young fellow probably found the situation less than amusing. "I'm sorry."

"No need to be. Mrs. Schmitt saved me. She said she wouldn't stay on without me."

"So you're not fired after all?"

He shook his head slowly.

She studied him with an inquisitive look. "Do you really know how my father could win the regatta next year?"

"Yes, but he wouldn't listen."

"Of course not, my father doesn't listen to anyone. You took a terrible chance, trying to give him advice."

"I know that now."

"Tell me—how can he win the regatta?"

"By changing the shape of his boat. I could do that for him. I could—"

Mrs. Schmitt returned with a cup of liquid as clear and pale as a peridot.

"Here you are, miss."

"Oh, thank you." Lorna took it and held it in both hands. Somehow, with the cook standing close, propriety reared its head and told Lorna she ought not be standing here discussing her family business with the kitchen help, no matter how interested she was in sailing. She cast a glance at the two maids, who still remained motionless, awestruck by her presence. Suddenly she realized she was keeping them from getting to bed.

"Well, thank you again," Lorna said brightly. "And good night."

The maids bobbed at the knees and blushed.

"Good night, Mrs. Schmitt."

"Good night, miss."

And after the faintest pause . . . "Good night, Harken." She threw one more glance into his very blue eyes. Outwardly, he neither smiled nor flustered but showed only the respect a kitchen servant should have for his betters. He simply nodded good night, but as she walked away his eyes scanned her rear profile from head to heel and his hands took a firmer grip on the broom handle. It was none of his business, but a man would have to be flat-out unconscious not to wonder. As she reached the servants' stairway and put her hand on the doorknob, his words stopped her.

"Might I ask, miss, which one you are? There are three of you, we are told."

She paused and looked back over her shoulder. "I'm Lorna. The oldest."

Lorna, the oldest, he thought, keeping the admiration from showing in his eyes.

"Ah," he said quietly. "Well, good night, then, Miss Lorna. Rest well."

She rested, however not at all well. How could she, when a kitchen servant's very blue eyes got between her and sleep? When that very same servant had had the temerity to slip a note to Papa and tell him how to win a regatta? When she herself was dying to know how to win a regatta? When the night's events had caused the most notorious set-to between Papa and Mama that *all* their friends were bound to be talking about tomorrow morning? When she had tasted her first judy and gotten the slightest bit flushed and fanciful from it? And taken over Mama's hostessing duties for even such a short and wonderful while, and played the piano for the guests, and exchanged secret messages with Taylor on the veranda, and felt sure that if they'd found a moment alone Taylor would have kissed her?

How could a young woman of eighteen sleep on a warm summer night when life was pushing at her bosom like a wing pushes at a chrysalis before it unfolds?

Chapter
TWO

I N the master suite of Rose Point
Cottage, Levinia donned a great
white tent of a nightgown with long, full sleeves, and in spite of the
heat buttoned it to the throat before stepping from behind her dressing room screen, properly attired for bed. Mattie, her maid, waited
beside the dressing table.

Wordlessly Levinia sat down. Mattie removed the silk organza
rose and combs and brushed Levinia's hair, then plaited it loosely in
a single thick braid. When the end was tied, she inquired, "Will there
be anything else, ma'am?"

Levinia rose, still regal in spite of relinquishing her crown. She
rarely thanked the help: Their pay was their thanks. Furthermore,
thanks spawned complacency, and complacency spawned laziness.
She tipped up her lips in a smile never quite realized, and said,
"Nothing more, Mattie, good night."

"Good night, ma'am."

Levinia posed as erect as a holy statue until the door closed, then
whipped up her nightgown and indulged in a frenzy of scratching at
the deep red ruts left in her belly by her corset stays. She scratched
until her skin grew raw, muttering bland expletives, then rebuttoned
the waistband of her cotton pantaloons, extinguished the gaslight and
entered the bedroom.

Gideon was sitting up in bed smoking a cigar, looking as if he
wanted to grind it out in the center of her forehead.

The mattress was high; she always felt conspicuous climbing up onto it when he was watching. "Must you smoke that detestable thing in here? It smells like burning dung."

"It's my bed, Levinia! I'll smoke in it if I want to."

She flounced onto her side, presenting her back, and jerked the sheet to her armpits, though even her feet were sweating. She'd be hanged if she'd lie on top of the sheet. Every time she did he came poking and prodding, expecting to do *that* again. She wondered for the ten thousandth time how old a man had to get before he grew tired of it.

He went on sullying the air above her head with that rank weed, because he knew how she hated it, and because he'd been bested by her tonight, which he hated.

All right, she thought, *two can play the same game.*

"I think you should know, Gideon, that Mrs. Schmitt refused to stay unless I kept Harken on, so I said he could stay, too."

Behind her he choked and coughed.

"You . . . did . . . *what?*"

"I told Harken he could stay. If that's what it takes to keep Mrs. Schmitt, that's how it'll be."

He gripped her shoulder and flattened her onto her back. "Over my dead body!"

She glared at him, her hands clutching the sheet to her chest. "You embarrassed me tonight, Gideon. You made us laughingstocks, raising such a furor in the middle of a dinner party, and all because nobody can tell you what to do. Well, *I'm* telling you, because it's the only way I can save face in front of my friends. The word will leak out—it always does. Our servants will tell the DuVals' servants, and theirs will tell the Tufts' and pretty soon the whole island will know that Levinia Barnett cannot command her own household staff. So Mrs. Schmitt stays and Harken stays, and if you're going to make a fuss about it and blow that stinking smoke all around the bedroom just because I have the upper hand for once, I'll be happy to go into the dressing room and sleep on the chaise."

"Oh, you'd like that, wouldn't you, Levinia? Then you wouldn't have to touch me, even in your sleep!"

"Let me go, Gideon. It's hideously hot."

"It's always hideously hot, isn't it? Or you're hideously tired, or you're afraid the children will hear, or my sisters will hear. There's always some excuse, isn't there, Levinia!"

"Gideon, what's gotten into you?"

Holding both her wrists crossed on her chest, he shucked down the sheet, reached beneath her nightie and began freeing the waist button on her pantaloons.

"I'll show you what's gotten into me!"

"Gideon, please don't. It *is* hot, and I'm very tired."

"I really don't care if you are or not. Once every three months I think a man has a right, Levinia, and tonight your three months are up."

When she realized there was no putting him off, she stopped resisting and lay like a hickory branch, her trunk stiff and her legs where he shoved them, enduring the ignominy that accompanied marriage vows. Midway through the ordeal he tried to kiss her, but sealing wax couldn't have made Levinia's mouth any tighter.

When the graceless debacle ended, Gideon rolled over, sighed and slept like a baby, while Levinia lay at his side with her mouth still pinched and ice in her heart.

In the room they shared, Agnes and Henrietta Barnett, too, used a dressing screen. Henrietta changed first. Henrietta took it as her God-given right to do things first; after all, she'd been born first. She was sixty-nine to Agnes's sixty-seven and had been keeping Agnes out of trouble their whole lives long. That wasn't about to change now.

"Hurry up, Agnes, and turn out that lamp. I'm tired."

"But I have to brush my hair first, Etta." Agnes stepped toward the dressing table, tying her nightgown at the throat. Henrietta reclined against two stacked pillows, closed her eyelids and tolerated the rosy gaslight against them while listening to Agnes putter around in her usual poky fashion, wasting time at the dressing table and keeping *everyone in the room* awake.

Agnes sat down, removed the celluloid pins from her rusty-gray hair and began brushing. A mosquito came and buzzed at the round globe of the gaslight, but she paid it no mind, stroking, stroking, tipping her head to one side. Her eyes were pale blue, with brows as finely arched and tapered as they had been in her twenties, though they, too, were fading from their earlier rich mahogany to gray. She was thin in both face and body, fine-boned, with delicate features that had attracted many a second glance over the past forty years. Recently her voice had developed a delicate tremble and her eyes wore an expression to match it.

"I think young Mr. DuVal is smitten with our Lorna."

"Oh, bosh, Agnes. You think every young man is smitten with every young woman he's seen with."

"Well, I think he is. Did you see them go out onto the veranda together tonight?"

Henrietta gave up and opened her eyes. "I not only saw them, I heard them, and for your information it was she who invited him outside and I intend to speak to Levinia about it. I don't know what the world is coming to when a girl of eighteen acts so bold! It's simply not acceptable!"

"Our Lorna's not a girl, Etta, she's a young woman already. Why, I was only seventeen when Captain Dearsley proposed to me."

Henrietta threw herself over to face the opposite wall and gave her pillow a plump. "Oh, you and your Captain Dearsley; how you do prattle on about him."

"I shall never forget how he looked in his uniform that night, with the gold braid on his epaulettes shining in the moonlight, and the . . ."

Henrietta joined in. " '. . . And the gloves on his hands as white as a swan's back.' If I hear that one more time, Agnes, I swear I shall be sick to my stomach." She glared over her shoulder. "Now turn down the gas and come to bed!"

Agnes went on brushing her hair dreamily. "He *would* have married me if he'd come back from the Indian wars. Oh, he would have. And I would have had a house this fine, and servants, and three sons and three daughters, and I would have named the first one Malcolm and the second one Mildred. Captain Dearsley and I had spoken about children. He wanted a big family, he said, and so did I. By now, of course, our Malcolm would have been in his forties and I would be a grandmother. Just imagine that, Etta: me a grandmother."

Henrietta twitched in exasperation.

"Ah, me ..." Agnes sighed. She set down her brush and began tying her hair back in a single tail.

"Braid your hair," Henrietta ordered.

"It's too hot tonight."

"A lady braids her hair at night, Agnes. When will you learn that?"

"If I had married Captain Dearsley, I'm sure there should have been many nights I would not have braided my hair. He would have asked me to leave it down and I would have." When her hair was tied, Agnes turned out the gas lamp, went to the window that looked out over the glasshouse and the side yard, where Levinia's prize rose garden spread an intoxicating scent upon the night. She lifted aside the curtain, listened to the fountain patter, breathed deeply, then padded barefoot to the carved bed and lay down beside her sister, where she'd been lying for as long as she had memory.

Through the wall they heard the muffled sounds of voices from the room next door. "Oh my," Agnes said softly, "it sounds as if Gideon and Levinia are still fighting." Abruptly the rumble ceased and a rhythmic thumping began against the common wall.

Henrietta lifted her head and listened a moment, then turned to her side and pulled a pillow over her ear.

Agnes lay on her back staring at the night shadows, listening to the sounds and smiling wistfully.

In a room across the hall Jenny Barnett sat cross-legged on her sister Daphne's bed. They were dressed in their nightclothes and the lantern had been extinguished. Jenny had already forgotten about Mama and Papa's quarrel and was rhapsodizing on her favorite subject.

"Lorna is so lucky." Jenny flopped to her back, one hand flung up to pluck at her hair, one leg over the edge of the mattress, its bare foot wagging. "He's *sooo* handsome."

"I'm going to tell."

"Oh no you won't, because if you do I'll tell about you smoking corn silk out behind the glasshouse."

"I did not!"

"You did too. Theron saw you and he told me. You and Betsy Whiting."

"I'm going to kill that Theron!"

Jenny continued swinging her foot. "Don't you just love Taylor's moustache and beard?"

"I think moustaches are dumb."

Jenny rolled onto her belly and lay her cheek on her doubled hands. "Not on Taylor they're not." She heaved a huge sigh. "Gosh, I'd give anything to be Lorna. Theron says Taylor kissed her down in the rose garden last week after they got home from the chautau-qua."

"Oh, yuk. You wouldn't catch *me* kissing Taylor DuVal! You wouldn't catch me kissing any boy! Boys are disgusting."

"I'd kiss Taylor. I'd even kiss him with my mouth open."

"With your mouth open! Jenny Barnett, you'll go to hell for talking like that."

Jenny sat up, cross-legged. She let her head loll back until her hair fell clear down to her waist, joined her hands and stretched them straight toward the ceiling, thrusting out her young breasts under her round-yoked nightie. "No I won't. Sissy told me that when you grow up everybody kisses like that. They even put their tongues in each other's mouths."

"I'm telling Mama you said that!"

Jenny let her arms fall and braced them on the mattress behind her. "Go ahead, tell her. Sissy says *everybody* does it." Sissy Tufts was Jenny's best friend, the same age as she.

"Well, how does Sissy know?"

"Sissy's done it. With Mitchell Armfield. She said it was terribly exciting."

"You're lying. Nobody would do such a putrid thing."

"Oh, Daphne . . ." Jenny eased off the bed, shoulders back and toes pointed like a ballerina crossing a stage toward her prince. "You're such a child." She fainted onto the window seat, where the moonlight flooded in thick as cream. Like a dying diva, she wrapped both arms around an updrawn knee and dropped her cheek upon it.

"I am not! I'm only two years younger than you!"

On her buttocks, Jenny pivoted a half-circle, imagining strings playing Tchaikovsky. "Well, all I know is, if some boy wants to kiss me I'm going to try it. And if he wants to put his tongue in my mouth I'll try that, too."

"Do you really think Lorna did that with Taylor?"

Jenny gave up her dancing, drew both feet onto the window seat and folded both hands over her bare toes.

"Theron saw them through his spyglass."

"Theron and his dumb spyglass. I wish Aunt Agnes had never given it to him. He carries it everywhere, and pulls it out and points it at my friends and makes this cackly laugh and says 'The eye knows' in a weird voice. Honestly, it's so embarrassing."

They sat awhile, thinking about how dumb twelve-year-old brothers could be, wondering when kissing would start for them.

In time Jenny interrupted the silence. "Hey, Daph?"

"What?"

"Where do you suppose your nose goes when you kiss a boy?"

"How should I know?"

"Wouldn't you think it would get in the way?"

"I don't know. It never gets in the way when the aunts kiss me."

"But that's different. When boys kiss you they do it longer."

After the two pondered silently awhile, Jenny said, "Hey, Daph?"

"What?"

"What if some boys tried it with us and we didn't know what to do?"

"We'd know."

"How do you know we'd know? I think we should practice."

Daphne caught her sister's drift and was having none of it. "Oh no, not me! Go find somebody else!"

"But, Daph, you're going to kiss boys someday, too. Do you want to be a dumb dodo who doesn't know the first thing about it?"

"I'd rather be a dumb dodo than practice kissing with you."

"Come on, Daphne."

"You're crazy. You've been gawking at Taylor DuVal too much."

"We'll make a pact. We'll never tell anyone else as long as we live."

"No," Daphne said stubbornly. "I'm not going to do it."

"Supposing it's David Tufts who tries to kiss you for the first time and you bump noses and make a fool out of yourself if he tries to put his tongue in your mouth."

"How do you know about David Tufts?"

"Lorna's not the only one Theron's used his spyglass on."

"David Tufts would never try to kiss me. All he ever does is talk about his bug collection."

"Maybe not this summer, but sometime he might."

Daphne considered awhile and decided there might be the slightest bit of merit in what Jenny said. "Oh, all right. But I'm not hugging!"

"Of course not. We'll do it like Sissy and Mitchell did. They were sitting on the porch swing when it happened."

"So what should I do? Come over there and sit by you?"

"Sure."

Daphne left the bed and joined her sister on the window seat. They sat side by side, with their bare toes touching the floor and their hair backlit by moonlight. They looked at each other and giggled, grew silent and uncertain, neither of them moving.

"Do you think we're supposed to close our eyes or what?" Daphne asked.

"I suppose so. It would be too embarrassing to do it with them open, like looking into a fish's eye when you're taking him off the hook."

Daphne said, "Well, let's do it, then. Hurry up. I feel stupid."

"All right, close your eyes and tip your head just a little."

They both tipped their heads and puckered their lips like sausage casings that have burst while cooking. They touched lips briefly, then backed up and opened their eyes.

"What did you think?" Jenny asked.

"If that's what kissing is like, I'd as soon look at David Tufts' bug collection."

"It was pretty disappointing, wasn't it? Do you think we should try it again and touch tongues?"

Daphne looked doubtful. "Well, all right, but dry your tongue off real good first on your nightie."

"Good idea."

They both pulled at their nighties and energetically dried their tongues, then quickly tilted their heads, scrunched their eyes shut and kissed the way they thought it ought to be done. After two seconds of contact, a snort of laughter came through Daphne's nose.

"Stop that!" Jenny scolded. "You blew boogers on me!" But she was laughing, too, hard enough to rock her backward, pulling them apart.

Daphne spit into a wad of nightgown and scrubbed her tongue as if she'd eaten poison. "Oh, ish! That was horrible! If that's what kissing is like, I'd rather *eat* David Tufts' bug collection!"

They laughed so hard they clutched their stomachs and doubled up, rolling on the window seat in the moonlight. Curled against the pillows, with their feet drawn up into the warm air stealing through the open windows, they became two young sylphs treading the brink of womanhood, hesitant to step in, knowing they would soon and trusting that when it happened they'd be ready. Their sprigged gingham nightgowns created two puddles of blue light on the darker blue cushion as they lay in relaxed coils, hushed now and tired, their attempt at kissing already mellowing into a humorous recollection they would recount for their own children well into their dotage. In time Jenny ventured to the stars outside, "I guess it only works if you do it with a boy, huh?"

"I guess," Daphne agreed, staring, too, at the stars.

Down on the lakeshore soft waves licked the sand. Frogs made the night pulse with their dissonant songs. From the gardens below lifted the smell of Mama's roses and the babbling of the fountains. Off in the distance the theater train could be heard chugging softly, bringing a load of summer people back from Saint Paul. In their blissful innocence, Jenny and Daphne drifted off to sleep, on their tongues not the taste of lovers' kisses, only that of starch from their own nightgowns.

In his room, with the lantern still hissing, surrounded by nautical paraphernalia, Theron Barnett lay on his back in a bed whose headboard and footboard were shaped like ships' wheels. His skinny right ankle rested on his updrawn left knee, and his nightshirt was shinnied around his hips. In his right hand he held a brass spyglass, extended full-length. He was driving it through the air, making flatulent sounds of propulsion with his mouth. He had studied the Civil War this past winter and was fascinated by the fight between the *Monitor* and the *Merrimack*.

"Vrrrtt!" Imitating an engine, he made his spyglass dive and rolled with it until his arms were hanging over the side of the bed and he was facing the floor with his chin screwed into the edge of the mattress. He raised both bare feet and flailed them some, crossed them, hummed a little and *thupped* the spyglass closed and open, closed and open. Abruptly he shot up and knelt in the middle of his bed, squinting one eye, peering through the brass piece at his wallpaper. A brigantine with furled sails loomed up in his sights.

"Ship ahoy! The brigantine *Theron* ten degrees off the larboard bow!" He had no idea what his words meant. He swung his spyglass around the room and found an entire army surrounding his ship. "Man the guns! All hands on deck!" Artillery fire hit his ship and he fell over, his eyelids shut and twitching, his fingers loosening on the spyglass.

As he sprawled across his wrinkled bedspread, he heard giggling from his sisters' room next door. He stood on the bed, reached for the high bracket and extinguished his gas lantern, hurried to the window seat and pushed the curtain back, training his spyglass on his sisters' bay window, which projected from the house on the same plane as his own. But their window was dark and all he could make out were white curtains and black window glass.

Disappointed that he, Black Barnett, the feared and hated Yankee spy, would witness no skulduggery tonight, he left his spyglass on the window seat and padded, yawning, to his bed.

The Sunday morning ritual at Rose Point Cottage began with breakfast at eight, followed by church at ten. Lorna awakened at six-thirty, shot up, checked her clock and flew out of bed.

Mrs. Schmitt had said the help were free as soon as breakfast was finished, which meant she had to corner Harken before eight if she wanted any questions answered.

At seven forty-five, all dressed and combed for church, Lorna once again entered the kitchen from the servants' rear stairs. Glynnis, the dining room serving maid, was back, coming out of the butler's pantry with a stack of clean plates. Mrs. Schmitt was coddling eggs; the red-headed kitchen maid was squeezing spinach dry in a tammy cloth, the other was mincing herbs on the chopping block. Harken was down on one knee on a piece of canvas, chipping ice with an ice pick. "Excuse me," Lorna said, once again arresting all motion.

After a first jolt of surprise, Mrs. Schmitt found her tongue. "I'm sorry, miss, breakfast isn't quite ready. It'll be on the sideboard at the crack of eight, though."

"Oh, I haven't come for breakfast. I want to speak to Harken."

Harken dropped a shard of ice into a cut-glass bowl and rose slowly, drying a hand on his trousers.

"Yes, miss?" he said politely.

"I want you to explain to me how my father can win the regatta next year."

"Now, miss?"

"Yes, if you don't mind."

Harken and Mrs. Schmitt exchanged glances before her eyes grazed the clock. "Well, I'd be happy to, miss, but with Chester still gone and breakfast expected at eight, I should be helping Mrs. Schmitt."

Lorna, too, checked the clock. "Oh, yes, how silly of me. Perhaps later, then? It's ever so important."

"Of course, miss."

"After church?"

"Actually . . . ah . . . ." He cleared his throat and shifted his weight from one foot to the other. He folded a thumb over the pointed end of the ice pick.

Mrs. Schmitt returned to coddling eggs and put in, "It's his day off, miss. He was planning to go fishing. Girls," she said to the maids, "finish them herbs and spinach now, hurry."

The two girls began packing spinach into boat-shaped molds and Lorna realized she was holding things up. To Harken she said, "Oh, of course, and I wouldn't dream of using up your day. But I do so want to hear more about your plan. I'd only take up a few minutes of your time. Are you fishing here on the lake?"

"Yes, miss. With Mr. Iversen."

"With *our* Mr. Iversen? You mean Tim?"

"Yes, miss."

"Why, that's perfect! I'll just sail the catboat over to Tim's as soon as we get back from church, and we can talk for a few minutes and you'll still get in a full afternoon of fishing. Would that be agreeable?"

"Yes, of course, miss."

"All right, then. I shall see you at Tim's the minute I can get away."

When Lorna had gone, Mrs. Schmitt shot Harken a sideward glance. She was whipping cheese sauce, her double chin flapping like a turkey wattle. "You'd best look out what you're doing, Jens Harken. You nearly lost your job once this week; this'll sure do the trick. And this time I won't be able to save you."

"Well, what should I have done? Refused her?"

"I don't know, but she's the gentry and you're the help, and them two never mix. You'd best be remembering that."

"We're not exactly sneaking out to meet in secret. After all, Iversen will be right there."

Mrs. Schmitt snorted and whacked her wooden spoon down. "All I'm saying is watch your p's and q's, young man. You're twenty-five and she's eighteen and it don't look good."

At breakfast Lorna was vaguely disappointed to see that Glynnis was serving their coffee instead of Harken. Papa and Mama were particularly silent this morning. Jenny, Daphne and Theron seemed lethargic after being up later than usual last night. Aunt Henrietta was busy telling Aunt Agnes how much food to take and to be careful of the spicy sausage as too much of it would give her dyspepsia. Aunt Agnes, as usual, was busy discoursing with the help.

"Why, thank you, Glynnis," she said when Glynnis served her coffee. "And how is your tooth today?"

Levinia glared at Agnes, who missed it and smiled up at the young woman in the white mobcap and apron. She was no more than eighteen and had pitted skin and a nose resembling a nicely risen muffin.

"Much better, mum, thank you."

"And have you heard from Chester?"

"No, mum, not since he left."

"How unfortunate that his father is ill."

"Yes, mum, though he's old. Seventy-seven, Chester says."

Levinia cleared her throat, lifted her cup and whacked it down on her saucer. "My breakfast will be cold if you don't move on with that coffeepot, Glynnis."

"Oh yes, mum." Glynnis colored and hurried along with her duties.

When she'd left the room, Henrietta scolded, "Mercy sakes,

Agnes, I wish you'd control your urge to visit with the help. It's quite embarrassing."

Agnes looked up innocently. "I don't know why it should be. I was just asking after the poor girl's tooth. And Chester has been with us so many years. Don't you care about his father being ill?"

Levinia said, "Of course we care, Agnes. What Henrietta is saying is that we don't discuss it with the help over breakfast."

Agnes replied, "You don't, Levinia, but I rather enjoy doing so. That Glynnis is ever such a nice young girl. Please pass the butter, Daphne."

Levinia's left eyebrow went up as she and Henrietta exchanged glances.

Lorna went to the sideboard and helped herself to fresh strawberries, taking a second look at the ice in the cut-glass bowl beneath them, recalling Harken on his knees chipping it with an ice pick a quarter hour ago. Returning to the table, she said, "If nobody's using the catboat, I'd like to take it out after church. May I, Papa?"

Gideon hadn't spoken a word through the entire meal. He did so now, with his eyes on his plate as he cut and stabbed a piece of sausage. "I don't condone women sailing, Lorna, and you know that." He popped the sausage into his mouth, leaving grease on his moustache.

Lorna stared at it, fighting for composure. If he had his way, she would remain in stays forever, sitting in the shade watching life sail by the way Mama did. She could fight him, but persuasion worked best with Papa. As long as he thought the final decision was his, the females in the family had a chance of getting their way.

"I'd stay close to shore, and I'd make sure I wore my bonnet."

"Why, I should think you'd wear your bonnet," put in Aunt Henrietta. *"With* a sharp hatpin!" Aunt Henrietta never stopped warning her nieces they must always wear a sharp hatpin. It was their only weapon, she held, though Lorna often wondered what man in his right mind had ever done anything to cause Aunt Henrietta to believe she needed a weapon. Furthermore, what man might do so to Lorna out in the middle of White Bear Lake on a bright Sunday afternoon?

"I'll make sure it's sharp," she agreed with feigned meekness. "And I'll be home at whatever time you say."

Gideon wiped his moustache and studied his daughter while reaching for his coffee cup. She could see he was in a rancid mood.

"You can take the rowboat."

They'd had a tremendous tiff when he'd learned—via Theron's tattling—that she had coerced one of the boys, Mitchell Armfield, into teaching her to sail his catboat.

"The rowboat," she wailed. "But Papa—"

"It's the rowboat or nothing. Two hours. And you'll take a life preserver with you. Why, if you capsized in those skirts they'd take you down like an anchor."

"Yes, Papa," she agreed. To her mother she said, "If it's all right, I thought I'd take a hamper and eat on the boat."

Sunday was the day this was most feasible on brief notice, with only a skeleton staff on duty and the day's noon and evening meals made up of cold foods.

"Very well," Levinia agreed. "But I *do* worry about you out on the water all alone."

"I could go along!" Theron put in hopefully.

"No!" Lorna cried.

"Please, Mother, can I?" Under the table Theron eagerly clapped his knees together.

"Mother, I took him into town with me this week when I'd rather have gone alone, and he tagged along with Taylor and me the other night to the band concert. Must I take him again?"

"Lorna's right. You can stay home this time."

Lorna breathed a sigh of relief and hurried to finish her breakfast before the others finished theirs. "I'll go tell Mrs. Schmitt." She gulped the last of her coffee, then hurried out before anyone could change his mind.

Jens Harken was in the kitchen when Lorna stuck her head into the room yet again. He was kneeling before the icebox, pulling out the drip pan from below it. When the door from the passageway swung open he looked up and met Lorna's gaze. His eyes were as blue as she remembered, his face as handsome, his shoulders as wide.

He stood, bearing the swaying water in the wide pan, and nodded silently in greeting as he headed for the back door to sling it into the herb garden.

"Mrs. Schmitt?" Lorna called, craning to peer around the edge of the door. Mrs. Schmitt came hurrying in from the butler's pantry, counting a handful of silverware in Chester's absence.

"Oh, miss, it's you again."

"Yes." Lorna flashed a smile, realizing that requests such as she was about to make cut into the few free hours the kitchen staff was allotted each week. Harken had returned and knelt to replace the drip pan.

"I was wondering if you'd pack me a hamper before you leave. Just a few things from the noon buffet that I can take on the boat."

"Certainly, miss."

"You can leave it at the back door and I'll come around and get it before I go."

"Very well. And I'll be sure to put in a couple of those currant cakes you like so much."

Lorna was nonplussed. Never in her life had she told Mrs. Schmitt she loved currant cakes.

"Why, how ever did you know?"

"The staff talks, miss. I know most of the foods you fancy, as well as the favorites of the others in the family."

Again Lorna smiled. "Why, thank you, Mrs. Schmitt, I'd love some currant cakes, and you have a nice afternoon off, will you?"

"That I will, miss, and thank you, too."

She left without another glance at Harken, though even after the door swung shut she was inappropriately aware of the fact that his forearms, below his rolled-up sleeves, had looked like knots in a piece of oak firewood, and his eyes had strayed to her more than once as he moved about his kitchen work.

She set out at noon with the hamper. Upon her head her leghorn bonnet was dutifully secured with a hatpin, freshly sharpened. Down her back streamed pale blue ribbons that matched the stripes in her sateen skirt. For her feet she had carefully chosen a pair of white canvas Prince Alberts, whose elastic gussets eliminated the need for troublesome buttonhooks. Twenty feet from shore she released the oars, reeved her skirts and tugged off the shoes, followed by her lisle stockings and garters, which she stowed in the picnic hamper. Reclaiming the oars, she took a bearing on the shoreline behind her and set out for Tim Iversen's place across the lake.

Tim Iversen was one of those rare people liked by everyone. By dint of his occupation, he had managed to breach the line separating the upper and lower classes, for as a photographer he worked for both. He wasn't rich by anyone's standards, yet he'd had a self-made log cabin on White Bear Lake since before the wealthy had built their fancy summer homes there. He called his cabin Birch Lodge and kept open house in it for any and all comers. He not only yachted with the wealthy, he hunted, fished and socialized with them as well, and he'd been chronicling it all in photographs since the rich had decided to make White Bear their playground.

Similarly, the working class found a friend in Tim. He had come from humble beginnings and refused to shun them. Furthermore, he was unpretentious and unpretty: As a youngster he'd lost his left eye in an accident involving an arrow made from a corset stay, and wore a glass eye. His remaining eye, however, served him well as a photographer of both classes. Not only had he set up a studio in Saint Paul, but he was garnering national acclaim as a stereophotographer, traveling the world over with a double-lensed stereo camera, producing side-by-side pictures for the stereoscope that had taken its place in every parlor of America and had created a national pastime.

Iversen's camera was nowhere in sight, however, as Lorna approached his dock. Instead, he and Harken, with their trouser legs rolled up, were manning opposite ends of a seine in the shallows along his shoreline. A goodly distance out, she stowed her oars and donned her shoes and stockings. Rowing once more, she glanced over her shoulder and found Tim waving. She waved back. Harken, with the net in his hands, only watched the boat come on.

When it reached the dock the two men were waiting in knee-deep water to stop it. Harken took the painter to pull the boat against the dock while Tim greeted, "Well, this is a pleasant surprise, Miss Lorna."

She stood up and caught her balance as the boat rocked.

"It's no surprise at all, Mr. Iversen. I'm sure Harken told you I was coming."

"Well, yes, he did"—Iversen laughed and vaulted onto the dock to offer Lorna a hand—"but I know your father's views on ladies yachting, so I suspected you'd have trouble getting away."

"As you can see, I had to settle for the rowboat," Lorna replied, taking Iversen's hand and stepping from the boat. "And I had to promise to be back in two hours."

Until now she had avoided glancing at Harken. She did so as he stood in the water, tying up the boat below her.

"Hello," she said quietly.

He lifted his face to squint up at her. His blond head was bare. His trousers were wet nearly to the crotch. The collar was missing from his wrinkled white shirt and its shoulders were dented by red suspenders. He gave a final tug on the knot.

"Hello, miss."

"I've interrupted your seining."

"Oh, that's all right." He flung out a glance that never quite reached the abandoned net and bucket. "We can finish later."

She strode the length of the bleached dock, followed by Iversen, who left wet footprints. Harken waded alongside and below her. They converged on the sandy shore, where the sun beat down and the placid water scarcely moved against it. The afternoon was hot and still. All around the sound of katydids created a piercing syllable that never ceased. In the nearby woods even the maples looked wilted. Along the shoreline overhanging willows appeared to be dipping their tongues to drink.

Lorna asked Tim, "Did Mr. Harken tell you I've come to talk about how to win a regatta?"

"Yes, he did, but did he tell you he's taken his idea to about half a dozen members of the White Bear Yacht Club and they've all told him he's crazy?"

She turned her gaze on the tall blond man again. "Are you, Mr. Harken?"

"Maybe. I don't think so, though."

"Exactly what do you propose?"

"A revolutionary new boat design."

"Show me."

His eyes met hers directly for the first time while he wondered why a pretty young thing like she wanted to know about boats. And could she understand? He'd sketched his ideas for yachtsmen far more experienced than she, and they'd failed to believe his reasoning. Furthermore, if her father found out about this clandestine meeting, he'd lose his job for sure, as Hulduh Schmitt had warned. But there she stood, looking up at him expectantly from the shadow of a straw bonnet, with a faint sheen of sweat on her brow and a hint of it dampening the armpits of her ham-shaped sleeves. From the waist down she was as slim as a buggy whip, while above she'd inherited her mother's generous breasts. A man would have to have *two* glass eyes not to notice all that plus her pretty face. Jens Harken, however, knew his place. He could easily keep propriety intact and treat her with the deference expected of the kitchen help, but he could not so easily cast aside the opportunity to talk about his boat to one more person. The boat would work. He knew it as surely as he knew he should not be standing on this lakeshore in his bare feet beside Miss Lorna Barnett in her pretty striped skirt and beribboned hat. But who knew which person might make the difference? It could turn out to be even so unlikely a one as this bored rich girl, who might possibly be doing nothing more than amusing herself with the kitchen help. On the off chance that her intentions were more honorable, he decided to show her.

"All right," he answered, retrieving his pail of minnows. He took three steps into the water, sent the minnows and lake water shimmering through the air, then filled the bucket once more. "Look out," he warned Lorna before swashing the water across the sand, creating a smooth, wet blackboard. From a nearby bush he snapped off a twig and returned to Lorna's side, where he squatted down with his weight on one heel.

"You sail a little, right?" he inquired as he began sketching.

"Yes, a little. Whenever I can sneak out to do it."

He smiled but kept his eyes fixed on the sand. "This is the kind of boat your father is sailing now. It's a sloop, and you know how a sloop is shaped underneath. . . ." He sketched a deep lower fin. "This keel configuration means that all this area from here . . . to here"—he sketched the waterline—"is displacing water. At the same time, when they're used for racing, they're carrying more and more sail, and to counterbalance that, there's more and more iron and lead being bolted onto the keel for ballast. And when even *that* won't keep them from tipping, they take on sandbags and the crew shifts them from side to side whenever she heels, you see?"

"Yes, I know all about sandbagging."

"All right now, imagine this . . ." He dropped both knees to the sand and began avidly sketching a second boat. "A scow, a light little thing with a virtually flat bottom that skims over the water instead of plowing through it. A planing hull versus a displacement hull, that's what we're talking about. We cut down on the sail area so we don't need all that weight on the hull. A thirty-eight-footer that would weigh, say, eleven hundred pounds with a displacement hull would weigh only about five hundred fifty with a planing hull. We'd save all that weight."

"But if you don't use lead ballast, what'll keep it from tipping?"

"Shape." He shot Lorna one quick glance—animated now—and drew a third picture. "Imagine it shaped like a cigar that somebody stepped on. It'll be only about three feet from the top of her deck to the bottom of her hull."

"So shallow?"

"Not only that, we do away with the long bowsprit—we don't need it anymore to hold the tacks of those ridiculously big sails. We'll use much smaller sails."

"But won't it nose into the water, being down so close to it?"

"No."

"You'll have a hard time convincing my father of that."

"Maybe so, but I'm right. I know I am! She might be shallow-hulled, but she'll still have a belly"—he pointed to the flattened cigar—"and because of her planing characteristics she'll have plenty of natural lift. When she's on a downwind run, the bow will lift instead of dip; and when she's sailing close-hauled she'll be heeled up so that very little wetted surface is in the water, versus the old design, where the hull is fully in the water, creating such a tremendous drag."

He paused for breath and sat back, hands on his thighs, looking straight into Lorna's eyes. His own, caught in the bright summer sun, became as brilliant as the sky behind him, and his breath seemed short from excitement.

"How do you know all this?"

"I can't say how. I just do."

"Have you studied?"

"No."

"Then how?"

He looked away, threw down the stick he'd been drawing with and brushed his palms together. "I'm Norwegian. I think it's in our blood, and besides, I've been sailing since I was a boy. My father taught me, and his father taught him."

"Where?"

"In Norway at first, then here when we immigrated."

"You immigrated?"

He nodded. "When I was eight."

So that accounted for his lack of accent. He spoke well-modulated English, but as she gazed up at his profile she saw very clearly the clean-lined Nordic features of his face—straight nose, high forehead, shapely mouth, blond hair and those discommoding blue eyes.

"Does your father agree with you?"

He gave her a glance, making no reply.

"About the boat, I mean," she added.

"My father's dead."

"Oh, I'm sorry."

He picked up the stick again and absently poked it into the sand. "He died when I was eighteen, in a fire at the boatworks where he worked in New Jersey. Actually I worked there, too, and I tried to convince them to listen to me, but they laughed at me just the way everybody else did."

"And your mother?"

"She's dead, too, before my dad. I have a brother, though, back in New Jersey." His smile returned, slightly mischievous this time. "I told him I'd come to Minnesota and find somebody to listen to me, and when I got rich and famous designing the fastest boats on the water he could come here and work for me. He's married with two little babies, so it isn't as easy for him to pull up stakes and move. Someday I'll get him here, though, mark my words."

They were both on their knees, intent upon each other with little sense of passing time. His hand was motionless upon the stick that protruded from the sand. Hers rested quietly on her thigh. His eyes were in full sunlight. Hers were shaded by the brim of her straw bonnet. She was wholly feminine in her high-necked white shirtwaist with its immense sleeves. He was wholly masculine in his wrinkled shirt, suspenders and bare feet. For just a moment they became two exceedingly comely people admiring each other for the sheer enjoyment of it.

Then propriety intruded and Harken dropped his eyes. "You're soiling your skirt, Miss Lorna."

"Oh." She looked down. "It's just sand. It'll brush off when it dries. So . . ." She leaned toward the drawing and outlined it with one fingertip. "Tell me, Mr. Harken, how much would it take to build this?"

"More than I have. More than I can convince the yacht club to put up."

"How much?"

"Seven hundred dollars, probably."

"Oh, that *is* a lot."

"Especially when they believe it'll tip right over on its side and sink."

"I must confess, some of that was hard for me to understand. The part about wetted surface. Explain it to me again so I can convince my father."

His expression opened in surprise. "Are you serious?"

"I'm going to try."

"You're going to tell him you were here, talking to me?"

"No. I'm going to tell him I was here talking to Mr. Iversen, and that he believes it'll work."

Harken's lips formed an unspoken O that remained a moment before he ventured, "You're a brave young lady."

She shrugged. "Not really. Tell me, Mr. Harken, have you ever heard of the novelist Charles Kingsley?"

"No, I'm afraid I haven't."

"Well, Mr. Kingsley holds that today's women suffer from a bevy of health problems, all of them caused by the three S's—silence, stillness and stays. I choose to reject all three and stay healthy, that's all. My father doesn't like it, but occasionally he gets tired of upbraiding me and I get my way. Who knows, perhaps this will be one of those times. Now, once more, Mr. Harken, explain your boat."

He had been doing so for some time when an explosion sounded nearby. They both started and looked up. There stood Iversen, surrounded by a cloud of smoke, withdrawing his head from beneath the black hood of his Kodak camera, which was standing on a tripod in the sand.

"Mr. Iversen, what are you doing!" Lorna cried.

"I have a hunch that those drawings in the sand might prove to be historic someday. I've simply recorded it for posterity."

She rose to her knees and lifted one hand in alarm. "Oh, but you mustn't."

Iversen smiled. "Don't worry. I won't show your father. At least not until the boat is built and Jens has sailed it across the lake without sinking. Beyond that, I can't promise."

Lorna relaxed and sat back on her heels. "Well, all right. But you must promise to keep the photograph hidden now. You know how my father is. After last night he isn't exactly congenial toward Mr. Harken, and if he thought for a minute that I was here discussing it with him, he'd have apoplexy. I'll need to convince him that you're behind Harken and that you believe this new boat will work. All right?"

"I *am* convinced his boat will work."

Lorna looked from Iversen to Harken to Iversen again. "Well then, why haven't you said so?"

"I have. They don't listen. You know what kind of a sailor I am." He had a reputation for losing every race he entered and on one occasion actually came in swimming behind his boat, claiming he could push it faster than sail it. He'd even good-naturedly named his boat the *May-B*.

Lorna clambered to her feet and approached Iversen. "Well, will you try again? With me? And with Harken if Papa will speak with him?"

"I guess I'd do that."

"Oh, thank you, Mr. Iversen, thank you!" Impulsively, she gave him a hug, then remembered herself and assumed a pose of demureness. "Oh, I'm sorry. Don't tell Mother I did that."

Iversen laughed.

"Or Aunt Henrietta, either." When Iversen's laughter once again faded, a lull fell. "Well!" Lorna said, throwing out her arms, then joining her fingers at her skirtfront. "I have a hamper and I'm starved. Would you gentlemen care to join me for a light repast?"

"Mrs. Schmitt's cooking?" Iversen replied, his eyebrows rising. "And me a bachelor? You needn't ask twice."

Harken had risen to his feet and stood beside the sketches, saying nothing. Lorna looked back at him. "Mr. Harken?" she invited much more quietly.

She had no idea what a lovely sight she made, with the sun slicing across her heart-shaped chin and her blue bonnet ribbons trailing down behind. No one need tell Harken it was as far from acceptable as anything could get to have a picnic with her. But Iversen was here with them, and it was only one stolen hour about which her father—she hoped—would never learn. Furthermore, after today Jens Harken would return to his kitchen and Lorna Barnett to her croquet games on the east lawn and neither of them would even bother to remember this odd, implausible encounter on a hot June afternoon.

"That sounds good," Harken answered.

Chapter
THREE

*I*VERSEN got an Indian blanket
which they spread in the shade
beneath the birches near his cabin. The three of them sat cross-
legged while Lorna produced from her hamper sliced ham, buttered
rolls, deviled eggs, fresh strawberries, pickled watermelon rind and
currant cake. She arrayed the foods at the rim of her skirt, which
surrounded her like a collapsed tent of blue-and-white stripes.

"Ah, it's much nicer here, isn't it?" she said.

Harken tried to admire the food instead of her, but it was difficult.
She lifted her arms and removed a hatpin, then the hat itself, tossing
it onto the grass and wildings at the edge of the blanket. She gave her
neck a little twist of freedom. "Ah, the shade is wonderful." Once
again she lifted her arms to do an all-around tucking job on her
looped-up hair. The pose threw her breasts into relief and brought
her immense white sleeves up about her ears. The cameo at her
throat disappeared beneath her chin while her tapered and tucked
shirtwaist strained against her ribs.

She dropped her arms and looked up, catching Harken's eye.
Immediately he looked away.

"Well!" she said, rubbing her palms together and leaning forward
to assess the food. "Strawberries, ham, eggs . . . Gentlemen, what
would you like first?" Holding a saucer, she gazed at Iversen.

"A little of everything."

She filled the saucer and handed it to him, leaning across her skirts, making them crackle.

"And you, Mr. Harken?"

"A little of everything except pickled watermelon rind."

"Oh, but they're quite exquisite." She selected eggs and berries while he watched her hand, with its little finger elevated, move over the colorful foods.

"You wouldn't think so if you'd helped Mrs. Schmitt can them. Makes the kitchen stink something terrible."

She was licking off a thumb and forefinger, which came out of her mouth slowly as she handed him his plate. "You helped can these?"

"I help with most of the canning. I wash the fruits and vegetables and do the lifting. Those boilers are pretty heavy for the women. Thank you, miss."

He accepted the plate and began eating while she considered the pickled watermelon rinds, realizing she had no idea what a boiler looked like, or how heavy it must be, or what all went into creating so simple a food as this.

"What else do you do?"

He met her eyes and spoke levelly. "I'm the kitchen odd-jobs man. I do what I'm asked."

"Yes, but what else?"

"Well, this morning was the gardener's day off, so at five-thirty I picked the strawberries, and after that—"

"At five-thirty!"

"Mrs. Schmitt believes that they're sweetest if they're picked before the sun dries the dew on them. Then, after I washed the berries I filled the woodbox for her, and built a fire, and helped polish the silver from last night, since Chester isn't back yet, and I squeezed oranges, and fetched a new block of ice from the icehouse and cracked some for under the berries, and put the rest in the icebox, and emptied the drip pans, and fetched the hamper from the storeroom and ran a hose over it, and swept the kitchen floor after breakfast, and hosed down the back stoop, and watered the herb garden. Oh, and I helped Mrs. Schmitt pack the hamper."

Lorna stared at him in stupefaction.

"You did all that this morning? On your day off?"

Harken's cheek was puffed out with a mouthful of bread and ham. He swallowed and said, "My day off starts when the breakfast work is done."

"Oh, I see. Still, all that before I was even out of bed."

"Early morning's the best part of the day. I don't mind getting up early."

She thought a moment, then inquired, "Why didn't the gardener's day off start after breakfast?"

"I believe he has a special arrangement with your mother, miss."

"A special arrangement? What sort of special arrangement?"

Harken toyed with the food on his plate, reluctant to go into detail about the absurd lengths to which the ladies went in their quest for one-upsmanship.

Iversen answered. "You know what a tremendous competition there is among the ladies out here, Lorna, when it comes to gardens."

"Well . . . yes?"

"And you know that Smythe is from England."

"Yes. His father gardened for Queen Victoria herself. I remember how Mother crowed about it when she hired him."

Harken explained, "Part of their agreement when he came here to work for her was that Smythe would have each weekend off from eight o'clock Saturday night until dawn on Monday morning."

"Oh, I see. So you pick the fruits and vegetables on Sundays."

"Yes, miss."

"And my mother takes the credit for growing the best produce and flowers in White Bear Lake, even though she does none of the work. I'll confess to both of you, I've always found it utterly silly the way the women compete to have the most spectacular gardens when they don't do any of the work themselves."

"It's no different with the men and their yachting," Harken said. "They own the boats but hire the skippers."

"Only for the really important regattas, though, like yesterday," Lorna said.

"And only because the Inland Lake Yachting Association allows it," Tim put in.

"Still, wouldn't you think they'd want to skip themselves?" Harken put in. "I would if I owned a boat."

"I guess you're right. There's really not much difference between Mama hiring a gardener and a boat owner hiring a skipper."

Iversen told them, "There's talk about the ILYA changing the rule, though, and demanding that the men who own the boats must skip them."

This brought about a lively discussion of the pros and cons of hired skippers, followed by a rehash of yesterday's regatta.

Lorna leaned forward, selected a strawberry and bit into it. "Now you, Tim"—she pointed at him with half the berry—"you've earned your reputation on your own."

"You mean on the *May-B?* Now, Miss Lorna, I'll thank you not to spoil a pleasant afternoon by reminding me of that."

They all laughed, and Lorna said, "I'm talking about your photography, not your sailing. Tell me, is it true that your boxed sets of stereophotos are going to be sold by Sears and Roebuck?"

"It's true."

"Oh, Tim, you must be so proud! And to think of your work being viewed in practically every parlor in America! Tell us about the pictures, and the places where you took them."

He described the Chicago World's Fair, which he'd photographed two years earlier, and spectacular places like the Grand Canyon and Mexico and the Klondike. He lit a pipe and settled himself against a tree while Lorna nibbled on a piece of currant cake and asked him where he might go this winter when he closed his little cabin for the season. He said perhaps to Egypt to photograph the pyramids.

She breathed, "The pyramids . . . oh my . . . ," and broke off another piece of currant cake and ate it, unaware of the fetching picture she made, rapt at Tim's stories, surrounded by a mound of crisp skirts, nibbling cake whenever she wasn't too mesmerized to forget it was in her hand.

Harken sat Indian fashion, elbows to knees, splitting a blade of grass, admiring her profile, her mannerisms, her quick laughter and naturalness. In time she said to Iversen, "Perhaps you'll go to New Jersey. Mr. Harken has a brother there."

She turned and smiled at Harken, catching him off-guard. He forgot to look away, and she chose not to. His thumbnail quit splitting the grass and they both became caught in an awareness that seemed to hum through their heads like the song of the katydids around them. The dappled shade, the post-picnic lassitude, the pleasant conversation—all had combined to steal wariness away and beg them indulge themselves in an exchange of silent curiosity that breached all class distinction. They simply looked their fill, admiring what they saw, filing away details to take out and explore later, when they lay in separate rooms on separate floors—the color of eyes, the curve of hair, the outline of mouths, noses, chins. Iversen leaned against his tree trunk, puffing his fragrant briarwood pipe and watching the two of them. Even his presence failed to end their folly, until finally his pipe burned out and he rapped out the dottle against a tree root.

With a start, Lorna emerged from her absorption with Harken to realize how long they'd ignored Tim. She reached for the first diversion she could find: the round tin.

"A piece of cake before I put it away?" She extended it to Iversen.

"No, thank you, I'm full."

"Mr. Harken?" She hadn't known offering a man cake could seem so intimate, but it felt that way, his being help with whom she'd never before associated.

"No, thank you, that was for you," he said, and forced himself to look away. His gaze settled on Iversen, whose mustachioed mouth wore a pleasant if knowing expression behind the empty briarwood pipe. Harken, too, realized it was time to call an end to this folderol.

"Well, Tim, are we going to catch those fish or not?"

Lorna moved as if she'd been stuck by a pin. "Gracious, I've been keeping you." On her knees, she began closing tins and jars and piling things back in the hamper.

"Not at all, Miss Lorna." Harken rolled to his knees to help her, placing the two of them in closer proximity than they'd been since they'd knelt over the drawings on the beach. She had a scent—warm, willowy, womany—that reached him as she moved about, putting her hat back on, driving the hatpin into place, closing the hamper, getting to her feet and swatting at her wrinkled skirts. She reached for the hamper but he reached, too.

"I'll get it," he said, expecting Iversen to rise and join them. When he didn't, Harken said, "Well, are you going to sit there all day, or are you going to see the lady back to her boat?"

Iversen got to his feet and said, "I'll put the blanket away." He took one of Lorna's hands. "Goodbye, Miss Lorna." He kissed it and said, "Good luck with your father."

Jens and Lorna left Tim shaking out the Indian blanket as they turned and walked, shoulder to shoulder, from the cool shade into the hot sun, across the shifting sand, onto the long wooden dock.

There were things he wanted to say, but knew he could not. She had said she must be home in two hours, yet more than two hours had passed and she seemed in little hurry. She walked like a woman reluctant to reach her boat. Turning his gaze, he granted himself one last study of her face. Downcast, it was, her chin lowered, creating a delicate pillow underneath and a puffed profile of her lips. Pinpricks of sunlight pierced her flat-brimmed bonnet and freckled her ear and jaw.

At her boat she stopped and turned, fixing him with a look so direct it could not be avoided. It entered his eyes and fragmented when it reached his chest, like a school of minnows when a rock is dropped among them.

"It's been a wonderful afternoon," she said gently, with an unmistakable note of regret at their parting. "Thank you."

"Thank *you*, Miss Lorna, for the picnic."

"I only brought it. You prepared it."

"My pleasure," he replied.

"I shall send word to you when I've spoken to my father."

He nodded silently.

Five seconds passed, motionless, bringing a faint weightlessness to both their stomachs.

"Well, goodbye," she said.

"Goodbye, miss."

She gave him her hand, and for the short spell while she stepped down into the rowboat, they knew the touch of each other's skin. Hers was soft as chamois, his tough as leather. She sat and he handed down the hamper. He knelt to untie the bow line, then reached down for the gunwale as if to push her off. Before he could do so she looked up and her bonnet brim nearly touched his chin. Their faces were very close while he knelt, motionless, above her.

"Will you be picking the strawberries tomorrow morning, then?" she inquired.

His heart gave a kick as he answered, "Yes, miss, I will."

"Then I shall have some for breakfast," she replied, and he pushed her away.

He stood on the dock watching while she rowed out stern first, then expertly turned the boat until she faced him. For a full five pulls on the oars she locked gazes with him, finally looking away to call, "Goodbye, Mr. Iversen," raising one hand and waving.

From the shadows of the trees, Tim called, "Goodbye, Miss Lorna!"

She neither smiled nor waved at Harken, nor could he make out her eyes in the shadow of her bonnet brim. Somehow he knew they were fixed on him, and he stared at her diminishing face until it was too far out to make out her features.

He thought of her that night as he lay on his narrow cot in his tiny third-floor room with its single window facing the vegetable garden. Tim had said only one thing when Harken had returned from seeing Miss Lorna off at the dock. He'd taken the pipe from his mouth, looked squarely at Jens with his one good eye, and said, simply, "Be careful, Jens."

Jens Harken would be careful, all right. In spite of all the ogling they'd done today, he wasn't fool enough to pursue even the most innocent exchange between himself and Lorna Barnett. He valued his job too much, and the proximity it gave him to men who could afford yachts and had the free time to sail them. But what in the world was she up to, trifling with the kitchen help that way? Undoubtedly she had suitors who'd be as rich as her old man someday, fluttering around the place and signing her dance cards. Richly dressed, boat-owning, acceptable young swains whom her mother greeted with a lifted cheek, her father with offers of expensive brandy when they entered the parlor.

One of them had been sitting beside her last night during dinner, Jens was sure.

So what could he make of today?

She didn't seem the flirtatious type, indeed her fascination with him seemed to have grown apace as the day progressed, just as his had for her: even more reason to follow Tim's advice. A slow-growing allurement held more dangers than a quick flirtation. He'd be better off encouraging the little kitchen maid Ruby, who'd shown overt interest in him recently. Ruby's frizzy red hair and freckles put him off, however, whereas Miss Lorna's hair was a deep, rich mahogany color, with a pattern of new growth around her face. Stepping from the boat, she'd been warm, and the fine whorls had clung to her temples and neck and had teased her ears. He'd always thought fine ladies spent the bulk of their summers devising ways to keep cool. Instead, she had rowed across the lake in the heat, had removed her hat and smoothed her hair and had shared a picnic with one for whom she should at the very least have shown total indifference, at the very most, disdain. That's how it usually was: The rich disdained those they employed.

Disdain, however, seemed wholly absent from Miss Lorna Barnett's demeanor today.

Lying in his servants' quarters, remembering, Jens tried to put her from his mind. His sheets felt sticky. He tossed over, flipped his pillow to the cool side and shut his eyes, but she was there again in memory, stepping down into the boat, taking the picnic basket from his hands, lifting her heart-shaped face and inquiring if he would be picking the strawberries for her breakfast tomorrow. He recalled her biting into one, then pointing it at Tim as she spoke—a glorious, unaffected creature with eyes brown as acorns and a beguiling smile, which she'd shown less and less as the afternoon progressed.

Was she, too, lying in bed restless, recounting the afternoon's events?

Miss Lorna Barnett most certainly was. She lay on her back with her hands stacked under her head, staring at the faint shadows delineating the ceiling medallion that surrounded her gaslight. When she'd set out in the boat today she hadn't half suspected what the afternoon would bring.

Jens Harken.

She thought about his given name, the name she dare not say, for to call him by it would be to cross a demarcation line that even she, with her independent spirit, would never breach. But simply to think it brought pleasure.

Jens Harken, a kitchen odd-jobs man . . . Merciful heavens, whatever had possessed her?

She had gone to Tim's merely to learn more about boats, for they fascinated her, and even though she wasn't allowed to sail yet, she would one day. When she did she'd organize the women into a yachting club of their own, and if they could sail revolutionary new boats that skimmed the water, why shouldn't they? If her papa was too obstinate to listen to Harken's ideas, she wasn't.

Papa—that stubborn, stubborn man. She had thought at first she would delight merely in getting him to change his mind for once and listen to Harken, perhaps end up in his good graces if Harken's plan worked and the White Bear Yacht Club eventually won the regattas. But her goal had taken on a new aspect once she'd knelt in the sand and watched Harken's wide, strong hands drawing boats in the sand. How could he know all that without any formal training in naval architecture? He had convinced her his plan would work simply by the strength of his conviction. In all the time they'd spent together today she was certain the only minutes he'd lost sight of the differ-ence in their stations was when he was slashing at the sand and talking about keel configurations. When she'd looked up into his face and asked him how he knew all that, he'd answered, "I don't know," and she'd thought, *Why, he really doesn't!* That was the moment when her fascination for him took wing.

She had knelt beside him, gazing up into his intent blue eyes and thought, *He can do this crazy thing. I know he can.* And upon the heels of that thought came another. *Oh dear, how incredibly handsome he is.*

His eyes, his face had captivated her time and time again today, try though she had to remain disinterested. Such a nice straight nose, and clear skin and a wonderful mouth, so visible without facial hair. She was accustomed to beards: All the men she knew wore beards, so Harken's shorn face had presented an almost startling novelty, apart from his handsomeness. He was muscular, too, from lifting all those blocks of ice and heavy boilers and who knew what else in the kitchen.

How long had he been here? Had he worked for them in town last winter? Had he worked here at the cottage last summer? The summer before? Why hadn't she thought to ask him? She suddenly wanted to know everything about him, about his mother and father and his trip across the ocean, and his childhood and his years on the East Coast, and especially she wanted to know how long he'd been in their kitchens, touching the foods she was served and the silverware she put in her mouth.

The thought seemed to bring her to her senses.

Abruptly she shot up in the dark, dropped her feet over the side of the bed and scratched her scalp with both hands, roughing up her hair in frustration. Lord, if only those crickets would stop. And the humidity drop. And a breeze come up! She lifted her hair from her hot nape, released a great sigh and let her shoulders slump.

She had to stop thinking of Jens Harken now. If she wanted to get spoony over a man, the one to get spoony over was Taylor DuVal. He was the one Mama and Papa intended for her to marry. She'd known it for quite a while already, even though they hadn't said so. Furthermore, twenty-four hours ago it was Taylor she couldn't wait to kiss on the front veranda. Tonight it was the kitchen help. But she'd better get that idea square out of her head!

She fell onto her side, mounding up the pillow beneath her cheek, bending one knee and pulling her nightdress up to let the air on her legs.

But she couldn't sleep. And she couldn't stop thinking of Jens Harken.

She overslept the next morning and missed breakfast. The dining room was silent and empty when she entered it, no linen on the table, no strawberries on the sideboard picked fresh by Jens Harken. The room smelled of a recent dusting with lemon oil. A new arrangement of flowers was centered on a lace runner, testifying to the fact that Levinia had been up long enough to arrange them. Lorna glanced at the passageway door to the kitchen: She could walk back there and ask for something—a logical excuse to see Harken, but a dangerous habit to form.

Instead she went into the morning room and found her mother there at her oak secretary, writing correspondence. The room, unlike the dining room, shimmered with morning light. It was decorated in shades of ivory and peach, with chintzes instead of jacquards, and French doors instead of casements. They were opened to the sunny east veranda, letting in a welcome breeze.

"Good morning, Mother."

Levinia looked up briefly, then continued writing.

"Good morning, dear."

"Where is everybody? The house seems deserted."

"Your father's gone back to the city. The aunts are on the back veranda in the shade and the girls went off to Betsy Whiting's. I'm not precisely sure where Theron is. He had his spyglass, though, so he's probably up in a tree somewhere getting his clothing dirty."

"Will Father be back tonight?"

"No, not until tomorrow."

"Oh Criminey, why not?"

"I've asked you not to use that vulgar expression, Lorna. What's so important that it can't wait a day?"

"Oh, nothing. I just wanted to talk to him." She headed for the door but Levinia stopped her.

"Just a moment, Lorna. I want to speak to you."

Lorna turned back and began explaining, "Mother, I know I said I'd be back in two hours yesterday, but it was so nice on the lake and—"

"It's not about that. Close the doors, dear."

Nonplussed, Lorna stared at her mother a moment before closing the pocket doors and crossing the room.

"It's about Saturday night," Levinia said. Her hard-edged lips looked as if they could cut glass.

"Saturday night?" Lorna lowered herself to the edge of a sofa.

Levinia sat back in her chair. "I noticed it, and Aunt Henrietta noticed it, so certainly others around the room did, too."

"Noticed what?"

"That you invited Taylor out onto the veranda." Lorna was already rolling her eyes before her mother went on, "Lorna, it simply isn't done."

"Mother, there were at least fifteen people in the room!"

"All the more reason for you to mind your manners."

"But, Mama—"

"You're the oldest, Lorna. You set the example for your sisters to follow, and frankly, dear, in this last year I've been growing more and more concerned about your flinging propriety to the winds. Now, I've talked to you about it before, but as Aunt Henrietta said—"

"Oh, blast Aunt Henrietta!" Lorna threw her hands in the air and popped to her feet. "She put a bug in your ear, I suppose. What's the matter with that woman?"

"Shh! Lorna, hold your voice down!"

Lorna lowered her voice but squared off to face her mother. "You know what Aunt Henrietta's problem is? She hates men, that's what. Aunt Agnes told me so. Henrietta had a beau she was engaged to, but he threw her over for someone else and she's hated men ever since."

"Be that as it may, she was only thinking about your welfare when she brought up the subject of you and Taylor."

"Mother, I thought you liked Taylor."

"I do, dear. Your father and I both like Taylor. As a matter of fact we've had frequent discussions about what a perfect husband Taylor would be for you."

Here it was, what Lorna had suspected.

Her mother's eyes dropped to the desktop while she lifted her pen horizontally and repeatedly touched it to her ink blotter. "I've never mentioned it before, but you're eighteen now and Taylor has been paying a lot of attention to you this summer. But Lorna, when his mother and father are in the room and you entice him onto the veranda—"

"I did not *entice* him! It was stiflingly hot in the house and the men were stoking up their cigars. And anyway, Jenny was with us every second."

"And what lesson does it teach Jenny when you take the lead in these amorous tête-à-têtes?"

"Amorous . . ." Lorna was so incensed her mouth dropped open. "Mother, I do not engage in amorous tête-à-têtes!"

"Theron has seen one of them through his spyglass."

"Theron!"

"The other night, when you and Taylor came home from the band concert."

"I'd like to ram that spyglass down Theron's gullet!"

"Yes, I'm sure you would," Levinia said, cocking her left eyebrow, dropping her preoccupation with the pen.

Lorna sank onto the arm of a sofa and said straight out, "Taylor kissed me, Mother. Is there anything wrong with that?"

Levinia folded her hands tightly on the desktop. "No, I suppose there isn't. One must expect young swains to do that, but you must never . . ." Levinia stopped and studied her joined hands as if search-ing for the proper phrase. She cleared her throat. Her face had turned bright scarlet, her knuckles white.

"Must never what, Mother?"

Staring at her hands, Levinia said, barely above a whisper, "Let them touch you."

Lorna, too, felt herself coloring. "Mother!" she whispered, abashed. "I wouldn't!"

Levinia met her daughter's eyes. "You must understand, Lorna, this is very difficult for a mother to say, but it's my duty to warn you. Men will try things." She reached out and touched Lorna's hand urgently. "Even Taylor. As fine a young man as he is, he'll try things, and when he does, you must withdraw immediately. You must come into the house or . . . or insist on leaving for home at once. Do you understand?"

"Yes, Mother," Lorna answered obediently. "You may trust me to do exactly that."

Levinia looked relieved. She sat back and relaxed her hands on her lap. The flush began fading from her face. "Well then, that unpleasantness is taken care of. And in the future, may I rely on you to let Taylor be the one to do the inviting during this courtship?"

"Mother, I'm not sure he's courting me."

"Oh, bosh, of course he is. He's simply been waiting for you to come of age. Now you are and I suspect things will advance quite fast this summer."

There seemed little more to say. Considering that the conversa-tion had clearly defined Levinia's and Gideon's approval of Taylor DuVal, the room held a lingering tension.

"May I go now, Mother?"

"Yes, of course. I must finish my letters."

Lorna walked slowly to the pocket doors, rolled them open and exited the morning room in a state of total confusion. What exactly had Mother been saying? That kissing was acceptable within bounds? That men would try to press those bounds by touching? Touching where? Mother's warning had been so vague, yet her blush spoke more clearly than her implications, suggesting that nothing further could be said on the subject.

One thing, however, was sterling clear. If Mother was displeased over Lorna's suggesting she and Taylor step onto the veranda, she would positively detonate if she learned Lorna had set up an assignation with a kitchen handyman and had had a picnic with him.

Lorna made up her mind she would steer clear of the kitchen and keep herself out of a potential pickle.

The remainder of Monday passed with stultifying uneventfulness. The range of activities available to those of the female gender left Lorna bored and restless. One could garden, fill scrapbooks, collect shells, butterflies or birds' nests, read, stitch, go shopping, have lemonade on the veranda, attend chautauquas or play the piano.

Lorna thought a game of tennis sounded much more exciting, but her friend Phoebe Armfield had taken the train into Saint Paul to shop, and Lorna's sisters were at Betsy Whiting's. As for sailing, Lorna was afraid to sneak out in the catboat after returning late yesterday. There was the rowboat, of course, but without Tim and Jens Harken waiting on the opposite shore it seemed pointless. After a light noon dinner (during which she wondered if Jens had picked and washed the vegetables) Lorna napped in the hammock. She played croquet with her sisters on the lawn in the late afternoon, and caught Theron in his room just before supper, issuing a warning that if he spied on her any more she was going to store his spyglass in his thorax.

He cackled and singsonged, "Lorna's sparking Taylor! Lorna's sparking Taylor!" and clattered down the front stairs when she tried to catch and throttle him.

Finally, in the early evening, Phoebe Armfield came to Lorna's rescue. She walked over from her parents' cottage four houses down the shoreline and said, "Come over and see what I bought today."

Walking west along the shaded road that bisected the island, Lorna exclaimed, "I'm so glad you came! I thought I would die of boredom today!"

The Armfields' summer retreat was no more a "cottage" than the Barnetts'. It had seventeen rooms on fifteen acres: Phoebe's father was the second generation of a mining empire which had accumulated its original wealth selling iron ore to the steel foundaries during the building of the railroads.

Phoebe's room was perched in a turret with a view of the lake to the north. The doors of her armoire were thrown open and hung with new frocks, which Phoebe modeled for her friend, one for an upcoming moonlight sail, which the yacht club had organized, and another for a dance aboard the excursion steamer *Dispatch* the following weekend.

"I'm going with Jack." Jackson Lawless was a young man who stood to inherit his father's hardware holdings in Saint Paul. The Lawless family's cottage was located in Wildwood, across the lake.

"Are you going with Taylor?" Phoebe asked, swirling about with the dress pressed to her front. She was a petite girl with hair the color of cinnamon apples, and a bubbly disposition.

"I don't know. I suppose."

"What do you mean, you suppose? Don't you *like* Taylor?"

"Of course I do. It's just that it seems as though he's everywhere our families are, his and mine. If I didn't like him, there'd be no way to escape him."

"Well, if you don't want him just let me know. I think he's cute, and Daddy says he's smart, too. He'll take his father's millions and double them in no time."

"Phoebe, do you ever get tired of having a father who has millions?"

Phoebe halted in mid-swirl and stared at Lorna in astonishment. She hooked the hanger over the top of the armoire door and rocketed onto the bed, making it bounce.

"Lorna Barnett, what's gotten into you? Are you saying you'd rather be poor?"

Lorna fell backward, staring at the crocheted tester above Phoebe's bed.

"I don't know what I'm saying. I'm in a mood, that's all. But just think of it, if we didn't have all this money, would our fathers care who we chose for friends, or whether or not it was ladylike to sail and play tennis? I'm so sick and tired of being told what to do by my father. *And* my mother!"

"I know. So am I." Phoebe became suddenly gloomy. "Sometimes I get like you. I want to just *do something!* To assert myself and make them realize I'm eighteen years old and I shouldn't have to live by all their silly rules."

Lorna studied her friend, suddenly bursting with her secret. Smugly she divulged, "I did something."

Phoebe came out of her torpor. "What? Lorna Barnett, tell me! What did you do?"

Lorna sat up, her eyes bright. "I'll tell you, but you must promise not to tell another living soul, because if my father found out he'd put me in a convent."

"I promise I won't tell." Phoebe crossed her heart and pressed forward eagerly. "What did you do?"

"I had a picnic with our kitchen handyman."

Phoebe's eyes and mouth formed three O's and stayed that way until Lorna put a finger beneath her chin and pushed.

"Close your mouth, Phoebe."

"Lorna, you didn't!"

"Oh, it's not the way it sounds. Tim Iversen was there, too, and we talked about boats; but Phoebe, it's so exciting! Harken thinks he can—"

"Harken?"

"Jens Harken, that's his name. He thinks he can design a boat that will revolutionize yacht racing. He says it'll beat anything on the water, but none of the yacht club members will listen to him. He actually went so far as to put a note in my father's dessert on Saturday night, and Papa got so angry he created a deplorable scene."

"So that's what it was all about! Everyone on the island is talking about it."

Lorna filled in the rest of the story, from her mother's and father's argument in the kitchen passage to her plans to intercede with her father on Harken's behalf.

When she finished, Phoebe asked, "Lorna, you aren't going to see him again, are you?"

"Goodness no. I told you, I'm just going to encourage Papa to listen to him. And besides, Mother spoke to me this morning about Taylor. She and Papa think he'd be the perfect match for me."

"And of course he is. You've told me so yourself."

Lorna, however, looked thoughtful. Her gaze rested on the crocheted bedspread as she unconsciously hooked it again and again with a fingernail and let it pull away.

"Phoebe, may I ask you something?"

"Of course . . ." Phoebe became concerned at Lorna's quick reversal of mood and touched her friend's hand. "What is it, Lorna?"

Lorna continued staring at the spread. "It's something Mother said to me this morning and it's . . . well, it's very confusing." Lorna raised her disturbed gaze and asked, "Has Jack ever kissed you?"

Phoebe blushed. "A couple of times."

"Has he ever . . . well, touched you?"

"Touched me? Of course he's touched me. The first time he kissed me he was holding me by my shoulders and the second time he put his arms around me."

"I don't think that's what Mother meant, though. She said that men would try to touch women—even Taylor—and that if he tried I must immediately come into the house. Mother was terribly embarrassed when she said it. Her face was so red I thought she might pop her collar button. But I don't know what she meant. I just thought maybe . . . well, maybe you'd know."

Phoebe's expression had turned sickly. "Something's going on, Lorna, because my mother had the same kind of talk with me one day this spring, and she got the same way, all red in the face and looking everywhere in the room but at me."

"What exactly did she say?"

"She said that I was a young lady now, and that when I went out with Jack I must always keep my legs crossed."

"Keep your legs crossed! What does that have to do with any-thing?"

"I don't know. I'm just as confused as you are."

"Unless . . ."

The flabbergasting thought struck them both at once. They stared at each other, unwilling to believe it.

"Oh no, Lorna, that's not possible." They considered awhile before Phoebe asked, "What did your mother say again?"

Neither of the girls realized they were whispering.

"She said that Taylor might try to touch me and I must not let him. What did your mother say?"

"She said when I'm with Jack I must keep my legs crossed."

Lorna put her fingertips to her lips and whispered, "Oh dear, they couldn't have meant there, could they?"

Phoebe whispered, "Of course they didn't mean there. Why would a man do such a thing?"

"I don't know, but why did our mothers blush?"

"I don't know."

"Why are we whispering?"

Phoebe shrugged.

After some more silent rumination, Lorna suggested, "Maybe you could ask Mitchell sometime."

"Are you crazy! Ask my brother!"

"No, I guess that's not such a good idea."

"He can teach us to sail whenever we can sneak out to do it, but I'd go to my grave ignorant before I'd ask him anything about something like this."

"All right, I said it wasn't such a good idea. Who else could we ask?"

Neither of them could think of a soul.

"Somehow," Lorna ventured, "this is all tied up with kissing."

"I suspected the same thing, but Mother never warned me not to kiss."

"Neither did mine, even when she found out I had been. That little pissant Theron was spying on me and Taylor and he told Mother. That's what started all this."

"Lorna, have you ever seen your mother and father kissing?"

"Heavens no. Have you?"

"Once. They were in the library and they didn't know I had come around the doorway."

"Did they say anything?"

"Mother said, 'Joseph, the children.'"

"'Joseph, the children'? That's all?"

Phoebe shrugged.

"Did he touch her?"

"He was holding her by the tops of her arms."

Silence again while the girls stared at their skirts, then at each other, coming up with nothing. First Lorna turned onto her back. Then Phoebe followed suit.

They stared upward a long time before Lorna said, "Oh, it's so confusing."

"And mysterious."

Lorna sighed.

And Phoebe sighed.

And they wondered when and how the mystery would be solved.

Chapter
FOUR

THE moonlight sail was rained out, forcing Lorna to postpone the talk with her father until Saturday night, when both she and Tim Iversen would be attending the dance aboard the steamer *Dispatch*.

She dressed in a gown of rich silk organdy in vibrant petunia pink. Its basque was trimmed with white point guipure lace and was shaped by graceful bretelles that erupted into billows upon her shoulders and met in points at the center waist, both front and back. The skirt, fitted in front, broke into pleats that fell behind and caught her heels in a miniature train as she crossed her bedroom to her dressing table.

The children's maid, Ernesta, was positively abysmal at dressing hair, especially at creating the new "Gibson girl" poufs, which Lorna herself had practiced for long hours before mastering, so Ernesta had been dismissed to see after Theron's supper while Lorna was preparing for the dance.

Jenny and Daphne had drawn up stools and sat flanking Lorna while she put the finishing touches on her hair. The younger girls watched, transfixed, while, with curling tongs, Lorna created a haze of fine corkscrews around her face and nape. She pulled at them, frowning as they sprang back, then with a wet fingertip touched a bar of soap and stuck two curls to her skin.

"Gosh, Lorna, you're so lucky," Jenny said.

"You'll be allowed at the dances, too, as soon as you're eighteen."

"But that's two whole years," Jenny whined.

Daphne crossed her wrists over her heart and faked a swoon. "And who will she *drooool* over when Taylor DuVal is already married to you?"

"You just shut up, Daphne Barnett!" Jenny retorted.

"Girls, stop it now and help me pin this in my hair." Lorna held up a cluster of silk sweet peas trimmed with wired teardrop pearls. Jenny won the honors and secured it in Lorna's hair while Lorna donned pearl earbobs and atomized her throat with orange-blossom cologne.

The final results awed even Daphne, who crooned, "Gosh, Lorna, it's no wonder Taylor DuVal is sweet on you."

Rising, Lorna petted Daphne on both plump cheeks, nearly touching her nose to nose. "Oh, Daph, you're so sweet." The two younger girls adulated their older sister as Lorna made her taffeta-lined train whistle across the floor to the free-standing cheval mirror. Posing before it, she pressed her skirt flat to her belly and twisted to see what she could of her train.

"I guess that'll do."

Jenny rolled her eyes and crossed the floor, playfully aping her older sister, lifting an invisible skirt, dipping her shoulders grace-lessly. "La-dee-da . . . I guess that'll do." Turning serious, she added, "You'll be the prettiest girl on that boat, Lorna, and don't pretend you don't know it."

"Oh, who cares about being pretty anyway? I'd rather be adventur-ous and sporting and interesting. I'd rather be the organizer of the first women's yachting club in the state of Minnesota or hunt wild tigers in the velds of Africa. If I could do that nobody would say, 'There goes Lorna Barnett, isn't she pretty?' They'd say, 'There goes Lorna Barnett, who sails as well as the men and hunts with the best of them. Did you hear she has a dozen loving cups on her mantel and the head of a tiger mounted above it?' That's what kind of woman I'd like to be."

"Well, good luck, because Papa would mount *your* head above the mantel if he found out you'd ever gone to Africa hunting. In the meantime, I guess you'll just have to settle for being Taylor DuVal's dance partner."

Lorna took pity on Jenny and petted her cheeks, too. "You're sweet, too, Jenny, and I'll tell Taylor that if you were eighteen years old you'd let him sign your dance card several times tonight, how is that?"

"Lorna Barnett, don't you *dare* tell Taylor such a thing! I'd positively die of mortification if you uttered one single word to him!"

Laughing, taking her ivory fan, waggling three fingers in farewell, Lorna swept from the room.

In the hallway she encountered Aunt Agnes just stepping out of her room.

"Oh my, it's little Lorna. Stop a minute and let me have a look." She took Lorna's hands and held them out from her sides. "Land, don't you look radiant. All grown up and off to the dance."

Lorna executed a twirl for her. "On the boat."

"With that young man Mr. DuVal, I expect." Aunt Agnes's eyes grew twinkly.

"Yes. He's meeting me at the dock."

"He's a handsome one, that one. I expect when he sees you he'll want to fill every spot on your dance card."

"Shall I let him?" Lorna teased.

Aunt Agnes's expression grew mischievous. "That depends on who else asks. Why, when I was being courted by Captain Dearsley I made certain I always danced with others, just to keep him guessing, though no one could dance like he." With a rapturous expression, she closed her eyes and tilted her head. One hand touched her heart, the other drifted into the air. "Ah, we would waltz until the room fairly spun, and the gold fringe on his epaulettes would sway and we would smile at each other and it would seem the violins were playing for us alone."

Lorna took Captain Dearsley's place and waltzed Aunt Agnes along the upstairs hall, humming "Tales from the Vienna Woods." Together they swirled, smiling, Lorna's gown rustling, both of them singing, "Da-dum, da-dum, da-dum . . . da daaa . . ."

"Oh Aunt Agnes, I'll bet you were the belle of the ball."

"I once had a dress very nearly the color of yours and Captain Dearsley said it made me look exactly like a rosebud. The night I first wore it he was dressed all in white, and I daresay every woman at the dance wished she were in my shoes."

They waltzed on. "Tell me about your shoes. What were they like?"

"They weren't shoes, they were slippers. White satin high-heeled slippers."

"And your hair?"

"It was deep auburn then, swept up into side clusters, and Captain Dearsley said at times it picked up the color of the sunset and shot it back at the sky."

Someone ordered, "Agnes, let that girl go! Her parents are waiting for her in the porte cochere!"

The waltzing stopped. Lorna turned to find her aunt Henrietta standing at the top of the stairs.

"Aunt Agnes and I were just reminiscing."

"Yes, I heard. About Captain Dearsley again. Honestly, Agnes, Lorna isn't the least bit interested in your witless fantasies about that man."

"Oh, but I am!" Aunt Agnes had clasped her hands as if about to wring them together. Lorna commandeered them for one more squeeze. "I wish you were coming to the dance tonight, and Captain Dearsley, too. Taylor would sign your dance card, I'm sure, and just imagine—we could exchange partners for a waltz!"

Aunt Agnes kissed her cheek. "You're a darling girl, Lorna, but this is your time. You just run along now and have a grand evening."

"I shall. And what are you going to do?"

"I have some flowers to press, and I thought I just might wind up the music box and listen to a disc or two."

"Well, have a nice evening. I shall tell Taylor that a little rosebud sent her hello." She bowed formally from the waist. "And thanks ever so much for the waltz." As she whisked by Henrietta, who wore her perennially scolding expression, Lorna said, "When Aunt Agnes cranks up the music box, why don't you ask her to dance?"

Aunt Henrietta made a sound as if she was clearing her nostrils, and Lorna went down the stairs.

She rode to the dance with her parents in their open landau. The ride took mere minutes, for Manitou Island itself was a scant mile long and covered only fifty-three acres. It was connected to land by a short arched wooden bridge, three blocks beyond which began a

string of stunning lakeside hotels, giving way to the town of White
Bear Lake itself.

Crossing the Manitou Bridge, the horses' hooves created a melodi-
ous echo, which turned blunt as the carriage swung southwest onto
Lake Avenue. The evening was glorious, eighty degrees and golden.
Beneath the trees contouring the lakeshore winsome ribbons of
shadow stretched eastward toward the azure water. Overhead, white
gulls hung like kites, while out on West Bay sailboats skimmed.

Lorna was watching them when Gideon, in formal black, with his
hands crossed on the head of a brass walking stick, remarked, "Your
mother tells me that she spoke to you about Taylor."

"Yes, she did."

"Then you know our feelings regarding him. I'm given to understand you're to be under Taylor's escort at the dance tonight."

"Yes, I am."

"Excellent."

"But that doesn't mean I won't dance with others, Papa."

Gideon glowered and his moustache bounced as he replied, "I
don't want you doing anything that will give Taylor the idea you
don't want to marry him."

"Marry him? Papa, he hasn't even asked me."

"Be that as it may, he's an ambitious young fellow, and a good-
looking one, too, I might add."

"I'm not saying he isn't ambitious or good-looking. I'm saying you
and Mother are putting words in his mouth."

"The man has been dancing attendance on you all summer. Don't
worry, he'll ask."

Since tonight was not the time she wanted to irritate her father,
Lorna prudently let the subject drop as they approached their desti-
nation.

The *Saint Paul Globe* had recently reported that the village of
White Bear Lake was home to more wealth than any other town in
the United States of America. When the Barnett landau pulled up,
the scene that greeted them might well have illustrated the article.
The members of the yacht club had chartered the steamer *Dispatch*
for the dance. It waited beside the Hotel Chateaugay dock, where a
crowd had already gathered beneath the roof of the dock gazebo.

Across the street the hotel itself reigned over Lake Avenue with its commanding view of the water. Turreted and gabled, it was painted white with green shutters and had a vast veranda that overlooked a finely shaded lawn dappled with hammocks and iron benches. Tonight the scene was studded with the jeweled hues of ladies' frocks, while their escorts in penguin colors paid dotage at their sides. On the street liveried carriage drivers drew up matched pairs and set wooden carriage blocks on the cobbles for the alighting gentry. The sound of hoofbeats mingled with the measured burps of the *Dispatch*'s engine, while liveried footmen hurried to scrape into their tin carry-aways any offensive nuggets dropped by the horses before the ladies' noses became offended or their trains tainted. From the upper deck of the *Dispatch* came the music of violins and oboes as a small orchestra struck into "The Band Played On," the signal for boarding.

Taylor spotted Lorna the moment she alighted. He left his parents and came from the shade of the hotel lawn wearing a broad smile.

"Lorna," he said, "how lovely you look." Taking her gloved hand, he bowed and kissed it. Like a proper gentleman, he immediately released it and greeted her parents.

"Mr. Barnett, Mrs. Barnett, you're both looking splendid this evening. Mother and Father are over on the lawn."

When the elder Barnetts had sashayed away, Taylor reclaimed Lorna's hand. "Miss Barnett." His eyes wore an especially appreciative light. "You look as delicious as an ice-cream sundae, all pink and white and smelling delectable, I might add."

"Orange blossom. And you're looking and smelling wonderful yourself."

"Sandalwood," he rejoined, and they both laughed as he offered his elbow.

He was an attentive partner, and undeniably attractive. As they boarded the *Dispatch* Lorna noted more than one gaze returning to them. Taylor's dark brown beard and moustache were trimmed to perfection, little disguising his firm jawline and attractive mouth. His nose had a faint crookedness that seemed to disappear in bold sunlight, but had its own engaging appeal when hit by shadows from a certain angle. His eyes were hazel and his brown hair parted just off-center, combed back above well-shaped if extraordinarily large ears. He did look attractive tonight, in his dress blacks with a white winged collar pushing up firmly against his throat.

Lorna told him, "My aunt Agnes sends her fondest hello. She wishes she could be here tonight."

"She's a darling."

"She and I had a waltz in the upper hall before I left."

He laughed and said, "If I may be permitted, you, Miss Lorna Barnett, are a darling, too."

Arm in arm, they boarded the boat.

Phoebe was already aboard with Jack Lawless and came to brush Lorna's cheek and say hello. When Taylor took Phoebe's hand in greeting she pinkened but declared, "I swear you two do turn heads." She smiled briefly at Lorna, much longer at Taylor. "But even so, I hope you won't forget, Taylor, that the rest of us plain Janes would like a dance sometime tonight."

Taylor replied, "All I need is a sharp pencil." He caught the one dangling from Phoebe's dance card while Jack, in return, signed Lorna's and suggested they all repair to the upper deck, where the band had struck into "Beautiful Dreamer."

Upstairs, the seven P.M. sun was blinding. A forward bell clanged twice and a moment later a thump and lurch sent the boat under way. The stutter of the engine quickened. The smoky blue smell of naphtha exhaust lifted momentarily, then the craft eased away from shore and the air freshened. The breeze fluttered Lorna's curls and ruffled her skirt. She shaded her eyes and searched for Tim, spotting him finally when the launch turned eastward and eased the golden glare.

"Tim!" she called, waving and moving toward him.

"Good evening, Miss Lorna," he greeted, removing the pipe from his mouth, his good eye assessing her squarely while the other seemed to look out over the aft rail.

"Oh, Tim, I'm so glad you're here."

"I told you I'd be here, didn't I?"

"I know, but plans can change. We'll talk to my father tonight, won't we?"

"My, you are impatient, aren't you?"

"Please, Tim, don't tease me. Will you do it tonight?"

"Of course. Jens is as impatient as you are to see what Gideon will say."

"But listen, Tim, let's not speak to him until the sun goes down and it gets cooler, because Papa hates the heat. And by that time he'll have drunk a couple of mint juleps, which will have taken the edge off his everlasting urge to dissent. Agreed?"

Tim leaned back from the waist, smiling at her speculatively.

"Do you mind if I ask, Miss Lorna, what stake you have in this? Because, as I remarked earlier, you seem unduly impatient to reverse your father's opinion of young Harken."

Lorna's eyes took on the roundness of professed innocence. Her lips opened, closed, then opened again. She tried valiantly to remain composed and keep her cheeks from coloring. Finally she replied, "Suppose he's right and his boat beats everything on the water?"

"You're sure that's the only reason you're pursuing this?"

"Why, of course. What other possible reason could there be?"

"Could I be wrong, or did I detect a faint attraction between the two of you on Sunday?"

Lorna's cheeks most definitely flared. "Oh, Tim, for goodness' sake, don't be silly. He's kitchen help."

"Yes, he is. And I feel obliged to remind you of that, because I am, after all, a friend to both your father and Jens Harken."

"I know. But please, Tim, don't mention anything about the picnic."

"I promised I wouldn't."

"You know my father," she said, squeezing his sleeve in appeal. "You know how he is about us girls. We're nothing to him but fluffy empty-headed matrimonial material to whom he gives orders which he expects to have obeyed without incident. Just once, Tim, just *once* I'd like my father to look at me as if he knew I had a brain in my head, as if he knew I had wishes and aspirations that go beyond catching a husband and running a house and raising children the way Mama's done. I'd like to sail. Papa won't let me sail. I'd like to attend college. Papa says it's unnecessary. I'd like to travel to Europe. He says I can do that on my honeymoon. Don't you understand, Tim? There is no way on this earth for a woman to gain an advantage on Papa. Well, maybe—just maybe—I might change that if he listens to Harken and finances his boat. And if it should win, might Papa not at long last consider me in a new light?"

Tim covered her hand on his sleeve with his own. The bowl of his pipe was warm against her knuckles as he gave her hand a squeeze.

"When you're ready to talk to Gideon, you give me a little whistle."

She smiled and let her hand slide from Tim's sleeve, and thought what a truly nice man he was.

She danced with Taylor and Jack, and Percy Tufts and Phoebe's father; with Taylor again, and once with Tim, and yet again with Taylor and with Phoebe's brother, Mitchell, who inquired how her sailing was coming along and offered to take her out for another lesson anytime she wanted. Though Mitchell was two years her junior, she detected an interest in her that went beyond nautical instructions, and found herself surprised by it, for she'd always thought of him as Phoebe's little tag-along brother, much as she'd thought of Theron. Mitchell had, however, grown tall, his shoulders had broadened, and he was doing his best to begin growing a beard, which presently had the appearance of a mouse with mange. When he released her and turned her over to Taylor, he gave her hand a secret squeeze.

The sun set behind a bank of violet clouds with brilliant pink and gold edges. The air cooled. The *Dispatch* cruised leisurely around all three petals of the clover-shaped lake, and the gentlemen's cigar coals burned red as lava against the fallen night.

Again Lorna danced with Taylor while her father observed with an expression of smug approval on his face. She smiled up at her escort for Gideon's benefit, wondering all the while if a flat-bottomed boat could keep upright, and how long it would take to build one, and if Jens Harken knew what he was talking about, and what he was doing at Rose Point Cottage at this moment, and if he had some young kitchen maid he was wooing, and where he might take her to do so.

Across Taylor's shoulder she noted that Tim Iversen had moved over to Gideon and struck up a conversation. When the dance ended she requested, "Leave me with Papa, would you, Taylor? And come back to get me after two songs or so?"

"Of course." As he walked her toward Gideon, under cover of darkness, his fingers rode the notch above her hip and his hand kneaded the shallows of her spine, alarmingly close to her right buttock. It shot blood to her cheeks and sent strange impulses racing along her spine. She started when he spoke close to her ear. "You don't mind if I ask his permission to drive you home, do you?"

"Of course not," she replied, certain that this was some of the touching her mother had warned her about, and surprised that it had begun right under her father's nose. She had expected such things occurred only under the most dark and clandestine of circumstances.

"Mr. Barnett," Taylor said, delivering her to her father. "Do you have any objection to my driving Lorna home tonight?"

Gideon removed a cigar from his mouth and cleared his throat. "No objection whatsoever, my boy."

"I'll be back," Taylor said quietly, and disappeared.

Tim told Lorna, "Your father and I were talking about next year's regatta."

Bless your heart, Tim, Lorna thought.

Gideon said, "It seems Tim here has got wind of that harebrained scheme our kitchen handyman came up with about how to build a faster boat. Seems the two of them have done some sailing together."

"Yes, I know. Tim and I talked about it on Sunday."

"So I heard. Clear across the lake you rowed."

"It was such a heavenly day, I couldn't resist. And I had enough food for two, so I shared my picnic with Tim and we got to talking about Harken's ideas."

Tim took over. "The fellow says the scow will plane, Gideon. And it makes a lot of sense to me that if it doesn't have to cut through so much water it'll be faster than the sloops by far. If I were you, I'd give Harken a listen."

"When everybody else laughed him away?"

Lorna put in, "But supposing, after they did, that you were the only one who'd listen, and Harken's scheme worked. You are, after all, the commodore of this yacht club. If his boat does what he says it will do, you could be immortalized."

Gideon puffed on his cigar and pondered. He loved being reminded he was commodore, except when being reminded as he'd been by last week's newspapers, which listed him as commodore of the losing yacht club. Those articles, accompanied by Tim's pictures, had undoubtedly been featured as far away as the East Coast, for the country was closely watching the heartland and following the formation of the Inland Lake Yachting Association, which was still in its infancy.

"Papa, listen," Lorna reasoned. "Look around you. There's more wealth on this very launch than can ever be spent in your lifetime. What good is all that money if you don't enjoy it? You won't even miss the piddling few hundred dollars it'll cost to finance the building of this boat. And if it capsizes, so what? Harken said—to Tim, that is—that it won't sink. It'll have a cedar hull instead of a metal-clad one, and the masts will be hollow, so they'll float. And he says that if she did go over, a five-man crew could right her like nothing, even without sandbags!"

They let silence drift awhile before Tim added, "He says a thirty-eight-footer will go eighteen hundred pounds instead of the usual twenty-five hundred. Can you imagine what a boat that light could do with a little wind, Gideon?"

"All we're suggesting, Papa, is that you talk to him."

"He can explain it a lot better than I can, Gid."

"And if you don't think his ideas have merit, don't put up the money. But he's your best chance to win next year and you know it."

Gideon cleared his throat, spit over the rail and flicked his ashes into the water. "I'll think about it," he told the two of them, and whisked the air with his fingers as if brushing crumbs from his lap. "Now go away and quit pestering me, Lorna. This is a dance. Go on and dance with young Taylor."

She grinned and curtsied playfully. "Yes, Papa. So long, Tim."

When she was gone, Gideon remarked to Tim, "That girl is up to something, and I'm damned if I know what it is."

The *Dispatch* docked at a quarter past eleven. Gas lanterns illuminated the gazebo as the yacht club members disembarked and broke into smaller groups. Some of the older set decided to take aperitifs and desserts at the Hotel Chateaugay. Lorna's and Taylor's parents went off with them. Lorna bid good night to Phoebe, and Taylor took her arm.

"The carriage is over here," he said.

"Do you have to come back and get your parents?" she asked.

"No. We took separate rigs."

They sauntered along the street beneath puddles of gaslight. Behind them the chugging of the naphtha launch quieted for the night. In the yard of the hotel the hammocks hung empty like cocoons whose inhabitants had flown. The smell of the lakeshore mingled with that of horses as they passed the row of sleeping animals still hitched to their conveyances. Several rigs went past, hoofbeats fading into the darkness as Taylor handed Lorna into the buggy, stepped to the side of the horse and tightened her bellyband, then boarded the rig himself.

"It's a little cool," he said, twisting around and reaching behind them. "I think I'll put the bonnet up." A moment later the light from a half-moon was cut off and the scent of leather freshened as the bonnet spread above their heads.

Taylor took up the reins and flicked them, but the horse set off at a lethargic walk.

"Old Tulip is lazy tonight. She doesn't like being awakened from her nap." He looked down at Lorna. "Do you mind?"

"Not at all. It's a heavenly night."

They plodded back to Manitou Island at the pace Tulip herself set, sometimes riding in deep shadow, sometimes turning into a plash of moonlight that turned Lorna's bodice lavender. On the island itself they passed beneath an allée of old elms that cut off any wink of light from overhead. The single road bisected the island, dividing its properties into northshore and southshore sites, each with its grand cottage and surrounding lawns viewed from the rear side through deeply wooded backlots. They passed the Armfields' but turned off the road well short of Rose Point, into a trail so narrow the spokes of the carriage wheels fanned the underbrush.

"Taylor, where are we going?"

"Just up ahead, where we can see the water. Whoa, Tulip."

The buggy stopped in a small clearing, facing the moonlight, with a bit of lakeshore visible through the willows ahead, and the backside of an outbuilding to their left. Somewhere in the nearby dark a horse whinnied.

"Why, we're out behind the Armfields' stable, aren't we?"

Taylor set the brake and tied the reins around its handle.

"Yes, we are. If we peered really hard through the trees we might even see Phoebe's bedroom light."

Taylor relaxed and stretched one arm along the back of the tufted leather seat while Lorna leaned forward, searching for Phoebe's light.

"I don't see it."

Taylor smiled and brushed her bare shoulder with the back of one finger.

"Taylor, there are mosquitoes out here."

"Yes, I suppose there are, but there are no little brothers or sisters." Indulgently he drew her back into the carriage, took her left hand and began patiently removing her glove. He did the same with her right and, when it was bare, held it in his own and searched her face.

"Taylor," she whispered, her heart racing, "I really should go home."

"Whenever you say," he murmured and shut out the moonlight with his head as his arms circled her and his mouth descended to take a first kiss. His beard was soft, his lips warm, his chest firm as he drew her against it. She put her arms around him and felt herself tipped and twined just so, until their fit became exquisite and Taylor opened his mouth wider. The heat and wetness of his tongue sent all thoughts of mosquitoes and Phoebe's light from her mind. He moved his head, slewing it in some canny motion that created magic within their joined mouths. Above her hip his right hand rested, kneading in counterpoint to his searching tongue. Somewhere in the distant rim of consciousness a bullfrog barked, and nearer, beneath the bonnet hood, the predicted mosquitoes arrived, buzzing, buzzing, landing, being brushed away while the kiss went on and on.

Its reluctant ending left them breathless, with their foreheads and noses touching.

"Am I forgiven for stealing you away into the woods?" he asked, nipping at her lips.

"Oh, Taylor, you've never kissed me like that before."

"I've wanted to. I knew from the moment you got out of your father's carriage tonight that I'd bring you here. How long do you think our parents will spend over dessert?"

"I don't know," she murmured.

His mouth descended once again, and hers lifted to meet it. With the second kiss his hands moved over her ribs and back as if chafing her warm after a thorough chilling. This, she supposed, could be none of the touching her mother had warned about, for it felt sublime and left her with no desire to run into the house.

Taylor ended the kiss himself, upon a grunt of amiable frustration, while thrusting both arms around her waist and reversing their positions, so she cut off the moonlight from his face. Listing to one side, he sprawled across the buggy seat and bent her forward atop his breast. "Lorna Barnett," he said against her neck, "you're the prettiest creature God ever put on this earth and you smell good enough to eat."

He licked her neck, surprising her and bringing out a giggle.

"Taylor, stop that." She tried to shrug him away, but his tongue made a hot wet spot and raised the scent of her orange-blossom perfume like a soft southern breeze through the soft northern night. She quit resisting and closed her eyes. "That must"—she struggled for breath—"taste awful." She tipped her head to accommodate him and felt a thrill shoot its warning from her middle. He bit her lightly, as stallions nip mares in the spring, and took her earlobe between his lips and suckled it before moving round to her lips again.

"Simply awful . . ." he murmured, transferring the taste of her own perfume from his tongue to hers. Where he led, she followed, opening her mouth to revel in exciting sensations. Kissing with open mouths . . . What a wondrous and mesmerizing convention. His hand on her side opened wide and his thumb moved across the silk of her bodice, its tip grazing the underside of her breast, sending delightful shivers everywhere.

She freed her mouth and whispered shakily, "Taylor, I must go home . . . please . . ."

"Yes . . ." he whispered, pursuing her mouth with his own, his thumb clearly stroking the underside of her breast. ". . . So must I."

"Taylor, please . . ."

He was showing signs of resisting when a mosquito came and took a drink out of his forehead. When he slapped it Lorna righted herself on the buggy seat, putting space between them though her skirt remained caught on his pantleg.

"I don't want my mother and father to beat me home, Taylor."

"No, of course not." He straightened up and ran both hands over the sides of his hair. "You're right."

She drew her skirt aright and tugged her bodice down all around, touched her hair and asked, "Am I mussed?"

With his hand he turned her face his way. His gaze, wearing a likable grin, went all around her hairline and came to rest on her mouth. "No one will guess," he answered. When she would have withdrawn, he held her as she was, swaying a thumb across her chin. "So very shy," he said. "I find that immensely attractive." He kissed the end of her nose. "Miss Barnett," he teased, "you may find me hanging around your doorstep a lot this summer."

She gazed up at him with the wonderment of a young woman led for the first time into the seductive realm of carnality, overcome by it and by him for being the first to teach her.

"Mr. DuVal," she replied without guile, "I certainly hope so."

Chapter
FIVE

O N Tuesday afternoon following the dance aboard the *Dispatch,* a small drawstring bag containing Levinia Barnett's loose change was delivered to the kitchen with orders that the coins were to be washed in soap and water. Jens Harken was busy doing so when the housekeeper, Mary Lovik, swept in.

She was a spare woman with a face like a waffle, fluted by its severe expression that reduced her mouth to a third its normal size and gave her unforgiving eyes the look of a weasel. She wore a white hat shaped like a soufflé, distinguished from those of the other female help by its pleats and diminutive size. Her hair was black, her dress gray and her apron starched so stiffly it gave off a *whang* like sheet metal when she walked.

Mrs. Lovik never moved amid her underlings without an air of self-importance. In the echelon of household help, she presided at the top, along with Chester Poor, the butler; everyone else fell beneath her, and she took contrary pleasure in reminding them at every turn.

"Harken!" she bellowed, flapping back the kitchen door and sweeping inside. "Mr. Barnett would like to see you in his study."

Harken's hands went motionless in the soapy water. "Me?"

"Yes you! Do you see anyone else in this room named Harken? Mr. Barnett doesn't like to be kept waiting, so get up there immediately!"

"Yes, ma'am. As soon as I finish these coins."

"Ruby can finish. Ruby, finish washing and drying Mrs. Barnett's change, and make sure every penny gets back to her."

Harken dropped the coins into the dishpan and reached for a towel to dry his hands.

"Do you know what he wants, Lovik?"

"It's *Mrs.* Lovik to you, and most certainly I don't know what he wants, though if he dismisses you over your outspokenness about the matter of the boats I shouldn't be at all surprised. Mrs. Schmitt! Has your help nothing better to do than stand and gape when someone walks into this room? Girls, get to work. Ruby, your apron is filthy. See to it that it's changed immediately. Harken, move!"

No sooner had Harken moved than Mrs. Lovik lambasted him again as he was about to push through the swinging door. "For pity's sake, turn your cuffs down and button your collar. You can't go into the master's study looking like kitchen riffraff."

Buttoning his collar and pushing the door with his backside, he replied, "But I am kitchen riffraff, Mrs. Lovik, and he knows it."

"I don't much care for your back talk, Harken, and I may as well tell you this, too—that if it were left up to me, you'd have been gone the very night you pulled that disrespectful stunt with the master's ice cream."

"But it wasn't up to you, was it?" He gave her a shameless grin, waved an arm toward the dining room passage and said, "After you, Mrs. Lovik."

She *whanged* along in front of him, with her snout in the air and her white cap bobbing. Officiously, she led the way to the foot of the main staircase and waved him on.

"Upstairs. And make sure you go back to the kitchen immediately when the master has dismissed you."

Upstairs.

Lord in heaven, they were some stairs. He'd never been up them before nor seen the gleaming mahogany handrail nor the cherubs on the newel post. The naked little fellows held up a gaslight and smiled down at him as he ascended upon a Turkish runner of blue, red and gold. Above, an arched window with a leaded-glass header looked down over the yard, and a second pair of cherubs held up another gaslight. Reaching it, he came to a T, where he stopped and looked left and right. Doors opened off the hall in both directions, with no clue as to which led into Mr. Barnett's study.

He chose left, coming first to a bedroom, where an old gray-haired lady sat asleep in a rocking chair with a book on her lap. He remembered serving her dinner that night in the dining room. He tiptoed past and peered into a bathroom with white-and-green granite tile on the floor, a china toilet with an oak water tank high on the wall above it, a pedestal sink and a huge sleigh-shaped bathtub with lion-paw feet. It smelled flowery and had a sunny window with a white curtain. Next he came to a boy's room, its wallpaper covered with windjammers on a blue background, its bed rumpled. Already he realized he'd chosen the wrong wing, but went on nonetheless, deciding to glance into the last rooms—more than likely the only chance he'd ever get.

He reached a doorway and stopped dead still.

There was Miss Lorna Barnett, sitting on a chaise longue reading a magazine. His stomach fluttered once at the sight of her. She was caught in the crossfire of light from two windows, and her hair was untended, her feet bare, her knees forming an easel for her magazine. She wore a pale lavender skirt and a white shirtwaist with a high stovepipe collar that was unbuttoned in the warm afternoon, wilting down over her collarbones. Her room was airy, with a view of the lake and the side garden. It was trimmed in the same pale blue as the striped skirt she'd worn a week ago Sunday.

She looked up when he stopped in the hall. Surprise clutched them both and turned them momentarily to statues.

"Harken?" she whispered, wide-eyed, coming to life muscle by muscle, lowering her knees and self-consciously covering her feet with her skirt. "What are you doing up here?"

"I'm sorry to disturb you, Miss Lorna, but I'm looking for your father's study. Upstairs, I was told."

"It's in the other wing. Second to the end on your right."

"Thank you. I'll find it."

He began to move away.

"Wait!" she called, throwing her magazine aside, dropping her feet to the floor.

He waited on the hall runner while she came and stood just within the doorway of her room. Her skirt was wrinkled and her shirtwaist limp. Her toenails showed below her hem.

"Has Father asked to see you?"

"Yes, miss."

Her eyes grew excited. "To talk about the boat, I'll bet! Oh, Harken, I'm sure of it."

"I don't know, miss. All Mrs. Lovik said was that I was to get myself up to the master's study and try not to look like kitchen riffraff while I was doing it." He glanced down at his trousers with damp spots on the belly, at his coarse white cotton shirt with black suspenders slicing it in thirds. "Seems I do, though." He lifted his wrists and let them fall.

"Oh, Mrs. Lovik." Lorna flapped a hand. "She's such a sour apple. Don't pay any attention to her. If Papa asked to see you we've got him thinking, and I'm sure it's about the boat. Just remember, there's nothing Papa wants so badly as to win. Nothing. He's simply not used to losing. So be convincing and maybe we'll see your boat built yet."

"I'll try, miss."

"And don't let Papa intimidate you." She pointed a finger to enforce her order. "He'll try, but don't let him."

"Yes, miss." He held his smile to a properly subdued one. How childishly enthusiastic she was, standing there improperly dressed, with her hair looking like burgundy wine splashed against a wall. It was dark and rich and stood out everywhere as if she'd been running her fingers through it while reading. Her state of dishevelment did little to disguise her natural beauty, which shone through without benefit of hats or curls or corset stays. He remembered she had said she'd forsaken the latter, and found himself charmed by the knowledge that she'd done the same with her stockings and shoes today. She was, without a doubt, the prettiest female he'd ever known.

"Well, I'd best not keep your father waiting."

"No, I guess not." She put two hands on the doorframe and leaned her top half out into the hall to point. "Down there. The one that's closed."

"Yes. Thank you." He headed away.

"Harken?" she whispered.

He stopped and turned.

"Good luck," she whispered.

"Thank you, miss."

When he got to Gideon's study door he looked back along the hall and found her head still poking out. She waggled two fingers at him, and he raised a palm to her, then knocked. She was still watching when Gideon Barnett ordered, "Come!"

Jens Harken entered a room with high, deep windows standing open behind a comma-shaped desk. At it Gideon Barnett sat, flanked by bookshelves on either side. The study smelled of cigar smoke and leather even though a brisk afternoon breeze flapped the heavy scarlet draperies at the windows. The room was a blend of light and dark, the light coming from the afternoon sun that slanted in obliquely, missing the desk itself but striking the spines of some books and one corner of the gleaming hardwood floor. The dark hovered in the sunless corners, where brown wing chairs surrounded a low table shared by a globe, a scattering of leather-bound books and a black lacquered humidor.

"Harken," Barnett said dourly in greeting.

"Good afternoon, sir." Harken came to a halt before the desk, remaining on his feet though there were four vacant chairs in the room.

Gideon Barnett let him stand. He stuck a cigar into his mouth and held it firmly with his teeth, drew his lips back and silently studied the blond man before him. The smoke lifted up and out the window. Barnett kept puffing, testing the man's mettle, waiting for the usual fidgeting to begin. Instead Harken stood at ease, his hands at his sides, his belly wet from some menial work he'd been doing in the kitchen.

"So!" Barnett finally barked, removing his cigar. "You think you know how to build boats."

"Yes sir."

"Fast boats?"

"Yes sir."

"How many have you built?"

"Enough. In a boatworks in Barnegat Bay."

Gideon Barnett hid the fact that he was impressed: Barnegat Bay, New Jersey, was a hotbed of sailing. The boating magazines were filled with articles about it. He pursed his lips, twirled his wet cigar tip around and around between them, and wondered what to make of the young whippersnapper who refused to be cowed by him.

"But have you ever built one of these things you're ranting about?"

"No sir."

"So you don't know if she'll capsize and sink."

"I know. She won't."

"You know," Barnett scoffed. "That's some flimsy conjecture to put money on."

Harken neither moved nor replied. His face remained impassive, his eyes steady on the older man's. Barnett found himself irritated by the fellow's unflappability.

"Some people around here are putting pressure on me to hear you out."

Again Harken said nothing, raising a commensurate urge in Barnett to fluster him.

"Well, say something, boy!" he burst out.

"I can show you on paper if you understand hull design."

Barnett nearly choked on his own spittle squelching the urge to throw the damned whelp out on his tailbone. Kitchen help intimating that *he*, Gideon Barnett, commodore of the White Bear Yacht Club, didn't understand hull design! Gideon threw down a pencil atop a stack of oversized white paper on his desktop. "Well, here! Draw!"

Harken glanced at the pencil, at Barnett, at the pencil again. Finally he picked it up, flattened one hand on the paper and began drawing. "Would you like me to come around there, sir, or will you come around here?"

A muscle in Barnett's jaw grew rigid, but he relinquished his position of superiority and walked around the desk while Harken continued drawing, one hand braced on the desk.

"The first thing you've got to understand is that I'm talking about two totally different kinds of boats here. I'm no longer talking about a displacement hull. I'm talking about a planing hull—light, flat, with very little wetted surface when it's heeled up." He went on sketching, cross-sectioning, comparing two yachts with two completely different outlines, explaining how the bow would lift when planing downwind, how the drag would be reduced when she was heeled up. He spoke of length and weight and natural lift. Of discarding the bowsprit, which would no longer be necessary because the sails would be much smaller. He spoke of gaff-rigging and sail plans and how much less they affected the scow's speed than did the overall boat shape. He spoke of a flat-bottomed sailboat without a fixed keel, something that had never been built before.

"So if there's no keel, where's your ballast?" Gideon asked.

"The crew acts as ballast, and there'll be no more need for sand-bagging."

"And they alone can keep it from capsizing?"

"No, not alone. The boat will have bilgeboards." Again he drew. "Instead of one fixed keel, we use two bilgeboards—sideboards, if you will—that can be dropped or raised as needed. You drop the leeboard when you're heeling, to prevent side drift, and just before tacking you change boards—up with one and down with another. See?"

Barnett thought awhile, studying the drawings.

"And you can design it?"

"Yes sir."

"And build it?"

"Yes sir."

"Single-handedly?"

"Pretty much. I might need one other man to help when I'm bending the ribs and applying the planking."

"I don't have a man to spare."

"I'll find one if you'll pay him."

"How much would it cost?"

"The whole boat? In the neighborhood of seven hundred dollars."

Barnett considered awhile. "How long would it take you?"

"Three months. Four at the most, including the work on the interior structure and the painting. I'd need tools and a shed to work in, that's all. I can build my own steam box."

Barnett stared at the drawings, snubbed out his cigar in an ashtray and walked to the window, where he stood looking out at the lake.

"The only thing I wouldn't make are the hardware and the sails. We'd farm out the sailmaking to Chicago," Harken told him, bringing Barnett's head around. "The boat can be done by fall and the sails made over the winter. I'll rig it myself. By next spring, when the season starts, she'll be seaworthy." Harken dropped his pencil and stood erect, facing Barnett and a glimpse of blue water behind him.

When Barnett said nothing, Harken went on. "I've sailed a lot, sir. My father sailed, and his father before him, and his father before him, clear back to the Vikings, I imagine. I know this plan will work as surely as I know where my love of water comes from."

The room fell silent while Barnett went on scrutinizing the younger man. "You're pretty confident, aren't you, boy?"

"Call it what you will, sir, I know that boat will work."

Barnett joined his hands behind his back, rose onto his toes once, settled back onto his heels and said, "I'll think about it."

"Yes sir," Harken replied quietly. "Then I'd best get back to the kitchen."

All the way to the study door he could feel Barnett's eyes burning into his back, could sense the man measuring him, could feel his reluctance to place faith in one of his underlings. Also he felt the depth of Barnett's obsession to be best at whatever he undertook. Miss Lorna had said her father hated losing, and that was obvious. Jens Harken wondered, should he be given the go-ahead to build this boat and it was as fast as he believed it would be, how a winning Gideon Barnett might repay him.

He took the straightest route back, noting that Miss Lorna's door was closed, tarrying not a moment. In the kitchen everyone was sitting around the table taking an afternoon breather over white cake and mint tea. They all jumped up and began babbling at once.

"What did he say? Is he going to let you build it? Did you go up to his study? What's it like?"

"Hold it, hold it!" He held up his hands to calm the excitement. "He said he'll think about it, nothing more."

The anticipation slid off their faces.

"I've got him thinking, though," Jens offered as consolation.

"What was his study like?" Ruby asked.

While he was describing it, the door from the servants' stairway burst open and Miss Lorna Barnett breached the kitchenhold again.

"What did he say, Harken?" she demanded, breathless, still wrinkled, but with her buttons closed and her shoes on. She came full into the room, crossed it and stood among the kitchen help near the scarred worktable in the center of the room, for all the world looking as if she'd been working among them all day. Her eyes were bright as sunstruck tea, her cheeks flushed from her run down the stairs, her lips open in excitement.

"He asked me if I could build a fast boat and I said yes. He asked me to sketch it on paper, and when I did he said he'd think about it."

"Is that all?" Her excitement vanished, then changed to vehemence. "Oh, he's so stubborn!" She rapped the air once with her fist. "Did you try to convince him?"

"I did what I could. I can't twist his arm, though."

"Nobody can. My father is immovable when he wants to be." She sighed and shrugged. "Ah, well . . ."

The room grew quiet, uncomfortably so. None of the kitchen help knew quite how to react to the presence of one of the family among them.

Mrs. Schmitt thought to say, "We have some cool mint tea, miss, and white cake. Would you care for any?"

Lorna glanced at the table and replied, "Oh, yes, it sounds good."

"Ruby, fetch a glass. Colleen, go out and get more mint. Glynnis, get a tray. Harken, chip some ice for Miss Barnett, please." Everyone bustled around, following orders, leaving Lorna to stand by herself beside the table, watching. Glynnis went into the butler's pantry and returned with a gold-rimmed plate and silver tray. The second kitchen maid, Colleen, washed the mint and bruised it in a mortar and pestle. Jens Harken found an ice pick and made it flash through the air—an arresting sight that caught and held Lorna's regard while ice chips scattered like diamonds onto the slate floor. While Ruby held a glass an ice shard slid from his fingertips into it. Mrs. Schmitt was carefully arranging everything on the tea tray when she discovered Lorna still standing beside the table, waiting.

"I can send Ernesta up to your room with it, miss, or out onto the veranda, if you prefer."

Lorna glanced at Harken, then at the table and inquired, "Couldn't I eat it right here?"

"Right here, miss?"

"Why, yes. It looks as if all of you were sitting here. Can't I join you?"

Mrs. Schmitt wiped the surprise from her face and answered, "Why, if you want to, miss, yes."

Lorna sat down.

Mrs. Schmitt brought the tray forward and set the whole works—gold-rimmed plate, silver fork, long-handled spoon, cutwork linen napkin, crystal glass and silver tray—upon the beaten tabletop, where the kitchen staff's ordinary tea things had been abandoned: thick white plates, plain glasses and dull forks still stuck into unfinished pieces of cake. The centerpiece of the table consisted of a lard pot, salt bowl, a tall crock full of butcher knives, a brass dispenser holding string for tying up vegetables and the supper's cucumbers waiting to be sliced.

The room fell silent.

Ruby hesitantly set the pitcher of tea on the table and backed away.

Lorna slowly picked up her fork while a circle of faces watched, not a soul in the room moving toward their chairs. She cut into her cake and paused, feeling more out of place than ever in her life. She looked up and sent Harken a silent message of appeal.

"Well!" He came to life, clapped his hands once and rubbed them together. "I could use another piece of that cake myself, Mrs. Schmitt, and a little more tea, too." He pulled out a stool next to Lorna's and mounted it from behind, cowboy-fashion, while reaching enthusiastically for the pitcher to pour himself a drink.

"A piece of cake it is," the head cook replied, and everyone took Harken's lead, filling the room with life once again. Ruby brought mint for him and inquired, "Don't you want ice?"

"Naw, this is fine." He refilled glasses on his side of the table, then passed the pitcher on, and soon they were all returned to their own places, taking their cues from him as he began chattering.

"So, how is Chester's father? Has anyone heard?"

"A little better. Chester says he's got his appetite back."

"And your mother, Mrs. Schmitt. I imagine you're going home to see her on Sunday?"

They talked, and ate cake, and passed a pleasant ten minutes while Lorna, internally attuned to his every motion, sat beside Jens as he downed three-quarters of a glass of tea in one tilt of the head, and ate a huge piece of cake. Afterward, he rolled up his shirt sleeves and leaned both elbows beside his empty plate and burped softly behind his curled hand. He teased Glynnis about a large sunfish she claimed to have caught, and leaned back to smile at Ruby when she came around and refilled his glass, and in doing so accidentally nudged Lorna's shoulder. He asked Mrs. Schmitt when she was going to make sauerbraten and dumplings again, and she teased him about a fish-loving Norwegian asking for such heavy, sour German food, and they laughed good-naturedly. Straddling his stool, laughing with Mrs. Schmitt, one of his widespread knees bumped Lorna under the table. "Sorry," he said quietly, and withdrew it.

In time Mrs. Schmitt pushed back her chair and looked at the clock. "Well, there's cucumbers to soak, and cardoon to wash, and potato crulles to get cut. Time moves on."

They all stood, and Lorna said, "Well, thank you very much for the cake and tea. It was delicious."

"You're most welcome, miss. Anytime." Mrs. Schmitt picked up her own empties.

Once again movement bogged down, everyone uncertain of what protocol demanded when Mrs. Schmitt had ordered them back to work before the young miss had taken her leave. Lorna gave Mrs. Schmitt a smile, let it speed across the others and headed toward the door to the servants' stairway. Jens made sure he got there first and opened it for her. Their eyes met for the merest second as she passed through, and she gave a smile so guarded it barely moved her lips.

He nodded formally. "Good afternoon, miss."

"Thank you, Harken."

When the door had closed he found everyone but Ruby back at work. She was holding some vegetables at the zinc sink, riveting him with a disapproving stare. When he walked past her she leaned back and murmured, "So why didn't she ask her father what he said to you? Makes more sense than herself running down here to ask you."

"Mind your own business, Ruby," he replied, and walked outside to bring in the cardoon which waited in a wheelbarrow beside the back door.

The following weekend, the White Bear Yacht Club set up a local race for its own members. Twenty-two boats entered. Gideon Barnett donned his official blue yacht club sweater and skipped his *Tartar* into a second-place finish.

Afterward, in the clubhouse over a glass of rum, he grumbled to Tim Iversen, "I lost a hundred dollars to Percy Tufts on that damned race."

Tim puffed his pipe and replied, "Well, you know the answer to that."

Gideon stewed awhile and said, "Don't think I'm not considering it."

He considered until the following evening, when he spoke to Levinia about it. They were in their bedroom, ready to retire. Gideon was standing before the cold fireplace dressed in his short-legged union suit, smoking a last cigar of the day when he announced out of the blue, "Levinia, you're going to have to hire a new kitchen handyman. I'm going to set Harken to building a boat for me."

Levinia paused in the act of climbing into bed. "Not if Mrs. Schmitt threatens to quit again."

"She won't."

"How can you be so sure?" Levinia climbed onto the high mattress and settled herself against the pillows.

"Because it's only temporary. It'll take him only three, four months at most, then he'll be back in the kitchen, where he belongs. I intend to speak to him in the morning."

"Oh, Gideon, it's such a nuisance."

"Take care of it, nonetheless." He stubbed out his cigar and joined her in bed.

Levinia thought about objecting further but, fearing a reprise of what had followed the last time she'd crossed Gideon, she swallowed her aggravation and steeled herself to the fact that she'd have to go through the tiresome ritual of finding temporary help.

The following morning at nine Jens Harken was again summoned to Gideon Barnett's study. This time the room was brighter, flooded with molten sun. Barnett, however, trussed up in a three-piece suit with a gold watch fob dangling across his belly, looked as gruff and stern as ever.

"All right, Harken, three months! But you build me a boat that'll beat those damned Minnetonka sandbaggers and anything on this lake, is that understood?"

Harken repressed a smile. "Yes sir."

"And when it's done you'll go back to the kitchen."

"Of course."

"Tell Mrs. Schmitt I'm not taking you away forever. I don't want any more blowups out of her."

"Yes sir."

"You can set up shop in the shed behind the glasshouse and gardens. I'll leave word with my friend Matthew Lawless that you'll be coming into his hardware and that you're to be given carte blanche buying any tools you need. Take the train into Saint Paul as soon as you've checked out of the kitchen. Steffens will drive you to the station. The hardware is on Fourth and Wabasha. As for lumber, same goes there—carte blanche here in town at Thayer's. You know where that is, don't you?"

"Yes sir. But if it's all the same to you, I prefer to pay for some of the lumber myself—whatever I'll need for the molds."

Barnett looked taken aback. "Why?"

"I'll want to keep them when they're finished."

"Keep them!"

"Yes sir. I hope to build a boat of my own someday, and the molds are reusable."

"Very well. Then about drafting tools . . ." Barnett scratched his brow, thinking.

"I have those, sir."

"Oh." Barnett dropped his hand. "Yes, yes of course. Well then." He put on his fiercest scowl and stood erect. "You answer strictly to me from now on, is that understood?"

"Yes sir. May I hire someone to help me when the time comes?"

"Yes, but only for the weeks it's absolutely necessary."

"I understand."

"You can eat your meals with the kitchen help the same as always and I'll expect you to work the same hours you did before."

"Sundays, too, sir?"

Barnett looked piqued by the request but replied, "Oh, all right, every Sunday off."

"And as far as going into town immediately, I'd rather have a look at the shed first, sir, if I may."

"Then let Steffens know when you'll need him."

"I will. And the train fare, sir?"

Barnett's mouth became pinched, his face ruddy. His upper lip appeared to tremble beneath his great drooping moustache.

"You will push and push until a man has all he can do to keep from throwing you out of the house, won't you, Harken? Well, I'm warning you, kitchen boy . . ." He pointed at him with a finger coiled tightly around a cigar. "Don't exceed your bounds with me or that's exactly where you'll find yourself." From his waistcoat pocket he withdrew a coin and dropped it onto his desktop. "There's your train fare, now go."

Harken picked up the fifty-cent piece, thinking he'd be damned if he'd dish out of his own pocket to make this rich man richer. He had plans for every fifty cents he could manage to save and they didn't include working in a kitchen until he was as old as Mrs. Schmitt. Furthermore, he understood something else about his employer: A man in his position wanted the esteem of his peers, and the household staff spread rumors. Being known as one who ordered his employees to take a train ride at their own expense would have left a curious if ironic dent in Gideon Barnett's pride.

Harken pocketed the silver coin without the slightest embarrassment. "Thank you, sir," he said, and left.

In the kitchen the news was greeted with a mixture of exuberance and worry.

Colleen, the little Irish second maid, teased, "Ooo, and aren't we rubbing elbows with the gentry now, hirin' out to build their playthings."

Mrs. Schmitt bemoaned, "Three months! Where do they think I can find somebody worth his salt to help me for three months? We'll end up doing it all ourselves."

Ruby chided, quietly, aside, "First upstairs in their study, next roaming around free on their grounds. Better be careful, Jens, you're not in their class and she knows it. So ask yourself why she's making eyes at you."

"You're dreaming, Ruby," he replied, and walked out the kitchen door.

Already he felt reborn, striding through the herb garden into the summer day. Lord, had herbs ever smelled so pungent? Had the sun ever been more dazzling?

He was a boatbuilder again!

He skirted the formal flower gardens, where the help was not allowed, and the picking gardens, which smelled strongly of petunias. Beyond them lay the glasshouse, where in winter fruits and vegetables were forced and in spring seedlings started. Behind the glasshouse a screen of columnar poplars circled the sprawling, meticulously tended vegetable garden. Cutting through it, he noticed the head gardener, Smythe, in the distance, wearing a straw hat, working between two rows of straw wigwams half again as high as himself. Though Smythe was a sour old fellow, Harken himself was in such a merry mood he couldn't resist calling, "H'lo, Smythe. How are your Baldwins this morning?"

Smythe turned and offered a limited smile as Harken approached and stopped to visit. "Ah, Harken, quite productive, I should say." Smythe had never smiled fully in his life, Harken was convinced. His correct British demeanor would not allow it. He had a long face with droopy eyelids and a nose as long and bumpy as one of his own white radishes. "I believe I'll have several quarts for herself by midweek."

The kitchen staff was well acquainted with Smythe's prized Baldwin blackcurrants and the mistress's predilection for them. He had devised a system of retarding the fruit by covering it completely with the outsized straw cones and removing them to let the sun ripen the berries only when Smythe or Levinia desired them ripened. By so doing he had prolonged their season a full two months.

"Mind if I try one?" Harken plucked a dark berry and popped it into his mouth before Smythe could reply. "Mmm . . . tasty. Yessir, Smythe, you really know what you're doing back here."

Smythe had cultured his expression of disapproval to a fine art. "*Miss*-ter Harken! You know the Baldwins are not for the kitchen help. The mistress has made that very clear."

"Oh, sorry," Harken replied blithely, "but right now I'm not the kitchen help. I'm heading for that shed back there in the trees to build the master a new sailboat. You'll be seeing me cut through here a lot this summer. Well, I'd better get to it." He headed on and threw back over his shoulder, "Thanks for the Baldwin, Smythe."

In jovial spirits he strode along through the rows of peculiar vegetables that gave evidence of the wealthy's desire to have the best and most unusual—Jerusalem artichokes, broccoli, leeks, fancy French climbing beans, salsify, scorzonera and the giant cardoons which resembled celery as tall as a man. He passed the more common ones—potatoes, turnips, carrots and the everlasting spinach, of which it seemed he'd washed haylofts full. *Three months,* he thought. *I don't have to wash any of that damned stuff for three whole months! And if this boat turns out to be the speed demon I believe it will, I might never have to wash it again!*

He passed fruit trees and hazelnut bushes, and a raspberry patch where the birds were pillaging. He helped himself to a handful and was eating them as he passed through the far screen of poplars into the cool of the woods beyond.

The shed was a long old clapboard structure that appeared never to have been painted. It had a pair of creaking crossbuck doors that turned back to reveal a crude plank floor, open rafters above and only two small, dirty windows on either side. There was a decrepit cutter inside with a broken trace, and some sacks of potatoes with sprouts growing up through the burlap, a rusty iron park bench, newspapers, barrels, bushel baskets and a variety of other flotsam that gave evidence of mice, squirrels and chipmunks having taken up residence. But as far as Jens Harken was concerned, it was paradise. It was cool, it smelled earthen, there were no sinks or iceboxes or hot, steaming kettles or imperious housekeepers ordering him what to do. No spoiled mistresses sending their dirty coins down for washing so their fingertips need not touch commoners' dirt. No horseradish to grate so tears streamed down his face, or teals to pluck or coppers to polish or rabbits to skin.

For three months he could work in this paradise, doing what he loved to do best, with only animals for company and the chirping of birds in the trees outside.

He walked the length of the building, looking up, checking out the rafters, which would need to be sturdy enough to support a winch. He decided where he'd run the stovepipe out the wall. It was July now. By September he'd need heat, and whether or not he finished in three months, the snow would be flying. He checked the grimy windows and found that with a little persuasion and a couple of sturdy clunks they would raise. The breeze blew in and brought the green smell of the woods. He imagined it filling sails, his sails, on a sleek, keelless beauty that would leap when it took the wind and disturb the water so little there would scarcely be a wake or a bow wave. His fingers itched to feel a plane in his hand and a length of spruce ripping and curling away as he fashioned a mast. He longed to smell a batch of white oak softening in a steam box, and hear his own hammer nailing ribs over a frame, and know the exquisite pride of watching a product of his own ingenuity take shape beneath his hands.

He stood with his elbows locked, the butts of both hands on the shoulder-high windowsill, and looked out into green trees and wild columbine and squirrels' nests. He thumped the gritty sill once with both hands and said with conviction, "Watch me. Just watch me."

Chapter
SIX

THE ride into town was heady for its sheer freedom. Summoning Steffens and the carriage, riding in the seat reserved for the privileged, Harken vowed one day he would own a carriage of his own and a fine bay to draw it. Boarding the train at the White Bear Beach Station, he reveled in being abroad at the time of day he'd normally be helping in the kitchen with the midday meal preparations. Alighting thirty minutes later amid the bustle of the downtown Saint Paul depot and making his way to the Lawless Hardware Store, he realized that Gideon Barnett, curmudgeon though he was, had given him the opportunity he'd been waiting for, and it was up to Jens Harken to make the most of it.

He selected the best tools money could buy, from the sandpaper paddle on which he'd sharpen his pencils to the seven-horsepower electro-vapor engine that would drive his saw. After arrangements were made for delivery, he spent an enjoyable hour walking the downtown streets, resisting the smell of spicy Polish sausages steaming in a street vendor's wagon, saving his nickel and eating the cold beef sandwich he'd brought from home, peering into windows, watching the streetcars and admiring an occasional silk bustle. The city was exciting—there was no doubt about it—but when he boarded the train for White Bear Lake, his anticipation made the allure of Saint Paul pale by comparison.

Back in White Bear, he walked from the depot to the lumberyard and ordered what he'd need to tide him over until his boat plans were complete, then walked the remainder of the way out to Manitou Island, skirting the lake, where few sails were visible on this midweek afternoon, but enjoying the view nonetheless.

At Rose Point he changed into rough clothes, scavenged for cleaning supplies and went out beyond the gardens to turn a shed into a boatworks.

Reaching his domain, opening the double doors wide, stepping into the long, deep coolness of the building, he felt again the ebullience of that morning, the determination to make something important happen here. He carried out the musty old potatoes and newspapers, burned a pile of junk and pushed the other castoffs into a corner. He raked the mice nests and acorn shells outside, swept the floor and began washing the windows. He was standing on a barrel in the midst of the job when the voice of Miss Lorna Barnett scolded from the great doorway.

"Harken, where *ever* have you been?"

She was standing with both hands on her hips, only a silhouette in the late afternoon light that filtered through the woodsy backdrop behind her. Her sleeves were big as bed pillows and her skirt shaped like a bell with a short train. He could make out a rim of pink outlining her clothing, and the bird's-nest shape of her hair, but beyond that he was blinded to any details.

"Your father sent me to town, miss."

"And didn't tell me a thing about it. By the time I got up he was already gone himself, and nobody seemed to know where you were. You're going to build the boat, aren't you?"

"Yes, miss, I certainly am."

She planted her feet wide, made two fists and punched them straight at heaven. *"Eureka!"* she yowled at the rafters.

A laugh pealed out of Harken as he dropped off the barrel, threw his scrub rag into a bucket of water and his drying rag over his shoulder. "I felt like doing the same thing when he told me."

She strode inside, her skirts sweeping the dirty floor. "You're going to do it here?" She came to a halt inches from him, breaching the shadows, bringing her face into detail, and pretty detail it was.

"That's right. He gave me the go-ahead to buy anything I need at the Lawless Hardware Store and at Thayer's Lumberyard. I went into town to order tools. Miss Barnett"—he glanced down at her hems—"you're getting your skirts filthy walking on this dirty floor. I swept it, but it's still none too clean."

She picked up her hems and gave them a whack. "Oh, who cares!" The dust flew as she dropped her clothing back into place, spreading the scent of orange blossoms into the dank old building. "I don't know why I wear these silly skirts with trains anyway. Mr. Gibson says they're out."

"Who's Mr. Gibson?"

Her expression grew artificially pained. "Oh, please, Harken, I didn't come here to talk about skirt lengths. Tell me more about what Papa said!"

Though she was an enchanting creature, he stepped away, putting a proper distance between them. "Well, he said that I have three months to build the boat and then I go back to the kitchen."

"What else?" She pursued him, eager-eyed, keeping close.

"Nothing else."

"Oh, Harken, that can't be *all!*"

"Well . . ." He thought awhile, then added, "He said I should tell Mrs. Schmitt it was only temporary because he didn't want any more blowups in the kitchen."

Lorna laughed, a measure of grace notes that transformed the rough building and made Jens Harken indulge in a covert assay of her. She was dressed in pink-and-white candy stripes today, with a white lace stand-up collar and cuffs and a form-fitting bodice that dipped down at the waistline in a tiny point and made her look as curvy as fruit. Furthermore, whenever he moved away, she advanced, without apparent compunction. Finally he stopped retreating and stood his ground, the two of them an arm's length apart.

"May I ask you something, miss?"

"Why, of course."

"Why don't you go to your father to ask these questions?"

"Oh, phoo!" She flapped both hands. "He'd answer me as if he were giving an order for tainted food to be buried and spoil the whole thing. You see, he resists you all the way."

"So I've noticed."

"Besides, I like you." She smiled up at him point-blank.

He gave a self-conscious laugh, looking first at the floor, then at her.

"Are you always this honest?"

"No," she replied. "I spend a lot of time with Taylor DuVal. Do you know Taylor? No, I suppose you don't. Well, anyway, I suppose you could say we're courting, but I've never told him I like him."

"But you do?"

She thought a moment. "After a fashion. Taylor doesn't believe in things, though, not the way you believe in your boat. His family is in flour milling, and frankly, it's a very tedious subject—the wheat crop, the projected market prices, the source of cotton bags. Of course, when we're together we talk about other things, but they're rather repetitive—my family, his family, what dances are coming up at the yacht club, and what chautauquas are coming up at the Ramaley Pavilion."

"Does he race?"

"His family does. They own the *Kite*."

"I've seen her. She's keel-heavy."

Lorna's eyes glinted with good-humored mischief. "But then, aren't they all, compared to what you propose to build?"

They stood awhile, smiling at each other, sharing the anticipation of building the boat and watching it sail for the first time, wondering for one reckless moment what might happen between now and then. A fly buzzed in some sunstream near the open doors and a transient breeze made a gentle mission through the trees, then went away.

Lorna Barnett was as charming a creature as he'd ever met. She seemed as down-to-earth as any of the kitchen staff, and as unpretentious. He decided to trust her.

"May I tell you something, Miss Lorna?"

"Anything."

"Once this boat races, I never intend to put foot in a kitchen again."

"Good for you, Harken. I don't think you belong there, either."

They stood close enough for Lorna to see the determination in his eyes and for Jens to see the corroboration in hers; close enough for him to smell the orange-blossom cologne in her clothes and for her to smell the vinegar water in his window rag; close enough to become aware of impropriety and disregard it.

"What will you do?" she asked.

"I want to own my own boatworks."

"Where will you get the money?"

"I'm saving. And I have a plan. I want to bring my brother from New Jersey so the two of us can run it together."

"Do you miss him?"

He answered with a click of the cheek and a wandering gaze that seemed full of memories. "He's my only family."

"Do you write to him?"

"Nearly every week, and he writes back."

She gave a conspiratorial smile. "Will *you* have something to tell him this week, huh, Harken?"

He smiled, too, and for a while they shared the moment of victory, commingled with an underlying sense of how much they were enjoying each other. The stretch of silence lingered, became an expanse of awareness in which they admired once again the mere visage of one another, for the first time ever in total privacy. Outside, the woods were still, not even a bird chirping. At the far end of the building the fly still buzzed, and the tea-green light threw leaf shadows along the crude floor and up the inside of one wall, making lacework of the grayed studs and the dirt-coated clapboards. Deeper within, where Jens and Lorna stood, the light from the half-washed window brightened only one side of their faces. Hers was smooth and curved, cupped high by the tight lace neckband that nearly touched her earlobes. His was dusty and angular, foiled by the open neck of a rough blue chambray shirt.

When they'd been silent and watchful too long, Jens spoke quietly. "I don't think your father would approve of you being here."

"My father is gone to the city. And my mother is napping with a cool cloth on her forehead. And furthermore, I have always been an unwieldy daughter and they know it. I'll be the first to admit, I haven't given them an easy time raising me."

"Why doesn't that surprise me?"

She grinned in reply. They were infinitely conscious of their aloneness as silence settled again and there seemed no acceptable way to fill it.

She looked down at her hands. "I suppose I should go. Let you get back to work."

"Yes, I suppose so."

"There's something I must say first, though, about yesterday."

"Yesterday?"

Her gaze lifted once more to his. "When I came to the kitchen and had cake with you. I realized, after it was too late, how uncomfortable I had made everyone. I just wanted to thank you, Harken, for understanding."

"Nonsense, miss. You had every right to be there."

"No." She touched his arm with four fingertips on the bare skin just above his wrist, a touch as brief as the sip of a hummingbird. Realizing her mistake, she withdrew quickly and curled the fingers into a tight fist. "I told you I'm unwieldy. Sometimes I do things I wish I hadn't. And when Mrs. Schmitt set down that silver tray with my cake on it, and the best silverware, and the good linen . . . well, I'd have given anything to be somewhere else. You knew it, and you did your best to ease my embarrassment. I simply didn't think, Harken. Anyway, thank you for your quick reaction."

He could have gone on insisting she was mistaken, but both of them knew she was not.

"You're welcome, miss," he replied. "I must admit, I feel a little more comfortable talking to you out here, away from the others. They . . ." He ended the thought abruptly, leaving her with the impression he wished he'd never begun.

"They what?"

"Nothing, miss."

"Of course it was something. They what?"

"Please, miss."

She touched his forearm again, this time insistently. "Harken, be honest with me. They what?"

He sighed, realizing there was no way he could sidestep her demand. "They sometimes mistake your intentions."

"What have they said about my intentions?"

"Nothing specific." He colored and looked away, pulling the dirty rag from his shoulder.

"You're not being honest with me."

When his eyes returned to her they wore the studied passivity of the trained household help. "If you'll excuse me, Miss Lorna, your father gave me a deadline, and I really should be getting back to work."

It had been a long time since Lorna Barnett had grown that angry, that fast. "Oh, you're just like him!" She rammed her fists onto her hips. "Men can be so infuriating! I can make you tell me, you know! You are, for all practical purposes, my employee!"

Jens was so taken aback by her sudden imperiousness he stood stunned and speechless. For a fleeting instant shock overtook his face, followed immediately by disappointment and a quick plummet back to reality. "Yes, I know." He turned away before she could see the patches of color ascend to his cheeks. Squatting, he recovered his rag from the bucket, wrung it out and, without further word, climbed back onto the barrel and resumed washing the window.

Behind him, Lorna's anger had collapsed as fast as it came. She found herself mortified at her thoughtless outburst. She took a step toward him, looking up.

"Oh, Harken, I didn't mean that."

"It's quite all right, miss." He could feel the heat climb his neck. How ridiculous he must have looked to her, losing sight of his station and allowing his attraction for her to show.

She advanced another step. "No, it's not. It just . . . just came out, that's all . . . please . . ." She reached out as if to touch his leg, then withdrew her hand. "Please forgive me."

"There's nothing to forgive. You were quite right, miss."

He would neither look at her nor stop going at the windowpane. His rag squeaked across the glass as he dried it and hid from her.

"Harken?" The appeal in her voice was lost on him. He stubbornly continued his work.

She waited, but his intention was clear, his hurt was clear, the barrier between them was as palpable as the shed walls. She felt like a quick-triggered misguided fool, but had no idea how to mend the hurt she'd caused.

"Well," she said in a small, remorseful voice, "I'll leave you be. I am sorry, Harken."

He need not turn to know she was gone. His body seemed to have developed sensors that prickled whenever she approached his sphere. In the silence following her leave-taking, the sensation withered, dulled, leaving him standing on the wooden barrel with the butts of both hands drilled against the lower window ledge and the rag hanging motionlessly from one. He turned his head, stared out across his left shoulder at the sunlit dust through which her petticoats had swept a trail. His gaze returned to the scene outside the window, a woodsy collection of sticks and leaf mold and greenery. He heaved an enormous sigh and stepped down slowly off the barrel. There he stood in the afternoon stillness. Motionless. Hurt. So she was just like her parents—aristocracy—and he'd best not forget it. Maybe what Ruby had hinted was right: Lorna Barnett was a bored rich girl playing games with the help simply to amuse herself.

With sudden vehemence, he pitched the rag into the bucket, spraying dirty water onto the floor, where it darkened the dusty planks. Then he kicked the barrel and sent it rolling.

For the rest of the day he was crotchety and malcontent. That evening he took Ruby out for a walk and kissed her in the herb garden when they got back to the kitchen door. But kissing Ruby was like kissing a cocker spaniel puppy—sloppy and difficult to control. He found himself anxious only to dry off his mouth and get her paws off his neck.

In his bed afterward he thought of Lorna Barnett . . . in pink-and-white stripes and orange-blossom cologne, with excited brown eyes and a mouth like ripe berries.

The woman had damned well better stay away from his shed!

She did exactly that for three days; on the fourth she was back. It was nearing three P.M. and Jens was sitting on a barrel, working at a makeshift table made of planks and sawhorses, drawing a long curved line on a piece of stiff manila chart paper.

He finished and sat back to study it, then felt eyes on him. He looked to his left and there she stood, still as a statue in the open doorway, wearing a big-sleeved blue shirtwaist, with her hands clasped behind her back.

His heart did a double take. His spine slowly straightened. "Well," he said.

She remained motionless, hands still clasped behind her. "May I come in?" she asked meekly.

He studied her awhile, pencil in one hand and a celluloid ship curve in the other.

"Suit yourself," he replied, and went back to work, poring over a numerical chart to the right of his partially finished drawings.

She moved inside with careful, measured footsteps to the opposite side of his table, where she stood before him in her pose of penitence.

"Harken?" she said very quietly.

"What?"

"Aren't you going to look at me?"

"If you say so, miss." Obediently he raised his eyes. Immense tears shimmered on her lower eyelids. Her bottom lip was puffy and trembling.

"I'm very, very sorry," she whispered, "and I'll never do that again."

Aw, sweet lord, did the woman not know what effect she had upon him, standing so girlishly with her hands clasped behind her back and tears the size of grapes making her eyes look devastating? Of all the things he'd expected, this was the last. The sight of her made his heart quake and his belly tense. He swallowed twice; the lump of emotion felt like a wad of cotton batting going down. *Miss Lorna Barnett*, he thought, *if you know what's good for you you'll get out of here as fast as your feet will carry you.*

"I'm sorry, too," he replied. "I forgot my place."

"No, no . . ." She brought a hand from behind her back and touched his chart paper as if it were an amulet. "It was my fault, trying to force you to say things you didn't want to, treating you like an inferior."

"But, you were right. I work for you."

"No. You work for my father. You're my friend, and I've been miserable for three days thinking I had ruined our friendship."

He refrained from saying he'd been, too. He had no idea what to say. It was taking a tremendous effort to remain on his barrel and keep the table between them.

Very softly, she said to the drawings, "I think I know what the kitchen help is saying. It wasn't too hard to figure out." She looked up. "That I've been flirting with you, isn't that right? Amusing myself with the help."

He fixed his eyes on his pencil. "It's just Ruby, but don't let it bother you."

"Ruby is the redheaded one, isn't she?"

He nodded.

"She particularly disliked my being there the other day. I could tell."

When he made no response, she asked, "Is she your girlfriend?"

He cleared his throat. "We've gone walking on our days off."

"She is."

"I suspect she'd like to be. That's all."

"So I embarrassed you, too, by showing up in the kitchen and insisting on having cake there."

"My father always said, one person doesn't embarrass another, one can only do that to himself. I told you, you had every right to be there and I meant it."

After an impacted silence during which he studied the chart paper, and she studied him, Lorna Barnett declared quietly, "I'm not amusing myself with you, Harken, I'm not."

He looked up. She was standing straight, eight fingertips resting on the edge of his rough table, the curve of her breast as smooth and flowing as if he'd drawn it with one of his own Copenhagen curves, her hair plumped up with a few tendrils floating loose around her face. That face—what a face—so sincere and pretty and vulnerable he wanted to take it between his two hands and kiss its trembling lips until they smiled once again.

Instead he could only say quietly, "No, miss."

"My name is Lorna. When will you start using it?"

"I've used it."

"Not Miss Lorna. Lorna."

In spite of the fact that she waited, he refused to repeat her name. That last formality was a necessary barrier between them, kept intact by Jens for both their good.

Finally she said, "Am I forgiven, then?"

Once again he could have insisted there was nothing to forgive, but they both knew she had hurt him.

"Let's just forget it."

She tried to smile but it didn't quite work. He tried to tear his eyes from her but it didn't quite work. In silence they confronted this unwise, unbidden attraction that was welling between them. It was drawn on their faces as plainly as the lines on his chart paper. He realized one of them had to be sensible and, as always, was the first to look away.

"Would you like to see my drawings?"

"Very much."

She came around and stood at his elbow, bringing along her familiar orange-blossom scent and the starchy blue presence of her clothing in his peripheral vision, her full sleeve so near his ear.

"They're not done yet," he told her, "but you can get an idea of the basic shape of the boat."

She reached for a loose piece of paper containing a rough sketch he'd done in about twenty minutes for her father.

"This is what it'll look like?"

"Roughly."

She studied it a moment then set it aside and took in the much larger, more precise drawing on which he was working. It was tacked down on the table.

"Do you always draw them upside down?"

"That's the way I'll build it, so that's the way I draw it."

"You'll build it upside down?"

"On these . . . here, see?" He pointed to one of several lines that vertically bisected the profile drawing of the boat. "There'll be one of these forms about every two feet down the length of the boat, and they'll stand on feet that'll support the whole thing. They're called cross sections or stations, and they form the basis of the mold. They'll be what determines the shape of the entire boat. Like this . . . see?"

He drew in the air with both hands but could tell she couldn't visualize it.

"It's hard to see from this one-dimensional drawing, but I'll do a fore-to-aft cross section, too, that will show each station. Then it'll be easier to see."

"How long will it take you?"

"To finish the drawings? Another week and a half or so."

"And then you can start building it?"

"No. Then I can start lofting."

"What's lofting?"

"Lofting? That's . . ." He stopped to think. "Well, it's fairing up a boat."

"What's fairing up?"

"Fairing up is making sure it doesn't have any lumps or bumps, making sure it has a good smooth even shape." *Like you*, he thought. "Like fruit," he said. "The surface of the hull has got to run smooth from any one spot to any other spot. Then she's fair."

Lorna Barnett looked down at Jens Harken, at the profile of his head and neck, at his black suspenders running in a tight curve from front to back, at the line his shoulder and arm made as he leaned his elbow on the table and concentrated on the chart paper.

Fair, she thought, *oh, yes, very fair indeed.*

Tempted to reached out and run a hand over that fine head and those solid shoulders, she decided she'd best get herself out of this shed and put some distance between them. Furthermore, she could see he wasn't getting much done with her interrupting. "Well, I'd better leave you to your work." She left his elbow and moved around the table. "May I come back again?"

Any other question would have been easier to answer. He wanted to say, No, stay away, but he could no more have denied her the right and himself the pleasure than he could have worked in a kitchen for the remainder of his life.

"I'll look forward to it," he replied.

She came frequently, dropping in to bother him not only when she was present, but after she'd left. She would inspect his drawings and ask questions, perch on the iron bench and chatter, watch him sometimes in silences so reaching they felt like strokes upon his flesh. She came one Friday when the drawings were nearly completed, and after inspecting his progress meandered around to the park bench. She spread its rusty seat with a piece of chart paper, sat down, pulled up her knees and wrapped them with both arms.

"Do you like band music?" she asked, out of the blue.

"Band music? Yes, as a matter of fact, I do."

"Mr. Sousa is coming tomorrow."

"Yes, I saw the posters."

"No, I mean he's coming here tomorrow, to Rose Point. Mother is hostessing a reception for him after the concert tomorrow night, then he's to be our overnight guest."

"So you're going to the concert."

She rested her chin on her knees. "Mm-hmm."

"And Mr. DuVal will be there?"

"Mm-hmm."

"Well, I hope you have a very nice time."

"Are you going?"

"No. I save my money."

"Ah, that's right. To start a boatworks."

She let him draw for a while, studying him, then abruptly changed the subject again. "When will you actually start building the boat?"

"Oh, another couple weeks or so."

"I'll help you."

She was a safe enough distance away that he could allow himself a protracted study of her. She wore pale yellow today. Her skirt had fallen over the edge of the bench like an inverted fan. Her breast was tucked fast against her thigh, and her hair looked soft as meadow grass. "Have you ever stopped to think what would happen if your father decided to walk out here and found you with me? I expect him to, you know, to check on the drawings."

"He'd be very angry, and he'd scold me and I'd argue that I have every right to be here, but he wouldn't fire you because he wants the boat too badly, and you're the only one who can build it for him."

"You're pretty sure of that, aren't you?"

"Well, aren't you?"

"No."

She only mused and lay her cheek on her knee, watching him unbrokenly.

"Is your brother like you?" she asked.

"No."

"What's he like, then?"

"He plods when I run. He stays behind in the East, where it's safe and he has a job, while I come out here, where there are none. But he knows boats."

"He worries about fair lines like you do?"

Jens merely shook his head as if to say, Girl, I can't keep up with you.

"Does he look like you?"

"People say so."

"Then he's handsome, isn't he?"

Jens colored. "Miss Barnett, I don't think that's appropriate for—"

"Oh, listen to him! Miss Barnett, in that tone of voice. And now I'm going to get preached to, I can tell."

He left his barrel, circled the table, took her by the calves and swung her feet to the floor. "Up!" he ordered. "And out! I have a boat to design!"

She got to her feet and walked backward to the door with him herding her. "Well, may I help you?"

"No."

"Why not? I'll be here anyway."

"Because I said so. Now get going, run off to Mr. DuVal, where you belong, and don't come back."

She turned, tossed her head, said with a great deal of assurance, "You don't mean that," and strode out the door. When she was gone he took a big deep swig of air, blew it out and energetically scratched the back of his head with eight fingers until his hair stood out.

"Jesus," he whispered to himself.

As she'd done once before when he'd stumbled upon her in her bedroom, Lorna Barnett stuck only her head back around the door, keeping everything else out of sight.

"Maybe I'll bring a picnic next time," she said.

"Oh, that's all I need!" he bellowed. "For you to go asking Mrs. Schmitt for—"

He was talking to thin air. She was gone at last, leaving him standing frustrated, tousle-headed and half-priapic in the middle of the cavernous shed.

On Saturday night, one hour before Mr. John Philip Sousa himself would raise his baton at Ramaley's lakeshore pavilion, the Barnett household was aflutter. The entire family was going to the concert, including the aunts.

In their room, Henrietta was scolding Agnes, "Don't be silly, you cannot go without gloves. It simply isn't done."

In Theron's room, Ernesta was parting his hair down the middle and greasing it back with brilliantine while he jiggled and squiggled and twisted to look behind him for his spyglass.

In their room, Daphne was teasing Jenny, "I suppose you're going to make goggle eyes at Taylor DuVal and make a dope of yourself again tonight."

In the master suite, Gideon happened to walk in on Levinia when she was only partially dressed. She shielded herself with a dressing gown and scolded, "Gideon, you could at least knock when you come in!"

In her room, Lorna needed help getting her dress buttoned up the back. Since Ernesta was busy with Theron, she went to the aunts' room.

"Aunt Agnes, will you please button me up the back?"

"Of course I will, dearie. What a lovely frock! Why, if you don't look like a regular little buttercup I don't know who does. Will young Mr. DuVal be there tonight?"

"Of course."

Across the room, Henrietta pursed her lips and put in, "Then be sure your hatpin is sharpened, Lorna."

They rode the steam launch *Manitoba* across the lake, boarding downtown at the Williams House Hotel and arriving at Ramaley's pavilion a good half hour before concert time. The pavilion itself was the most imposing structure on the lake, châteauesque in design, with turreted corners topped by finials, and a busy roofline broken by spires, pinnacles and gables. Its open-arms steps lifted to a quartet of doors topped by an elaborate plaster cartouche above which towered a roof peak shaped like a candlesnuffer. The second floor was a ballroom, surrounded by French doors giving onto pillared porticoes, while its third floor, circled by twenty-foot-high Renaissance arched windows, was devoted entirely to an auditorium. The auditorium seated two thousand and was lavishly appointed with red velvet and gilt.

The Barnetts entered their private proscenium box and seated themselves on opera chairs, all but Gideon, who'd gone backstage to deliver a personal welcome to Sousa.

The aunts grinned, whispered to each other and pointed with their folded fans at familiar faces. Daphne and Jenny peeped over the balustrade and giggled when young men tipped their heads in salute. Theron peered through his spyglass and said, "Wow, I can see the hair in that fat woman's nose!"

"Theron, put that down!" his mother scolded.

"Well, I can! And it's a big nose, too. Gosh, her nostrils are big as hoofprints, Mama, you should just see 'em!"

Levinia gave Theron a whack on the back of his head with her fan.

"Ouch!" He lowered his spyglass and rubbed his noggin.

"When the music begins you may use that thing. Not before."

He slumped in his chair and muttered, "Jeez."

"And watch your tongue, young man."

Taylor DuVal came in and greeted everyone in the box, kissing all the ladies' hands and taking a look through Theron's spyglass. Theron leaned close to him and, shielded from his mother, pointed and whispered, "There's a fat lady down there in a blue dress and you can see the hair in her nose."

Taylor took a look and whispered back, "I think I see some in her ears, too."

To Lorna, he said, with a special, private smile into her brown eyes, "I'll see you during the intermission."

The concert was inspiring. Sousa's original American music raised the hair on Lorna's arms and made her insides tremble. It brought thunderous applause and smiles to everyone in the audience.

At intermission in the lobby Taylor said to Lorna, "I've missed you."

"Have you?"

"I certainly have. And I intend to make up for it later at your house."

"Taylor, shh. Someone might hear you."

"Who's going to hear? Everyone's busy talking."

He took her hand and laid it over his palm and ran his own over it time and again, as if smoothing a curled page. "Did you miss me?"

She hadn't. "A lady wouldn't answer that," she replied.

He laughed and kissed her fingernails.

The reception at Rose Point was attended by fifty of White Bear Lake's elite. The dining room was festooned with red, white and blue flowers. A cake shaped like a bass drum was emblazoned with an American eagle clutching golden arrows in its claws, surrounded by the aurora borealis. The tea was flavored with rose geraniums and the finger sandwiches were fanciful enough to be mistaken for jewelry. The crowd was noisier than usual, their mood enhanced by the presence of the gentle but fiery patriot whose fame was spreading beyond America's shores since he'd resigned his post as conductor of the United States Marine Band and begun touring the world. In his goatee, oval spectacles and white uniform with three medals on his chest, Sousa bowed over Aunt Agnes's hand while Lorna watched from a distance. "Watch Aunt Henrietta," Lorna told Taylor. "As soon as Sousa turns away she'll say something to dampen Aunt Agnes's joy."

Sure enough, Henrietta's mouth drew tight as a drawstring purse as she delivered some stern reprimand to her sister. Agnes's fluttering immediately ceased.

"What makes people like that?"

"Lorna, your aunt Agnes is a bit daffy. Henrietta simply keeps her in line."

"She is not daffy!"

"The way she's always mooning about her young Captain Dearsley? You don't think that's daffy?"

"But she loved him. I think it's very sweet how she remembers him, and Aunt Henrietta can be so cruel. I've told Mother I believe she hates men. One of them spurned her when she was young, so she has nothing good to say about any of them."

"And how about you?"

When she made no reply, Taylor said, "I think I've upset you, Lorna. I'm sorry. Tonight of all nights, I didn't mean to do that."

Taylor was standing directly behind Lorna. In the lee between their bodies she felt him caress the center of her back. Shivers radiated up her arms, along with surprise, for they stood in the crowded hallway, her father only a few feet away in the archway to the morning room and her mother at the far end of the dining room.

Such audacity right under her parents' noses. Taylor asked, "Do you think we'd be missed if we went out into the garden for a few minutes?"

Curiously, she thought of Harken at that moment, Harken, who occupied her thoughts most of the time she was away from Taylor. "I don't think we should."

"I have something for you."

She glanced back over her shoulder, her temple almost bumping Taylor's chin. His dark beard was beguiling, his eyes and lips smiling down at her—this man her parents wanted her to marry. "What?"

In the secret space between them his fingertips seemed to be finding and counting her vertebrae within her dress. "I'll tell you in the garden." She was a young, nubile woman, susceptible to each subtle nuance of courtship, to its touches and its flatteries and its very suggestibilities.

She turned and led the way toward the door.

Outside, Lorna walked beside him along the graveled paths between her mother's prized roses, around the splattering fountain, beyond the picking beds with their fragrant night-scented stocks and chrysanthemums and marigolds. When she stopped in the moonlit path, visible from many windows, he caught her elbow and said, "Not here."

He took her to the farthest side of the garden, into the glasshouse, where it was damp and private and smelled of humus. They stood on a flagstone walk between rows of clay pots holding shoulder-high blackberry canes being propagated by Smythe for winter bearing.

"We shouldn't be in here, Taylor."

"I'll leave the door open, so if anyone comes looking for us we'll hear them." He took both her hands and held them loosely. "You look pretty tonight, Lorna. May I kiss you . . . at last?"

"Oh, Taylor, you put me in a predicament. What exactly do you think a lady should answer?"

He turned her right hand palm-up and kissed the pads of four fingers. "Then don't answer," he said, and placed both her hands on his shoulders. His own went to her waist as his head dipped down and cut off the starlight shining through the glass roof. His lips met hers discreetly, warm and closed within the sleekness of his beard, hinting at opening, not quite doing so. He kept the kiss brief, then stepped back and reached inside his suit jacket to the watch pocket of his waistcoat. From the pocket he withdrew a small velvet pouch.

"I've known for some time that our parents would be very much in favor of you and me marrying, Lorna. My father spoke to me about it nearly a year ago, and since that time I've been watching you grow up, admiring you. Unless I'm mistaken, your parents would be as much in favor of our marriage as mine are. So I've bought you this . . ." From the pouch he emptied into his palm a piece of jewelry that gave a golden wink as it fell. "It's not a betrothal ring, because I think it's a little soon for that. But it's the next thing to it, and it comes with my sincere intention to ask for your hand when we both believe we've come to know each other well enough. So this is for you, Lorna."

He put it in her hand, a tiny gold bow from which was suspended a delicate oval watch.

"It's beautiful, Taylor."

"May I?"

What could she say? That she'd been flirting with their kitchen handyman lately in a shed behind the garden? That she'd been thinking of him much more often than of Taylor? That she'd been trying to get him to kiss her and he wouldn't?

"Oh, yes . . . of course."

He took the watch from her hand and pinned it on her bodice, exceedingly careful to avoid touching her breast, his very carefulness seductive in its own right. The faint brush of his fingertips on her garments, and the garments on her skin provoked a sensual reaction along the surface of her breasts. When the watch was in place she touched it with her fingertips and looked up into Taylor's shadowed face.

"Thank you, Taylor. You're a very sweet man."

He took her chin between thumb and forefinger and tipped it up. "I'm sure you know, Lorna, that I'm falling in love with you." He kissed her once more, starting gently, waiting until he sensed her reserve yield to curiosity, only then becoming more exacting. His lips opened and he drew her flush against his length in an embrace such as Lorna had recently been imagining with Harken. How many times had she stood near him, every meeting of their eyes a collision, willing him to break down and kiss her this way, hold her against his long body and answer so many vague questions about which she'd wondered? Only, he hadn't. Now here was Taylor, with his tongue in her mouth, his left arm clamped firmly around her waist, and his right hand, finally, wholly, covering one of her breasts. In all her life no single touch had ever radiated as this one did, to regions far removed from the touch itself, like a snagged thread puckering distant points. No wonder Mother had warned her.

They both regained propriety at once, ending the kiss suddenly, their chins downturned, heads close while their breathing evened.

No apologies came from Taylor.

None came from Lorna.

The last two minutes had been too momentous to warrant apologies. Finally they stepped apart, Taylor finding and keeping Lorna's hands.

Belatedly, she said, "We must go back in now, Taylor."

"Yes, of course," he whispered thickly. "What are you doing tomorrow?"

"Tomorrow? I . . ." Tomorrow was Sunday. She'd been planning to row over to Tim's and see if she could find Harken there again.

"Will you go sailing with me?"

At her pause, Taylor encouraged, "I'll sail over and pick you up at your dock at two o'clock. What do you say?"

Harken, she realized, was an impossibility. Not only was he remaining stubbornly polite and subservient, if he ever broke down and satisfied both their curiosities, where could it lead? Even he realized what was best when he'd sent her packing with an admonition to fly to Taylor, where she belonged.

Lorna heard herself answer the way circumstances dictated she answer.

"All right. Shall I ask Mrs. Schmitt to pack us a picnic?"

Taylor smiled. "It's a date."

Chapter
SEVEN

THE watch from Taylor raised a
stir among Lorna's family. Ev-
eryone took it for a betrothal gift in spite of her protestations it was
not. Her mother smiled smugly and said, "Wait till I tell Cecilia
Tufts." Her father set no limit on her sailing time with Taylor. Her
brother said, "I told you Taylor and Lorna were sparking." Daphne
got starry-eyed while Jenny looked glum, realizing it was only a
matter of time before she lost her idol completely and irrevocably.
Aunt Henrietta issued her warning about wearing a hatpin on the
boat. And Aunt Agnes said, "Aren't you lucky. I never got a chance
to go sailing with Captain Dearsley."

Taylor picked up Lorna at two o'clock. They spent the entire
afternoon on the water in Taylor's catboat. Lorna was in her glory
crewing for Taylor, though the boat had only a single sail. He let her
handle the rudder, and sometimes the winch during tacking. They
sailed from Manitou Island into Snyder's Bay, then east to Mah-
tomedi and from there around West Point, up the Dellwood shore,
where they passed Tim's cabin. But no one was about. Then south
again toward Birchwood, off whose shore they reefed the sail and ate
their picnic lunch bobbing on the water. Lorna had no need to use
her hatpin, nor would it have been possible, for she'd removed her
hat well over an hour earlier and sat with the sun on her face.

While they ate, the wind freshened, and as they crossed the lake yet again Lorna, exhilarated, pointed her nose to the wind like a figurehead on the prow of a great windjammer. Her dress front was damp and her hair tangled as they sailed the rim of the fishing bar in North Bay, where several rowboats were anchored and their occupants dozed in the late afternoon sun with cane poles in their hands.

Lorna picked him out immediately by the set of his shoulders and the overall familiarity of his form. Even in a wide straw hat, with his lower half hidden by the boat, she knew who it was. He was with another man, a stranger Lorna had never seen before.

Oddly, she could tell he spotted her at the same moment she did him. Even across the blinding water she had a sense of connection with him at the precise moment they recognized each other.

She smiled, stood and waved broadly above her head. "Jens! Hello!"

He waved back. "Hello, Miss Lorna!"

She cupped her mouth. "How are they biting?"

He leaned over the side of the boat and lifted a stringer of good-sized fish. "See for yourself!"

"What are they?"

"Walleyes!"

"My favorites!"

"Mine too!"

"Save one for me!" she joked, then sat down as the catboat sailed out of range and left Harken only a bump with wavy edges against the shimmering water.

Watching her smile after the boat, Taylor inquired, "Who was that?"

"Oh." She recovered quickly. "That was Harken, our kitchen handyman."

Taylor studied her closely. "You called him Jens."

Too late Lorna realized her slip and tried to make light of it. "Yes, Jens Harken, the one who's building the boat for my father."

"And just where might you be eating fish with him?"

"Oh, Taylor, don't be silly. I didn't mean it literally."

"Ah," Taylor said. But Lorna could tell he was not convinced. Furthermore, after the encounter with Jens her day seemed to go flat.

Her zest for sailing lost its headiness, her damp clothes seemed cloying and she began to feel the sunburn on her face.

"If it's all right with you, Taylor, I'm ready to go home."

Taylor studied her so intently she turned away and reached for her hat to escape his scrutiny. She flattened it on her wind-whipped hair and rammed the pin home. "I think I've got a sunburn and Mama is going to kill me if she sees me in this wet dress."

"Then maybe we should wait until it dries."

"No, please, Taylor. I don't want to get a chill."

Finally he answered, "Whatever you say," and headed back toward Manitou Island.

Jens Harken cleaned the fish and left them in the icebox with a note asking Mrs. Schmitt to fry them for the staff's breakfast the following morning.

At five-thirty A.M. when he walked into the kitchen she was filling his request, dipping the fish into buttermilk and cornmeal while Colleen fetched lard for the skillet and Ruby set the table.

"Morning," Jens greeted.

Mrs. Schmitt replied, "Maybe."

He came up short and glanced from Ruby to Colleen to the streaked bun on the back of Mrs. Schmitt's head. "You're in a fine mood this morning, I see."

She went on coating the fish. "I hope you went out to get these fish alone."

"As a matter of fact, I didn't."

"Jens Harken, you ain't got the sense God gave a tree stump if you had that girl along with you!"

"What girl?"

"What girl, he says. Lorna Barnett, as if you didn't know."

"I did not have Lorna Barnett with me!"

"Then what was she doing ordering a picnic for two yesterday?"

"How should I know? She's got friends, hasn't she?"

Mrs. Schmitt gave him *that look*. It nearly pulled her eyeballs out of her left ear and said, *Don't you lie to me, young man!*

"I had a new friend with me, Ben Jonson, if you must know. I met him at the lumberyard, and he's about my age, single and has his own fishing boat, so the two of us went out together."

Mrs. Schmitt slipped a metal spatula under a fish fillet, whupped it over, sending up a lardy sizzle, and said to the frying pan, "Well, that's better."

Ruby, however, continued shooting daggers at Jens from the corner of her eye while thudding plates onto the table as if she were dropping anchors.

He ignored her and said to Mrs. Schmitt, "Fry it all. I'll take the extra out to the shed to eat at noon. That way I won't have to come back here, where all the old hens are waiting to peck my eyes out."

She'd come. He knew as surely as he knew the shape of his own hands that she'd come to explain why she'd been sailing with Taylor DuVal. The man in the catboat had been DuVal, Jens was sure, a damned handsome fellow in a fancy yachting cap with a white crown, black visor and gold braid trim—the kind of a fellow she belonged with.

It was a drizzly day the color of pewter. The rain had begun well before dawn and continued into the late morning, a steady garden soaker. On the roof of the shed intermittent plops sounded as the moisture collected on leaves and dropped in syncopated beats. On the two small windows, droplets coalesced before tumbling in zigzag rivulets down the panes.

Inside, the place was dry and fragrant, lit by a gas lantern, filled with new lumber: white oak, mahogany, spruce and cedar. The cedar above all raised an aroma so rich and redolent it seemed edible. It stood to one side, stacked on wood slats.

Jens had spent the morning on his knees, nailing sheets of fir onto the floor, creating an expanse of pale grain a full thirty-eight feet long and then some. It had brightened the room considerably, spreading its peachy glow toward the murky rafters and broadcasting its fresh-milled smell. Around the edges of the new wood the old floor formed a frame of dirty gray. Upon it he'd left his thick boots and worked stocking-footed, measuring, marking, tacking down a black rubber batten much longer than himself on the unsoiled sheets of fir.

He heard the door squeak and looked up.

As he'd expected, Lorna Barnett came inside and closed the door behind her.

"Hello," she said from two-thirds of a building away, so far her voice echoed.

"Hello."

"I'm back."

Back and wearing something sleek below, puffed at the sleeves that showed off a set of fair lines as pretty as any boat he'd ever seen. He let his smile answer, remaining on his knees with one hand draped over the head of a hammer and its handle braced on his thigh.

"Gracious, it smells good in here," she remarked, sauntering toward him.

"New lumber."

"So I see." She walked around the edge of the fir past the stacked lumber. "And new lamps." She looked up at them while coming to a halt at a point nearest where Jens knelt.

"Yes." He sat back on his heels and studied her as she moved from shadow into light. Her skirt was patterned with blue morning glories, her shirtwaist solid white. Her face, lifted briefly to the lantern, turned his best intentions to foolhardiness.

"Looks like you got a little too much sun yesterday," he remarked.

She touched both cheeks. "I'd have been all right if I hadn't taken my hat off, but I couldn't resist."

"Does it hurt?"

"Yes it does, actually, but I'll live." She glanced at a series of dots he'd drawn on the clean wood, connected by the long graceful curve of the black batten.

"What are you doing?"

"Lofting, at last."

"So this is lofting . . . fairing up the boat, right?"

"Right."

"Making sure it has no lumps and bumps, right?"

"Right."

"Making sure it's smooth as fruit."

Jens only smiled.

"How does it work?"

Explaining was much safer than admiring her, so he struck in. "Well, I do a full-scale drawing of the boat—a side profile first—and then a fore and aft drawing of all the cross sections sort of nested together. When I'm all done there'll be a whole series of dots on the floor. When I connect any of those dots with the batten it'll show me if all the curves are fair. If they're not, let's say one of them bulges by even an eighth of an inch, that station of the boat will be hideous when it's done. So I change the curve of the mold in that spot and fix it *before* I make the mold."

"Oh."

He could see she didn't understand his verbal explanation, but the curve of the batten on the floor was unmistakable.

"Well, go ahead," she said, "don't let me stop you."

He laughed softly and replied, "You already have. I might as well have my dinner." He pulled out a pocket watch and checked it. "Hoo! Where did the morning go? Last time I looked it wasn't even nine yet." Actually, he'd been starved for over two hours but had put off eating on the chance she'd get here beforehand: It was a matter of some fish she'd asked for. "Do you mind if I eat while we visit, Miss Lorna?"

"Not at all."

He left his hammer and tacks, rose and crossed the fir planking in stocking feet to fetch a tin from atop the stack of lumber and remove its lid.

"Care to join me?" he asked, returning to Lorna, extending the tin.

She peered inside. "What's in there?"

"Fried walleye."

"Why, it is!" Her face blossomed in surprise: eyebrows up, cheeks rounded, smile anchored by a bite on her bottom lip. "It's the fish you caught yesterday!"

"You said to save some for you."

"Oh, Jens, what a surprising man you are! You really brought some for me?"

"Of course." He gestured toward the rusty park bench. "Would you care to sit?"

She looked around and said, "All right, but not there. Let's sit in the boat instead."

"In the boat?"

"Certainly, why not? We can have our first picnic in it before it's even on the water."

He chuckled and said, "Whatever you say, Miss Lorna. Hold on while I find us a tablecloth." While he went off to get a piece of chart paper she removed her shoes and left them beside his boots.

"Oh, you don't have to do that," he called. "The wood will get dirty eventually anyway. I just like to enjoy it clean for a while."

"If *you* take off your shoes, *I* take off my shoes." Her heels made hollow thumps on the floor as she crossed it. Her shoes, perched beside his boots, made an intimate picture as he passed them to put the chart paper down in the curve of the batten and set the tin of fish upon it. He enjoyed the sight of her dropping down Indian fashion, her flowered skirt flaring like a morning glory. Her shirtwaist had the usual huge sleeves, lots of skinny pin tucks up the front and a good thirty buttons holding it closed clear up past her throat. Just above her left breast was pinned a tiny pendant watch he'd never seen before, drawing attention to that lush curve. He pulled his eyes away from it and dropped down facing her.

"Help yourself."

She reached into the tin, plucked out a piece of fish and flashed him a smile.

"Our second picnic," she said.

He, too, helped himself and the two of them, riding an imaginary boat upon a sea of fragrant fresh-cut fir, ate cold fish with soggy breading and thought no fare had ever tasted finer, for they were together, as they loved to be, talking, smiling, exploring with their eyes.

"You really did get a sunburn," he said. "Your poor little nose looks like a signal light."

"It kept me awake most of the night."

"Did you put anything on it?"

"Buttermilk. But it didn't do much good."

"Try cucumbers."

"Cucumbers?"

"That's what my mother used to put on us when we were boys. Ask Mrs. Schmitt for one, or just pick one out of the garden on your way back to the house."

"I'll do that."

He studied her face critically, the sunburn an excuse to do so for a protracted length of time. "It's probably going to peel, anyway."

She touched her nose self-consciously. "And I'll look like a scaly old scrub pine."

"Mmm . . . I don't think so. I don't think you'll ever look like a scaly old scrub pine, Miss Lorna."

"Oh, won't I?" Her expression turned saucy over the backward compliment. "What will I look like, then?"

Their eyes locked in good humor. He bit, chewed and swallowed, enjoying this mildly flirtatious wordplay as much as she. Finally, with a one-sided grin, he ordered, "Eat your fish."

They finished their first pieces and started on seconds.

"Was that your Mr. DuVal with you yesterday?" Jens asked.

"It was Mr. DuVal. It was not *my* Mr. DuVal."

"I figured it was him. He was the one sitting beside you the night I served dinner in the dining room. He's a fine-looking fellow."

"Yes, he is."

"A decent sailor, too."

"I'll bet you're better."

"You've got to have a boat before you can be a sailor."

"You will have, someday, when you own your own boatworks. I know you will." She licked off a finger.

"So you and DuVal had a picnic yesterday, did you?"

"Lordy, that kitchen staff is gossipy."

"Yes, ma'am, they are. Trouble is, they thought you were out there having a picnic with me."

"What!"

"Mrs. Schmitt likes to mother me, but yesterday she outdid herself. She gave me a proper scolding about taking you out fishing with me and how inappropriate it was. But don't worry—I set her straight. I told her it wasn't me. I was with somebody else."

"And are you going to tell me who he was or not?"

"A new friend, Ben Jonson. I met him at the lumberyard when I went in to order all this wood. It was his boat."

"A new friend—good. My best friend is Phoebe Armfield. I've known her since we were little girls. Tell yours I'm glad he invited you. The fish were delicious."

Again she licked off her fingers, looked around for something with which to wipe her mouth but found nothing. Still sitting cross-legged, she doubled forward, fished for a hem of her petticoat and used that.

Surprised, Jens laughed, looking down at the back of her head. "Miss Lorna, what would your mother say?"

"What mother doesn't know won't hurt her. Or me." She flipped down her skirt and said, "Thank you. I'm sure I shall never forget this wonderful picnic."

He smiled into her eyes. She smiled into his. As always, he was the one to keep things light between them.

"So tell me, how was Mr. Sousa's concert?"

"Rousing. Patriotic."

"You met him?"

"Absolutely. He has splendid bearing and wears tiny oval glasses with gold wire rims and a miniature moustache and goatee that looks quite stunning with his uniform. It was white, by the way, with gold trim, and a captain's hat. Oh, and white gloves, which I never saw him remove, even once, not even when he ate finger foods. Mama's soiree was a great success."

"And Mr. DuVal was there, too?"

"Yes," she replied, finding Jens's eyes and keeping them. "Mr. DuVal is everywhere I go, it seems." Nearly whispering, she added, "Except here."

It took Jens a beat to recover and reply sensibly, "That's to be expected; after all, you're courting."

"Not quite."

"You're not? But you told me you were."

"I may have said that, and I may spend a lot of time with him, but don't say we're courting! Not yet!" As she spoke, her voice became more agitated. "It's enough that my family is all saying so, but then I suppose they have good reason. . . . Oh, Harken, I don't know. I'm so confused."

"About what?"

"This." She touched the watch above her breast. "It's from Taylor, you see." Jens gave the watch a second look and felt jealousy billow. "He gave it to me Saturday night after the concert and said it's not a betrothal gift, but everyone in my family thinks it is. And I don't want to be betrothed to Taylor yet, don't you see?"

Jens said what he thought he ought. "But he's fine-looking, and wealthy, and one of your class. He treats you well, your parents approve of him. It makes good sense to marry a man like that."

He knew even before she spoke, from the sincere and troubled softening about her eyes, that her following words would be better left unsaid. She said them quietly, looking straight into Jens's eyes.

"But what if there's someone I like better?"

Time reeled out while her admission bore down on them both. He could have reached out and simply taken her hand and the course of their lives would have changed. Instead, he chose the prudent road, replying, "Ah, well, then that's a dilemma, Miss Lorna."

"Harken—"

"And you'd better do some long hard thinking before you pass up an opportunity like DuVal."

"Harken, please—"

"No, Miss Lorna." He reached for the tin and shifted in preparation for rising. "I've said my piece, and it's good advice, I think. But in the future I think it might be better if you talked to someone else about this." He picked up the tin and carried it away.

She followed him with her eyes. "Who?"

"How about your friend Phoebe?"

Lorna rose, got her shoes and sat on the park bench to pull them on. "Phoebe is no good. She's so smitten by Taylor herself that she hasn't got an ounce of objectivity in her body. All she ever says is, 'If you don't want him, I'll take him.' "

"Well, there . . . see? He's a good catch."

Jens turned from placing the tin on the stack of lumber and found Lorna coming toward him. She didn't stop until she was so close he could have rearranged her hair with his breath.

"You can be very exasperating, do you know that?" she said.

"So can you."

"You don't like it when I come here?"

"Of course I do. But you know the problem as well as I do."

She studied him at close range, her deep brown eyes importuning him for the kiss he wisely had decided never to give. When she saw she was getting nowhere, she glanced aside, absently studying the stacked lumber awhile. Raising her eyes abruptly, she astonished him by asking, point-blank, "Aren't you ever going to kiss me, Harken?"

He released a breath containing sound: half laugh of surprise, half self-protection.

"Sure," he said, "the day they let me join your father's yacht club."

He began to turn away but she stopped him with a hand on his arm. Five little suns seemed to rest where her fingers did, burning their shape into his flesh.

Nothing moved. Not he, not she, not the earth, not time. Everything halted in anticipation.

"I've considered ordering you to do so, but I tried that once before and it didn't work so well."

He bent down and kissed her so lightly and briefly it was over before either of them had a chance to close their eyes.

"Harken, don't," she chided. "I'm not a child. Don't treat me like one."

They stood in the throes of temptation, the blood caught in their throats, the moment sensitized by the realization that kisses between them were strictly taboo. Yet they had breached that taboo a dozen times already by meeting, picnicking, becoming friends. What paltry dictum carried any weight when balanced against what they already felt for one another?

"All right," he said. "Once, and then you go."

"And then I go," she agreed.

He knew once he did it he'd be doomed, but he put his hands round her starchy sleeves nevertheless, and took a single fateful step that brought the tips of her breasts against his suspenders. His head tilted at the very heartbeat in which hers did. Their eyes closed, their lips joined, bringing rampant stillness to all but their hearts. Above her elbows his grip tightened and the angle of his head deepened. They opened their lips and tasted for the first time, trespassing into the texture and wetness of each other until some lovely motion began, one head swaying above another while all around them the rain serenaded and the perfume of cedar flavored the shed.

One kiss. Only one.

They made it last . . . and last . . . and last . . . until all within them ached at the idea of ending it.

A bump sounded on the shed roof: They startled apart, looking up as a squirrel landed and skittered across the shingles.

They looked down into each other's eyes, their mouths still parted, breaths tripping fast, Lorna's bodice rising and falling rapidly like the belly of a sleeping kitten while Jens continued gripping her sleeves, rubbing the white cotton with his thumbs.

When she spoke her voice sounded reedy.

"Someday, when I'm as old as Aunt Agnes, I shall tell my grandchildren about this moment, just as she's told me about her lost love, Captain Dearsley."

Jens smiled and traversed her face with his eyes—lips, cheeks, eyelids, hairline, where the dark mass of her hair drooped, framed by flossy stragglers.

"You have romantic notions, Miss Lorna, that are very unwise."

She studied him with a blissful expression in her eyes, as if his kiss had transported her above a temporal plane.

"How was I to know," she returned, "unless you kissed me?"

"Now you know. Are you any happier?"

"Yes. I am infinitely happier."

"Miss Lorna Barnett"—he wagged his head—"you're an impetuous young woman and you make it hard for a man to turn you out." He dropped his hands from her sleeves. "But I must." Gently, he added, "Go on now."

She sighed and looked around as if coming back to earth. "Very well, but on second thought, I just might talk to my friend Phoebe. She may not have any judgment where Taylor is concerned, but she *is* my best friend, and if I don't talk to someone about this, I feel I shall burst."

What in the world could he do with a woman like her? She laid out her feelings like a grocer displaying his finest produce, proud of its bright color and freshness, inviting him to pick it up, squeeze and judge for himself.

"Do you think that's wise?"

"Phoebe can be trusted. We've shared a lot of secrets before."

"All right, but just remember, this isn't going to happen again. Agreed?"

With her lower lip caught between her teeth she studied his blue eyes. "I'm not going to make any promises I can't be sure to keep."

He simply gazed at her, wondering how it was possible an ordinary man like himself could put such a lovestruck expression on the face of a beautiful, privileged girl like her.

"Walk me to the door?"

She plodded with reluctance in every footfall. He followed at her shoulder, wishing she could stay the rest of the afternoon and keep him company while he worked, wishing for the first time ever that he was a rich man. At the doorway she paused and turned.

"Thank you for the fish."

"You're welcome, Miss Lorna."

"There you go with your Miss Lorna again. Doesn't it matter that you've just kissed me?"

He put a wealth of feeling into his reply. "It matters a great deal."

She captured his eyes while they both felt the tug of parting wrenching them in two directions. He could see very clearly she wanted to kiss him again. He wanted to kiss her, too. He opened the door a shoulder's width and they stood in a shaft of outside dampness while raindrops made *blip-blips* on the carpeted forest floor.

He wanted to say, Come back again, I love having you here, talking about the boat with you, sharing my dreams with you; I love your hair and eyes and smile and a dozen other things about you.

Instead he said, "Don't forget those cucumbers."

She smiled and replied, "I won't."

The last he saw of her she was running down the path holding her skirt up to her knees.

Lorna Barnett found herself surprised by her unwillingness to divulge anything to Phoebe Armfield about her tête-à-tête with Jens Harken. She hugged the knowledge to herself and retired early that night to draw it out and examine alone in the darkness. Lying flat on her back with coins of salady-smelling cucumber covering her face, she brought it all back. In memory, the entire afternoon took on a rich texture comprised of wood and rain, simplicity and honesty. What pleasure she had found in the plebeian pastime of sitting cross-legged in the middle of a fresh-wood floor and picnicking on leftover fish. What joy she had taken in facing Jens Harken at close range and watching his facial expressions run a range of responses, from laughter to thoughtfulness to admiration. And finally, when the kiss had ended, the same naked yearning she felt.

Her mother would be mortified if she knew.

Lorna was not—she was discovering—like her mother. She was a sensitive and sensual human being to whom Jens Harken had become a man, not hired help but someone respectable, likable, admirable, even, who dreamed a dream and acted upon it. Her physical attraction to him did not merely breach the barriers of class distinction; it negated them. When they were together they were simply a man and a woman, not a poor man and a rich woman. To be in his presence created happiness. To watch him work fascinated. To listen to him speak was as arresting as listening to John Philip Sousa's marches.

She found herself stunned by her intense reaction to his simplest physical aspects. His face, of course, his handsome Norwegian face; but also his hands, neck, the veins along his inner arms, his crossed suspenders, even the belled toes of his stockings—looking at any of them created a tempest of feelings within her, simply because they were part of him. When he moved, each angle of his limbs became in her eyes balletic, each turn of his head perfection. Even his clothing seemed to rustle differently than other men's.

And kissing him—oh . . . oh . . . kissing him was delight of unimagined magnitude. He had smelled like the shed, all cedary and woodsy, almost tasted that way, and when his tongue had touched hers it felt as if he'd drawn all the warm peachy glow from their surroundings into that one spot and transferred it inside her. She grew desirous simply thinking about it. Lying in her bedroom, one floor below his, she made up her mind that nothing short of incarceration could keep her from kissing him again.

Jens Harken had discovered it was far easier to escort Lorna Barnett out of his shed than out of his head. For the remainder of the afternoon she beset him, smiling from his memory, tipping her face up to be kissed, leaving it tipped when the kiss ended.

Damned adorable, incorrigible girl.

In his own room that night she was still there inside his head, very nearly inside his heart. To keep her from making further inroads in that direction, he wrote to his brother.

Dear Davin,

I think I've made some headway at last. I've finally got someone to finance the flat-hulled boat I've talked about for years—my employer, Mr. Gideon Barnett, would you believe. He's set me up in a shed, let me buy tools and wood, and I'm already doing the lofting. He still thinks I'm crazy, I believe, but he's willing to gamble his money on the off chance that I'm not. He's given me three months, even though the boat won't race until next summer. When it does, be ready to come out here. It'll win and win big, and the whole country will hear about it, and you and I will be in business. I've been saving every cent I can. I hope you have been, too. We'll need it if we want the Harken Boatworks to become a reality. When it does we'll have something to start with, because I've paid for the materials for the mold myself, so I can keep it afterwards, which is more than we had when I was out East.

I wish you were here now so we could talk about the boat design and work on it together. I've met a new friend named Ben Jonson, and I think I'll ask him to help me when it comes time to bend the ribs. He's a Norsky, as you guessed, and nobody can fair up a boat like us Norskies, yes, little brother? He works at the lumberyard where I bought my lumber, but work slows down there in the fall, when building season is over, so I think he'll be able to help me. He took me fishing on Sunday and we caught us a nice mess of walleyed pike, which are plentiful here.

Oh, by the way, I shared some of the fish with a lady.

I shared some of the fish with a lady. It was as much as Jens Harken trusted himself to say. The onslaught of feelings Lorna Barnett had stirred up in him demanded that he say that much, for, like her, he felt he would burst if he didn't tell someone. But he'd tell no more.

When the letter was sealed and the light off, he lay once more in his attic bedroom, much as she lay in hers below him, resurrecting her image and the pleasure of spending time with her, kissing her.

He closed his eyes, laced his fingers across his chest and realized something momentous. Up until now when he'd dreamed about building a fast boat, he'd dreamed of building it for himself, for the pleasure of watching it fly with the wind, and for the eventualities it would bring about: a business of his own and his brother, Davin, at his side with more customers than they could accommodate.

Now, for the first time, he dreamed of winning for her, so that he would be worthier in her father's eyes and would garner the respect of other men like her father, and would no longer be ordered back to a kitchen.

He pictured the regatta with himself skipping—always himself skipping—and Lorna Barnett on the shore, standing with the other parasolled women, cheering him on as he planed downwind with the bow of the boat lifted and the sails bellied. He pictured the boat shooting past the home buoy, and heard the applause of the crowd from the clubhouse lawn as he brought her in, and imagined Tim Iversen taking his photograph for the yacht club wall, and Gideon Barnett shaking his hand, saying, "Well done, Harken."

One kiss had enlarged his dreams to this extent. Yet he knew in his heart all this was not possible. He was not a yacht club member and probably never would be. Neither would he probably ever skip this boat, for they hired skippers with winning records and brought them from all over the country in their efforts to win the big races. He had no record, no boat of his own, no wealth, no status.

And absolutely no right to be falling in love with Gideon Barnett's daughter.

Chapter
EIGHT

THOSE were the sun-strewn days of July. The weather turned hot, the rain disappeared and the gardens flourished. Levinia's roses flaunted themselves. Smythe's berries became grandiose. The lawns surrounding Rose Point Cottage seemed to hum daily with the whir of mowers, followed by the herbal scent of shorn grass. Out in the boat shed beneath the vaulty trees, the great double doors remained open fourteen hours a day, welcoming the summer breeze inside along with Miss Lorna Barnett whenever she chose to come.

She waited four days to return. On the day when she did, she went first to find her mother in the picking gardens, where Levinia was collecting long blue spikes of delphiniums in a flat basket hung over her arm.

"Mother . . . good morning!" Lorna called.

Levinia looked up, squinting from beneath the brim of a wide straw bonnet. She wore green gloves and held pruning snips.

"Good morning, Lorna."

"Isn't it a glorious day?" Lorna scanned the skies.

"It's going to be beastly hot, and you should have a bonnet on."

"Oh, I'm sorry, Mother. I forgot."

"Forgot? When you're still peeling from your last sunburn? Next you'll get freckled, and then how will you get rid of the ugly things?"

"I'll try to remember next time."

"What have you there?"

"Cookies. I smelled them baking and went down to the kitchen to investigate. Cinnamon and apple. Would you like one?"

Lorna opened the white napkin. Levinia pulled off one glove and helped herself.

"I'm taking the rest out to Mr. Harken in the shed, if it's all right with you."

"Gracious sake, Lorna, I don't like you loitering around the help that way."

"I know, but he sometimes works right on through lunch, and I thought he might like a little tideover. Is that all right, Mother?"

"Well . . ." Levinia glanced dubiously toward the vegetable garden and the woods beyond, back at Lorna and the napkin in her hand. "That's not our good linen, is it?"

"Oh, no. It's one for the staff's use, and I'll be sure to tell Harken to return it to the kitchen when he's done."

Again, Levinia threw an undecided glance toward the shed. "Well, I guess so, then."

"I've been going out occasionally and visiting with him and checking the progress on the boat. It's quite fascinating, actually. He's drawing it out full-scale, right on the floor. Would you like to come with me?"

"To that musty old building? Heavens no. Besides, I have bouquets to arrange."

"Well then, I guess I'll just go alone." Lorna sent her gaze in an appreciative arc across the gardens. "Mother, your flowers are truly breathtaking this summer. May I take one of these?"

"Help yourself . . . but, Lorna, you won't stay out in that shed very long, will you?" Levinia looked worried.

"Oh no." Lorna selected a delphinium and sniffed it. Surprisingly, it had no smell. "Just long enough to see how the work is going and give these cookies to Mr. Harken, then I thought I'd walk down along the shore to Phoebe's house. She's invited me for lunch on the veranda."

"Oh, how nice." Levinia looked relieved. "Tell her hello from me, and her mother, too. What time will you be back, then, dear?"

Backing away, Lorna shrugged. "Not late. By three for sure, then if it's not too hot I might try to talk Jenny into a game of tennis. Goodbye, Mother."

Levinia watched after her daughter, in her hand the cookie with a single bite taken from it. "Now, remember," she called, "you won't stay long!"

"No, Mother."

"And next time wear your hat."

"Yes, Mother."

Levinia sighed and watched her willful daughter disappear.

Lorna cut around the glasshouse, skirted the vegetable garden and entered the woods. She heard the engine even before she reached the shed. *Pup . . . pup . . . pup:* little explosions with long pauses between. She listened a moment, then continued along the short path to the sharp right curve that would deliver her to Harken's doorway. There at the curve, she paused to inspect herself. Juggling the cookies and delphinium in one hand, she checked her hair, running a palm over the smooth pouf to two fat ornamental hair brooches that protruded from her Gibson droop like pearl-headed chopsticks. She tugged at her skirt, looking down her midriff at the green-and-white stripes meeting like arrows down her center front. She touched the grosgrain cravat bow at her throat.

At last, satisfied, she transferred the delphinium to her right hand and stepped to the doorway of Harken's domain.

He was sawing a piece of wood, unaware of her presence. Waiting out the piercing shriek of the saw, she pleasured herself with the sight of him in a very faded shirt that had probably once been the color of tomato juice. It was so worn and thin that it draped from his limbs like jowls from an old jaw. With it he wore the usual black suspenders and black trousers. He worked bare-headed, and the rim of his hair was wet with sweat, darkened to the color of year-old grain.

The saw stopped whining but the engine continued its intermittent *pup . . . pup.* Whistling softly, he examined the piece of wood he'd just cut, running his fingertips over its sawn edge.

"Hello, Jens."

He looked up. His fingers stopped examining. Their ill-advised kiss was there between them as if it had just happened, demanding remembrance while they both knew it must be forgotten.

"Well, look who's here."

"Bearing gifts, too." Lorna went inside, approached him with her napkin-nest and flower, while he waited beside his sawing rig. "It was my turn. Cinnamon-apple cookies today, fresh from Mrs. Schmitt's oven . . . and something to match your eyes."

She offered him the delphinium first. He looked at the flower, at her, hesitated while the allure they possessed for each other smote them both with lovestruck quietude. Beside them the engine made another *pup*. He reached out to accept her gift: Its delicate blue petals painted a striking contrast to his soiled hand and faded work clothes.

"What is it called?"

"A delphinium."

"Thank you."

The flower did, indeed, match his blue eyes. It took an effort for Lorna to drag her gaze from them and recall she'd brought something more. "And here are your cookies." She put the napkin in his wide hand.

"Thank you again."

"I can't stay today. I'm going to Phoebe's for lunch on the veranda, but I just wanted to come by and see how you're doing."

He turned away, walked to the engine and touched something that shut it off. "I'm doing fine," he said, from a safer distance. "And see what I've got. Your father allowed me to buy this wonderful electro-vapor engine."

"Electro-vapor."

"Four-horsepower."

"Is that a lot?"

"You bet. It takes a spark from this little battery here and runs on illuminating gas."

"On illuminating gas . . . my."

"All I have to do is turn the switch and I can saw wood without using any elbow grease. Isn't that some miracle?"

She gave her attention to the engine. It had a big flywheel with long pulleys connecting it to the saw. He'd walked the length of those pulleys to put distance between them.

"My, yes, quite a miracle. I see you've done some cutting with it already." Across the floor where the battens had lain the last time she was here five molds stood, two feet apart, shaped like upside-down cross sections of the boat. Already she could see how they'd define the shape of the hull. He had been cutting another when she'd interrupted.

"You're making progress."

"Yes."

"I wish I could watch you work awhile, but I'm afraid I have to go. I'm supposed to be at Phoebe's by noon."

"Well . . . thanks for the cookies. And the flower."

"You're welcome."

She studied him for a very long moment, from a good ten feet away and, just before turning to leave, said, "Yes, I was right. They are very much the color of the delphinium."

At Phoebe's house, Lorna was directed to the cool seafoam-green summer room, where Mrs. Armfield was writing letters, seated on a chair by an open French door with a portable desk on her lap. She offered both hands, then her cheek for kissing. "Lorna, how nice to see you. I'm afraid Phoebe's not feeling too well today, but she told me to be sure to send you up to her room."

Upstairs, Phoebe lay curled on her bed, hugging a pillow to her abdomen.

"Phoebe . . . oh, poor Phoebe, whatever is wrong?" Lorna swiftly crossed to the bed and sat down beside her friend. She combed Phoebe's hair back from her temple.

"What's wrong every month at this time. Oh, I just hate being a girl sometimes. I get such bad cramps."

"I know. Sometimes I do, too."

"Mother had the maid bring me some warm packs to put on my stomach but they haven't helped at all."

"Poor Phoebe . . . I'm sorry . . ."

"I'm the one who's sorry. I've ruined our luncheon plans."

"Oh, don't be silly. We can have lunch any old time. You just rest and tomorrow I'm sure you'll feel better. If you do, should we have lunch then?"

They made the plan, and Lorna left her friend still coiled around the pillow.

She took the less-used shoreline rather than the road back to Rose Point property, silently thanking Phoebe for giving her an excuse to return to the boat shed, armed with her mother's reluctant approval, and the realization that nobody was expecting her back at the house till midafternoon. Picking her way through the woods, approaching him, she felt again the wondrous exhilaration that accompanied every trip she made to Jens Harken. He would put up barriers, she knew, but she understood why.

He was gone, however, when she got there. The delphinium she'd given him was lying on the sill of the north window, where the breeze ruffled its petals. The cookies were gone, but the napkin lay folded in fourths on a stack of lumber. The engine was quiet, the flywheel still. She walked near them, stooping at the stack of sawdust beneath the sawblade, picking up a handful, lifting it to her nose and letting it drift back down—fragrant, wispy evidence of his morning's labor. She examined his work in progress, running her fingertips over pencil lines he'd drawn on wood, and edges he'd cut with the saw, much as he did after he made them. She recalled his excitement over having such fine tools with which to work. She moved through the space he'd moved through, touched the things he'd touched, breathed the smells he'd breathed, and discovered that this mundane setting had been transported, in her eyes, simply because he'd been in it.

She sat on the iron bench and waited. He returned after thirty minutes, and she heard his approaching footsteps just before he reached the open double doors.

He stepped inside and halted, discovering her there. As always, a force field seemed to generate around them.

"Phoebe is ill," she told him, "and no one is expecting me till three o'clock. May I stay?"

He neither answered nor moved for the longest time. Standing as he was, with the light behind him, Lorna could not make out his features. But his pause was clear enough: It was caution, pure and simple.

"Why don't you go ask your parents and see what they say?"

"I already did. I asked my mother before I brought you the cookies."

"You asked your mother!"

"She was picking delphiniums in the garden and I stopped by and told her I was bringing the cookies to you and asked if I could have a flower."

"And she said yes?"

"Well . . . I'll have to admit, she didn't know I was bringing the flower to you."

"Miss Lorna, you know I love to have you here, but I don't think it's a good idea for you to come so often."

"Don't worry. I won't make you kiss me again."

"I know you won't because I'm not going to!"

"I just want to watch."

"You distract me."

"I'll be as quiet as a mouse."

He laughed aloud. She laughed, too, realizing what a magpie she was.

"Well, maybe not quite that quiet," she admitted. "But please let me stay anyway."

"Suit yourself," he finally conceded.

There was no more kissing. When she left, he did not invite her back again. But the next time she came, the rusty iron bench had been painted.

So began the parade of visits when Lorna would take up her station on the bench and keep Jens company while he worked. She came most often in the early afternoon, when her mother napped, sometimes bringing delectable tidbits of food she and Jens could share, sometimes sharing some sweet he brought from his noon dinner in the kitchen, explaining that the kitchen staff ate different desserts from the family. These—he thought—were often better than the fancy things served in the main dining room, which tended to be more looks than sugar.

Oh, how they would talk. Lorna especially. She would cross her ankles Indian fashion on the seat of the bench and chatter about her life. If she'd been to a chautauqua or a concert or a play, she described it in detail. If there was a soiree afterward, she would describe the food. He asked her who Mr. Gibson was, the one she'd once alluded to so briefly, and she told him about the previous summer, when the famous artist had been their houseguest and had influenced her so profoundly she'd changed her dress and hairstyle. They spent a long time discussing whether Lorna herself more closely fit into the category of Gibson's "boy-girl" (who was a sport and would enjoy losing her life on a runaway horse more than gaining the attentions of a lovesick man) or "the convinced" (who set a certain goal and pursued it without taking a single side step). They decided that if anyone was "the convinced" type, it was Harken himself, since he had left his only family to pursue his goal as a boatbuilder.

Jens spoke of his brother, Davin, and how he missed him. "I've written and told him all about this boat I'm building, and he's nearly as excited as I am. He says if it wins the regatta next year, he'll get here if he has to crawl all the way, so we can set up business together."

"I cannot wait to meet him. Did you tell him about me?"

"I told him I fed you fish."

"That's all?"

"That's all."

"Tell me what your parents were like," she said one day.

He told of a stern patriarch and a hard-working housewife who left their families behind to build a better life for their sons in America. He told of working with his father at the boatworks, prying answers out of the reticent man, who could never understand where Jens's questions came from, nor find the wherewithal to answer in a manner that would satisfy the curiosity of a young boy whose passion for boats soon outstripped his father's knowledge of them.

"So you truly didn't learn all you know about boats by working in the boatworks."

"No. Some of it just comes from in here." Jens tapped his temple. "I picture a boat and I know how it will act in the water."

Watching him work on the present one, she believed this fully.

He said to her one day, "It must be nice to have so much family, to have even your aunts live with you. I would like that."

"You only think you'd like that. There are so many people in our family it's hard to find any privacy." Lorna went on to tell Jens about her aunt Henrietta, who always seemed to know when she was going out and accosted her with humorous if aggravating reminders to always carry a sharp hatpin as a weapon. She told about Aunt Agnes's long-lost love, Captain Dearsley, and how Agnes's devotion to him had never waned, but shone like a hopeless beacon through the old woman's lonely years of being admonished and reprimanded by her older sister.

"I love my aunt Agnes," Lorna told Jens. "But I merely tolerate my aunt Henrietta. I've often thought that if I could have one wish in my life it would be to bring back Captain Dearsley for Aunt Agnes."

"You wouldn't wish for something for yourself?"

"Oh no. I have my whole life before me to work toward my wishes. Aunt Agnes is old, though, and it must be sad to see your life running out and never have love and children and a home of your own."

"So to you wishes are something you work toward, they're not pipe dreams?"

That set off a whole new avenue of discussion, which led eventually to the subject of luck and whether or not it was granted by fate or created by each person for himself.

During those days of discussion the work on the boat progressed. The cedar cross sections were completed and set in their proper relationship to one another along the length of the shed, like slices of salmon on a cutting board. These were strung together by a backbone and two side stringers made of spruce, laid in notches cut into the cross sections to receive them.

Ah, those cedar-scented, green-dappled days of deep summer. While they progressed, Lorna and Jens nurtured one another as confidantes and friends. As lovers, though, they stood fast in their resistance to each other, upholding their agreement not to kiss again. Until the day Lorna brought a bowl of the prized blackcurrants, sugared and creamed and smuggled out of the house in a Sevres china sauce dish folded inside a boating magazine. Jens saw her arrive and left his work to meet her.

"Look what I've brought!" She unveiled her prize. "Ta-daa!"

"Blackcurrants?" Jens laughed robustly. "If Smythe ever found out he'd pop a gasket."

"Aaand . . ." Lorna drew out the word like a fanfare, then proudly produced one silver spoon.

"Only one?" Jens asked.

"One is all we need."

They dragged the iron bench out to the very verge of the wide doorway and sat with their bodies inside, heels out, ankles crossed, eating blackcurrants and cream and sugar, taking turns with the spoon until, at the end, Lorna scraped every last vestige of purple juice from the side of the bowl and held it up to feed to Jens.

"You eat it," he told her. "It's the last of it."

"No . . . you," she insisted.

He was sitting with one wrist hooked casually over the backrest of the bench beyond Lorna's shoulder, the rest of him outwardly relaxed. She held the spoon in the air, waiting, her brown eyes locked with his blue ones, bent upon giving the last taste to him. Finally, his head dipped forward and he opened his mouth. She caught a glimpse of his tongue and watched, fascinated, as his lips closed around the spoon . . . and the spoon rearranged them . . . then lingered . . . lingered . . . inside his mouth . . . while that single shattering kiss came back to beguile them.

Finally she slipped the spoon free. It made a soft clink settling into the bowl, the bowl no sound at all nestling into the folds of Lorna's skirt. The only sound they heard was that of magnified heartbeats and breathing—their own—while a fine and unwelcome tension built and budded between them. For days they had been good, and careful, and discreet, and politic. But it had failed: They could not be merely friends when it was lovers they wanted to be.

Long before he moved, they both knew he would.

His arm left the bench and carried her toward him in one definite sweep as she lifted her face to his descending one. His fingers curved into her warm armpit as she reached up for his neck. There was no pretense of reserve, no coquettish or polite first affectation. Their kiss was lush, intimate, dense from the moment of contact. It involved tongues and teeth and a very stubborn gravity that seemed unwilling to allow them close enough, skewed as they were on the bench. It tasted of blackcurrants and temptation and lasted longer than the flavor of the berries, which they took from each other's tongues. It ended with Jens drawing back to rid them of the bowl and spoon before reclaiming her again. She went against him eagerly, her freed hands spreading on his back like sun on a prairie. Their mouths opened. They caressed the allowable spots—ribs, backs, napes, waists —while those crying out to be touched went unsatisfied. When at last the kiss ended they drew apart, smileless, their breaths beating on each other's faces, in plain view of anyone who happened to come around the curve in the path.

He broke free and ordered, "Come with me," led her by one hand from the bench, inside, where the wall hid them. There in the shadows, he drew her home against him and she went gladly, up on tiptoe, her arms thrown round his shoulders. Length to length, they kissed, discovering the wonder of fitting together as they'd so often imagined. The minutes stretched into the shadowy stillness of the afternoon while his hands played over her back, down her sides, bearing down upon her hips before sliding up till the butts of them rested against the side-swells of her breasts, very near indiscretion.

He lifted his head and their eyes met.

"Lorna," he said. Simply Lorna.

"Jens," she replied, experiencing the same urge to speak his name.

For some time they merely gazed, having reached this plane at last.

"Could I say it now?" he wanted to know.

"Yes . . . anything."

"You're the most beautiful woman I've ever known. I thought so from the first night you came into the kitchen."

"And I thought you were the handsomest man. It's been very hard not saying so."

"It's been very hard not saying a lot of things."

"Say them now."

"Beautiful girl, do you know how many times I've thought about doing this?"

"Kissing me?"

"Kissing you, holding you, running my hands over your fair lines." With his palms still at the sides of her breasts he stretched out his thumbs and stroked, narrowly missing two most sensitive spots.

"How many?"

"Fifty, a hundred, a thousand. So many that it kept me awake nights imagining it."

"Me too. You've truly ruined my sleep."

"I'm glad."

She took the next kiss, rising up on tiptoe and opening her mouth with an invitation he gladly accepted, delving into it fully. Their sleek tongues moved in ballet, deep, shallow, deep again. He bit her upper lip in pantomime, then licked as if to heal the unrealized hurt, and centered the kiss once more. In the midst of it, he moved his hands, slid them inward and covered both her breasts, held them gently.

Against his cheek she quit breathing.

Against his mouth, hers went lax. "Oh . . ." she whispered, and "Oh . . ." again, then stood very still with her eyelids closed and her arms over his shoulders. His caress was slow and easy, knuckles turned outward as if holding a globe, giving her time to acclimate to his touch. When she had, he explored with his thumbs.

Her eyelids flickered open. The tip of her tongue showed between her teeth. Her breasts rose and fell in his hands, marking the rhythm of her taxed breathing. He went on making small circles over those pleasure spots until a shudder quaked through her, then he put his arms around her again and gathered her close.

He spoke against her hair. "It's not safe here."

"Then we must meet someplace where it is."

"Are you sure?"

"Yes. I've been sure long before today. Oh, Jens." She gripped him tighter, feeling as thwarted and threatened and frustrated as he, unaccustomed to making plans for this sort of thing, uncertain, even, if *this sort of thing* was what they were agreeing to. There was a faint sense of transgression, an even greater one of inevitability. They felt bonded by both.

"Can you wait until Sunday?" he asked.

"If I must, but I feel as if I shall die when I walk away from you."

"There's a stretch of woods south of Tim's, where the beach is poor and rocky and nobody comes. Meet me there. I'll borrow Ben's boat. One o'clock?"

"One o'clock."

"And, Lorna?"

"Yes, Jens?"

"If you know what's good for you, you'll wear a very sharp hatpin."

* * *

On Sunday it was sunny. Lorna took a picnic. And a blanket. She wore blue and stuck a nine-inch cloisonné hatpin, freshly sharpened, into her hat. She rowed across the lake and found Jens's boat already there, on a rocky section of shoreline with a bit of a bluff leading up to the woods above. As she approached, he appeared from the trees and came down a path to wait on the shoreline, wearing a black Sunday suit and a black derby. She glimpsed his attire over her shoulder while he stood with his weight borne on one hip, the opposite leg cocked, his foot on a rock.

"Hello," he called, while she stowed the oars and the boat drifted in.

"Hello." He was waiting to take her bow line and tie it to a willow bush. The boat bumped and scraped along scarcely submerged rocks as Lorna stood up and steadied herself. She stepped over the seat to hand him the blanket and hamper, then poised before taking his waiting hand and making the leap to shore. He landed her safely, swinging her half behind him and planting her gracefully on the uneven ground.

He kept his hands at her waist. She kept hers on his shoulders. They stood immobilized by each other's presence and this summer day's bounty of time.

She took in his appearance, very different in the formal Sunday clothes, the suit over a white shirt and black tie, the hat that changed the overall shape of his face. Such a surprise it was.

He took in her appearance, pleased she'd chosen the same blue striped skirt she'd worn the day of their first picnic, the same billowing white sleeves, the same straw hat with its blue trailers.

"Hello," he said again, softer, smiling almost shyly.

She answered with a shy laugh and a very, very soft, "Hello."

Of the tens of things they'd planned to say or do at this moment, none came to mind, only to stand beneath the beating sun, resplendent in their newfound feelings for each other.

There were boats on the water within visible distance. He bent to retrieve the blanket and hand it to her. Carrying the hamper himself, he led her by the hand up the bank, where rocks and wild grasses made the footing precarious.

"Careful, it's steep."

When she began skittering backward he hauled her up to safety until they reached at last a plateau above, where the woods was heavy enough to hide them yet provided a view of the water to the west. There, beneath the birches and maples, they spread her tartan plaid blanket and pretended picnicking was what they had come here for.

There were glimpses, though, stolen and admiring. He caught her at one—it had turned into an outright stare—just as he straightened from setting the hamper on the blanket. They stood on the grass with the prepared place between them.

"Is something wrong?" he asked.

"I've never seen you in a suit before."

He looked down his front.

"It's a very old suit. My only one."

"Or a hat."

He removed it and stood with it in his hands, a courtesy he'd never before had the opportunity to show. "It's Sunday."

"No . . ." she said, "don't take it off. I like it on you."

"Very well." He put it back on, using two hands, tipping it ever so slightly off level. "For you."

She studied him, letting her glance drift from the derby to his freshly shaved face to his necktie, which formed a thick knot between the tips of a rounded shirt collar. His jacket, which was fully buttoned, appeared to be slightly too snug and short in the sleeves, as if he'd grown since it was purchased. To Lorna, it only emphasized his pleasing proportions.

"I suppose a lady shouldn't say a man looks breathtaking."

Jens couldn't restrain his smile. "No, I believe it's the man who tells the lady that." He removed the smile and added, "You look breathtaking, Miss Lorna. I hope you'll take it as a compliment when I say that I've always admired your fair line in those big sleeves and skinny skirts."

"You have?" She looked down and plucked at her sleeves as if to put more air in them. "I shall take it as my favorite compliment, even though the sleeves are forever catching on doorways and touching dusty things and getting crushed. And the skirt is only skinny in the front. In the back it's quite full . . . see?" She whirled, presenting her back—shapely, too—with the skirt poufing, the boned shirtwaist hugging and the blue bonnet ribbons trailing. When she faced him once more, her cheeks were pink. "Fair line, indeed," she teased with a smile.

He could think of nothing except how badly he wanted to kiss her, but the picnic should be had first, and some polite conversation shared, and things like the weather and the local fishing and the progress on the boat commented upon lest he appear indecently eager.

"Would you sit down, please, Miss Barnett, so I can sit down, too?"

"Oh, my goodness, I didn't realize." She knelt and watched his tall form bend and fold and find a comfortable, relaxed pose, his weight on one buttock with one foot extended and the other knee raised, one palm spread on the blanket behind him.

They looked at each other. They looked at the water.

"We couldn't have asked for a nicer day, could we?" he remarked.

"No, it's perfect."

"Lots of fishermen out."

"Yes."

"And lots of sails too."

"Mm-hmm."

"It feels good to be out of that shed for a day."

He'd covered the niceties, though he knew he'd done so too expressly for strict politeness. Their eyes were drawn to each other again, expressions painted by the unsaid.

"Shall we have our picnic right away?" she asked.

"That's fine. What have you got in there?"

She opened the hamper and began spreading things out on the blanket. "Cold chicken with a special mushroom ketchup, Jerusalem artichokes wrapped in bacon, almond tarts and glacé pineapple pears."

"You'll spoil me."

"I should love very much to spoil you." She made the remark while occupied with the foods, filling a plate. "However, I think it would take more than glacés and Jerusalem artichokes to rid you of your predilection for cold fish. This is what I love about our picnics.

Mine are exotic and yours are satisfying. So we learn a little bit about each other, don't we?"

She handed him the plate with a flash of a smile and began filling one for herself. He watched her, admiring each motion, each feature, her delicate fingers, long throat in its cylinder of white, so many, many buttons up her center front, the way her hair ballooned beneath her bonnet brim, the delicate puff of her chin when it was tucked down.

"Did you ask Mrs. Schmitt to pack the hamper?" he inquired.

"Yes, I did."

"What did she say?"

She went on filling her plate but her diction became clipped. "She isn't paid to *say* anything. Furthermore, I don't answer to Mrs. Schmitt and neither do you. Did you borrow your friend's boat?" She hit him with a direct look.

"Yes, I did."

"What did you tell him?"

"The truth. That I was meeting a girl."

"Did he ask who she was?"

"He knows."

"He does?"

"He found the blue delphinium on the windowsill and asked how it got there. I'm no good at lying." A stretch of silence scintillated between them, rife with hinted truths about their feelings and the significance of these clandestine meetings. At length, Jens went on. "I want you to know, Lorna, that if we're ever discovered, if word ever gets to your mother and father and they confront me with it, I'll tell the truth."

She looked him straight in the eye and replied, "So shall I."

They each held a plate filled with excuses. Across the top of the picnic hamper their gazes declared very clearly that this willful postponement of kisses was becoming more than either could tolerate.

Jens set his plate on the grass. He reached across the hamper and commandeered hers, set it aside, too, along with the hamper and tins. Next, he removed his hat. "It's such a pretty little lunch," he said, "but I'm not the least bit hungry."

Lorna's cheeks blazed pink and her heart knocked as Jens knelt before her, his eyes steady on her upturned face, his pose filled with intention while she sat primly on her heels, her hands joined in her lap. He gripped her arms, crushing her starched sleeves, and drew her up . . . up . . . into his embrace. She went joyously, into a kiss of greatest import, for it was the first they had willed—mutually—long before this day arrived, this hour, this minute. In their beds alone at night, they had willed it. Trudging through the hours of the days, they had willed it. Rowing to this trysting spot in separate boats, they had willed it. Now at last it happened, callow as it began, for he'd had to bend down and dip his head beneath her hat brim to reach her lips. Joined like a wishbone, with their mouths softly engaged, they said their true hello. Jens parted Lorna's lips with his tongue, felt the tip of hers come shyly to meet it and stroked it: *Come hither, don't be afraid, let me woo you.*

Some gulls flew by, squawking. Some flies buzzed over their plates. In the distance a steam whistle blew. They heard none of this, heard only the voices in their heads that said, *At last, at last.*

The earth sighed. . . . Or was it the breeze? The summer trembled, or was it their touch? Two glad lovers neither knew nor cared as Jens blindly lifted his hands to her hat, found the pin and removed it, then the hat itself from her head. Lorna reached up reflexively, interrupting the kiss, just as the hat sailed away to join his on the grass. Her chin dropped down and she touched her hair with the same momentary shyness of earlier, feeling for any strand loosened by the departing straw. He took her face in his hands and lifted it to his intense regard.

Only summer was there to witness as they itemized and idolized—eyes, noses, lips, chins, shoulders, hair, eyes again.

"Yes," he said, "you're as perfect as I remember."

His head lowered, his arms surrounded her, drawing her flush against his black Sunday suit. At last they were body to body, mouth to mouth. All they'd been wishing they felt: fully-matched desire. He held her low across the spine, waltzlike, against his sturdy hips. His knees remained widespread. Her skirts puddled around them. She clung to his shoulders.

They twisted till their fit became grassy—two blades blown by the same wind—and the kiss became a wild suckling of mouths, wet and unrestrained in that awful burst of impatience between arousal and denial. She felt her mouth freed and exulted, "Jens . . . Jens . . ." while their arms crushed one another and beyond his shoulder she saw the birch branches swaying overhead.

"I can't believe this," he told her in a stranger's voice, a voice constricted with desire.

"Neither can I."

"You're really here."

"And you're really here."

"I thought this afternoon would never come, and when it did, I was sure I'd wait here for nothing."

"No . . . no . . ." She drew back and gave his mouth a brief and darting kiss, then another to his cheek. "How could you think that? I've always come to you, haven't I?"

"You know I'd come to you if I could." He captured her hands, kissed both her palms, then pressed them to his chest.

"Yes, I do know that now." She knelt with her hands spread flat upon him, upon his woolen jacket that felt warm and scratchy and marvelously exotic for belonging to this special man.

"Every time you come to the shed and I look up and find you standing there in the doorway, this happens to me."

"What?"

"This." He pressed her right hand even harder against him.

"This?" Looking into his blue eyes she slipped three fingers beneath his lapel and centered her hand over his clamoring heart. His white shirt was smooth with starch, his suspender textured, the flesh beneath it solid as hickory, and ever so warm. *Th-thup, th-thup, th-thup:* His heart felt as if it might bruise her palm.

"Oh . . ." she breathed, kneeling very still, concentrating. "Just like mine . . . for hours after I see you."

"Really?" he said softly, while absorbing the thrill of her hand inside his jacket. "Let me feel."

When she made no reply he laid his hand carefully on her heart—a big, rough boatbuilder's hand on the closely tucked fine white lawn of her blouse. He counted the heartbeats that seemed to have accelerated to the same pace as his own. He watched acceptance find and dwell in her eyes. And finally he let the hand drop gently to cover the fullest part of her breast. She closed her eyes and teetered. Her fingers clutched his shirtfront. Her breath came in tiny patters that pushed her flesh against his palm in rapid beats.

She thought, *Oh, Mother . . . Mother . . .*

Then, *Oh, Jens . . . Jens . . .*

She felt his mouth come down upon hers, and the shift of his body as he took her with him off her knees onto her back. His weight came down, too—a great, wonderful, welcome weight securing her beneath him—while his hand continued shaping and reshaping her breast, his mouth shaping and reshaping her mouth. Below, his body beat a rhythm upon hers, his foot hooked her left knee and drew it aside, creating a cradle within which he lay.

When the kiss ended she opened her eyes to see his face framed by green leaves and blue sky. The rhythm below stopped . . . a pause only, before resuming . . . slower . . . It stopped again. No smiles. Only pure involvement with the tensions in their bodies, recognizing them, allowing them, saying so with their eyes. His hand moved slower on her breast, exploring lightly while he looked down at it, then placed breathy kisses on her nose, eyelids and chin.

He found her hand, carried it to her own waist. "Unbutton this," he whispered, and pushed himself back to kneel with one knee on either side of her right leg, pressing her skirts intimately against her. He sat back heavily upon her leg, removing his jacket while she began freeing the thirty-odd buttons of her shirtwaist.

Thirty buttons were a lot: He finished first and loosened his necktie, then said, "Here . . . let me," and bent forward to take over her task. His eyes followed his fingers; hers followed his eyes. When he reached her chin she raised it to clear the way. The last button fell free, leaving a hesitation beat while both of them struggled for breath. He put both hands inside her bodice and spread it wide, exposing her collarbone and throat, her white chest and her whiter shift with its shoulder straps edged in lace and a new set of buttons.

He undid these, too, but left the panels overlapped, her breasts still covered as he tipped forward, braced a hand beside each of her ears, closed his eyes and began touching his open lips to her collarbone . . . throat . . . chin . . . putting space between his mouth and her skin until she was unsure if she was being kissed or only breathed upon.

Something warmed the underside of her jaw—lips? breath?—and tarried just above her left breast until she thought she must certainly either be touched there or die.

She became touched. There ... upon her breast, which he gathered in a hand, shift and all, as he toppled to one side, collecting her against him and slipping an arm between her and the ground. Her breast was full, heavy, supple. He held it like a pear in his palm, then explored it through white cotton—its full, resilient perimeter, its aroused tip. Momentarily, he abandoned it to rub her shift back from her shoulder, exposing the single breast to summer shadows and his enamored gaze. Its aureole was copper-hued and stood like a gem in a high mount. Its orb was covered with a haze of ultrafine hair.

"My mother said ..." she murmured behind closed eyes, and let the fragment trail as his wet mouth stole rational thought and made of her breast a lovely thing filled with life, warmth, need. From it a river seemed to unleash, some shimmering, sparkling flow running to the nether reaches of her body.

Then the shift was down at her waist and his open mouth had left one breast wet and moved to another as her shoulders arched up to meet him.

"Oh ..." she breathed, her hands in his hair, "this is wicked, isn't it, Jens?"

He lifted his head and kissed her mouth. His was wet beyond the perimeter of his lips. "Some people would say so. Does it feel wicked?"

"No ... oh no ... I've never felt this way before."

"Your mother warned you against this—is that what you were going to say?"

"Don't talk, Jens. Please ... just ..." Her fingers were laced through his thick blond hair as his face loomed above hers. She circled the helix of his ears with her thumbs, and gently drew his head down. And it all began again, all the smoldering, kissing, wetting, grinding introductions that led only to frustration which Lorna did not fully understand. Jens did, though. When it reached a peak he could no longer handle, he guttered, "Lorna, we've got to stop," and rolled off her abruptly. He lay on his back, panting, with one wrist over his eyes.

"Why?"

"Just be still," he said, and reached over to grip her thigh through her skirts, his fingertips nearly at her groin. "Just be still."

She rolled her head to study him but his eyes were closed beneath his wrist. He gripped her leg hard. She looked up at the trees and tried to catch her breath, all the time aware of his hand and where it was. Someplace in the woods a squirrel chattered. Beside her Jens's chest rose and fell like a fevered man's. His hand began moving, up and down, rubbing her own underwear against her leg, his fingertips forcing petticoat and skirts and pantaloons to brush a hidden part of her that sent out startling reactions. Was this a caress? This tight, tight grip that moved first up and down, then sideways, twisting?

She had no idea what to do, say, think. She lay as still as if asleep, only stiffer, quite afraid, while all the feelings inside her seemed to rush to the private swell of flesh near his fingertips.

His wrist remained over his eyes. His sleeve touched her bare right arm.

I must go, she thought, but before she could voice the words his hand went away. He lay motionless for some time. Finally his head turned and she felt herself being studied at close range. She concentrated on the overlapped leaves above, delicate serrated edges shifting and changing the pattern of the blue backdrop behind them. Moments and moments passed before Jens finally spoke, giving her the impression he'd done some hard thinking before doing so.

"Do you know what all this leads to, Lorna?"

"Leads to?" She was afraid to look at him since he'd touched her that way.

"You don't, do you?"

"I don't know what you mean."

"Your aunt Henrietta's warning about the hatpin. Do you know what it means?"

Confused, she kept silent.

"I suspect your mother warned you about all this wickedness."

"She didn't say it was wicked."

"What did she say?"

With no answer forthcoming, Jens took Lorna's chin and made her meet his eyes.

"Tell me what she said."

"That men would . . . would try to touch me, and when they did I must immediately go into the house."

"She's right, you know. You should be heading back to the house right now."

"Are you telling me to go?"

"No. I'm telling you it would be best for you. But I want you here with me every minute you can stay."

"Oh, Jens, I really don't understand."

"You've never done this before, have you?"

She colored and would have sat up, but he was too quick, keeping her where she was.

"You have!" he said with some amazement, leaning over her to see straight down into her eyes. "With DuVal?"

"Jens, let me up."

"Not until you've answered me." He took her chin. "Was it with DuVal?"

Forced to meet his eyes, she found lying difficult. "Well . . . a little."

"A little?"

She found some spunk. "All right, yes."

"He kissed you there, the way I did?"

"No, he only . . . you know . . . touched me, sort of . . . like you did in the shed."

"Touched you."

"But I always did what my mother said—I went in the house right away."

"You were very wise."

"What's wrong, Jens? I shouldn't have done this with you and now you're angry with me, is that right?"

"I'm not angry with you. Get up." He took her hands and made her sit. "I'm not angry—you mustn't think that. But it's time you got dressed."

For the first time guilt assailed her. She hung her head as she threaded her arms through her shift and drew it together to cover herself. He saw and took pity, untwisting one strap on her shoulder, then sitting back and watching as she began the slow process of closing thirty-three buttons: He counted them this time. Lifting her sagging chin, he placed a soft kiss on her mouth. "Don't look so forlorn. You haven't done anything wrong." His words did little to remove the sudden glumness from her face. It remained downcast while he touched the fine curls at her forehead. "Your hair's come down. Do you have a comb?"

"No," she said to her knees.

"I have." He withdrew one from a pocket. "Here."

She wouldn't look at him all the while she found her scattered hairpins on the blanket, combed her hair up and did simple things to it. When she'd restored it to its bird's nest shape, she handed him the comb.

"Thank you," she said so meekly he scarcely heard.

He retrieved her hat, watched her pin it on and searched for some way to make her happy again.

"Should we have our picnic now?" he asked.

"I'm not very hungry."

"I am," he replied—anything to see her smile return.

"Very well." Obediently, she turned to get their plates. The food was crawling with ants. Not only crawling: swimming. To Lorna's dismay her eyes had filled with tears. She kept her head turned to hide them, trying to control her voice. "I'm afraid our picnic is r . . . ruined. The ants are all . . ." She tried for one more word. ". . . All ov . . ." She swallowed hard, but the tears kept coming, and her throat had closed up. A sob broke forth as she went limp, doubling forward to drop the plates blindly on the ground. There she slumped, the plates pressing the backs of her hands to the grass.

Immediately Jens went to his knees, turning her into his arms. "Oh, Lorna, what is it? Don't cry, sweetheart, don't cry . . . you'll break my heart."

She clung to his neck. "Oh God, my God, Jens, I love you."

He closed his eyes. He swallowed. He crushed her to his breast while she sobbed out broken words. "I love you so m . . . much that nothing else m . . . matters anymore, only seeing you, b . . . being with you. Oh Jens, what's g . . . going to happen?"

He had no answers. All of these days leading up to this moment he'd needed none because the words had gone unspoken. Now they were in the open, joined by more which spilled forth from Lorna. "To think that this spring when I came out here to the c . . . cottage

I didn't even know you existed, and now your v . . . very existence is the most important thing in my life."

"If we stopped this right now—"

"No! Don't say it! How can I stop this when it's all that matters? When I have been more alive since I've met you than ever before? When my days begin with thoughts of you and end with desire for you. When I lie in my bedroom and think of you above me and imagine myself sneaking up the servant's stairway and finding your room."

"No! You must never do that, Lorna, never!" He pulled back and held her sternly by the sleeves. "Promise me!"

"I won't promise. I love you. Do you love me, Jens? I know you do. I've seen it in your eyes a hundred times, but you're not going to say it, are you?"

"I thought . . . if I didn't say it, it might be easier."

"No, it will be no easier at all. Say it. If you feel it, say it. Give me that much."

Her challenge hung in the air between them until at last he said, almost defeated, "I love you, Lorna."

She dove against him and held him as if to keep him near her forever. "Then I'm happy. For this one moment, I'm happy. I think I knew this could happen right from the first. From the night I walked into the kitchen and demanded to know what had happened to set my father off. When you admitted you'd put the note in his ice cream I began admiring you on the spot."

"Damn that note anyway," he despaired.

"No," she breathed. "No. It was meant to happen, this was meant to happen. Can't you feel it?"

They shared some quiet time, holding each other, but in his soul Jens knew heartbreak lay ahead for both of them. He sat back and held her hands loosely, rubbing her knuckles with his thumbs. "What about DuVal?" he asked. "What about the watch he gave you, and your parents' wish that you marry him? And the fact that I'm the kitchen help?"

"Never!" Her fierce expression demanded no more rebuttal. "Never again, Jens Harken! You're a boatbuilder, and one day you'll have a business of your own, and people from all over America will come to you to have you build boats for them. You've told me so."

He put a hand on her jaw, silenced her lips with a thumb. "Ah, Lorna, Lorna . . ." He sighed, long and wearily. He looked off into the woods. A long time passed.

She broke the sad silence, asking, "When can we meet again?"

He seemed to pull his thoughts from the middle distance and drew her to her feet. Tenderly, he looked into her eyes.

"Think about it. Think if you really want to, and all the times you'll cry if we keep seeing each other, and all the sneaking and lying we'll have to do. Is that what you want, Lorna?"

It wasn't, of course. Her eyes told him so.

"You said you wouldn't lie," she reminded him.

"Yes, I did, didn't I?" The unspoken truth said they'd both do so if forced to. Each of them disliked knowing this about themselves.

"It's late," he said. "You have to get going."

Tears brimmed in her eyes as she shifted her gaze to the plates, still crawling with ants.

"Yes," she whispered lifelessly.

"Come, I'll help you put the picnic away."

They knelt and spilled their lovely food into the grass, stowed the plates and folded the blanket in forlorn silence. He took the hamper, she the blanket, and they walked back to the crest of the footpath. He led the way down, steadying her with one hand as she followed. At the boats, he stowed things, freed the painter for her, then turned. They stood facing each other on the gray rocks.

"I didn't even ask you how your boat is coming," she said.

"Fine. Just fine. I'll be steaming the ribs soon."

"May I come and watch?"

He tipped his face to the sky, closed his eyes and swallowed.

"All right," she relented. "I won't. But tell me you love me one more time, just so I can have it to remember."

He kissed her first, covered her delicate jaws with both hands and held her mouth firmly in place beneath his, trying to put into the kiss all the heartbreak he, too, felt. Their tongues joined in sad goodbye while above them the sun blazed and beside them the blue water glinted. "I love you," he said, and watched her leave with tears in her eyes.

Chapter
NINE

ETURNING home after her tryst
with Jens, Lorna felt grateful it
was Sunday. A cold supper buffet meant she need not face her parents
over a formal dinner table. She had no appetite anyway, and spent
the supper hour alone in her room, sketching Jens's name in rococo
letters surrounded by roses and ribbons and forget-me-nots. She
dipped her pen and began adding a bluebird. With only one of its
wings complete, she dropped the pen, covered her face with both
hands and pressed her elbows to the dressing table.

Did he mean never to see her again? Was that his ulterior meaning
when he'd said, Think if you want to, Lorna. . . . Think of all the times
you'll cry and all the sneaking and lying we'll have to do.

She was so close to crying now.

This was love, then, this aching, forlorn dolorousness within. She
had not suspected it would affect one so wholly, that it would take
a life whose course had always been set and cast it adrift this way; that
it could turn a gay nature into a gray one.

She drew his name again, trimmed in flowers with drooping heads.
On the flowers she put faces raining teardrops. When her own threatened, she hid the sketches inside one of her summer hats and put the
cover back on the bandbox.

She wandered the house listlessly. Her sisters were looking
through scrapbooks. Theron had gone to bed. Gideon was smoking

a cigar on the back veranda. Levinia and Henrietta were absorbed in a game of backgammon. Intent upon the board, they failed to look up when Lorna wandered to the morning room doorway. She stood a moment, watching the two women, who looked as if they were piqued with each other's recent plays, then returned upstairs and knocked softly on Aunt Agnes's door.

Agnes answered, "Come in," and put down her book face first on the bedcovers.

Lorna wandered in and found her aunt against her pillows with the coverlet turned back across her lap. Like a little girl lost, she inquired, "What are you reading?"

"Oh, just one of my old favorites from *Harper's*. *Anne* it's called."

"Perhaps I shouldn't disturb you."

"Oh, heavens, don't be silly. I've read that old story a hundred times. Myyyy my, my, my, my, my . . . What is this?" Aunt Agnes pulled a long face. "You do look the very picture of dejection. Come here, child." She held out one arm and Lorna fell across the bed into its shelter.

"Tell your old aunt Agnes what's wrong."

"Oh . . . nothing. And everything. Growing up, minding Mother, these quiet Sunday nights."

"Ah, yes, they can get long for us single women, can't they? Where is that young man of yours? Why aren't you doing something with him?"

"Taylor? Oh, I don't know. I just don't feel like it tonight."

"Did you have words with him? Could that be the reason you're so glum?"

"No, not exactly."

"What about your sisters, and Phoebe—where are they?"

"I just didn't feel like being with them."

Agnes accepted this and stopped probing. Gloaming settled outside the window while Lorna lay ensconced by the comforting smells of starched cotton, violets and camphor.

After a while, Lorna said, "Aunt Agnes?"

"Hm?"

"Tell me about you and Captain Dearsley . . . what it was like when the two of you fell in love."

The old woman retold her timeworn stories, about a man in a white uniform with swaying gold-braided epaulettes, and dress military balls, and a woman overcome by love.

When the narrative ended, Lorna lay as before and stared across her aunt's breast at the roses and ribbons climbing the wallpaper.

"Aunt Agnes . . ." She composed her words carefully before going on. "When you were with him, did you ever feel tempted?"

Agnes thought, *Ah, so that's what this is about.* Wisely, she refrained from voicing the remark. Instead she answered truthfully, "It is the nature of love to tempt."

"Did he feel tempted, too?"

"Yes, Lorna, I'm quite certain that he did."

A long spell passed while the two communicated in silence. Finally Lorna spoke aloud. "When Aunt Henrietta warns me to make sure I wear a hatpin, what is she really warning me about?"

It took some seconds before Agnes responded. "Have you asked your mother?"

"No. She wouldn't answer me honestly."

"Have you and your young man been spooning?"

"Yes," Lorna whispered.

"And it has gotten . . . personal?"

"Yes."

"Then you know." Agnes hugged her niece tighter. "Oh, Lorna, darling, be careful. Be so very, very careful. Women can end up in terrible disgrace if they do those things with a man."

"But I love him, Aunt Agnes."

"I know. I know." Agnes closed her wrinkled eyelids and kissed Lorna's hair. "I loved Captain Dearsley, too. We went through all the same things you're going through right now, but you must wait till your wedding night, then there are no bounds to restrict you. You can share your body without shame, and when you do there shall be only the greatest joy for you both."

Lorna tipped her face up and kissed her aunt's cheek. It was downy and softened by age. "Aunt Agnes, I love you. You're the only one in this whole household I can talk to."

"I love you, too, child. And—believe it or not—you're the only one I can talk to, too. Everybody else thinks I'm dottier than a case of chicken pox, just because I enjoy my memories. But what else have I got besides your mother's short shrift, and Henrietta's constant belittling, and your father—well, I'm grateful for the home he gives me, but he treats me like I'm an idiot, too. Never asks my opinion of anything that matters. You, though, child. You're the special one. You have something more valuable than all the money and power and social standing it's possible to achieve in this world. You have a love of people. You care about them, and that's what makes you special. Many's the day I've said a prayer of thanks for you in this house. Now . . ." Agnes slapped Lorna's rump. "I think I hear my sister coming. She'll have some cutting remark to offer if she finds you wrinkling her side of the bed. You'd better get up."

Before she could, Henrietta came in. She halted at the sight of Lorna clambering off the bed, then closed the door.

"I should think, young woman, that you'd know better than to climb on someone else's bed in your shoes. And you, Agnes, should know better than to let her."

To make up for Henrietta's barb, Lorna knelt on one knee and stretched across the bed to kiss Agnes's cheek.

"Love you," she whispered. Passing the other aunt, whose mouth looked as if she were spitting out a cricket, Lorna said, "Good night, Aunt Henrietta."

The following day—only one day after Lorna's picnic with Jens— her mother had scheduled a croquet match. She had done so two weeks before, making it impossible for Lorna to avoid attending. Levinia had planned the event for early evening, a get-together for the young people, she said: Croquet at six P.M. followed by a twilight supper on the lawn.

That evening when the guests arrived, the grass looked plush in the long shadows. Against its emerald nap, the men's white trousers and the women's pastel skirts appeared paler, richer. Even the white wickets and stakes made a show against it. Tables for four dotted the south edge of the lawn. Each was draped with pristine battenberg lace, drawn up at the hems by nosegays of pink roses and white orchids with ribbons trailing down to lie curled on the grass. Upon each table a hurricane candle awaited the dusk, its glass globe ringed by flowers matching those below. The scene was sumptuous in every detail, with the lake in the background and the ladies all in wide-brimmed hats, these, too, laden with flowers.

Lorna wore one, a new white one with yards of gauzy tulle twisted round and round its crown like the work of a thousand spiders, and in this haze, a trio of lavender cabbage roses matching her trim-waisted dress.

She had overcome her blue mood of the day before and was actually enjoying the croquet match. Some of the very young set were included—Jenny, of course, and her friends Sissy Tufts and Betsy Whiting. Jackson Lawless and Taylor were there, as well as Phoebe and her brother, Mitch. There were sixteen in all, creating two even teams playing on two parallel courts. Mitch had ended up on Lorna's team and had been flirting with her ever since the game began, suggesting they go sailing once more before it was time for him to return to school in the city. She had laughingly refused for the third time when Mitch gave his blue-striped ball a solid rap that sent it smack up against hers.

Swaggering over, grinning, he studied her red-striped ball with wicked intent in his eyes. "Well now . . . I could be generous and leave you where you are . . . or I could send you to kingdom come. Which one will it be?"

"Mitch, you wouldn't!"

"Why wouldn't I? Maybe if you'd have been nice and said yes you'd go sailing with me, I might take pity on you."

"Oh, Mitch, please . . ." She began to fawn over him. "Look how close you are to that wicket. Why, with your two free shots you could be through it and halfway to the next wicket!"

Instead, he lined up to send her ball to kingdom come. She gave him a jostle that toppled him off-balance, and he pushed her aside to get back at her ball. A good-natured scuffle ensued.

"Brat!" she teased.

From across the court Taylor called, "Lorna, is he going to send you?"

"I think so! Will you come and beat him up if he does?"

"Here goes." Mitch butted the balls, anchored his own with a foot and—*crack!*—sent Lorna's red striped one rolling off the lawn, across a graveled walk and into a privet hedge bordering the gardens.

Lorna turned to watch it go. "Mitch, you big bully. Wait till—"

The words died in her throat. Coming toward her along the edge of the garden through which he was not allowed to walk was Jens Harken. He still wore his work clothes, the knees white with sawdust, the shirt sleeves rolled to the elbow. Obviously he was heading toward the kitchen for his supper. He stopped when he saw her. The two of them stared, transfixed.

Behind her, Taylor came to deliver mock punches to Mitchell, then drop a possessive hand on Lorna's shoulder. "I fixed his wicket, Lorna," Taylor said.

She had no delusions about how this tableau appeared to Jens: A privileged rich girl, cavorting with her peers on the verdant croquet court while behind them the tables, festooned with flowers and lace, awaited the hour when the hired help would bring out a fancy meal. Then the young men in their white linen suits would seat the young ladies in their expensive hats and gowns while the candles held back the gloaming. In the midst of all this frolicked she, the woman who had yesterday professed to love Jens Harken, wearing a small gold watch on her breast, caught in the midst of playful antics with— among others—the handsome young flour-milling heir her parents expected her to marry.

Staring at Jens Harken through the late summer twilight, Lorna wanted to drop her mallet and run to him, reassure him: What you've witnessed means nothing; it's how we live, but not always how we want to. I'd rather be with you in the boat shed than here at this soiree my mother arranged. I'd rather be watching your hands shape wood than holding it with my own, rapping a silly ball around the grass.

"Lorna?" Taylor said behind her, squeezing her shoulder. "I think it's your turn."

She glanced back to find his eyes fixed on Jens, who moved on toward the house.

From the other croquet court someone called, "Hey, DuVal, what are you doing over there? You're playing on this court!"

"Yeah, Taylor, get back here!"

"Lorna?" he asked, frowning. "Is something wrong?"

"No!" she answered too brightly, wishing he'd go away, drop his hand from her shoulder, stop studying her eyes so closely. "Just that

I've got to try to get this ball out of the privet hedge now, that's all." She shrugged away from his touch and said with false gaiety, "Thank you for defending me."

But who would defend her before Jens Harken? Who would tell Jens how she hurried to the privet hedge to hide the fact that her eyes were gleaming with tears? He would think—with good reason—that she was plying her womanly wiles on two men at once. Three, even, for there had been Mitchell, a full two years younger than she, with whom she'd been involved in a playful scuffle just as Jens came along the path. Why would it not look as if she was playing the role of the consummate flirt? Furthermore, why would a poor, struggling boatbuilder believe a woman with such a privileged life would find it the slightest bit constricting?

"Supper! Supper, everyone!" On the far side of the lawn, Levinia was waving a handkerchief. "You'll have to call this last game a bye!"

Gideon stood behind her, his forefingers and thumbs in his vest pockets as he observed the young people. On the tables behind them the candles had been lit. Compotes of fruit had been delivered to each place setting, the facets of the crystal stemware catching the candlelight and scattering it around the scene like fallen stars.

"Come along now! Put those mallets down!"

Taylor slipped up behind Lorna and captured her elbow, tucking it firmly against his ribs. "Come along now," he gently mimicked Levinia, taking Lorna's mallet from her hand. "Put those mallets down and come to supper with the fellow who thinks you're the prettiest girl on the croquet court. Unless, of course, you were planning to sit with Mitchell Armfield, who is—in case you hadn't noticed—still wet behind the ears."

Here was Taylor, commandeering her elbow. And there was her father, watching. And her mother, whose only achievements were measured by the successes of her supper parties. And all around were Lorna's peers, laughing and happy and unaware of the drama that had just occurred at the edge of the garden where the kitchen handyman cum boatbuilder had confronted the society belle whom he had secretly kissed and caressed just yesterday.

Trapped in a social web from which there seemed no escape, Lorna allowed Taylor to escort her to the table.

* * *

Sleep came reluctantly that night. She felt she owed Jens an explanation, an apology. The nights had grown cooler and smelled of chrysanthemums, the harbingers of autumn. Not long now and September would arrive, and with it chill nights, then frost, threatening the water pipes in the house and sending the family back to Saint Paul for the winter. When they returned to the Summit Avenue house, Jens Harken would be left behind to complete the boat he had begun. What then? Would this summer's rendezvous be relegated to nothing more than a memory—best forgotten—of a tryst between a misguided young girl and a lonely immigrant who found temporary pleasure in each other's company?

It felt like more.

It felt like love.

It *was* love; thus today demanded both explanation and apology.

The following morning immediately after breakfast Lorna headed straight for the boat shed. She smelled it long before she reached it: wood scent so heavy in the air she was sure her clothing would smell of it when she returned to the house. She reached the open double doors and found herself face-to-face with the reason why: Inside, Jens had rigged up a steam box for bending the ribs of the mold. It was fired up, loaded and sending out small plumes of white mist at the smallest breaks in the pipes. Standing before the steam box, inspecting the operation, was her father. Beside him was Ben Jonson, whom she recognized from the fishing boat. Photographing the events for the yacht club wall and any newspaper interested was Tim Iversen.

Gideon saw Lorna the moment she saw him.

"Lorna, what are you doing here?"

"I came to see the progress on the boat. After all, if it hadn't been for me it wouldn't have been designed. Good morning, Mr. Iversen. Good morning, Mr. Harken." Not for nothing did Lorna possess some of Gideon's own backbone: She entered the shed as coolheadedly as if she'd fully expected her father to be there. "I don't believe we've met," she said to Jonson. "I'm Lorna Barnett, Gideon's daughter."

He slapped the cap off his head and accepted her handshake. "Ben Jonson. I'm happy to meet you, Miss Barnett."

"Do you work for my father?"

"Not exactly. I work at the lumberyard, but things are slacking off over there now that the season's ending, so I'm taking the morning off to help Jens bend these ribs."

"I hope you don't mind if I watch."

"Not at all."

Gideon interrupted. "Does your mother know you're out here?"

Lorna's voice said, "I don't believe she does." Her eyes said, *Hadn't you noticed, Father—I'm eighteen years old?*

"This is men's work, Lorna. Go back to the house."

"To do what? Press flowers? With all due respect, Father, how would you like to be told to go back to the house when there's a boat being built that may change yachting history, right out here in our very own shed? Please let me stay."

Tim interrupted. "While you're deciding, Gid, do you mind if I take a picture? I've got the camera all ready." He moved toward his tripod and black hood. "In the annals of the White Bear Yacht Club it could be important someday—boatbuilder, boat owner and boat owner's daughter, who convinced him the idea had merit. Don't forget, Gid, I was there when she asked you."

"Oh, all right, take your infernal picture, but make it quick. I've got a train to catch."

Tim took that infernal picture, and a lot more, and Gideon Barnett forgot about catching the train into town because the actual ribbing process was about to begin, and he was as fascinated with it as was his daughter. Jens had made his steam box out of a large-diameter metal pipe, plugged at one end by a wooden stopper, at the other by rags, fed by steam from a hot water boiler. The boiler created a quiet sizzle and took the faint touch of chill off the morning as Jens explained his work.

"An hour in the steam box is all it takes to expand the grain of the wood enough to make it pliable. When that white oak comes out of there it'll be as limp as a noodle, but it won't stay that way for long. That's why I needed Ben today. The mold is all ready, as you can see. . . ." He turned toward it. "The notches are all cut in the stringers." There were three longitudinal stringers. "And the board-boxes are in and the gunwale on. Now all we need is those ribs. What do you say, Ben"—Jens and Ben exchanged a bright-eyed look of eagerness—"you ready to play hot potato?"

The two men donned gloves and Jens removed the rag from the end of the pipe. A cloud of fragrant steam billowed out. The moment it cleared, he reached in and pulled out a length of white oak. It was an inch thick and an inch wide and, indeed, as white and limp as a cooked noodle. Ben took one end, Jens the other, and together they hurried to fit it across the boat, from gunwale to gunwale, into three clean notches waiting to receive it.

"Woo, she's a hot one!"

Working one on either side of the frame, they smoothed it in, removed their gloves and nailed it to each of the three stringers. With their knees they bent it down over the gunwale, cut it off with handsaws and nailed it to the gunnel on each side. The entire process had taken a matter of a few minutes.

"When we're done ribbing 'er up, the fair lines will show almost as clear as on the finished boat, and I guarantee you, Mr. Barnett, she'll be as fair as a boat can be. Another rib coming up," Jens announced, and withdrew a second one from the steam box, flopped it over the mold, and the two men repeated the process: fit, nail, trim, nail. Every six inches along the cross sections: fit, nail, trim, nail.

Their gloves got wet and they handled the hot ribs gingerly. Sometimes they yelped. Sometimes they blew on their reddened fingers. Their knees got wet and, more than once, burned.

Lorna watched, wholly fascinated as the shape of the boat appeared, rib by rib. She watched this man she loved, tugging off gloves with his teeth, wielding a hammer, cleaving with a saw, sweating as he advanced along the length of the mold, leaving a fragrant, white skeleton behind. She observed his pleasure in his work, the deftness and skill of his every movement, his keen sense of oneness with Jonson as they toiled in tandem. The two men matched motions until they'd perfected their timing and each of them finished a rib at the same moment. A look would pass between them as they'd step back from the newly applied rib, a look of satisfaction and concord that recognized—each in the other—purpose, talent and mutual skill.

Then, amidships, Jens would squat on his heels, peer along the snowy oaken ribs and view the fair line from this angle, that, and another. He would walk to the opposite end of the frame and peer outward toward the open doorway—port side, starboard side— bringing Lorna an even clearer understanding of the importance of all those dots on the floor during lofting. Their exactitude, transferred finally into three dimensions, brought satisfaction to the Scandinavian boat designer.

"Yup, she's fair," he'd murmur, more to himself than to anyone else in the shed.

In less than two hours the entire mold was ribbed up. Gideon Barnett was still there, watching. Tim Iversen had taken many photographs. Lorna Barnett had watched the entire process and was still waiting to be recognized in any way by Jens Harken.

He walked to the far side of the building and came back with a long batten. Against the mold, Jonson held one end while Harken held the other. "This is her sheer line," he told Barnett. "Not much boat in the water, is there?"

"Not much," Barnett agreed, "but will she heel over and sink, that's the question."

Harken turned away but there was an undeniable note of superior knowledge in his question: "What do you think?"

Barnett bit his tongue. Actually, the longer he watched this Harken, the more he came to believe, as did the cocky young boatbuilder himself, that this craft would do what he said: It would make every other one in the water look like an albatross.

Into the void, Iversen spoke, removing his pipe from his mouth. "What do you intend to name her, Gid?"

Gideon transferred his gaze to Tim's good eye. "I don't know. Something fast—like the *Seal*, maybe, or the *Gale*."

"How about something faithful instead?" Tim's eye skimmed Lorna, then returned to Gid. "Like Lorna here, who believed in it well before you did. I think it would be fitting if this yacht were named after your daughter. What's your middle name, Lorna?"

"Diane."

"How about the *Lorna D?* It's got a nice ring. I like the hard *D* with the soft *A.*" Tim puffed a couple of times on his pipe, sending a fruity tobacco aroma to mingle with that of steamed wood. "The *Lorna D.* What do you think, Gid?"

Gideon pondered some. He bit on the left corner of his beetling moustache. He studied Lorna, who was assiduously avoiding studying Jens, and had been all morning.

"What do you say, Lorna? Do you want this yacht named after you?"

She thought of Jens, here in this shed, shaping the *Lorna D* day after day with his big, wide, capable hands, running them over the boat's fair lines, making her swift and sure and responsive.

"Do you mean it?"

"Divine justice, I suppose you'd call it. Especially if she wins."

"Those are your words, not mine." Even chiding her father, Lorna found it impossible to keep the excitement from shining in her eyes. "I'd love it, Papa, and you know it."

Gideon realized how true it was when he heard his daughter call him Papa, which she hadn't done much since she'd matured. Only when he was very much in her favor did the word escape her lips.

"Very well. The *Lorna D* it is."

"Oh, Papa, thank you!" She pranced across the shed and hugged his neck while Gideon cocked forward at the hips and searched for a place to rest his hands, ever in a quandary when his girls showed affection in such a way. He loved his daughters—of course he did— but his way of demonstrating it was by issuing gruff, authoritative orders, the way a proper Victorian father ought to, and by footing the bills for their expensive soirees and clothing. Returning hugs while other men looked on was beyond Gideon Barnett's pale. "Damnation, girl, you're going to tear my collar right off its buttons."

By the time Lorna released him, Gideon was flustered and harumphing.

"May I tell my friends?" Lorna asked.

"Your friends . . . well . . . hell, I don't care."

"Then it's official?" Lorna tipped her head to one side.

Gideon flapped a hand. "Go ahead, tell them, I said."

"And may I bring them here to see it?"

"And overrun the place?" Gideon blustered.

"Not all of them, just Phoebe."

"I swear, you young females are getting to act more like tomboys than anything I ever saw. Oh, all right, bring Phoebe."

"And I shall want to come often to check on the *Lorna D*'s progress. You don't mind, do you, Papa?"

"You'll be in Harken's way."

"Oh, fiddle. There were three of us here today, plus a camera, and we weren't in his way, were we, Harken?" She fired the challenge straight at Harken's eyes. It was the first solid contact they'd exchanged since she'd entered the shed.

His glance quickly veered to her father. "I . . . ah . . ." He cleared his throat. "No, I don't mind, sir."

"Very well, but if she gets to be a pest, throw her out. I swear to God, I don't know what I'm doing, letting a girl hang around a boat shed. Your mother will have a conniption." While upbraiding himself, Gideon tugged at his watch fob and slid a golden hunter out of his vest pocket. "Damnation, it's nearly noon. I've got to get into town before it's time to come back home! Harken, see me about a check when you're ready to order the sails from Chicago. And Jonson, what do I owe you for helping out today?"

"Nothing, sir. My pleasure, just to work on a boat again."

"Very well, then. I'm off. Lorna, you too. Do me a favor and give your mother at least a crumb of time spent at ladylike pursuits this afternoon."

"Yes, Papa," she replied meekly.

"I'll be leaving, too," Tim said. "Thanks for letting me horn in and take pictures. You'll see them soon, Jens."

With nothing resembling a personal farewell, Lorna took her leave with the others.

When they were gone the shed grew quiet. Ben and Jens worked for a while cleaning up the place, sweeping up the sawdust and the stub ends of the ribs from the floor, hammering in a nail more securely here and there on the mold. Moving around it, Jens whistled softly through his teeth: "Oh, Fetch the Water," an old Norwegian folk song. He touched the oak ribs in many places, pinched them, tried to jiggle them, but found them firm.

"They've already taken the mold," he remarked.

"Yup."

Jens put away some nails. Hung up a hammer. Ben's eyes followed him. Speculating. Jens whistled another verse. Ben leaned back against the mold with his arms and legs crossed. "So . . ." he said, "is she the one you met on Sunday?"

Jens's whistling stopped. His head snapped up. "What makes you ask a thing like that?"

"You didn't look at her once in all that time she was here."

Jens went back to work. "So?"

"A girl that pretty?"

"You think she's pretty?"

"Prettier than the sunset on a Norwegian fjord. Brighter, too. I had trouble keeping my eyes off her."

"So?"

"So, she didn't look at you, either. Until she tricked her father into agreeing to let her come out here whenever she wants to. And now you're whistling 'Oh, Fetch the Water.' "

"You know, Jonson, you must've gotten too close to that steam. Maybe it boiled your brains a little bit, huh? What in the world has 'Oh, Fetch the Water' got to do with Lorna Barnett?"

Jonson began singing the old love song in Norwegian, very softly, wearing a three-cornered grin that followed his friend around the boat shed till the last lines:

> But when it is the one I love
> Then life is surely worth the living.

By the time he finished, Jens had quit creating busyness to occupy his hands. He stood beside the stove with its coals dwindling, staring at the cooling boiler and steam box.

"You're right." He shifted his gaze to Ben. "We've got some feelings between us, Lorna and me."

"Aw, Jens," Ben said sympathetically, his teasing gone. "You haven't."

"We didn't mean for it to happen, but there you are."

"I figured something like this that day she stood up in the boat and waved to you. Just the way she did it—like she wanted to jump in and swim over."

"She's a fine girl, Ben, as fine as they come, but independent. She started hanging around here, asking questions about the boat, then about me and my family. Pretty soon we were talking like old friends. Then one day she asked me to kiss her." Jens ruminated awhile before shaking his head at the floor. "Worst mistake I ever made, kissing her."

Jens found two pieces of sandpaper and handed one to Ben. They both began sanding the ribs.

Ben said, "I imagine if her old man knew, you'd be out of here on your ass, and that'd be the end of your boatbuilding."

"Yup."

"You should have known, Jens. Our kind, we kiss the kitchen maids."

"I tried that." The two men exchanged wry glances. They went on sanding. "Ruby, her name is."

"Ruby."

"A redhead with freckles."

"And?"

The sandpaper rasped on. "Remember when you were a boy and you got a new puppy? You'd go off to school all day long, then when you'd come home that little thing was so happy to see you he'd lick you up one side and down the other. Well, that's what kissing Ruby was like. I just kept wishing I had a towel."

Both men laughed. A while later Ben asked, "So how far has this thing gone with you and the girl whose father would tack your hide to the door if he knew about it?"

"Not as far as you're thinking. But it could if we keep seeing each other. I decided last night that we're not going to. It's over. It's got to be, because she doesn't belong in my world any more than I belong in hers. Lord, Ben, you should have seen her last night. . . ."

Jens described the scene he'd come upon while walking back to the house for supper, sparing no details, not even about Lorna's relationship with Taylor DuVal. ". . . And there she stood with DuVal's hand on her shoulder and his watch on her breast, right where my hand had been the day before. Now you tell me—what business have I got with a woman like that anyway?" Speaking the words, Jens felt anger and hurt well up within. "If she comes around here again I'm ordering her point-blank to *get out!* Finishing this boat and getting a boatworks of my own mean more to me than Lorna Barnett anyway."

He wanted to mean it. All during that afternoon after Ben left, while Jens worked on the mold alone, while he listened to the monotonous *shh-shh* of sandpaper on wood, and felt the heat rise against his palm, and registered the shape of each rib through his callused hands, he wanted the boat to mean more to him than Lorna. But every thought of her brought longing. Every memory brought wishes.

At seven o'clock he closed the shed doors, put a stick through the hasp, then stood a moment, listening to the soprano section of crickets tuning up. An evening chill had arrived, gathering dampness from the earth. He drew on a plaid wool jacket. Turning down his collar, he looked at the sky—peachy in the west, violet overhead, overlaid by leaves and branches already blackened to silhouettes. He moved down the worn path toward the poplars. Over the vegetable gardens the bats were out, fluttering past as quickly as illusions. The tomato bushes smelled tangy. Some of the early-bearing vegetables had already been pulled up—pea vines, beans—and new ones undoubtedly started by Smythe in the glasshouse for the family's winter use in town. Jens's face collected a spiderweb that seemed suspended in midair: a sure sign of approaching fall.

He was unaware of Lorna's presence until she brought him up short with a "Psst." She stood between the poplars, as straight and still as they, camouflaged by their foliage and the deep shadows of evening. Around her shoulders she wore a short knit cape, gripped in both hands at her throat. "I've been waiting for you."

"Lorna . . ." He left the path and blended into the poplar shadows with her. "You've got to stop doing this."

How comely she looked with the dusk shading her skin faintly blue, and her eyes gleaming like polished agates as they found and held him with an expression of bald adoration. "I know I should stop, but I can't seem to." In a whisper, she appealed, "What have you done to me, Jens Harken?"

His heart began a crazy dance and all his good intentions fragmented. She moved at the same moment as he, a loved-starved lunge that opened her cape and closed it around both their shoulders as they clung and kissed. His tongue was swift and sleek in her mouth, opening it, invading it, spreading the flavor of wood and desire and frustration that had been increasing during their past two encounters of maneuvering around each other with false indifference. She kissed him as one ending a long deprivation, her tongue darting and licking and demanding a fulfillment of which she was ultimately ignorant. He clasped her body hard and took a spraddled stance into which he could mold and hold her. His hands dropped down, caught her buttocks within her skirts and bent her forward along his frame while he tipped back and made a bow of his body. Her toes lost purchase and dangled above the grass as she lay cast over his body, her breasts and belly yielding to his.

When he set her down they were breathless, their eyes avid and burning with impatience. They spoke in a rush.

"You were angry with me today," Lorna said.

"Yes, I was."

"About last night?"

"Yes, and about you coming to the shed when your father was there, about DuVal. About everything!"

"I'm sorry about last night. I didn't want to be with him, but I didn't know how to get out of it. My mother planned the whole evening and I had no choice."

"You belong with him."

"No. I don't love him. You're the one I love."

He held her by the head and looked into her face with an expression of aggravated frustration on his own. "You belong with him and that's what makes me the angriest, because I know it's true, and nothing can change it. Your world and his are the same, don't you see? Sousa as your houseguest, and discussions with Mr. Gibson, and croquet suppers on the lawn. That's a world I'm not allowed in. I can only live it by listening to you tell me about it."

When he'd finished she stared at him and whispered, "You haven't said you love me."

"Because it hurts too much." He gave her head one shake. "Because every time I do you believe a little stronger that it can work, and it can't. You took a big chance today, coming out here when your father was here."

"But now I have his permission, don't you see?"

"Not to do this. Don't fool yourself, Lorna."

"Oh, Jens, please don't be angry with me anymore. You still are—I could tell when you kissed me."

"You're so damned innocent," he railed, and kissed her again, the same as before, his entire body torn between inveighing and inviting. He moved his hands over her, touching her gingerly when he wanted to touch her passionately. "My hands are dirty. . . . I've been working all day."

"No . . . no . . ." She captured one and plunged her face into its palm, kissing it. "I love your hands. I love them on your work. I love them on me. They smell like wood." She spread his palm on her face, as if it were a balm she would apply to heal herself.

The simple act of affection turned his heart over. He bent and scooped her up in his arms and carried her back along the path to the boat shed, through the woods where full dark had fallen. She curled her arms around his neck and put her mouth against his jaw, where a day's growth of whiskers abraded her lips.

"Will you be missed?" he asked, bearing her along with her hip bumping his stomach.

"My mother and father are at the Armfields' playing loo."

At the shed he set her on her feet and removed the stick from the hasp. He opened the door a narrow space. "Go inside and put some wood on the coals. I'll be right back."

"Where are you going?"

"Just do as I say, but don't light the lamps."

He ran into the dark woods, elbows up to deflect branches as he jogged in the opposite direction from the house, toward the northerly lakeshore. Reaching it, he stripped and plunged headlong into the water, gasping when he emerged into the brisk night air. He scrubbed everywhere, the best he could without soap, then stood on the bank and gave a canine shake of limbs and head before donning his trousers and snapping his suspenders up over his bare shoulders. Into his shirt he rolled his boots and remaining clothing, then returned through the woods to the shed and the woman who waited.

Inside, all was black but for two glowing spots: the open stove door and Lorna's face as she hunkered before it with both arms wrapped around her knees.

The shed door creaked.

"Jens?" she whispered, startled, her head snapping around toward the black end of the building.

He closed the door and answered, "Yes, it's me."

Her shoulders wilted with relief as she peered into the inkiness and watched him emerge from it, clothed in nothing but trousers and black suspenders. She rose slowly, as if spellbound, her eyes riveted on his naked chest, its golden fleece picked out by the flickering firelight.

"I took a quick bath," he said, shivering visibly, running his wadded-up clothing over his trunk, then casting it aside.

"Oh," she said, glancing away, unnerved by his unexpected appearance in such a state.

He reached up with both hands and fingercombed his wet hair, then dried his palms on his trousers and stood before her, ruffled all over with goose bumps. Her eyes returned to the golden V of hair on his chest and the nipples within it, then veered off shyly. "You must be freezing." She began to turn away as if to give him her place before the open stove door.

He caught her arm at the crook of her elbow, in a grip so tight it would have stopped her had his words failed.

"Lorna . . . don't turn away." His fingers left wet spots on her sleeve. She returned to him in the slow movements of a lover facing her chosen one at the momentous confluence of two lives. He pulled the knit cape from her shoulders and discarded it in the shadows somewhere at their feet. Her eyes were wide upon Jens's, then closed as he drew her into a tender embrace and kissed her with cold, wet lips and a warm, wet tongue. Her arms rose to his shoulders, her sleeves stuck to his damp back and her bodice to his damp chest. His flesh was puckered with goose bumps as she opened her hands on it. A cold droplet fell from his hair onto her face. Another followed . . . and another . . . and the trio ran in a rivulet down her cheek. The kiss gained motion, became a graceful swan dance of heads and hands. She gripped the edges of her cuffs to stretch her sleeves taut, then began blindly drying his back. He dipped his knees and clasped her to him, then surged up against her, wholly aroused. One of them shuddered . . . or was it both? Was it from the cold or from the quick release of suppression, neither could tell.

He found buttons along her back and began releasing them—down to her shoulder blades only before tugging the hem of the shirtwaist from her waistband and stripping it up over her head. Hairpins fell to the wooden floor as she emerged with her hair disarrayed and her eyes wide and bright with expectation.

Her shift was made of soft white lawn and was shirred by a blue ribbon into a scooped neck with buttons below. He gathered the garment into his two hands, and her breasts along with it, looking into her eyes as his thumbs changed her to the shape of desire.

"Are you afraid when I touch you this way?" he asked.

"I was at first."

"And now?"

"Now . . . oh, now . . ." She relaxed against his caress and let herself be swayed by it. He lifted one breast high and bent to it, kissed it through the thin lawn, and bit it gently. He treated the other to the same blandishment, then held both in his hands and smiled down into her blissful face.

"There are other ways a man touches a woman. You don't know about them, do you?"

"No . . ." she whispered.

"Here . . ." He dropped one hand down the front of her skirts and rubbed it softly against her pubis. "Like this"—he curled his fingers until they conformed to her hidden shape—"and like this . . . It's part of loving. Do you know why?"

She shook her head, once again mesmerized by his voice and touch.

"To make babies."

"B . . . babies?" She started and pulled back, her eyes disbelieving.

"Sometimes. Sometimes just for pleasure."

"Babies? When you're not married?"

"I didn't think you knew, and I wanted to warn you that could happen."

Suddenly her mother's warning became startlingly clear. She pulled away from him sharply, feeling cheated, foiled. All the lovely billowing feelings she held for Jens seemed like a mean trick nature had played on them both.

"I cannot have a baby. My mother and father would . . . would

. . . Oh, gracious, I don't know what they would do." She looked genuinely horrified.

"I've frightened you. I'm sorry." He took her arms lightly and drew her near once more. "You're not going to have a baby, Lorna, it doesn't happen that easily. It takes more than touching, and even then, it doesn't happen all the time. And it won't happen at all if we stop in time."

"Oh, Jens . . ." She fell against him and doubled her arms around his neck. "I'm so relieved. You scared me. I thought I should have to go back to the house when that's the last thing I want to do." Her grip tightened, her plea became impassioned. "I want to stay here with you, until dawn if I could, and on into tomorrow, and the tomorrow after that. There's no other place I want to be than right here in your arms. If that isn't love I cannot imagine what is. Oh, Jens Harken, I love you so much that everything in my life has changed."

Her outpouring led to another kiss—a frantic seeking that dragged his open mouth across her face, and hers across his, to rejoin and reclaim and resurrect the passion interrupted earlier. Mouth to mouth, hand to breast, body to body, they strained ever nearer love's ineluctable conclusion. He lifted her skirt in both hands, found his way beneath it to her hips and bracketed them in a grip that drew her flush against him and tipped her to an obliging angle. Like waves against a shore, he taught her to move, and there, where their bodies hove together, urgency spread. He kissed her roughly, a lusty mingling of two wet mouths, then caught her lower lip between his teeth and held it as if to say, *Be still,* while sliding one hand down her shift with its long placket running from front to back. He gripped her firmly, through the damp white overlapped lawn, as if she were a handful of turf he might lift from the earth and fling over his shoulder. By his teeth and one hand, he held her, rocking the butt of that hand gently, rhythmically, until her mind went hot with colors— splendid sunrise colors that seemed to infuse her core and limbs. In time those limbs became limp, then jolted once in untutored surprise as he slid his hand inside her shift and found his way within her body.

"Oh, Jens . . ." she whispered as his touch went deeper and her head hung back.

"Lie down," he whispered, and supported her while lowering them both to the fragrant wooden floor, where he'd once lofted a boat that was named after her. Beside it now, he came to know her shape, as he knew the shape of the *Lorna D*. Over her his hands curved, as they'd curved over the white oak mold that hovered above them. Within her, warmth flowed, as warmth had flowed from the wood itself when he'd sanded it smooth earlier that day. He touched her in myriad intimate ways, beckoning, until her hips rose from the hard spruce floor to seek more and more.

He turned her skirts back and braced on one elbow beside her, watching desire distort her features as her throat lifted toward the rafters overhead, and the meager firelight painted the periphery of her face. Her eyes were closed, her arms flung wide, her shoulder blades scarcely touching the floor.

"Lorna, Lorna . . . beautiful creature . . ." he murmured, "this is how I've imagined you."

Her eyelids fluttered open as his touch left. He opened the few buttons on her bodice and turned it back, exposing her breasts. There, he kissed her, adored her, washed her with his tongue and shaped her with his lips. Again, he reached low to touch her intimately. At his return her eyelids closed and she cooed, a soft throaty sound while coiling half onto one side, her arms and one leg forming an arabesque around him.

There came that moment when he felt compelled to seek her eyes once again, his own lit by mere pinpricks of light from the dying fire beside them. "I love you so much," he whispered.

"I love you, too. I shall always, always love you, no matter what."

He put his parted lips very lightly upon hers and whispered, "It's all right if you touch me, too." He could tell from her stillness she wasn't sure where and how. "Anywhere," he invited.

She touched his bare chest and he abandoned her mouth to watch her eyes follow her hand. Timidly it explored, learning as it went: the texture of the golden hair, the firmness of his ribs, the silken hair again, diffidently avoiding his nipples.

"You're all golden. Like a Viking. Sometimes I think of you that way—as my golden-haired Norwegian Viking, sailing in on a great ship to sweep me away." She caught his head and drew it down for a kiss, and returned her hand to its preoccupation with his naked chest, slipping beneath a suspender and riding it to his jutting shoulder.

"Push it down," he whispered against her mouth. "It's all right . . . push it down."

She pushed the suspender over his shoulder. It fell limp upon his arm.

"Now the other one," he whispered, and shifted his weight, giving her access.

The second suspender fell and her hands played over him—shoulders, throat, ribs and chest, until all his senses reached outward toward her and all below yearned to be couched within her. He caught her hand and carried it downward, urging, "Don't be shy . . . don't be scared . . . here . . . like this . . . ," and she came to feel his warmth and hardness for the first time through a layer of scratchy wool. He cupped her hand beneath his and shaped it like himself. He uttered her name, the name he so loved—"Lorna . . . Lorna . . ."—and moved both their hands, teaching, beseeching, until hers moved of its own accord. In time he opened four buttons and slid her hand into the warm, dark secrecy awaiting within. At the moment of intimate encounter they were lying on their sides, each with an ear upon a bent arm, staring into each other's eyes.

His closed at her touch, and his breast rose and fell as if from hard labor.

"Oh," she said, the word a note of wonder and discovery at his heat and shape. "Oh . . . I had not dreamed . . ." He taught her what instinct had not, made of her hand a sheath and returned his own hand to her waiting body. Together, so bound, they reveled in the wondrous beck and call of their young bodies, their young love. They kissed sometimes. Other times they murmured inarticulate sounds composed of passion and promise and puissance that issued from their throats while splendid desire rose and demanded its due. At the breaking point, he knocked her hand away and turned upon her, kneeling, hauling her over his lap and supporting her from beneath until her body bowed like a wind-filled sail, her head and shoulders barely grazing the floor. Through the barrier of wool and lawn, they mimicked the consummation of love, until those flimsy, false, frail obstacles called clothing could no longer be tolerated.

He fell to all fours above her and ordered between racked breaths, "Lorna, open your eyes." She did, and looked up at him from the halo of dark hair that lay tangled on the rough floor. "Do you understand now? Me . . . inside you . . . that's how it happens; but if we do it you could end up with my baby. I don't want that to happen."

She caressed his face, beside his mouth, with one hand.

"I love you. . . . Oh, Jens, I love you so much. . . . I didn't know it would be like this."

"We can stop, or we can take a chance that it won't happen from just one time."

"Stop? Oh . . . I . . . please . . . please, Jens, no . . . will it happen?"

"I don't know. Maybe not. I . . . oh God, Lorna, I love you, too. . . . I don't want to hurt you or get you in trouble."

"The only way you could hurt me would be if you ever stopped loving me. Please, Jens, teach me the rest."

He crooked his elbows, bringing his face down to hers. He kissed her mouth in love and apology and desire, then said, "Wait . . . ," and reached back into the dark for his roll of clothing. One tug and the boots went tumbling and thumped to the floor. "Lift up," he ordered, "I'll put this under you." Beneath her hips he spread his shirt. "You're going to bleed, but don't be scared. It only happens the first time."

"Bleed? But, Jens . . . your shirt . . . Jens, it will get all—"

His kiss cut off her concerns. "Lie still . . ." he whispered, and placed himself just within her, while their hearts beat in frantic anticipation and all the world waited.

"Jens," she whispered, gripping his shoulders.

"Be still."

"Jens . . . oh . . ."

"It might hurt some. . . . I'm sorry. . . ." In a whisper, "I'm sorry."

With a gentle thrust he bound them, body and soul.

She caught her breath and arched up, as if prodded between the shoulder blades. He lay utterly still, watching her face, wishing away her hurt, until she slowly relaxed and opened her eyes to find him bearing his weight on strong arms above her.

"All right?" he asked.

She released a breath and nodded.

"I wish I had a fine featherbed for you right now," he told her as he began moving, "and a soft pillow that we could lie on, and some flowers from the picking garden—some of those blue delphiniums, maybe, like you brought me that time, and a rose or two for the good smell. I would put them on your hair, and watch your face put the flowers to shame. Aw, Lorna . . . sweet, darling Lorna . . . we're as close as two people can be now, and for the rest of our lives we'll be changed because of this minute."

She tried to keep her eyes open, but they became weighted by pleasure. "I think"—she struggled for breath between words—"that I should be the proudest . . . woman in the world . . . to have your baby . . . and that I . . . Oh, Jens . . ." She gasped and arched up high against him, her head tipped back at a sharp angle. "Oh, Jens . . . oh . . . ohahhhhhhh . . ."

At the moment of her cry, he withdrew and spilled his seed on his own shirt, atop her virgin blood, in the hope that she would never have to suffer disgrace because of him. Then he fell, depleted, upon her heaving chest. Her breath beat at his ear and their heartbeats played in counterpoint. He rested heavily upon her while her fingers ran up his skull again, and again, and again.

Beside them, the fire had dwindled to coals.

Above them, the skeleton of the boat loomed.

All about, the stillness of the late-summer night kept their secret. They thought about their future—the certain parting that lay ahead—and beyond, the hazy afterward and the forces that would try to keep them apart, the impossibility of being so after this.

"I would do it again," she said. "I would do this shameful, wonderful, incredible thing again with you, knowing full well what might happen if I do. Does that make me bad?"

He levered the brunt of his weight from her and looked down into her beautiful brown eyes. "It makes you mine, the way no wedding vows could, the way no promises could. How will I ever say goodbye to you when they take you back to town?"

"Shh . . ." She covered his mouth with her index finger. "Don't speak about that. That won't happen until the frost comes and the pipes are in danger of freezing up. We have at least five weeks till then. Maybe six, if we're lucky."

"Mid-October. Is that when you usually move back to the city?"

She nodded solemnly. "But I don't want to talk about it." She clasped him close, already in slight desperation. "Please, Jens, let's not talk about it."

"All right, we won't." He held her awhile, suspecting that there were tears in her eyes, though the room had grown too dark to see. "Stay where you are," he said, and slipped into the darkness, found some wood tailings and dropped them into the stove. Waiting for them to ignite, he pulled up his trousers and buttoned them, but left his suspenders hanging at his sides. When the wood flared he turned back to Lorna and drew her up by one hand. In the lambent orange light, he sat beside her and touched her face.

"I'm sure you don't know . . ." These things were hard to say, in spite of the intimacy they'd just shared: these less than romantic facts of life.

"Don't know?"

He drew a deep breath and faced what must be faced. "If your monthly doesn't come you must tell me right away. Promise."

"My monthly?" She, too, grew embarrassed, threaded her arms into her shift and drew it together to cover herself.

He told her, "If it's ever late it could mean you're going to have a baby, and if you are you must come to me and tell me right away, and we'll figure out what to do. Promise me."

"I promise," she said to her lap.

They sat awhile silently, imagining it, hoping it would never happen that way. Lorna slowly buttoned her shift. When she reached the top button he brushed her fingers aside and tied the blue bow, his fingers thick and clumsy on the fine, smooth silk. When he was done they sat on, facing one another, each occupied with his own approaching sadness.

Jens took both Lorna's hands loosely.

"I love you," he said. "I want to marry you, but it'll take some time. If we asked your father now he'd throw me out. Next year, if things go the way I plan, I'll have my own boatworks, and I can take care of you then. Could you be happy on a boatbuilder's wages, Lorna?"

She stared at him in stunned amazement. "Yes," she uttered as if coming out of a stupor. "Oh, yes!" she exclaimed, and flung both arms around him. "Oh, Jens, I was so afraid you wouldn't ask. I thought that maybe . . . maybe after what we just did . . . I don't know what I thought."

He took her by both arms and pressed her back so he could see her face.

"You thought maybe I would do that to you, then act as if it had never happened?"

"I don't know. It only struck me afterwards, when we were lying so quietly together—I should not want to lie that way with any other man. I couldn't after doing it with you, but if you didn't ask me to marry you, then what?"

"I am asking. Will you marry me, Lorna Barnett, as soon as my boat wins that race, and I have my own boatworks with plenty of customers to make us a decent living?"

She beamed. "Yes, I said. Nothing can stop me. Not my father, not my mother, not Mr. Taylor DuVal, not all the social expectations they've set for me, because between you and me it simply must be. Especially after tonight."

"Oh, Lorna . . ." He clasped her to him. "I'm going to work so damned hard for you, and I might never get as rich as your father, but I'll give you a good life, you'll see."

"I know you will, Jens."

"And we'll have babies, and teach them to sail, and take them on picnics; and when they're old enough I'll teach them to build boats with me."

"Yes," she breathed, "yes."

They sat back and held hands and smiled at each other some more.

"Now you'd better get dressed so you can get back to the house before your parents get home."

"When will I see you again?"

"I don't know."

"Tomorrow. I'll bring Phoebe to see the boat."

"The mold. It's not a boat yet."

"Yes, the mold. I'll bring Phoebe, all right?"

"All right. But I'm not promising I can keep the truth from showing. I'll probably grab you on the spot and kiss you whether Phoebe's there or not."

She slapped him playfully on the chest. "You will not. You'll be perfectly proper, just as you were today."

"It'll cost me, though."

"Good," she teased, and touched his lower lip with an index finger.

After moments her hand slid down and rested on his chest, then captured his. Time was moving on: They knew they must part, but stole one more minute, holding hands like innocent children, adoring each other, sating themselves for the separation ahead.

"You have to go," he said softly.

"I know."

"Let me help you with your dress."

He pulled her to her feet and buttoned the back of her shirtwaist while she held her hair aside. When the garment was closed up to her nape, he put his hands at her waist.

"Lorna, about DuVal . . ."

She dropped her hair and turned. "I'll speak to my mother about him immediately. Papa will be a little more difficult, so I'll start with Mother, and get her used to the idea that he's not for me. The sooner they understand that I'm not going to marry him, the better."

Jens looked relieved.

"And I promise," Lorna added earnestly, "that I shall never wear his watch again. That promise I can keep from this moment forward, and I shall. I vow on my love for you."

He squeezed her hands and told her with his eyes how very grateful he was for her promise.

"Fix your hair," he said.

"Oh, dear." She reached up to it. "I forgot my comb. Do you have one?"

He shrugged—"Sorry"—and tried futilely to arrange it with his fingers.

"Oh, it's no use. It'll need much more than fingers."

She scraped at it while he knelt to find her hairpins on the dimly lit floor.

"How about these? Will they help?"

She did the best she could, bending forward at the waist and flopping the heavy, dark fall forward, then grasping it in both hands and trying to reconstruct the nest-and-pouf while he watched.

Each motion, each pose went into his treasured storehouse of memories, to be drawn out later, in the lorn hours of midnight, while he slept in the room above hers.

"I've never told you before—I love your hair."

Her hands stalled, putting in the last pin. She dropped them slowly, filled with love so pure and fine it seemed her very heart had left her body to dwell in his.

"I would like to watch you someday," he went on, "put it up in that pretty bird's nest you wear. I picture you doing it—when I'm alone in my room at night. Every time I imagine it you're dressed in the white-and-blue outfit you wore the first day, with huge sleeves that lift up around your ears when your arms go up, and your breasts lift, too, and your waist is as thin as a sapling. And I put my hands on it so that when you lower your arms they come around my neck, and you say my name. Jens . . . just Jens, the way I love to hear you say it. And that's the simple dream I have of you."

She smiled, and in the darkness felt her cheeks heat with joy.

"Oh, Jens, what a lovely man you are."

He chuckled, suspecting he'd waxed too romantic for manly ways, yet it was the truth, something he'd wanted to tell her all summer.

"When I'm your wife," Lorna said, "you can watch me every morning."

Her hair was up. Her dress was buttoned. The hour was late.

"I must go," she said.

He laid her knit cape upon her shoulders. They walked to the door. He pushed it open and it creaked a farewell song. Outside, they held each other one last time, silent, wishful. He drew away, caught her by the sides of her neck and kissed her forehead for several heartbeats, then stepped back and let her go.

Chapter
TEN

PHOEBE was duly impressed by both the *Lorna D* and its builder. She exclaimed the moment the two girls were alone, "He's the one!"

Lorna crossed her lips with a finger. "Shh!"

"But he's the one you told me about. The one you had the picnic with, and you're sweet on him, aren't you?"

"Phoebe, be quiet! I'll be in real trouble if anyone hears you."

"Oh, who's going to hear me out here in the garden. Come on, let's go sit in the gazebo, where we can talk. If anybody comes around we'll see them."

They sat in the gazebo on the wooden benches with their backs to the latticework, soaking up the afternoon sun that had grown much less intense as August became September.

"All right," Phoebe demanded, "what's going on between you and that handsome Norwegian boatbuilder? Tell me right now!"

Lorna spoke as if giving up. Her inflection lacked all girlish giddiness when she replied, "Oh, Phoebe, promise you won't tell?"

"Cross my heart."

"I'm in love with him, Phoebe. Heart and soul, forevermore, in love with him."

Lorna's seriousness, her quietness, her straightforward manner conveyed as much as her words. From that first revelation, Phoebe believed her.

"But Lorna." She, too, lost her flighty manner. "What about Taylor?"

"I've never loved Taylor. My parents are just going to have to understand that I can't see him anymore."

"They'll never understand. They'll be very upset."

"Yes, I suppose they will, but it wasn't my fault, Phoebe. I saw Jens the first time and something happened inside here." Lorna touched her heart. "From the very first time we spoke there was a certain knowledge between us, as if we were fated to meet and be more than passing acquaintances. We both felt it, long before we spoke of it or . . . or kissed."

"He's kissed you?"

"Oh, yes. Kissed me, held me, whispered endearments to me, as I have to him. When we're together it's impossible not to do those things."

Phoebe, looking troubled, took Lorna's hand. "Then I'm afraid for you."

"Afraid?"

"He's a commoner, an immigrant; he has no family or money or social position. They'll never let you marry him, never. From the moment they find out they'll do everything in their power to see that it doesn't happen."

Lorna gazed off across the garden. "Yes, I imagine they will."

"Oh, Lorna, you're going to get hurt."

Lorna sighed and closed her eyes. "I know." She opened them again. "But please don't warn me not to see him anymore, Phoebe. I couldn't stand that. I need at least one ally I can trust, one who'll believe that what I'm doing is right . . . for me and for Jens."

"You can trust me, Lorna. You have my promise I'll never try to change your mind about him, because I can see it's true that you love him. You've already changed because of it."

"Changed? Have I?"

"There's a serenity that I've never seen before."

"A serenity . . . yes, I suppose so. That's how I feel inside . . . as if all my life I've been peering through a dusty window, frustrated because I could not see clearly, and finally someone has washed it clean. Now here I stand, gazing through at the world in all its bright, sparkling colors, and I wonder, How could I not have noticed before how beautiful everything is? Oh, Phoebe . . ." Lorna turned to her friend with a radiant face. "It's impossible to describe how it feels. How when I'm away from him everything around me seems gray and lifeless, then when I step into his presence all of life abounds once more. It becomes splendid, and meaningful. And when he speaks, his voice is more than just . . . just vocal intonations. It's a refrain. And when he touches me I know why I was born; and when he laughs I am happier than when I laugh myself; and when we part . . ." Lorna leaned her head back against the lattice and turned her face toward the distant boat shed. "And when we part . . . it is the November of my heart."

The girls sat in the silent sun, stricken—both—by Lorna's poignant soliloquy. In the gaillardia patch insects droned. Out beneath an oak tree at the far side of the yard Smythe raked up acorns. From the house Aunt Agnes came toddling through the flower beds, her hat left behind, her hair shining in the sun as she stretched forward to whisk a net at a butterfly.

"Here comes Aunt Agnes," Lorna said, melancholically.

"Catching butterflies for her collection."

The old woman swiped again at a cosmos blossom and placed her prey in a brass cricket box.

"Poor Aunt Agnes, pressing flowers and collecting butterflies, pining her life away for her dear lost love."

Agnes spied them, raised her hand and waved. The girls waved back.

"All she ever wanted in her life was her beloved Captain Dearsley."

"Then she'd understand how you feel about Jens."

The girls rolled their heads and exchanged gazes. The unsaid scintillated between them: Lorna would need such understanding in the days ahead.

"Yes, I believe she would."

September suddenly turned hot. The migratory monarchs came through and Aunt Agnes mounted several. Theron, Jenny and Daphne—as well as Mitch Armfield—took the train daily into the city to attend school, returning in the late afternoon and complaining about the heat on the train, the heat in their schoolrooms, the heat in their bedrooms. Lorna blessed each eighty-five-degree day, for it meant no plans were yet in the offing for the family's return to the house on Summit Avenue in Saint Paul.

Taylor invited her to take the theater train into the city to see May Irwin in *The Widow Jones*, but Lorna declined with the excuse that she was not in the least inclined to watch the buxom, boisterous blonde gambol around the stage singing this new profanity called ragtime. Taylor suggested perhaps another show, another night, then inquired why he hadn't seen her wearing the watch he'd given her. She touched her bodice and told a bald-faced lie. "Oh, Taylor," she said, "I'm so sorry. I lost it." That night she went out to the end of the dock and flung the watch into the lake.

Her mother planned a dinner party for twelve and placed Lorna's place card next to Taylor's. Lorna came along as Levinia was putting the finishing touches on the dining room, and switched hers to the opposite end. Levinia pursed her entire face and said, "Lorna, what in the world are you doing?"

"Would you be terribly disappointed, Mother, if I sat next to someone else?"

"Someone else—whyever, Lorna?"

Willing her face to remain pale and inscrutable, Lorna gripped the back of a rosewood chair and faced Levinia across the elegantly appointed table. "I suppose you won't believe me if I tell you that Taylor and I are not well suited."

Levinia looked as if her underwear had just come up missing. "Twaddle!" she exploded. "You're suited and I won't hear another word to the contrary!"

"I haven't any feelings for him, Mother."

"Feelings! What have feelings to do with it! Your marriage to Taylor will put you in a house as grand as our own, and you'll move among the cream of society. Why, I daresay it won't be a year or two before Taylor will even have a summer home out here."

"Is that what you married Father for? A grand house, and a place in society and a summer home on White Bear Lake?"

"Don't you be impertinent with me, young lady! I'm your mother and I—"

"And you what? You love Father?"

"Hold your voice down!"

"I am holding my voice down. You're the one who's shouting. It's a simple question, Mother. Do you love Father? I've often wondered."

Levinia's face had turned as maroon as the papered walls. "What's gotten into you, you insolent child?"

"The realization that when Taylor touches me I want to run in the house."

Levinia gasped. "Oh dear . . ." She came rushing around the table, leaving her stack of place cards behind, whispering, "Oh, gracious dear, this is distressing. Lorna, he hasn't taken advantage of you, has he?"

"Taken advantage?"

Levinia seized her daughter's arm and shepherded her toward the morning room, where she closed them in with the pocket doors.

"I warned you about men. They're all the same in that regard. Has he . . . well, has he . . . you know . . ." Levinia stirred the air with one hand. "Has he done anything untoward when you were alone together?"

"No, Mother."

"But you said he's touched you."

"Please, Mother, it's nothing. He's kissed me, that's all." Lorna spoke with conviction, for she knew now, fully well, that what she and Taylor had done together truly was nothing.

"And embraced you?"

"Yes."

"And that's all? You're sure that's all?"

"Yes."

Levinia wilted onto a settee. "Oh, thank goodness. Nevertheless, given what you've told me, I think it's time we set a wedding date."

"A wedding date! Mother, I just told you, I don't want to marry Taylor!"

Levinia went on as if Lorna hadn't spoken. "I'll speak to your father at once, and he will speak to Taylor, and we'll get the plans nicely under way. June, I should think, here in the garden when the roses are in bloom. We always have lovely weather in June, and the yard can hold as many or more than Saint Mark's. Oh dear . . ." She pinched her lower lip and gazed toward the window. "The best of the summer vegetables won't be ready yet, but I'll speak to Smythe and see if he can force them this winter. Yes, that's what I'll do—and the raspberries, too. Smythe can do magic with anything that grows, and we'll have dinner on the lawn. Oh!" She pointed at Lorna. "And the vows will be spoken in the gazebo, of course. I'll have Smythe plan some early-blooming flowers for around it—something showy since the clematis won't be in bloom yet—and of course your sisters will be bridesmaids, and you'll want Phoebe, too, I'm sure. Lorna? . . . Lorna, where are you going? Lorna, come back here!"

Lorna ran straight to Jens, panic-stricken and needing the reassurance of his arms around her, only to find two of her father's friends there, members of the yacht club, looking over the boat mold and asking questions about its design. She did an about-face in the path and ran to find Aunt Agnes. Agnes, unfortunately, was napping in her room with an afghan pulled over her thin shoulders, and Lorna had too much heart to awaken her. She ran downstairs and was slamming out the front door when Levinia called from the morning room doorway, "Lorna, where are you going?"

"To Phoebe's!" she shouted, and streaked as if a tornado were at her heels.

Phoebe—bless her soul—was home, playing the piano in the parlor when Lorna burst in.

"Phoebe, I need you."

"Lorna, hello . . . Oh dear, what's wrong?"

Lorna slid onto the piano bench and flopped into her friend's arms. "I'm scared and angry and I want to tie my mother to her stupid gazebo with her own clematis vines and leave her there for the winter!"

"What's happened?"

"I told her I didn't want to marry Taylor, but she said she's going to set a date anyway. Phoebe, I won't marry him! I won't!"

Phoebe held Lorna fast and searched for any rejoinder that wouldn't sound placative. Since all did, she held them inside and let Lorna rage.

"I won't end up like my mother. I just couldn't live my life like that. Phoebe, I asked her if she loved my father, and she couldn't even lie about it. She just didn't answer. Instead, she started running off on a tangent, planning my wedding, talking about Smythe and r . . . raspberries and J . . . June in the gaz . . . gaz . . ." Lorna broke into tears.

"Don't cry . . . Oh, Lorna, please, darling, don't cry."

"I'm not crying. Well, yes, I am, but I'm as angry as I am distraught." Lorna sat back and made fists in her lap. "We're nothing, Phoebe—don't you see? What we want, what we feel, who we love is dismissed simply because we're women, and worse yet, women who belong to rich men. If I wore trousers I could say marry me or don't marry me and nobody would bat an eye. Instead, look what they do to us—parcel us off as social chattel. Well, I won't be parceled off! You'll see, I won't!"

Phoebe was trying hard not to laugh, biting her lip because Lorna looked so fierce and pretty at the same time.

"All right, laugh if you want!" Lorna scolded.

Phoebe did. She released a frisson that relieved all the tension in the room. "I can't help it. You should see yourself. You should hear yourself. Why, if I were your parents I'd be scared half to death to tangle with you. Does this Jens Harken know what a hellcat he's getting?"

Phoebe could not have chosen a more perfect comeback. Lorna succumbed to her humoring.

"You've guessed, of course. He *has* asked me to marry him—or did he? Telling you now, it hardly seems as if either one of us asked. We simply agreed, as though it had to be. But he's got to finish the *Lorna D* first, and it's got to win that regatta so he'll have established a reputation. Then Father will see that he's going to be somebody. Oh, he is, Phoebe, I just know it."

"So all you really need to do is hold your mother off until next June, when the regatta will be run."

"But she's talking about a June wedding."

Phoebe ruminated awhile. "Maybe you could promise her an August one."

"I can't lie anymore. I've already lied once. I threw Taylor's watch in the lake and told him I lost it."

"Forget I suggested it."

Lorna sighed. She turned to the piano keys and played a minor chord, letting it ring through the parlor until it became a memory.

"Life is so complicated," she lamented, dropping her hand to her lap, staring at some black notes dancing along some white staff paper on the music holder of the piano.

"And growing up is so hard."

When Lorna and Phoebe were children they sometimes played duets together. The aunts would applaud and ask for another rendition, and the parents would brag about how bright and talented their daughters were. Times had been so simple then.

"Sometimes I wish I were twelve again," Lorna replied.

They sat on, pondering the difficulties of being eighteen. After a while Phoebe asked, "Did you talk to your aunt Agnes?"

"No. She was sleeping."

"Talk to her. Confide in her. Maybe she'll intercede for you with your mother."

The thought terrified Lorna. She dropped her head into her hands and her elbows made the piano go *Daang!* There she sat, miserable. Suppose Aunt Agnes did just that and her mother told her father, and her father dismissed Jens. Suppose Lorna herself came right out and declared she was in love with Jens Harken. It wouldn't surprise Lorna if her mother advanced the wedding date even farther.

Similar thoughts struck Phoebe. She herself was walking out with Jack Lawless when the one she had eyes for was Taylor DuVal. The day could very well come when her mother and father would set down edicts about whom she would marry, and it very likely would be Jack.

"Tell you what . . ." she said, rubbing Lorna's bowed back, jostling her affectionately. "How about if I go to your mother and tell her I'll marry Taylor, and the sooner the better. Would you untie her from the gazebo and let her plan *my* wedding feast? I don't think there's a woman in White Bear Lake who could do it any better."

Lorna laughed and slung her arms around Phoebe, and they sat on the piano bench with no more answers than they'd had when Lorna had arrived.

*   *   *

That evening she told her mother she wasn't feeling well and shunned the dinner party. Theron stuck his head into her room around eight o'clock and said, "You sick, Lorn?"

She was sitting on her window seat in her nightgown with her knees against her chest. "Oh, hi, Theron. Come on in. No, I'm not too sick, not really."

"Then how come you're not down at the party?" He came and sat at her feet with one buttock cocked on the padded seat.

"I'm just sad, that's all."

" 'Bout what?"

"About grown-up things."

"Oh." His expression grew thoughtful, then he screwed up his face in conjecture. "Like finding good help and the price of commodities?"

She reached forward and tousled his hair, smiling in spite of herself. "Yeah, something like that."

"Hey, I know!" he exclaimed, suddenly bright. "Wait here!"

Off the window seat he shot, and ran out the door. Lorna heard his heels thumping down the hall to his room, a pause, then the slam of a door before his footsteps returned. He whipped around the doorway, breathless, and charged to the window seat. "Here." He thrust his spyglass into her hands. "You can use this for a while. Nobody can feel sad when they can have the birds right in their room, and sleep in the trees and sail in a big ship. Here, I'll pull it out for you." He did, and handed it back. "Just stick it up to your eye and close the other one. You'll see!"

She followed orders and the moonlit dock jumped into her room. "Shiver me timbers," she said, and scanned around to Theron's face. "There's a pirate in my room. Captain Kidd, I believe."

He giggled, and she felt better.

"Thanks, Theron," she said sincerely, lowering the brass piece, smiling at him affectionately. "It's just what I needed."

He got embarrassed then and didn't know what to do. He scratched his head with stubby nails and left his hair standing up like hard-crack taffy. "Well, I guess I gotta go to bed."

"Yeah, me too. See you tomorrow. Sleep tight . . . and don't let the bedbugs bite."

His face got disgusted. "Aw, come on, Lorn, that stuff's for babies."

"Oh, sorry."

He headed for his room.

"Thanks again, Theron."

At the door, he turned and sent a last loving look at his spyglass. "Hey, Lorna, don't leave it outside overnight or anything. And don't get any sand in it."

"I won't."

"How many nights you think you'll need it?"

Till the regatta next summer, she thought. "Oh, two or three should be enough."

"Okay. I'll come back for it, but don't leave it where Jenny or Daph can find it."

"I won't." With the telescope she saluted.

"Well, see ya," he said, and left.

When he was gone she held the spyglass in her lap until the brass grew warm across her palm. She studied it, this gift of love, and found tears in her eyes. Finding good help and the price of commodities— she smiled through her tears. Did he even know what a commodity was? Dear, sweet Theron. Someday he would grow up and become a man, more like Jens than Papa, hopefully. She became overpowered by the tenderest, most touching love she had ever felt for her brother. Suffused by it, she sat on her window perch a long time, discovering something she had not known until now: that love feeds upon itself, multiplying as it is given. Just as her love for Jens had opened her senses to her physical surroundings, it had opened her heart to a truer love for those around her. Even for Mama, with her misguided priorities, and Papa, with his bluff, unaffectionate demeanor. She loved them, truly she did, but they were wrong, wrong, to dictate her affections. Father, of course, would go along with Mother when she said it was time to set a date for Lorna's wedding. And at the yacht club and at afternoon teas they would speak about it with Taylor's parents, and it would be treated as preordained that Lorna should be Taylor's wife.

How could she change their minds? It would be difficult, but she knew she must try, and she intended to do so tonight.

* * *

She was still awake when the dinner party ended, lying in bed, listening to the sounds of her parents ascending the stairs, using the bathroom and retiring to their room for the night. Slipping from her bed, she donned a wrapper and went to their room.

Her knock was followed by a surprised silence, then her father's voice, "Yes, who is it?"

"It's Lorna, Father. May I come in?"

He opened the door himself, dressed in his trousers over a short-sleeved summer union suit with his suspenders trailing. Levinia, she saw, was already in bed. The scent of cigar smoke was strong in the room.

"I must talk to both of you."

This was a room into which she rarely stepped, as an adult. She had never understood why until this moment. Levinia was clutching the covers to her chest, though she was covered to her ears in white cotton.

Lorna closed the door and stood with her spine against the knob, holding it behind her.

"I'm sorry I didn't come down to dinner tonight, and I'm sorry I lied. I was not feeling ill. I simply didn't want to be with Taylor."

Gideon spoke up. "Your mother has told me about this preposterous declaration you've made, that you don't want to marry him. Girl, what in blue blazes has gotten into you!"

"I don't love him, Father."

Gideon's eyes narrowed to pinpoints while he stared at her in derision. Then he snorted and spun away. "That is the singularly most asinine statement I've ever heard."

"Why?"

"Why!" He spun back to her. "Girl, if I have to tell you you're dumber than I think! I'm in total agreement with your mother. Taylor DuVal worships the ground you walk on. He's ambitious, and bright, and will have earned a fortune in his own right by the time he's thirty, just as his father did before him. He's part of our social circle, and his parents are as pleased as we are about the two of you keeping company. Now, the matter is settled! You're marrying him in June at whatever function your mother plans!"

Lorna stared at him, helpless, angry, her insides trembling.

"Papa, please . . . don't—"

"The matter is settled, I said!"

She compressed her lips. Hard. Tears built. Spattered. Spinning, she flung open the door and slammed it so hard the ash fell from Gideon's cigar in the ashtray. Everyone in the house heard her footsteps pounding down the hall, then her own door slamming as she careened toward her bed and bounced onto it, face down, weeping her heart out.

Ten minutes later she was still sobbing when Jenny crept in and approached the bed uncertainly. Lorna was unaware of her presence until Jenny stroked her hair softly.

"Lorna? . . . Lorna, what happened?"

"Oh, Jennneeeeee . . ." Lorna wailed.

Jenny clambered onto the bed and Lorna curled into her sister's arms.

"They're making me marry Taylor, and I don't want to."

"But Taylor's so handsome. And nice."

"I know. Oh, Jenny, I wish I admired him the way you do, but I love someone else."

"Someone else?" Jenny whispered, more awed by this news than by Lorna's weeping and door slamming. "Gosh."

"Someone they wouldn't approve of."

"But who?"

"I can't tell you, and you mustn't tell them. They don't know about it yet. I know I'm a coward not to come right out and tell them, but they're so . . . so forceful and righteous about it, ordering me around and . . . and telling me what I have to do. You know how they can be. But I just can't stand it anymore."

Jenny went on petting Lorna's hair. Never in her life had the older sister been succored by the younger. First Theron, now Jenny: They had come, sensing they were needed, and Lorna was deeply touched by their caring. Momentarily one more voice whispered timidly out of the dark.

"Jenny? What's the matter with Lorna?"

Daphne materialized like a child-spirit floating toward the bed from the doorway.

"She's had an argument with Mother and Father. Go back to bed, Daphne."

"But she's crying."

"I'm all right, Daph." From the sanctuary of Jenny's lap, Lorna reached out a hand. Daphne came to take it and lean against the edge of the bed. "Truly I am."

"But you never cry, Lorna. You're too old."

"A person is never too old to cry, Daphne, remember that. And I feel ever so much better now that you and Jenny and Theron have visited me."

"Theron was here?"

"Before his bedtime. He brought me his spyglass."

"His spyglass . . . gee . . ." Breathless wonder haloed the word.

Jenny asked, "Are you feeling better now, Lorna?"

"Oh, yes . . . thank you both. Now I think you'd better go back to bed before you get in trouble with Mother, too."

Jenny plumped Lorna's pillow, and Daphne gave her a quick kiss on the mouth. "I'll play tennis with you tomorrow, Lorna," she offered.

"And I will, too," Jenny added.

"I'd love that. Thank you. You're both dear sisters."

"Well, good night, Lorna."

"You sure you won't cry any more, Lorna?"

"I'll be just fine."

They lingered in the dark, unsure if they should abandon her yet, finally tiptoeing away as if she were an infant they had just rocked to sleep.

In their absence, Lorna's world grew dreary once more. The love shown by her siblings created a deep and touching afterglow, but it was tinged by an inexplicable sadness different from that of earlier. It was the sadness of the lovelorn who, when sundered from their beloved, find tears in all things happy.

Jens . . . Jens . . . you're the only one who can make me happy. You're the one I want to be with, laugh with, cry with, love.

She heard the old Chesterfield clock chime in the downstairs hall. Not a soul in the house astir.

A quarter hour.

A half hour—was it one-thirty? Two-thirty?

The three-quarter hour . . . in the deep of night.

No one to hear.

No one to know.

She lay flat on her back with her hands locked, pressed hard between her breasts, her heart pounding in trepidation. Jens . . . Jens . . . sleeping above me in your tiny attic room.

No one to hear.

No one to know.

Her bed was high. It seemed to take a long time for her feet to find the floor. When they did, she took neither wrapper nor slippers, but went barefoot, straightaway, across her room, down the hall and up the servants' stairway with its narrow walls and high risers and the trapped smell of the day's cooking. She had been up here several times and knew the layout: three rooms on the right, three on the left, all squashed beneath the roof like hair under a dunce's cap. Jens's was the middle door on the left.

She opened it without knocking, slipped inside and closed it deftly without making a sound. Inside, she stood motionless, her heart hammering, listening to Jens's breathing from the amorphous white shape of the bed. It stood to her left, against a wall. Beside it a single eyebrow window bent the shingles up scarcely enough to offer a breeze when dropped inward on its hinges. The room was very hot and smelled like a sleeping man—of warm breath and warm skin and the faint stuffiness of worn clothing. His clothing hung on hooks to her left: dark streamers against the lighter wall, created by the trousers and shirt he'd worn today.

His bed was single. His left arm cantilevered off it, its wrist pointing toward her as he lay on his side. He snored lightly, a sound resembling a curtain flapping against a window casing in a back breeze. Did he dream of sailboats? Of steamed wood? Of her?

She approached the bed and squatted beside it on her heels, next to his outstretched arm.

"Jens?" she whispered.

He slept on. In her life she had never approached the slumbering form of a man. His shoulders were bare. His chest, too, down to the waist, where a sheet covered him. The underside of his outflung arm appeared pale and vulnerable. She touched him there, with four hesitant fingertips, on the soft, warm, unflexed muscle of his biceps.

"Jens?"

"Hm?" His head came up and stayed so, his body registering the awakening before his mind did. "Whss . . ." he whispered, confused. "What is it?"

"Jens, it's me, Lorna."

"Lorna!" He sat up abruptly. "What are you doing here?"

"I came to be with you . . . to talk . . . I have some terrible news."

He took a moment to clarify his mind, glancing over to the eyebrow window, rubbing his face.

"Sorry . . . my mind is fuzzy. What happened?"

"They're going to marry me off to Taylor. Mother says she's going to set a date—next June. I pitched Taylor's watch in the lake, and pleaded with them, and told them I don't love him, but they're dead set against me, and angry to boot. They say I'm going to marry Taylor whether I like it or not. Oh, Jens, what am I going to do?"

"What time is it?"

"I don't know exactly. Close to two, maybe, or three."

"If you get caught here they'll crucify you . . . and me, too."

"I know that, but I won't get caught. They all just went to sleep about an hour ago. Jens, please, what are we going to do? I cannot marry Taylor after lying with you, but I'm afraid to tell them the real reason yet."

"Of course you can't." He raked back his hair, tugging the sheet closer to his hips and waist, casting around in the dark for good judgment in the midst of this muddled midnight morass. He had no more answers than she. "Here"—he reached for her arm—"come on up here."

She sat on the edge of his bed facing him while he gripped her arms through the sleeves of her cotton nightgown. "I don't know what we're going to do, but it's not this. We're not going to put you at risk by meeting up here where anyone could find out about it. You're going back down to your room and we'll take it a day at a time."

Plaintively she asked, "Would you marry me now, Jens?"

He dropped his hands from her warm, resilient flesh and tried not to think of it beneath a single layer of loose white cotton. "I can't marry you now. What would we live on? Where? Everybody I know knows your father. He'd make sure no one would hire me, and besides, I thought we agreed I wasn't going to be a kitchen handyman anymore. I'm going to be a boatbuilder. I can't do that until the *Lorna D* is finished."

"I know," she whispered, dropping her chin guiltily.

With the edge of a finger he tipped it up. "Right now there's no danger. They aren't saying you have to marry him tomorrow."

She told him calmly, "They had a dinner party tonight. I was supposed to sit next to him. Do you know what it's like to sit next to one man, pretending you're amused and attracted by him, while you love someone else? I've been doing that most of the summer, and I cannot do it anymore. It's dishonest. It's unfair to Taylor, and to you, and to me. And I love you too much to continue the pretense, Jens."

They sat in silence, linked only by a short stretch of sheet that flowed between his hip and hers, aggrieved by their love and its attendant heartbreak, wishing at times they had never met. They thought about addressing her parents, facing them with the truth. They knew such an act would be folly, for along with the right to love they both wanted a good life, and speaking to her parents now would nearly guarantee anything but.

"Have you ever thought," he asked, "how much simpler our lives would be if you'd never come back into the kitchen that night?"

"Many times."

"And then you feel guilty for thinking it."

"Yes," she whispered.

"Me too."

They let some silence pass. He sat with one hand propped on the mattress behind him. Reaching across his hip, he took her hand.

"If this ever works out, and we have children of our own, we're never going to dictate who they can love."

Their thumbs played a sad game of roundabout. Minute upon minute disappeared, and the sadness became supplanted by temptation, no matter what he'd said. They were two in love, in a warm attic bedroom, dressed in little, fighting memories of the first time they'd made love. They sat a long time, linked by only their fingers, while images of a more intimate link trespassed in their minds. They studied their joined hands, scarcely visible in the unlit room, while their thumbs circled . . . circled . . .

Then stopped.

He looked up first. At her face, or the place where it bowed low in the darkness. She looked up, too, as if in answer to his silent call. They sat helpless, hapless, in the tug of this merciless seduction perpetrated upon them by their own bodies. Such pounding. Such rushing. Such persuasion they felt.

Such knowledge of wrong, of right, of risk.

An admission left his lips, a word, uttered in a pleading whisper: "Lorna . . ."

And with it they moved.

Mouth to mouth, breast to breast, they ended the separation and yearning, and silenced the voices of common sense in their heads, falling from grace with all but each other. Over he took her, in a desperate tumble, and shifted her legs down along his own almost roughly. They kissed, matching their mouths, and rolled, matching their lengths, and lifted knees and opened legs and confirmed suspicions that there was nothing more than one sheet and one nightgown separating their skins.

"My beautiful Lorna," he praised, filling his hands with her breasts, then her hips, and finally her nightgown, hauling it out of their way. It caught on her left arm and became part of their rolling embrace.

"I tried not to come," she whispered beneath the onslaught of desire. "I stayed in my room willing myself to go to sleep . . . not to think of you . . . not to leave my bed. . . ."

His touches on her naked skin were swift and well aimed. "I tried, too . . ." He was touching her, inside, before the pillow changed shape beneath her head. She arched back and caught him behind a hip with her heel, her lips drawn back and her eyes closed. He grabbed the sheet and kicked it to the foot of the bed while she searched low and caressed him. Sharing those first impatient pleasures, they gave their bodies license, letting muscle and sinew celebrate this call to life. And all those days and hours of longing came into play—a summer's worth of looking away, looking toward, warning themselves one thing, feeling another. Their sexual encounter in the boat shed became part of tonight as well, its lessons well enjoyed and mulled, brought forth now to be repeated and elaborated.

"You . . ." he quite growled, a man overcome, ". . . driving me crazy night and day. Why didn't you stay away, you rich man's daughter?"

"Ask the moon to stop turning the tides. . . . Why didn't you turn me out, you poor boatbuilder's son?"

In answer he only growled, rolled flush upon her and entered her body to be caught from behind by both her heels.

Tensile and silent, they arched. And breathed through clamped teeth.

Those minutes of conjunction became fine in both their flamboyant and meditative moods. They discovered some rarified truths: that a cataclysmic first joining soon gives way rather than burn out too soon; that the ensuing expanse of lush, lazy caresses fills a need equally as vital; that it is hard to whisper when one feels like shouting exuberances to the heavens; that though a man's intentions may be noble, his actions don't always carry through. When they were wrapped in shudders and Jens had his hand clapped over Lorna's open mouth to keep her from calling out, he asked the moon to stop turning the tides, but the moon only smiled, and Jens remained in Lorna's body till the final slump and sigh.

Chapter
ELEVEN

SEPTEMBER aged. The brief spate of hot weather cooled and dawn began shrouding the lake with mist as its chill air kissed the warm water. The choiring of frogs ceased. The rusty creaking of Canada geese took its place, lifting faces skyward. In the marshes along the shoreline the cattails had exploded into powder puffs, forlorn now that the red-winged blackbirds had deserted them and headed south. At sunset the skies burned in vivid hues of heliotrope and orange as refracted light shimmered off the dust of harvesttime. The air became fragrant with leaf smoke and wheat chaff, and at night the moon donned a halo, warning of colder weather ahead.

In the boat shed the planking had begun. Daily now, the steam box hissed, loaded with fragrant cedar, perfuming the place with humidity and flavor so heavy and rich the sparrows pecked at the windowpanes as if begging to be let inside. Six inches wide and a half inch thick: steam it, glue it and screw it into place, then overlap that plank with another and another. The boat became a reality, a thing with a real fair line and a sheer line. The planking was completed and the caulking began: strips of cotton batting forced into the plank butts with a sharp-edged disk roller, waiting for water to swell and expand them and make the craft seaworthy. The countersunk screw holes were filled with wooden plugs. Then came the part Lorna loved best.

From the first time she watched Jens planing, she thought it the most arresting motion she'd ever seen. With the tool in both hands he would twist and lean and lunge, his shoulders slanted at an oblique angle, shifting and flexing as he labored with a love as true as any she'd ever seen a person display for his work. He whistled a lot and dropped often to a squat, eyeballing the length of the boat with one lid closed. On the balls of his feet he would balance among the curled cedar shavings that were as blond as his hair and from which it seemed to take its fragrance.

"When I was a boy," he said, "I caught plenty of hell from my father if I tried to get by without fairing up a boat good with the hand plane before sanding 'er down. My dad . . . he was a fussy one. Sometimes even before we started planing, when we'd be making the mold, he'd see one station that was bulging, and he'd say, 'We got to rework that one, boys,' and we'd groan and complain and say, 'Aw, Dad, it's good enough.' But now I thank my lucky stars that he made us do it over till it was right. This boat here . . . this little beauty will have a fair line the wind won't know is there."

Lorna listened, and observed, and admired the fine articulation of muscle on Jens's arms and shoulders as he moved and moved. She thought she could go on forever watching this man build boats.

She told him, "That time I came into the kitchen when you were all eating cake and Mrs. Schmitt asked you to chip some ice for my tea . . . You squatted down and started chipping away with that ice pick, and a little space appeared between your waistband and your shirt. It was shaped like a fish and I couldn't take my eyes off it. You were wearing black trousers and a very faded red shirt—I remember thinking it was the color of an old tomato stain that's been washed a lot. And your suspenders cut right down through the middle of that bare piece of skin, and while you were chipping, the pieces of ice went sailing over your shoulder to the floor. Then finally you got a big piece off and cupped it in your hands and let it slip off your fingertips into my glass . . . and you dried your hands on your thighs." Jens had stopped planing and stood looking at her. "Watching you push that hand plane," she concluded, "does the same thing to my insides."

Wordlessly he put down the tool and crossed the room to her, took her in his arms and kissed her, bringing the smell—the near taste—of cedar along with him.

When he lifted his head his expression still wore a hint of astonished surprise. "You remember all that?"

"I remember everything about you from the first moment we met."

"That my shirt was red and faded?"

"And crept up . . . back here." She touched him in the Y of his suspenders, drawing three light circles with her middle fingertip.

"You're a very naughty girl, Lorna Diane." He grinned. "Here." He found a piece of sandpaper for her. "Put yourself to use. You can sand behind me." She smiled and kissed his chin, then together they returned to the *Lorna D* to labor side by side on this boat that symbolized their future.

She went often to his room during those last weeks before the family moved back to the city. After they'd made love they would lie entwined, whispering in the dark.

"I've made a decision," he told her one night. "When the *Lorna D* is done, I'll come back to town to work in the kitchen until spring."

"No. You don't belong in a kitchen."

"But what else can I do?"

"I don't know. We'll think of something."

Of course, they thought of nothing.

The members of the White Bear Yacht Club beached their crafts and turned their interests to hunting. Wild ducks and geese began appearing on the supper table at Rose Point Cottage. The second week in September, Levinia began to make lists of what should stay and what should go. Then in the third week of September an unseasonably early frost came and killed all of her roses. Gideon and his cronies decided they were leaving for a five-day hunting trip to the Brule River in Wisconsin, and Levinia announced at supper that she was having the pipes drained the following morning and everybody should have their things packed and be ready to go back to town in the afternoon.

That night when Lorna went to Jens's room their lovemaking held a desperate undertone. They clung harder. Spoke less. Kissed a little too frantically.

Afterward, lying in his arms, she asked, "When will the boat be done?"

"Two months. That's longer than your father gave me, but I can tell I'll never finish in one more month."

"Two months . . . how shall I stand it?"

"By remembering that I love you. By knowing that somehow, someday, we'll be together as man and wife." He kissed her to seal the promise, holding her head firmly between his hands, then lifting his head as they searched each other's sad eyes.

"So you'll come back to town when the boat is done?"

"Yes."

They had argued further about it and decided it was best, only till next summer.

"And you'll be staying at the Hotel Leip till then?" Most of the lake hotels closed in the winter, but the Leip reduced its rates and stayed open as a boardinghouse.

"Yes. Your father's paying my room and board. You can write to me there."

"I will. I promise. And you can write to me, but send the letters to Phoebe. Use her middle initial, *V,* so she'll know it's for me. Now, I'm getting too sad talking about us being apart, so tell me about the *Lorna D.* Tell me what you'll do next and next and next between now and winter, when I'll see you again."

He spoke in a monologue, his words meant to hold eventualities at bay for as long as possible. "A lot more hand sanding, then I'll paint the outside. Green, of course. It's got to be green. Then cut the planking even with the ribs and release the boat from the mold. Then I'll start the work on the interior structure. I'll have to laminate the center backbone, and put on the deck beams over the internal framework, and cover them with cedar planking. Then more planing and fairing, of course, and after that I'll cover the deck with canvas. Next comes a mahogany wood molding to cover the nails that are holding the canvas on. Then there's molding to be put on around the cockpit—mahogany, too. Then I drill the rudder hole and install the shaft, and put on the deck hardware and—"

She flung herself into his arms, cutting off his words, holding her sobs captive in her throat.

"So much work," she whispered. "Will you have time to be lonesome for me the way I will be for you?"

"Yes, I'll miss you." He rubbed her naked spine. "I'll miss your showing up in the doorway with delphiniums and blackcurrants, and your incessant questions, and the smell of your hair and the feel of your skin and the way you touch me and kiss me and make me feel like I'm a vital piece of this universe."

"Oh, Jens, you are."

"Since I've fallen in love with you I am. Before that I wasn't sure."

"Of course you were. Remember how you used to tell me you were certain you could build the fastest boat ever? And how you'd change the face of inland racing? Your self-confidence was one of the first things I admired about you. Oh, Jens, I'm going to miss you so much."

They clung, and counted off the minutes of the escaping night, and dreaded parting.

"What time is it?" she'd ask at intervals, and Jens would get up, turn the face of his watch to the eyebrow window and read it by the negligible moonlight that oozed in.

"Three-twenty," he answered the first time.

Then, "Nearly four."

And finally, "Four-thirty."

Returning to his narrow bed, he sat beside Lorna and took her hand. One of them had to be sensible. "You have to go. The kitchen staff will be getting up soon, and we can't risk you running into one of them in the hall."

She sprang up and flung her arms around his shoulders, whispering, "I don't want to."

He put his face to her neck and held her, impressing this moment in his memory to sustain him through the months ahead, thinking, *Let her be safe, and not pregnant, and keep her in love with me this much until I can be with her again, and don't let them talk her into marrying DuVal, who is so much better suited to her kind than I am.*

They kissed one last time, each of them trying to be strong for the other, Lorna failing.

He had to put her from him. "Lorna . . . where is your nightgown?" he asked gently. "You've got to put it on now."

She rummaged in the dark and found it but sat with her head

hanging, the garment slack in her hands. He took it from her lifeless fingers and found its neck hole, and held it for her. "Here . . . put it on, darling."

She lifted her arms and the gown collapsed around her. He settled it into place and fastened all but the top two buttons, dipping his head and kissing her between her collarbones before buttoning them, too.

"Just remember . . . I love you. You mustn't cry now, or your eyes will be red in the morning, and what will you say when they ask about it?"

She flung herself upon him. "That I love Jens Harken and I don't want to go back to town without him."

He swallowed the lump in his throat and stood, forcing her arms to slide free of his neck.

"Come," he said, "you're making this awfully hard for me. Another minute and you'll have me in tears."

Immediately she obeyed—she could do for him what she could not for herself—leaving the bed and walking beside him to the door. There he turned and pulled her gently into his arms.

"It'll be the fastest, finest boat ever," he promised. "And it will win you for me—you'll see. Think about that when things get you down. And remember, I love you and I *will* marry you."

"I love you, too," she managed as her long-held weeping broke forth.

Their mouths collided in one last smeared, tormented kiss while she clambered barefoot onto the tops of his feet. His eyes stung. The kiss became anguish.

Finally Jens tore himself away, gripped her arms firmly and ordered, "Go."

A grievous pause punctuated by her soft sobs in the dark, and she was gone, leaving only a rustle of cotton and a vast emptiness in his heart.

Levinia spurted, in the midst of their leave-taking nine hours later, "What in heaven's name is wrong with you, girl? Are you sick?"

"No, Mother."

"Then put that hat on and get moving! Mercy sakes, you act as if you have Addison's disease!"

To Lorna, returning to the Saint Paul house felt like going to prison. It was her home, but so much less homelike than the cottage at White Bear Lake. Situated on Summit Avenue among the crème de la crème of Saint Paul's mansions, Gideon Barnett's town house had been erected as a monument to his success. The address in itself was one of superlative prestige, for the list of property owners along Summit included those with the oldest money in Minnesota—industrialists, railroad barons, mining executives and politicians who need only take a short carriage ride down the hill to be at the State Capitol. The house itself was constructed of gray granite mined at Saint Cloud, Minnesota, from one of Gideon Barnett's own mines; it had been erected by German stonemasons brought to America expressly for the job by Barnett himself. It was Gothic, burly, a massive pile of dinge with cubelike lines broken primarily by a high square tower at the center front, which housed the main stairway. Its doors were elaborately carved, with ornate bronze hardware shaped like gargoyles baring canine teeth. As a baby, Lorna had closed her eyes and burrowed her face against her mother's shoulder when being carried into the house to avoid confronting those scary beasts.

Inside, the place was overburdened with treacle-colored woodwork and mahogany furniture whose legs were as thick as human waists. It was accessorized by joyless pieces like malachite urns, French bronzes, stuffed stags' heads (Gideon's hunting trophies) and dark, busy Kirman rugs. Its immense chandeliers hovered overhead like the wrath of God, while its fireplaces—all eight of them—hove at the house's inhabitants like great, gaping maws. Add to all this windows set too deep to allow enough light inside, and there waited a place darksome enough to not only match but to augment Lorna's heartsickness.

She lived with that heartsickness daily, from the time she opened her eyes in her thick-posted satinwood bed to the time she appeared at supper in the gloomy dining room with its shroudlike wallpaper swallowing up all the light from the ugly chandelier worked in the shape of Indians bearing bows and arrows.

She felt as if she had left her heart at Rose Point Cottage and in its place lay a lifeless mass she carried around as one would a purse with no money, something that merely rode along without being opened to anyone. A week went by and Lorna remained listless and quiet. Two weeks, and Levinia grew concerned. She came, eventually, to press Lorna's forehead in search of fever. "Lorna, what is it? You haven't been the same since we came home from the lake."

"It's nothing. I miss the gardens, and the bright house, and the wide open air, that's all. This house is so dominating and dark."

"But you haven't been eating, and your color has been so sallow."

"I tell you, Mother, it's nothing. Really."

"Say what you will, I'm concerned. That day we were leaving Rose Point I made some remark about Addison's disease to get you going, but I've been watching you ever since, and yesterday I actually looked up Addison's in our *Health and Longevity* book. Lorna, you have many of the symptoms."

"Oh, Mother . . ." Lorna flounced to the other side of the room, displaying more energy than she had in two weeks. "For heaven's sake!"

"Well, it's true. You've been in a state of prolonged languor. Your appetite is capricious, and you seem to show a special repugnance to meats. Have you been vomiting, too?"

"No, Mother, I haven't been vomiting. . . . Now, please . . ."

"Well, don't get so upset with me. Every other symptom fits, and they say the vomiting comes only in more advanced cases. Nevertheless, I think we should take you to see Dr. Richardson."

"I'm not going to Dr. Richardson. I've just been a little tired is all."

Levinia considered, then rose to her full height as if she'd made a decision. "Very well. If you're not sick, it's time you end this moping and join the human race again. Dorothea DuVal has invited the two of us to lunch at her house this coming Thursday and I've accepted. She and I believe it's time to begin making wedding plans. Next June isn't that far away, you know."

"But Taylor and I aren't even officially engaged!"

"Yes, I know. But Dorothea says you will be soon."

The empty purse of a heart Lorna believed she carried showed it had a rich cache of objections that jingled around, wanting to be spilled: exasperation at her mother's refusal to listen, anger at both Levinia and Dorothea for railroading her this way, gut denial that any such wedding would ever take place.

Realizing, however, that her objections would again be overridden if voiced, she surprised Levinia by answering calmly, "Whatever you say, Mother."

She left the room and went directly to seek out Aunt Agnes, finding her in the music room with the lace curtain flipped back to let in extra light. The old woman was sitting in a sewing rocker beside a piecrust table doing some fancywork.

"Aunt Agnes, may I talk to you?"

Agnes removed a pair of spectacles and laid them on the table beside her thimble keep.

"Of course. I can do this anytime."

Lorna closed the pocket doors and drew a low footstool near her aunt's chair.

"Aunt Agnes," she said, curling her shoulders and propping her elbows on her knees, looking up into a pair of kind blue eyes. "I must trust you with the most important secret of my entire life."

"If you do, I shall honor that trust to my grave."

Lorna touched the backs of Agnes's shiny, mottled hands. "Remember when I talked to you about the man I love? Well, that man isn't Taylor DuVal. He is someone Mother and Father will strongly object to. He's one of their employees, Jens Harken—the one who's building the boat for Father. Until he began on the boat he was our kitchen odd-jobs man, but it doesn't matter to me at all—I love him as deeply and as truly as you loved Captain Dearsley. I want to marry him."

Aunt Agnes's eyes grew tender. She reached out both hands, her fingers permanently crooked and knotted, and took Lorna's face as if to place a kiss upon it. Instead, she spoke lovingly. "Dear child, then you have found it. You're one of the lucky few who've been blessed by it."

Lorna smiled. "Yes, I am."

Agnes dropped her hands. "And you're willing to fight for it— you'll have to be, because Gideon and Levinia will snarl and yelp and lay down laws."

"They already have. Mother and Dorothea DuVal are meeting over lunch on Thursday to start making wedding plans. They want me there, too. I've told and told Mother I don't want to marry Taylor, but she simply won't listen."

"Because she and your father were not blessed like you and I. They don't understand."

"What should I do?"

"Can this young boatbuilder support you?"

"No, not yet. In another year, maybe."

"Have you broken it off with Taylor?"

"No. I've just been avoiding him in the hope that he'll get the hint."

"Mmm . . . not a very honorable way to conduct yourself."

"I know," Lorna whispered.

"Nor a very effective way. If you want him to stop calling—and giving your mother ideas—tell him so. If you must, tell him you love another man. It will hurt him, but who of us hasn't been hurt by love? Hurt serves its purpose—it intensifies our joy when it finally arrives. So the way I see it, the first step is to sunder your tie to young Taylor in an absolutely clear-cut fashion. Mothers have been able for centuries to force their daughters to the altar, but they haven't been so successful with sons. If neither of you wants the marriage, perhaps those two meddlesome women will desist. The sooner you speak to Taylor the better."

This time it was Lorna who took Agnes's face between her hands. She kissed the old woman squarely on the mouth and told her sincerely, "I can see why Captain Dearsley loved you so much. Thank you, dear Aunt Agnes."

The following day Lorna dressed for the weather and took the streetcar down the hill into Saint Paul's business district, to the offices of the DuVal Flour Milling Company, which hovered at the base of a forest of tall grain elevators on the west shore of the Mississippi River. The place was dusty and smelled pleasantly oatsy, its air astir with fine particles of grain.

Taylor, wearing leather sleeveguards, was working at a desk within a glassed-in office when Lorna was announced. His surprise showed plainly: He shot to his feet and glanced up eager-eyed, searching her out on the other side of the glass. She waved inconspicuously. He smiled and came striding around his desk, removing the sleeveguards and leaving them behind as he swept through his door.

"Lorna," he said, reaching out with both hands. "What a surprise this is!"

"Hello, Taylor."

"I couldn't believe it when Ted said your name. I thought he was joking."

"So this is where you learn your father's business."

"This is it." He gestured. "Dusty, isn't it?"

"Pleasantly so." She looked to her right. "And that is your office."

"With its very dusty window."

"Could we go inside a minute, Taylor?"

Her tone took the smile from his face and turned it somber.

"Of course." He touched her elbow and followed, closing the door behind them. From a wooden armchair he removed a flat of grain samples, then dusted the seat and placed it beside his desk.

"Please . . . sit down."

She did, gingerly, with her back several inches away from the vertical ribs of the backrest. He sat, too, in a well-used wooden swivel chair, whose springs twanged loudly.

When they quieted, so did the room.

Into that uneasy silence Lorna spoke. "I came to talk to you about something very important, Taylor. I'm sorry to do it here in the middle of your workday, but I simply didn't know what else to do."

He sat waiting, his forearms resting on an open ledger as large as a tea tray. He was dressed in a gray striped suit, a white shirt with a high, round collar and a black tie. For the dozenth time she wondered why it had not been possible for her to fall head over heels in love with this man: He was so perfect.

"Has your mother spoken to you recently—about us?" she inquired.

"Yes, as a matter of fact, she has. Just last night."

"Taylor, you must know that I think a great deal of you. I admire you, and . . . and I've had a lot of fun with you. This summer when you gave me the watch, you said it was intended as a token of your intention to marry me. Taylor"—she stumbled and looked down at her gloves—"this is so hard to say . . ." She raised her eyes to his. "You're a fine man, an honest man, a hard-working man, and I'm sure you'll make a wonderful husband, but the truth is . . . I'm so very, very sorry, Taylor . . . I don't love you. Not the way I think a woman ought to love the man she's going to marry."

Taylor's moustache lowered slightly on the left side, as if he'd caught his upper lip between his teeth. He sat motionless, his hands flat on the ledger page, separated by four inches of blue-lined paper. His calmness rattled Lorna: She chattered on to cover her discomposure.

"Our mothers have their heads together and they want me to join them tomorrow over lunch, to make plans for our wedding. Taylor, I beg you . . . please help me convince them this is not the right thing to do, because if you don't they're going to forge right ahead and plan a wedding that should not take place."

Taylor moved at last. He tipped back his chair, blew out an immense gust of breath and scrubbed one hand down over his face. It covered his mouth and chin while he studied her with troubled eyes. Finally he dropped his hand and admitted, "I suppose I'd guessed." He lined up the ledger with the edge of the green blotter, very precisely—something to occupy his eyes. "You've been avoiding me much of the summer, though I didn't know why. Then I noticed you weren't wearing the watch. I guess that's when it struck me. I just kept hoping you'd change . . . that one day you'd be the way you were those first nights we were alone together. What happened, Lorna?"

He looked so hurt she felt cruel and glanced aside.

He tipped his chair forward and joined his hands on the ledger, speaking earnestly. "Did I do something wrong? Did I change some way?"

"No."

"Did I offend you with my advances?"

She looked at her lap and whispered, "No."

"Then what is it? I deserve to know. What changed your mind?"

Her eyes had taken on a faint sheen of tears. In spite of them, she faced him squarely. "I fell in love with somebody else." Disbelief seemed to render him speechless. He stared at her while in the anteroom four workers stitched flour bags and a cat stalked for mice. Through the floor came the faint rumble and vibration of the nearby mill wheels grinding.

Lorna told him, "I'm being honest with you, Taylor, because I *am* guilty of hurting you—it's true—but I want you to know I never intended to do so."

He became animated at last, gesturing wide. *"Who* could you possibly have been seeing that I don't know about!" His cheeks had grown ruddy above his beard.

"I'm not allowed to divulge that. To do so would be to betray a confidence."

"It's not that young whelp Mitchell Armfield, is it?"

"No, it's not Mitch."

"Then who?"

"Taylor, please. I cannot tell you."

She watched his ire grow, though he tried to curb it. "Obviously your parents don't know about him." When she refused to reply, he continued speculating. "Which means it's someone they don't approve of, right?"

"Taylor, I've been truthful with you, but in the strictest of confidence. I must ask you not to reveal what we've said here today."

Taylor DuVal left his chair and stood at the dusty glass, knuckles to hips, facing the workroom, where clerks and seamstresses moved about their daily business, all making money for him, money this woman could have shared—a life of luxury this woman could have shared. And he would have been good to her! Generous to a fault! He'd given her a betrothal watch while she'd been two-timing him. Two-timing him, for God's sake! He wasn't such a bad catch. As she'd said, he was honest, hard-working and loyal—by God, he'd been scrupulously loyal to her! And if it came down to it, he was pretty easy on the eye. So, to hell with her. If all that wasn't enough for the woman, he didn't need her!

"All right, Lorna." He turned brusquely. "You'll have your way. I'll speak to my mother and tell her my future plans have changed. I won't bother you again."

She stood. He remained across the room.

"I'm sorry, Taylor," she said.

"Yes . . . well . . . don't be. I won't be unattended for long."

Lorna colored. It was the truth, she knew. He was far too plum a catch for the ladies to ignore, once they realized he was on the marriage market.

* * *

At the news, Levinia went into a decline. She took to falling back into chairs with her eyelids closed, speaking in a puling voice and sprinkling iris water into her handkerchief, then pressing it to her nose while her eyes brimmed once more.

Gideon swore a blue streak and called Lorna a stupid twit.

Jenny wrote to Taylor, expressing her apologies for the broken engagement and offering a friendly ear should he need someone to talk to.

Phoebe beamed and asked, point-blank, "So now he's fair game?"

Aunt Henrietta hissed, "Ungrateful girl, someday you'll regret this."

Aunt Agnes opened her arms and said, "We romantics must stick together."

Lorna wrote to Jens:

> My Dearest One,
>
> Bleak are these days without you, though I have some news to cheer us both. I have taken command of my own life and have severed my relationship with Taylor DuVal, once and for all.

Jens wrote back:

> My Beloved Lorna,
>
> This boat shed without you is like a violin without strings. No music happens here anymore. . . .

Lorna wrote:

> Jens, my darling,
>
> Never have so few weeks felt like so many. I don't know if it's being separated from you that causes this lethargy, but I have been feeling so lifeless, and even food has lost its appeal. Mother fears it's Addison's disease, but it isn't. It is simply loneliness, I'm sure. She wants me to go to the doctor, but the only cure I need is you. . . .

Jens wrote:

> Dearest Lorna,
>
> I grew terrified when I read your letter. If you're ill, please, darling, do as your mother suggests and visit the doctor. If anything should happen to you I don't know what I'd do. . . .

Lorna's lethargy persisted. Food, especially the odor of cooked meat, seemed to turn her stomach. Most upsetting, that symptom of Addison's which signaled its advancement—vomiting—happened one morning, and in its wake, Lorna, too, grew terrified.

She went straight to Aunt Agnes.

Agnes took one look at Lorna's blanched face and flew across the room. "Good heavens, child, what's wrong? You look as though you left all your blood in a jar in your room. Sit down here."

Lorna sat, shaken. "Aunt Agnes," she said, clinging to her aunt's hands, lifting her terrified eyes. "Please don't tell Mother, because I don't want to scare her yet, but I think I really do have Addison's disease."

"What! Oh, surely not. Addison's disease—why, what gave you that idea?"

"I looked it up in the *Health and Longevity* book and it's just as Mother suspected. I have all the symptoms, and now I just vomited, and the book says that means it's in its advanced stages. Oh, Aunt Agnes, I don't want to die."

"Stop it this minute, Lorna Barnett! You're not going to die! Now tell me about these symptoms."

Lorna described them, still clinging to Agnes's hands. When she finished, Agnes sat down beside her on the chaise.

"Lorna, do you love me?" she asked.

Lorna blinked, then stared, digesting this unexpected question. "Of course."

"And do you trust me?"

"Yes, Aunt Agnes, you know I do."

"Then you must answer a question, and you must answer it truthfully."

"All right."

Agnes squeezed Lorna's hands tighter. "Did you do with your

young boatbuilder what a bride does with her groom on her wedding night?"

Lorna's cheeks flared. Her gaze dropped to her lap as she answered in a guilty whisper, "Yes."

"Once?"

Again a whisper. "More than once."

"Have you missed any of your fluxes?"

"One."

Agnes whispered, "Dear God." Quickly, she took control of her emotions. "Then I suspect this isn't Addison's, but something even worse."

Lorna feared asking.

"Unless I miss my guess, you're in a family way, dear."

Lorna spoke not a word. Her hands slipped from Agnes's, and one rested on her heart. Her gaze turned toward the window and her lips formed a silent O. She had two thoughts: *Now they'll have to let me marry him,* and, *Jens will be so happy.*

Agnes rose and paced the room, pinching her mouth. "I must think."

Lorna murmured, "I'm going to have Jens's baby."

Agnes said, "The first thing we must do is find out if it's true, but I see no reason for your mother to know unless it is. So here's what we'll do. I shall find a doctor, perhaps one in Minneapolis who wouldn't know us, and I'll take you there myself. We'll tell your mother that you and I are going out for tea and shopping, and we'll take the train. Yes, that's it. We'll take the train. Listen, dearling, it'll take me some time to arrange, but I'll do so as quickly as possible. Meanwhile, eat lots of fruits and vegetables and drink milk if nothing else will stick with you."

"Yes, I will."

"I must say, you don't look as upset as most young girls in your predicament would be."

"Upset? But don't you see—they'll have to let me marry him now. Oh, Aunt Agnes, this is the answer to our prayers!"

Agnes cranked her face into a whorl of creases that could have meant a dozen different things. "I don't believe your mother will think so."

*   *   *

To Lorna's surprise, on the day they went to the doctor Aunt Agnes told a pack of lies worthy of a patent medicine salesman. First she made Lorna don her own engagement ring, which had not been off her finger since Captain Dearsley had put it there in 1845. Then, when arriving at the doctor's office, she gave her name as Agnes Henry, and Lorna's as Laura Arnett. When the doctor confirmed that Lorna was carrying a child who would be born probably next May or June, Agnes told him she was absolutely delighted because, as "Laura's" legal guardian, she considered the baby her first grandchild. Too, she confided that Lorna's husband would be in for the delight of his life, since the two of them had been trying for two years already, with no success till now. She paid the doctor in cash, thanked him with a smile and said they would be back in two months, as recommended.

Over lunch at Chamberlain's, Lorna remarked, "You surprise me, Aunt Agnes."

"Do I?" Agnes sipped her coffee with one finger raised, a faint tremble in her hand.

"Why did you do that?"

"Because your father is a wealthy socialite and the word would spread like wildfire if it got out. He and your mother would know before your lunch is digested . . . or thrown up, as the case may be."

Lorna's heart filled with love. "Thank you."

"You have a right to see your young man first, so the two of you can confront your parents together. If he loves you as you say, and if you have a solid plan to marry, your parents' shock might only last twenty-five years, instead of fifty. At least, if it had happened to me and Captain Dearsley, that's how I'd have wanted it to be."

Lorna's eyes glowed. "Oh, Aunt Agnes, I'm so happy. Imagine, I'm carrying his baby right now. I'm not looking forward to facing Mother and Father—that's bound to be a horrible scene—but once it's over, I'm sure they'll help us."

That night, when Agnes said her bedtime prayers, she included a very, very brief one of contrition for her lies, and a much longer one asking that for once in their lives her brother and his wife might put their daughter's feelings first, before considering the petty, snobbish reaction of their own social circle.

Chapter
TWELVE

AFTER the family left Rose Point
Cottage, it wore an abandoned
look, its windows covered from within, its verandas cleared of wicker,
gardens mulched for winter, docks drawn up onto the lawn and masts
gone from the lakeshore. Even more noticeable, the silence: no car-
riages coming and going, no doors slamming, fountains burbling, boat
whistles shrilling; no voices from the water or the croquet court or
the gardens. Only Smythe, puttering about his glasshouse, tipping
and burying the roses for winter and swaddling the berry canes in
warm wraps.

Jens saw the gardener occasionally through the trees, whose leaves
had fallen, the Englishman slightly stooped, wrapped in a muffler
over his black jacket. Sometimes the sound of wheels would carry
across the back lot as Smythe pushed his garden cart along the gravel
paths.

Mornings and evenings, Jens made the forty-minute walk to and
from the Hotel Leip, observing the shortening of days, noting the
frantic activity of the squirrels, the thickening of the morning frost,
adding a sweater beneath his jacket, heavier gloves on his hands. In
the boat shed he would build a fragrant fire of cedar scraps, and add
maple stovewood that burned slow and hot and made the air smell
like a smokehouse. On the fender of the stove he'd put a potato, and
eat it, piping, for his lunch, often studying the floor where the marks

from his lofting still outlined the spot where he and Lorna had picnicked during those days of first acquaintance. On the windowsill her delphinium remained—dry, crisp, but blue as the skies of summer that had watched them fall in love.

Tim came sometimes, bringing his pipe smoke and easy smile, taking a photograph or two, leaving the place lonelier than ever when he departed.

Jens completed the bottom of the boat, varnished and dried it, then began work on the interior structure. He laminated the center backbone, constructed two bilgeboards, put them in place and began the framework of the deck beams. Over it he nailed cedar planking, then once more spent time planing, sanding, fairing. Running his hands over the *Lorna D* he might have been running them over the woman herself, so vivid were his memories of touching her, loving her, rubbing her back in the suspended serenity of afterlove. Often, bending to his work, he reheard her words: *Watching you push that hand plane does things to my insides.* He would smile wistfully, recalling the day she'd said that, what she'd worn, how her hair was arranged, how she'd studied him while he worked, and described the clothes he'd worn one time while he was chipping ice. It had struck him fully that day—she really loved him. Why else would she have clung to such detailed memories of that inconsequential kitchen scene?

Fairing up the boat without her he felt a great, hollow loneliness inside.

Her letters said she missed him, that she felt ill from missing him, that all she needed was to see him again and her lethargy would vanish. *Let it be nothing more,* he thought, *nothing but loneliness.*

October waned and turned nasty. A rim of rime appeared at the edge of the lake and the first snow fell. The deck planking was complete and Jens needed a pair of extra hands to help him stretch a layer of canvas over it. He called upon Ben. One blustery day the two of them were working together in the cozy shed. The wood stove was stoked; the strong smell of paint and turpentine permeated the place. They had painted the deck to dripping wet and were stretching the canvas over the sticky paint, tacking it all around the outside edges.

Ben spit the last tack into his left hand and began hammering with his right. "So . . ." he said. "What do you hear from Lorna Barnett?"

Jens missed a beat with his hammer. "What makes you think I'd hear from Lorna Barnett?"

"Aw, come on, Jens. I'm not as ignorant as I might look. Ever since the family went back to town you've been gloomy as a November wake."

"It shows that much, then?"

"I don't know who else notices, but I sure do."

Jens stopped working and flexed his back. "She's a hard woman to forget, Ben."

"They usually are when you think you're in love."

"With us it's more than thinking."

Ben shook his head. "Then I pity you, you poor sap. I wouldn't be in your shoes for all the boats in the White Bear Yacht Club."

Ben's pessimism took hold of Jens. He grew silent and morose, wondering if he and Lorna were deceiving themselves, if they'd ever fight their way free of her parents' tentacles and actually get married. Suppose they did, would she be happy as the wife of a boatbuilder who could never give her the riches to which she was accustomed? Perhaps he'd be most kind to release her, send her back to DuVal, where she'd be assured of wealth, prestige and her parents' approval.

These black thoughts persisted, turning Jens wretched within himself. They robbed him of sleep at night and peace during the day, left him feeling fickle and unsteadfast, unworthy of Lorna's faithfulness, which rang forth clearly from her every letter.

He had reread those letters until he knew them by rote. He missed her, pined for her, needed a glimpse of her, a smile, a touch to see him through these times of separation and misgiving.

After the canvas was stretched and dried Jens worked alone applying the coaming around the cockpit: steaming it, clamping it on, tamping it into place with a mallet and securing it flush with the underdeck. He'd chosen the finest Honduran mahogany, as smooth beneath his fingertips as sterling silver, only warmer. Working it brought him great satisfaction, its grain close and its color warm as human blood. On a day in early November he was standing in the cockpit, a brace and bit in his hands, drilling a hole through the maroon wood when the hinges creaked and the door opened.

He swung around just as a blue coat and bonnet appeared. With her back to him, a woman closed and latched the cumbersome door.

"Lorna?" His heart burst into double time as she turned to face him. "Lorna!" He dropped the tool and vaulted over the side of the boat.

He ran.

She ran.

They collided off the starboard bow in a jubilant and frantic embrace. The impact swung them around, bruised their mouths, braided them into one. They drew back to see each other. "Sweet savior, you're here!" He grasped her head and stamped kisses everywhere, so untempered they bumped her about like a rough boat ride. His thumbs skewed her eyebrows as he kissed her mouth disbelievingly again and again.

"Jens . . . let me see you . . . Jens . . ." She took a turn beholding his face, touching it, exulting, "My love . . . my love . . ."

He held her fast against his body, nearly crushing her ribs. "Lorna, what are you doing here?"

"I had to see you. I simply couldn't wait another day."

"I think you saved my life." He closed his eyes and smelled her, ran his hands over her. She smiled and clung while they rocked from side to side.

"Where did you tell them you were going?"

"To Phoebe's."

"You took the train out?"

"Yes."

"How long can you stay?"

"Till three."

He withdrew a watch from his pocket—ten forty-five—and when he'd put it away, chuckled. "I'm still in shock. Let me see if you're real."

She was real, all right, and warm, and compliant as they kissed again, hoarding each other and making up for five weeks' separation. When the kisses ended her coat was unbuttoned and he was cupping her breasts through her thick winter suit.

"I missed you so much," she murmured.

"I missed you, too, like I hadn't imagined I could miss anyone." His eyes squeezed shut upon the memories of his weakheartedness.

How could he have believed for a moment that he could turn her away? Send her to another man?

She admitted unabashedly, "I missed your hands on me."

He drew back and adored her upturned face, too rapt for smiles. "Did you get my letters?" he asked.

"Yes. Did you get mine?"

"Yes, but I worried so. Are you all right now?"

"I'm fine. Really, I am. Come . . ." She took his hand and led him to the wrought-iron bench, which was pulled up near the stove. "I have something to tell you." They sat close, knees to the heat, holding hands like minuet dancers. She studied his knuckles as she told him calmly, quietly, "It seems, Jens, that I'm in a family way."

She felt his fingers go slack, then tense. "Oh, Lorna," he whispered. She watched his breath grow ragged, his face blanch, then he gripped her in an awkward embrace, their knees intruding. "Oh, Lorna, no." He swallowed convulsively against her ear.

"Aren't you happy?"

When he made no reply, terror swelled her chest.

"Jens . . . please . . ."

His death grip relaxed. "I'm sorry," he said in a raspy, terrified voice. "I'm sorry. I'm . . . I just . . . God in heaven . . . pregnant. Are you sure?"

She nodded, growing more fearful by the moment. She had expected reassurance. She had expected concern. She had expected a tender hug and a caring expression in his eyes while he said, "Don't worry, Lorna. Now we can get married."

She had not cried since hearing the news, but her tears threatened while he sat with a sickly expression on his face.

"Oh, Jens, say something. You're scaring me to death."

He set her back and held her by both arms. "I didn't want it to happen this way, not . . . not with you in disgrace. Do your parents know?"

"No."

"You're absolutely sure it's true?"

"Yes. I've seen a doctor. Aunt Agnes took me."

"When is it due?"

"May or June, he wasn't sure."

Jens rose and began pacing, his brow furled, his gaze distant. She grew more disillusioned with each step he took. The stove threw out cloying heat. The smell of paint and glue began making her dizzy. Sweat broke out beneath her arms and on the back of her neck. Fear congealed into one sickening lump that lay in her stomach like a helping of bad fish.

She took control of her emotions and ordered, "Stop that, Jens, and come here."

He spun in his tracks and halted.

"It never occurred to me to be scared . . . until now," she said, forcing calm into her voice.

His preoccupation vanished. He rushed to her and dropped down on one knee. "Forgive me. Oh, sweetheart, forgive me." He took her hands and kissed them in apology, leaning over her lap. "I didn't mean to scare you. It was the shock, that's all. . . . I'm trying to figure out what to do. Did you think I was wondering how to get rid of you? Never, Lorna, never. I love you. Now more than ever, but we have to do the right thing. We have to . . . Aw, Lorna, sweetheart, don't cry." He touched her face tenderly, swiping at her tears with a thumb. "Don't cry."

She lunged into his arms, another awkward embrace with Jens kneeling and she curling above him. "I haven't until now, honest, Jens, but you scared me so."

"I'm sorry, oh, darling girl, of course you were scared with me charging back and forth like a mad bull and not saying a thing about the baby. Our baby . . . Lord in heaven, it's hard to believe." He opened her coat and touched her stomach reverently. "Our baby . . . here, inside you."

She covered his hands with her own and felt their warmth seep through her clothing. "It's all right. You can't hurt anything."

He stretched his hands wider, staring at them and the flattened plaid wool of her suit jacket. He lifted his gaze to her face.

"Ours," he whispered.

She dropped her forehead to his and they both closed their eyes.

"You're not disappointed?" she whispered.

"Aw, girl, no. How can I be?"

"When I found out I said to Aunt Agnes right away, Jens will be so happy. Now they can't keep us apart."

He sat back on one heel and took both her hands. Earnestly, he said, "We must go to your parents and tell them immediately. This is their grandchild. Surely they'll give us their blessing when we tell them we love each other and want to get married right away. I'll find us a place out here—it'll be small, but inexpensive: So many places are empty for the winter, and in the spring my brother will come, and we'll open our boatworks immediately. Why wait for the regatta? The word about the *Lorna D* has spread, and there are plenty of yacht club members who'll be waiting in line to have me design a boat for them. We won't be rich, not at first, but I'll take care of you, Lorna, you and the baby, and we'll have a good life, I promise."

She cupped his face and smiled into his dear blue eyes.

"I know we will. And I don't need to be rich, and I don't need to have a fancy house. All I need, Jens Harken, is you."

They kissed with renewed tenderness, almost as if each was kissing their unborn child and sealing a pact with him. Jens drew Lorna to her feet and wrapped both arms around her. They stood a long time, peaceful, hopeful, embracing with their baby pressed firm against its father's belly.

"So tell me . . . just how have you been feeling?"

"Mostly tired."

"Are you eating properly?"

"As properly as I can. Meat makes me sick, though, even the smell of it."

"Fruits and vegetables?"

"Yes, they still taste good."

"Thank heavens for old Smythe and his glasshouse. I'd like to run and find him right now and tell him thank you."

Lorna smiled against his shoulder. "Oh, Jens, I love you."

"I love you, too."

"Do you suppose we'll have lots of babies?"

"I'm sure of it."

"What do you think this one will be?"

"A boy. A boatbuilder like his papa."

"Of course, how silly of me to ask."

"The second one can be a girl, though, a little dark-haired beauty like her mother, and after that I'd take a couple more boys, because by then the boatworks will be thriving, and someday we'll call it Harken and Sons."

She smiled again, imagining it and loving the image of her future life.

Finally Jens drew back. "Did you rent a coach to bring you out here from the depot?"

"Yes, but I dismissed him."

"How do you feel about a forty-minute walk in the snow?"

"With you? Foolish question."

"Then here's what I think we should do. We'll walk back to the Leip and you can wait in the lobby while I take a bath and change into my Sunday suit. Then we'll take the train into town together and we'll talk to your mother and father right away, tonight. Once we get that behind us I can begin making plans for where we'll live, and you can begin making plans for the wedding."

"What about money?"

"I've saved every penny I could since I've been here. I've got enough put by to see us through the winter, maybe even longer."

She didn't ask if any would be left to start his business: one giant step at a time.

They walked arm in arm through a day with a marbled sky of gray and white. What little snow had fallen resembled marbling, too, lying in veins of white upon the frozen tangle of spinach-colored grass beside the road. Some crows had spotted an owl and scolded it, circling a tree in the distance. A wagon came by, loaded with casks that resounded like timpani as they thumped against one another. The driver raised a red-mittened hand and received a wave in return. Where the road neared the lakeshore the wind became icier and bore the musty scent of muskrat houses and decaying cattails. Near town, the expensive hotels had traded their June resplendence for the bleaker aspect of winter, their abandoned park benches, gazebos and lawns mere reminders of the gayer season. At the Leip an American flag clapped in the wind, shortened by two twists around its standard. Inside, a black potbellied stove warmed the lobby, which was otherwise deserted. Jens took Lorna to a horsehair chair near the stove.

"Wait here. It won't take me long. I'll see if I can get you something hot to drink while you wait."

He went to the desk and rang the bell but nobody came. "Be right back," he told Lorna, and went into the kitchen, which was also abandoned. Winter board at the Leip included breakfast and supper: Now, at midday, no meals were in progress or promised. He opened a reservoir on the stove, found some lukewarm water inside and took a pailful with him on his way back through the lobby.

"I'm sorry, Lorna. Nobody's around."

"Oh, I'll be fine. It's warm here by the stove. Don't worry about me."

"If anyone comes, tell them you're waiting for me."

She smiled. "I will."

Nobody came. She read a newspaper during the thirty minutes Jens was gone. He reappeared, freshly shaved, dressed in his Sunday suit, a heavy wool coat and his black bowler.

"Let's go."

So formal. So somber. In keeping with their mission today.

On the train to Saint Paul they clasped hands on the seat beneath Lorna's coat but found little cheerful to say to each other. Outside, a wispy snow began and the countryside became pale, as if viewed through a bride's veil. They crossed a trestle over the Mississippi River and slowed beneath the wooden canopy of the downtown depot.

From the depot they rode a hansom cab to Summit Avenue, still clasping hands, Lorna's fingers curled over the edge of Jens's palm—tighter and tighter—while he smoothed them repeatedly as if to stroke away her mounting dread.

On Summit Avenue, as they approached the great gray hunk of stone where they would confront her parents, Lorna said, "No matter what happens in here tonight, I vow I will walk out of this house with you."

He kissed her mouth briefly as the horse's hooves came to a halt beneath the porte cochere. Lorna reached for her reticule, but he laid a hand on her arm. "You're my responsibility now. I'll pay."

He paid the cabbie while the horse shook its head and jingled its harness, then the rig pulled away, leaving them before the door with its bare-toothed gargoyles. Lorna refused to acknowledge them. She looked up at Jens instead.

"Mother will probably be in the drawing room, and Father doesn't get home until around six o'clock. I don't want to approach them till they're both here. Would you mind terribly waiting in the kitchen? I'll come for you as soon as Father is home."

Inside the massive entry hall their luck ran out. Just as they entered, Theron, believing himself alone, came sliding down the banister, his hand squealing on the polished wood. Lorna glanced balefully at Jens and decided in this case offense was the best defense. As her brother hurtled off the end of the railing and landed with a thud, she scolded in a whisper, "Theron Barnett!"

Theron spun around in surprise.

"Mother would blister your backside if she caught you doing that."

Theron covered his rear flank with joined hands. "You gonna tell?"

"I should but I won't—not if you don't tell on me."

"Why? What'd you do?"

"Sneaked out to see the boat."

"You did!" His eyes grew great. "How does she look?"

"Ask Mr. Harken."

"Oh, hi, Harken. Is the boat all done?"

"Just about. All but the hardware and rigging. Had to come in and talk to your father about those."

"He ain't here."

"He's not here," Lorna corrected.

"He's not here," Theron repeated.

"I know," Harken replied. "I'll just visit in the kitchen awhile, how's that?"

"Can I come with you?"

It took great effort for Jens to resist telegraphing a silent question to Lorna. Quickly he reasoned that if the boy was with him for an hour he wouldn't be in the drawing room reporting Jens Harken's presence to the mistress of the house.

"Sure, come on," he said, reaching for the lad's head, steering him ahead of himself. "I'll tell you all about the *Lorna D.*"

In the kitchen, Hulduh Schmitt looked up and threw both hands in the air. *"Mein Gott!"* she exclaimed, followed by a spate of German while she waddled across the floor and grasped Jens in a breasty hug. "What are you doing here, boy?"

"Reporting to Mr. Barnett on the progress of the boat."

Everyone accepted his explanation. The kitchen maids came to say hello, Ruby hanging back coyly to be the last and offer an especially personal smile of welcome, which left Jens wondering how it was possible he'd ever found her attractive enough to kiss. He shook hands with his stand-in, a flat-faced fellow named Lowell Hugo, whose breath stank of garlic. To celebrate Jens's visit, Mrs. Schmitt authorized the tapping of a precious gallon bottle of last summer's homemade root beer, and they sat around the center worktable taking a rare fifteen minutes from their duties to visit and ask dozens of questions about the boat, and its prospects for winning, and Jens's plans if it did, and his lodging out at White Bear, and if he'd seen Smythe, and how the gardener was faring, and if the old Englishman was as irascible as ever.

After forty-five minutes, when Jens was beginning to worry about Theron's continued presence, the children's maid, Ernesta, came sweeping in, breathless and distraught. "Oh, there you are, bothering the kitchen help again! Your mother will be coming up to your room any minute to inspect your schoolwork and if you know what's good for you, you'll be there!"

Off Theron went, with Ernesta's fingers prodding the back of his neck.

Shortly after six P.M. Lorna appeared, wearing a form-fitting dress of forest green taffeta with an ivory collar and cuffs, her hair freshly combed and her cheeks unnaturally pink.

"Harken," she said formally, "my father would like to see you now."

"Ah . . ." He left his chair. "Very well, Miss Barnett."

She turned her back on him. "Follow me."

He did precisely as ordered, three steps behind her whispering taffeta that seemed to resound through the granite foyer like the rising of an entire church congregation at the entrance of the minister. Someone was playing the piano in the music room. As they passed its open doorway, Daphne looked up from the sheet music, and the two aunts from their tatting, but Lorna kept her eyes straight ahead on the doorway of the library. As luck would have it, Jenny happened along the upper hall at that moment and paused at the head of the stairs to watch in surprise the two passing below.

Lorna fixed her eyes on the library entrance and led Jens to it. Inside, Gideon Barnett sat in a brown leather wing chair with his knees crossed, holding a cigar between his teeth and a newspaper on his lap. The room smelled of burning things: the expensive tobacco, the birch in the fireplace and illuminating gas—faintly sooty. It held hundreds of leather-bound volumes reaching clear to the ceiling, with its ornate molding, center medallion and five-globe chandelier. On the table beside Gideon another single gas globe illuminated his newspaper. On the wall above a hide settee a mounted stag head held two guns across its antlers.

Gideon's gaze shot up the moment Lorna and Jens paused in the doorway.

"Hello, Father."

He removed the cigar from his mouth in slow motion, making no reply. His eyes flicked from Jens to Lorna.

"Where is Mother?" she asked.

"Upstairs with the boy." The boy was Theron.

"I thought she'd be down by now."

Barnett's stare became riveted on Harken. He pointed with the wet end of his cigar. "What's he doing here?"

"I invited him. We need to speak to you and Mother."

"You *invited* him?" Finally Gideon's attention snapped to Lorna. His eyes bulged and his color began to rise. "What do you mean, you *invited* him?"

"Please lower your voice, Father." Lorna turned and said to Jens, "Wait right here. I'll go find Mother."

Halfway up the stairs, Lorna met Levinia coming down. The older woman's face was ruched with worry. She descended hurriedly, clutching her skirts in one hand and the handrail in the other. "What's wrong? Jenny said that boatbuilder is down here with you."

"Could we talk in the library, Mother?"

"Oh dear," Levinia's voice trembled and her breasts bounced as she hastened after her daughter. Once again Lorna caught a glimpse of Jenny at the top of the stairs but chose to ignore her.

In the library, Gideon was on his feet, pouring himself a bourbon from a crystal decanter. Jens waited where Lorna had left him. Levinia circled wide around her ex–kitchen helper, as if he were someone brought in off the streets and not yet deloused.

"Gideon, what is it?"

"Deuced if I know."

Lorna closed the pocket doors to the hall. To her right, a second set of pocket doors—closed—led to the adjacent music room, where the piano music had stopped. She experienced a moment of grave doubt: Her father would soon be shouting while the remainder of the family would likely be poised beyond those doors, bent forward at the waist.

She stationed herself beside Jens. "Mother, Father, would you both please sit down?"

"Like hell I will," Gideon rumbled. "I sense disaster here, and I always meet disasters on my feet. Now get on with it, whatever it is."

Lorna looped her hand loosely through Jens's arm.

"Jens and I would very much like—"

Jens pressed her fingers to silence her. Then he took over.

"Mr. and Mrs. Barnett, I know it will come as a surprise to you, but I've come here to tell you that I have fallen most deeply in love with your daughter and I respectfully ask your permission to marry her."

Levinia's mouth fell open.

Gideon's expression turned thunderous. "You've what!" he bellowed.

"Your daughter and I—"

"Why, you impertinent young whelp!"

"Father, it isn't only Jens asking, it's me, too."

"You shut your mouth, young woman! I'll deal with you later!"

"I love him, Father, and he loves me."

"The kitchen handyman! Jesus Christ, have you lost your mind!"

In the music room Aunt Agnes began playing "Witch's Revel" in fortissimo: Lorna recognized her missed notes and deplorable technique.

"Oh, Lorna," Levinia moaned. "Is this why you threw Taylor aside?"

"I know all the arguments you two are going to give me, but none of them matter. I love Jens and I want to marry him."

"And live on what? Where?" Gideon shot back. "On a handyman's salary in his bedroom on the third floor? Wouldn't that look just ducky? Is that where all our friends should come to call on you for afternoon tea?"

"We'll live in White Bear Lake, and Jens intends to open up a boatworks there."

"Don't you mention the word boat to me!" Gideon roared, his face rubicund and trembling. "All this started because of that boat, and *you* . . ." He stabbed a finger at Jens. "You underhanded sonofabitch! Sweet-talking my daughter while I gave you advantages I wouldn't have *dreamed* of giving anyone else! Why, I wouldn't let her marry you if you were Christopher Columbus himself!"

Levinia touched her lips and wailed, "Oh, I knew something was wrong. I just knew it. So many times I tried to find you and couldn't—you were out there in that boat shed with him, weren't you?"

"Yes," Lorna replied, still pressed to Jens's sleeve. "I spent a lot of time with Jens last summer. I got to know him as well as any friend I've ever had—better. He's honest, and brilliant, and hard-working and kind, and he loves—"

"Oh, stop . . ." Gideon pulled a disgusted face. "You're making me sick."

"I'm sorry to hear that, Father. I should think it would matter a great deal to you that the man your daughter wants to marry is one she loves very much, and who loves her equally as much."

"Well, it doesn't! What matters is that you're not marrying any kitchen handyman, and that's final!"

Jens spoke up, moving behind Lorna and resting his hands on her shoulders. "Not even if she's carrying his baby, sir?"

Gideon reacted as if he'd been poleaxed. Levinia covered her mouth and let out a squeak. Beyond the wall a tortured "Witch's Revel" still clanked.

"My God in heaven," Gideon finally breathed, his color receding. Then to Lorna, "Is it true?"

"Yes, Father, it is. I'm carrying your grandchild."

For a moment Gideon appeared defeated. The starch left him and his shoulders slumped. He ran a hand through his hair and began pacing. "Never in my worst nightmares did I imagine one of my daughters shaming us this way! Sinning with a man . . . laying with him and baldly admitting it! Don't you ever call the spawn of your sin my grandchild! Dear God, we'll be outcasts!"

Levinia's knees buckled and she wilted to a wing chair. "Lord have mercy, the disgrace. What will I tell my friends? How shall I ever again hold my head up in public? And you—don't you realize decent people will shun you after this? They'll shun our whole family."

"Mother, you're overdramatizing."

Gideon recovered first. His shoulders squared, his fists clenched and the color returned to his face. "Take her upstairs," he ordered his wife.

"Father, please, we came here honorably to speak to—"

"Take her upstairs, Levinia, and lock her in her room! Harken, you're fired."

"Fired—but—"

"Father, you can't do that! We came to you for help and instead you—"

"Levinia, take her upstairs!" Gideon roared. "And lock her in her room, where her brother and sisters cannot see her or speak to her. Harken, I want you out of my sight before I count to three, or so help me God, I'll take the gun from that rack on the wall and kill you where you stand."

Levinia, becoming terrified, caught hold of Lorna's arm. Lorna struggled free. "Father, I love this man. I'm going to have his baby, and no matter what you say, it's my right to marry him!"

"Don't you speak to me of rights! Not after you've lain with him like some . . . some common slut! You gave up all your rights when you did that—the right to this family, to this house, to my support and your mother's concern. Now you'll live without all that and see how you like it! And you'll start by going upstairs without a whimper, because, by the Almighty, if your sisters get wind of this disgrace you've brought upon us, I'll take it out on your hide, pregnant or not! Now go!"

"No, Father, I will not," she replied defiantly, moving closer to Jens, finding his hand.

"By the devil, you will!" Gideon raged. "Levinia, take her this moment!"

Levinia clutched Lorna's arm. "Upstairs!" she ordered.

"No, you can't make me! Jens . . ." She was crying, reaching for Jens with one outstretched arm while Levinia dragged her away by the other. "Lorna . . ." He caught her hand.

Gideon barked, "Get your hands off her, you filthy swine. You've touched her all you're ever going to! I want you out of my house and off my property, and if you ever try putting foot anywhere on it again I'll have the law on you, and don't think I haven't got the connections to do it!"

"No! Jens, take me with you," Lorna pleaded.

Levinia tried force once again. "Girl, don't you defy your father!"

Lorna swung around and gave her Mother a shove. "Leave me alone, I don't have t—" Levinia stumbled back against a chair leg and nearly fell. Her hair jounced to one side and sat off center.

Gideon stormed across the room and struck Lorna once. The blow snapped her head to the side and left her cheek red, her eyes wide and stunned.

"You will go with your mother at once!" he roared.

She gaped at him through shimmering tears, pressing a palm to her cheek.

"Why, you bastard!" Jens lunged and grabbed Gideon's coat front. "You'd strike your own daughter!" He shoved the older man into an upholstered chair with enough force to teeter it backward. Gideon rebounded in one motion, coming at Jens with furor and fists.

"You filthy low-life scum! You got my daughter pregnant!"

"And I'll kill you if you touch her again!"

The two were ready for mortal combat when Levinia's voice called for common sense.

"Stop it! Stop it, everyone! Listen to me, Lorna..." She swung nose to nose with her daughter. "See what this has started already? Fisticuffs, enmity, rage. And you're at fault! You, who were taught right from wrong from the time you were in pinafores. Whether or not you see this as a disgrace, it is. You think you can walk out of here with him and everything will be all right! Well, it won't be! You have two fine and unsoiled young sisters but what you've done will reflect on them the moment you leave this house. It will reflect on us. They will have no suitors and we will have no invitations. Our friends will titter behind their hands and blame us for what you've done. We'll be disgraced right along with you because good girls simply don't perform the sinful act it took to get you in this condition! You don't seem to realize that. It's sinful! Shameful! Only the lowest creatures disgrace themselves as you have."

Lorna had dropped her chin and was staring at the carpet through her tears. Levinia went on pressing her advantage.

"What shall I say to your friends? To Taylor and Phoebe and Sissy and Mitchell? Shall I say to them Lorna went off to marry the kitchen helper whose bastard she's carrying? Don't fool yourself for a moment that they won't be shocked. They will be, and their parents shall forbid them to keep company with you, just as I would if it were one of them who were in this trouble."

In a cool, controlled tone, Levinia reiterated, "This is a bastard you're carrying, Lorna. A bastard. Think about that. Think about all it implies and if you want your child to go through life carrying that label of disgrace, for he will be disgraced time and again if you keep him."

The room had grown silent. Jens retained a light hold on Lorna's arm. "Lorna . . ." he said softly, uncertain of what to do.

Levinia said, "I'm asking you to be sensible. To go upstairs and give your father and me time to discuss this situation, to decide what is best for all concerned."

Lorna lifted her brimming eyes to the man she loved. "Jens," she whispered brokenly, "m . . . maybe . . ."

He held her wrist with one hand and rubbed her elbow with the other, up and down, up and down while their eyes remained locked in a sad soliloquy of silence.

"Maybe we all need to . . . to think things through," she whispered. "I'm going to need their help as well as yours in the months ahead. Maybe I should . . . should go with my mother now."

He swallowed once. His Adam's apple made a slow rise and fall. "All right," he whispered. "If that's what you want."

"It isn't what I want. It's what's wisest."

He nodded, dropping his eyes to her sleeve because they were at last filling with tears.

"I'll see you soon. I'll find you," she said.

He nodded again, drew her to him by both arms and kissed her cheek.

"I love you, Lorna," he whispered. "I'm sorry this had to happen."

"It'll be all right," she replied. "I love you, too."

They stood in a tiny universe of their own until Gideon straightened his clothes, moved to the hall door and wordlessly rolled it open.

He stood back while Lorna submitted to her mother's guiding hand and allowed herself to be ushered from the room. Just before they reached the doorway Levinia ordered in an undertone, "Get rid of those tears."

From somewhere deep within, Lorna found the gumption to do as ordered. She sniffed and dried her face with the backs of her hands as she walked into the hall and encountered her sisters and brother, wide-eyed, hovering near the newel post, and Aunt Henrietta lingering in the door to the music room, where, at the piano, Aunt Agnes had finally desisted and quit trying to cover the sound of the squabble with her terrible playing.

Levinia feigned a put-upon air. "All this fuss over sailing, if you can imagine. Honestly, who ever heard of a woman in a regatta anyway?"

Lorna marched past her siblings without meeting their glances, conscious of Jenny's gaze assessing her wet eyelashes and the dark tear splotches on her taffeta dress. Behind her she heard murmured goodbyes and knew Jens was leaving. She heard the outer door opening and closing and fortified herself with the silent promise that nothing could keep them apart as long as they loved each other.

In her bedroom Lorna moved stiffly to her bed and sat down, staring at an eye-level flower on the wallpaper. Levinia closed the door, dropping darkness upon them, making no move to light the lamp beside Lorna's bed.

She spoke with absolute authority. "I'm not going to lock you in. I know I don't have to, because you'll wait here until your father and I have had a chance to talk. Don't speak to anyone, do you understand?"

"Yes, Mother," Lorna answered dully.

"And don't even think about running away with that . . . that penniless, uncouth *immigrant!*"

"No, Mother."

Silence awhile before Levinia disparaged, "Well, I hope you're satisfied with yourself. Some example you've set for your sisters to follow, isn't it?"

Lorna made no reply. She kept thinking of the word *bastard* and wondering if it was true that her sisters would be shunned by all the young men they knew.

"If word of this leaks out, no decent man will ever speak to you again, to say nothing of marrying you. Women who fornicate give up all chances of that. God forgive you, I don't know how you could do such a filthy, base thing. Your father and I will never be able to hold up our heads in polite society again. You've sullied the name of this entire family, and I must say, the shock is probably going to be more than I can stand. But I shall bear up—I swear I shall—until we can think of what to do about this sorry state of affairs. Now you wait here like your father ordered, young miss, is that understood?"

"Yes, Mother."

The door closed behind Levinia and her footsteps faded down the hall. Lorna sat motionless in the dark, both hands wrapped around her unborn child, wondering where its father would go, what he would do, and when she would see him again.

Chapter
THIRTEEN

THE train ride home found Jens tormented for having left Lorna. But what else could he have done? The almighty Gideon Barnett! Jens should have known better than to trust the man to react sympathetically to any plea for understanding. He should have taken Lorna and married her and told her parents afterward!

The fact remained he had not. He'd done the forthright, the honorable thing. With these disastrous results.

What should he do next? Storm the house? Abduct his bride? Elope with her? Confront Barnett and beat the hell out of him? (How satisfying that would be.)

The fact was, Jens Harken had no idea what to do next, so he went back to the Hotel Leip to lie awake until well after four A.M. and gnash his teeth about it.

In the morning he'd made two decisions: to remove his boat mold from Gideon Barnett's shed, and to speak to Tim Iversen about storing it at his place. He washed, dressed and went downstairs for breakfast, only to receive the news that if he was to eat, he'd pay for it himself: Gideon Barnett had already slammed the door on any further financial subsistence.

He ate, paid and took the train back to Saint Paul. From the depot he walked to Iversen's photographic studio on West Third Street. Though visiting it for the first time, he found it with no difficulty and entered to discover the place looked as much like a greenhouse as a photo studio. Plants flourished everywhere: filling the box window facing the street, in pots on the floor, in fern stands at the rear. Geraniums bloomed, violets rioted, potted trees thrived and ferns cascaded. Amongst these, George Eastman's patented Kodak cameras were offered for sale in a glass case while at the far end of the room, against a curtained wall, small furniture awaited subjects for the next picture. Near the front window, Iversen himself toyed with a stereo camera containing two lenses set three inches apart.

He craned around—sharply, to accommodate his single eye—at the sound of the bell on the door. Immediately he smiled, came forward and took the cold pipe from his mouth.

"Well, if it isn't my friend Harken. What in blazes are you doing here? Did you lose your boat?"

"As a matter of fact, I did. That's what I came to talk to you about."

"This sounds dour. What's happened? Come here . . . come, come . . . take your coat off and warm up by the stove."

Removing his coat, Jens followed Tim to an oval heater stove against the west wall of the room. Tim poured a cup of coffee and scraped two chairs forward.

"Well, I might as well give it to you straight," Jens said, accepting the cup and seating himself. "Barnett gave me the sack and the boat along with me."

Tim paused in the act of filling his pipe. "You don't say. What got into him?"

"I asked his permission to marry his daughter."

Tim's one good eye settled on Jens and probed while he struck a match, puffed, blew a cloud of fragrant smoke and waved out the flame.

"Aye, I can see how a request like that would set Gid off. He's stopped progress on the *Lorna D*, you say?"

"Yup. He wants me off his property for good, says if I put foot on it ever again he'll sic the law on me. Well, I got off, but I won't leave my boat mold behind. I paid for the materials to make it and he agreed that it would be mine once the *Lorna D* was finished. My only problem now is finding a place to store it. I came to ask if I could put it in your cabin till I can find a place of my own."

"I don't see why not. It's not being used for anything else right now."

"Thanks, Tim."

"And what about you? I don't imagine Gid is footing the bill for you up at the Leip anymore either."

"Nope. He cut me off before I could get down to breakfast this morning. Must've sent a telegram to get word there that fast."

"So what are you going to do?"

"I don't know. I'm not broke, but the money I've saved I intended to use to open my own boatworks. My plan was to wait until after next year's big regatta, but it looks as though I don't have much choice. I'll have to start my business now."

Tim grinned with the right side of his mouth and his one good eye. "Sometimes it takes adversity to spur a man to action. So what about Lorna? You still intend to marry her?"

"You bet I do. Nobody's going to take her away from me. Nobody!"

Tim crossed his arms, stuck the pipe back in his mouth and said around its stem, "It's odd, but I feel partially responsible for your predicament."

"You?"

"I saw what was happening between you and Lorna and I abetted it more than once."

"It would have happened with or without the picnic at your place. Lorna and me . . . well, it's strong between us, Tim, real strong. As if fate planned us to be together. And we will be, but first I've got to get established as a boatbuilder. I figure old man Barnett didn't do me so bad after all. There's been so much talk about the *Lorna D* that everyone in White Bear Lake knows my name by now. I've got about four hundred and twenty dollars of my own, and the rest I'll get a bank loan for. I should be able to find somebody willing to take a risk on me. One more favor I need to ask of you—could I have just one or two good photographs you took of the boat last time? I might not have much money to put up, but I've got a good head, and damned good boat sense, and when I show those photographs to a banker, he'll see for himself that I'm a good risk."

"One or two good photographs, huh?" Tim puffed on his pipe,

striping the air with wispy gray fragrance. He puffed and thought, and thought and puffed, and finally said, "Come over here."

He led Jens to the camera he'd been puttering with near the front window. "See this?" He placed his hand affectionately atop the black box, which stood on a shoulder-high tripod. "You might say this is my *Lorna D.*" He gestured to include the rest of the shop. "All of that—portraits—that's what I do out of obligation. This is what I do out of love. Travel the world taking my stereo camera with me, capturing all the places the ordinary man can never see any other way than in his living room looking through his stereoscopic viewer. Did you know I've been to the Klondike? Imagine that. And Mexico and Palestine and the Chicago World's Fair two years ago. Next week I'm leaving for Sweden and Norway, then at the end of the winter I'll be in Italy and Greece. And from all those places I'll bring home my little twin pictures, and do you know what I'll do with them? I'll not only sell them here, I've got a contingent of salesmen who are making me money all over the United States selling them door-to-door, to say nothing of Sears and Roebuck mail-order catalogues. I'm a rich man, Jens, as you've probably guessed. But I've got no wife, no family, nobody to spend all that wealth on." Tim paused for a breath.

"Now you come along. And I think you're a damned smart man who's designed a damned smart boat that's going to show a few of my good friends they should have paid attention to you when you asked them to. You need backing. I have money. So here's what I propose.

"You go ahead and take your mold out of Barnett's shed, but don't leave it in my cabin for long. The cabin, by the way, is yours until next spring, when I come back from my travels. It's colder than the devil—you'll be growing a beard to keep your face warm at night— but you can hug the stove when you have to, and cook your own meals, and pump your own water, and what more does a man need? When I get back in the spring I'll want it back—without a bunkmate, thank you.

"Meanwhile, find a decent building for the Harken Boatworks— rent one, buy one, whichever you prefer—and put your mold to work. You invest three hundred dollars, and I'll invest the rest and you start building those squashed cigars with sails and I suspect within two years—one, maybe—you'll have the busiest boatworks in the state of Minnesota. We'll set it up so that when you begin making a profit you can either buy me out or pay me back, with a little interest for my trouble. Now, what do you think about that?"

Flabbergasted, Jens only stared at his friend.

"Well, say something," Tim said.

"I can't. I'm speechless."

Tim chuckled deep in his throat, went to the stove, removed a lid and rapped out the dottle from his pipe, then slipped the pipe into his pocket. Turning back to Jens, he wore the smile of a man who enjoys seeing others thunderstruck. "Well, what do you think, mister boatbuilder? Shall I set up a bank account for you?"

"You'd do that? You'd do everything for me?"

"Mmm . . . not quite everything. I can't get your girl back for you. You're going to have to do that yourself."

"The hell you can't. This will do it! Don't you see? All I needed was a way to support her, and you're giving me that."

"Don't underestimate her father, Jens. You'll play billy hell trying to change his mind, even if you become as rich as Barnett himself, because he grew up rich, you see. You were beneath him when he met you, and beneath him you'll remain. No, I wouldn't plan on marrying his daughter unless you do it against his wishes, and that could be disastrous for your business. His best friends will be your best customers."

"What about you? You're his friend. Don't you fear his retribution?"

"Not particularly. I, too, grew up poor, and I don't want to marry one of his daughters. If he snubs me, I can tolerate that. As for my business—well, I just got done telling you I have the support of Sears and Roebuck, as well as my friend George Eastman, whose cameras I sell exclusively in Minnesota. Sure, word will get around the yacht club circle that I backed your business, but if there's one thing that crowd respects it's people who know how to make money. When they see your enterprise succeed, they'll congratulate us both."

"All but Gideon Barnett," Jens concluded.

"All but Gideon Barnett."

On that doomful note, their discussion ended, yet in spite of it Jens felt borne by hope. What a friend he'd found in Tim Iversen. What a genuine, good, foresighted man. Jens found himself overcome with gratitude. He felt the way a parent feels when another has saved the life of his child: No thanks are adequate. He attempted them none-theless, clasping Tim affectionately while bidding goodbye.

"I cannot thank you enough. You're a good, good friend and I will make you happy you took a chance on me. I'll work hard to make my boatworks succeed. You'll see."

"You don't have to tell me that. I know a man with a dream when I see one, and they're the best kind, the wisest ones to invest in. I know, because I was one myself and someone helped me. Old feller name of Emil Zehring, who was a friend of my dad's. He's dead now, so the only way to repay him is to pass on the tradition, which I hope you'll do one day, too, when someone younger and needier than yourself needs a boost."

"I will. I promise."

"Well then, what are you waiting for? Go! Get that boatworks started so I can get my money back!"

Leaving Tim's, Jens found himself smiling. Yes, his life had taken on new promise. All would be perfect, if only he could marry Lorna. He had no delusions, however, about the welcome he'd get if he went to the door with the gargoyles and asked to see her. Instead, he decided to write to her with his good news, sending the letter through Phoebe, as earlier agreed, and set up a secret meeting.

That night he wrote:

Darling Lorna,

So much has happened since I saw you twenty-four hours ago. I hardly know where to begin. First, let me tell you I love you and that our future looks rosier than ever before. Last night was the worst day of my life—yours, too, I think—but we cannot let it deter us, especially after what happened today.

I went to see Tim, and unbelievable as it seems, he's going to set me up in business. I'm writing this from his cabin. Not only has he given me the use of it for the winter, he's putting up whatever money I need to start the boatworks. I've already walked the length and breadth of White Bear Lake searching for an empty building that would do, but everything is filled up with boats in winter storage. So I've found a lot that's for sale and tomorrow Tim is coming out to look at it and if he likes it, we'll build a new building on it that will be the home of Harken Boatworks. It's not far from Tim's cabin, between it and the yacht club, on a nice stretch of land that will need a little clearing first, but I don't mind that. I've got a strong back and a good axe, and that's all a Norwegian needs to survive. I've decided to build the place myself and save all that labor cost. Ben is going to help me, as the lumberyard in town has laid him off until spring. Another piece of good news is that Ben has found a sawmill we can use to make our own boards, so we'll save on lumber costs, too. It will be a lot of work but I don't mind. By spring the building will be up and ready well before the baby comes, so that by the time he gets here I'll be an official boat-builder. What do you think about that?

I guess you can tell I'm pretty excited.

Everything we want is going to come true. The only hard part will be that we'll have to get married without your mother and father knowing. Lorna, it broke my heart to see her herding you out of the room like some criminal. For me, getting shouted at and called names didn't hurt near as bad as watching you get treated that way. I see that I was wrong in guessing they'd treat us kindly when they found out about the baby, so we'll never do that again. From now on, all our plans will be secret. Now, Lorna, sweets, we're going to have to meet so that we can make some arrangements. I've thought a lot about it today, and I think that what you should do is come out on the 10:30 A.M. train next Friday. Buy a ticket for Stillwater instead of White Bear Lake. Too many people know you in this town, and I don't want your father getting wind of this. When you get to White Bear, I'll board the train and we'll go on together to Stillwater to the courthouse there, and get our marriage license. Stillwater's got so many churches we can pick which one we want to get married in, and afterwards we can live at Tim's for the winter, then in spring, when the boatworks is done, it'll have a loft we can use for our home until we get on our feet and can afford to build a real house somewhere. I know it's a big step down for you, living in a log cabin and a loft above a boatworks, but it won't be forever. I'll work harder than you ever saw a man work, to get you the kind of things you deserve, sweetheart, and someday your dad will eat his words.

I just read what I wrote and on second thought maybe we better make it next week Tuesday when you come out on the train, to give this letter time to reach Phoebe and Phoebe time to get it to your place and you time to get some excuses dreamt up for leaving the house.

Well, Lorna Diane, that's what we're going to do. I hope my plans are all right with you. We're going to be so happy. I love you so much, darling girl, and our baby, too. Give the little feller a pat on the head and tell him it's from his papa and that in my spare time this winter I'll be making him a cradle with wood from our own land (at least it will be someday).

Now, don't be sad. Smile and think of me and of next week when we'll be Mr. and Mrs. Jens Harken.

> Your loving future husband,
> Jens

He posted the letter the following day and went ahead with his plans. Tim thought the lot looked fine. It had some good trees on it that could be harvested and it was close to his cabin, so he could check on his investment readily come spring, when it was open for business.

They bought it.

Jens rented a freight wagon and went out to the boat shed at Rose Point to get his molds. Finding the door already padlocked, he broke the lock, took what was his and left with only one regret: that he'd never get the chance to finish the *Lorna D,* which looked forlorn in the shadows of the sprawling old shed that had already begun to smell stale from disuse. One last time he laid a hand on the boat's flaring side and said, "Sorry, old girl. Maybe I'll see you on the water sometime."

Out at Tim's, he hauled his precious mold inside the cabin—contrary to Tim's suggestion—and leaned the pieces against the wall of the main room, where they were out of the weather and he could look at them nights and picture the boats that would someday be formed around them.

At the new land, he and Ben set up a sawmill and began felling trees. They rented a pair of big, muscular Percherons from a nearby farmer and set to work making lumber, much to the delight of both men: two young Norwegians with the tang of new-cut wood in their nostrils, and sawdust on their boots, and horses to talk to.

Jens thought a man would have to be in heaven itself to be any happier.

On Tuesday he arose early, heated water and washed his flannel bedsheets and hung them over the boat molds to dry. He heated a second batch of water and bathed every inch of his hide, put on clean woolen underwear, his Sunday suit, a warm jacket and a cap with earlaps and walked four miles into town to meet the ten-thirty train.

He waited as it pulled in, his heart lifting half his gullet into his throat with each beat. While the train slowed, he shifted from left foot to right, right to left, scrunching his cold hands into fists inside his mittens and curling his cardboard train ticket in his palm. He watched the coach windows pass, searching them for Lorna's smile and wave, wondering which car she'd be on.

When the air brakes hissed and the couplings clanked, and with the depot platform vibrating beneath his feet, he waited where he was, expecting her to appear on the steps of one of the last cars and wave him in.

He waited and waited. Three passengers got off. The porter removed their luggage from the train and they carried it away. The station agent came out with a pouch of mail and stood a moment in friendly conversation with the porter. Up ahead, the steam whistle wailed and the porter called, " 'Boooooard!" then bent to pick up his portable step.

Jens shouted, "Just a minute! I'm boarding!"

He ran and mounted the steps in two leaps, his heart banging hard. The first car turned up no Lorna. As he entered the second, the whistle sounded and the train began moving, rocking him back on his heels. He clutched a seatback and waited out the momentum, then proceeded into the next car and the next, his dread growing with each passing seat. When he reached the coal car, he turned around and backtracked, clear to the caboose, getting his ticket punched midway.

Lorna was nowhere on board.

They were a third of the way to Stillwater by the time he sank into a seat and gave in to the trembling fear in his stomach. He sat staring out the window, swaying listlessly while the half-snowy November landscape swept by the window. At crossings, the train whistle would keen. A woman across the aisle from him asked if he was all right, but he didn't hear her. He saw a fox once, running along on a distant hillside with its tail straight out behind itself, but the animal failed to register as Jens stared and stared and wondered and wondered.

At Stillwater he went into the station and purchased a ticket for Saint Paul, then sat beside a hot iron stove, too preoccupied to realize he was sweating inside his warm winter outerwear. The inbound train came through shortly after noon. By one forty-five P.M., he was standing on the sidewalk before Gideon Barnett's house on Summit Avenue, glancing from the servants' entrance to the front one, wondering which was best to take. If he went in through the kitchen he'd surely get questioned by his friends, and he was in no mood to pretend blitheness.

He chose the front entry and raised a hand to the bronze gargoyle knocker with its bared canine teeth.

The door was answered by Jeannette, one of the downstairs maids, whom he recognized.

"Hello, Jeannette," he said. "I've come to speak to Miss Lorna. Would you mind going to get her for me?"

Jeannette, never cordial to him, was even less so today. Her mouth pursed. She held the door open so narrowly only one of her eyes showed.

"Miss Lorna is gone."

"Gone! Where?"

"I'm not at liberty to say, nor to allow you inside. Word's come down."

"But where is she?"

"Off to school somewhere, that's all we heard, and as you know, it's not our place to ask questions."

"School—in the middle of November?"

"As I said, it's not our place to question."

"But, doesn't anybody know?"

"None of the help, no."

"How about Ernesta, she must know. She's Lorna's maid."

Jeannette's single visible eyebrow quirked superciliously.

"The young miss is gone, I said, and Ernesta don't know no more than I do. Good day, Harken."

She shut the door in his face.

Feeling as if he were moving through a nightmare, he went around to the kitchen door. It was half below ground level, down a set of concrete steps.

Mrs. Schmitt said, "Oh, it's you again."

He minced no words. "Do you know where Miss Lorna is?"

"Me? Ha."

"Do you know when she left?"

"How would I know—the cook who never sees nothing but these four kitchen walls."

"Ask the others—somebody must know."

"Ask them yourself."

He was just about to do so when from the opposite side of the kitchen a door opened and Levinia Barnett flew inside, obviously informed by Jeannette of Jens's presence. She crossed straight to him and pointed out the door. "You've been dismissed, Harken. Now get out of my kitchen and quit slowing down my staff."

Jens Harken had been pushed to his limits. He'd been denigrated, shouted at, called names, turned out, treated like tripe. And now this woman—this detestable, manipulative, insufferable witch—was withholding from him the whereabouts of the woman who was carrying his child.

He grabbed Levinia Barnett's wrist and hauled her outside through the servants' entry. She let out a yelp and began swatting and clawing at his face. "Let me go! Let me go!" He slammed the door while she screeched, "Help! My God, somebody help me!" He crossed her forearms and shoved them hard against her breasts, flattening her against a concrete wall. Her silk dress caught on the concrete and pinioned her against it like a thousand porcupine quills.

"Where is she?" Jens barked. "Tell me!"

Levinia screamed again. He pushed her harder against the wall. One of her sleeve seams ripped. Her screaming stopped and her eyes bulged. Her skinny lips flopped open in fear.

"Listen to me, and listen good!" He loosened his hold. "I don't want to hurt you. I've never manhandled a woman in my life, but I love your daughter. That's my baby she's carrying. When I—"

The kitchen door opened and the new man, Lowell Hugo, stood there bug-eyed and going about a hundred and thirty pounds. Jens could have driven him into the ground like a tent stake with one bong on his pointy little head.

"Let her go!" Hugo demanded in a wimpy voice.

"Get back in there and shut the door!" Jens put one hand on Hugo's chest and shoved him six feet into the kitchen. Hugo tripped on the threshold and fell on his rump.

Jens dragged Levinia Barnett along the wall and slammed the door himself.

"Now listen and listen good! I'm not a violent man, but when you take away Lorna and my baby, I fight back. I love her. She loves me. You don't seem to understand that. Now, one way or another we're going to find each other, and if you don't think she'll be looking for me as hard as I'm looking for her, you don't know your daughter very well. So you can give your husband this message—Jens Harken was here, and he'll be back. As many times as it takes until I find his daughter." He released her cautiously, taking one step backward. "I'm sorry about your dress."

Levinia Barnett had gone so limp with fright she appeared to be hanging on the wall by the silk threads alone.

The kitchen door whapped open and Hulduh Schmitt emerged, brandishing a rolling pin.

"Get away from her!" Hulduh yelled, and cracked Jens a good one on his right temporal bone. He got an arm up to deflect the blow but its force dumped him back against the cement steps. He scuttled backward, on all fours.

"You get out of here or I'll give you another one!" Hulduh yelled, coming for him.

He turned and ran.

Behind him the kitchen help swarmed around their queen, caught her as her knees buckled and carried her back into the kitchen.

Within one hour, in the walnut-walled offices of Gideon Barnett's lumber empire, a stir escalated.

"Sir, you can't go in there! Sir!"

Jens Harken paid little heed, stalking through the corps of Barnett's underlings, peering into one glass office after another until he spotted Barnett himself, looking fat and walrus-y behind his desk, while two men sat on chairs before it.

Jens opened the door without knocking and stood like a warrior just inside the room.

"Tell them to leave," he ordered.

Barnett flushed above his thick gray moustache as he rose slowly to his feet. "Gentlemen," he said without a glance at either of them, "if you'll excuse us for a minute."

The two men rose and went away, closing the door behind them.

With distaste written on every muscle of his face, Barnett hissed, "You . . . low-life . . . immigrant . . . trash. I should have expected something like this from you."

"I came to ask you how much a woman's silk dress is worth, because I just ruined one of your wife's." Jens withdrew some bills from his pocket and laid twenty dollars on the desk. "You'll hear about it as soon as you get home, I suppose, probably sooner. This low-life immigrant trash who's in love with your daughter and who's the father of her baby just tried to force your wife to tell him where you've hidden her. You'll want to have me arrested, of course, so I came by to tell you where the law can find me. I'll be at Tim Iversen's cabin for the rest of the winter, or if not there, just a half mile or so north of there, putting up my own boatworks. Just listen for the saw—you can hear it for a couple of miles. But before you send the sheriff, think of this. Arrest me and there'll be a trial, and at that trial I'll tell them why I was at your house questioning your wife. I'll tell them I was fighting for Lorna and for our baby. And someday when I find her, and she never speaks to you again, you'll ask yourself if it was all worth losing a daughter over . . . and a grandchild along with her. Good day, Mr. Barnett—sorry I interrupted your meeting."

Chapter
FOURTEEN

I N her room the night Gideon and Levinia learned she was in a family way, Lorna had waited—less obediently than apathetically. They had wielded the mightiest weapon of all: shame. Against her father's furor or her mother's reproach Lorna might readily have rebelled. But humiliation had done its dirty work.

Belittled, spiritless, she sat in the dark feeling for the first time ever like a sinner. Until her mother's denunciation Lorna had considered her love for Jens a hallowed thing. It had made of her a better person rather than a small one: benevolent where she might have been petty; generous where she might have been stingy; complimentary where she might have been critical; patient where she might have been intolerant; cheerful where she might have been morose.

Cheerfulness, however, had been snuffed out by Levinia's tirade. After her mother left the room, Lorna sat at the foot of her bed staring at the undrawn draperies, too dispassionate to get up and close them or light a lamp. She sat instead in the dark, enumerating the number of ways her family might be hurt if she ran away with Jens. Was it true? Would they and she be shunned forever by their former friends? Would her sisters be sullied by her reflected shame? Would her mother's friends whisper behind her back and her father's business associates avoid him? Would she herself lose Phoebe's friendship? Would her child suffer the name "bastard" for his entire life?

She considered the word *fornication* again and again. Never before had she put such a name to the act that had seemed so resplendent between herself and Jens. She'd considered it a wondrous manifestation of the love they felt for each other, a fitting celebration of that love.

Levinia, though, had called it low, base, filthy.

Shameful.

The night deepened and Lorna remained alone. Despondent. No dinner tray was delivered. None of her family came near. The piano kept silent. Jens left and stillness lurked in his wake. The house exuded a clandestine air as of whispered secrets being discussed behind closed doors. After a long, long time Lorna tipped to one side and drew her feet onto the bed. Fully clothed, she lay with her knees updrawn, eyes open, not even a pillow beneath her head. In time she slept, roused partially and shivered, slept again, awakened sufficiently to loosen her dress, remove her shoes and climb beneath the covers.

She awakened near eight A.M. to the sound of three knocks on her door.

"Your breakfast, miss."

A tray thumped the bottom of the door. Footsteps tiptoed away. Light shone through the west-facing windows, which gave the morning a questionable quality of dulled luminosity. A cold backdraft threaded down the fireplace, smelling of charcoal. Lorna lay supine, resting the back of a hand on her forehead, wondering where Jens was, what he would do to support himself now that Gideon had fired him, if he would come to the house again trying to see her, if he'd write to her, what would happen to each of them, if he had spent the night in the same blunt agony as she.

As shamed as she.

She collected her breakfast tray but ate nothing, drank only a cup of tea and a glass of some dark maroon juice that activated her saliva glands and made the inside of her mouth feel rough.

She lit a fire and stared into it, picturing Jens's face. Writing in her journal, she fell asleep with her head on her arm, sitting at her tiny writing desk. Downstairs a door closed, awakening her. Outside, horses' hooves pattered. Shortly before noon Lorna's bedroom door opened without any knock and Aunt Agnes slipped inside. She came straight to the desk and wordlessly embraced Lorna, holding the younger woman's head in both arms as if it were a load of Turkish towels gathered from a clothesline.

Aunt Agnes's dress smelled of her familiar musty rose dusting powder, a scent Lorna had always associated with loneliness. With her head on Aunt Agnes's breast, she tried not to cry. "Mother says I'm not supposed to speak to any of the family."

"Typical of Levinia. She can be such an imperious ass without half trying. Forgive me, Lorna, but I've known her longer than you so I feel I've earned the right to speak my mind. You can love her, but don't you ever—ever!—admire her!"

Lorna smiled wanly against Aunt Agnes's dress front, then drew back. "What's going to happen?"

"I don't know, but something's afoot. They know better than to let me in on it, but I can listen at keyholes better than anyone else in this family, and believe me, I will." The tremble in Agnes's voice, usually slight, was more pronounced today.

"Thank you for playing the piano last night when all that was going on in the library."

"Oh, child . . ." Agnes petted her niece's hair. It was all ascraggle and framed a face so laden with sorrow it shredded the older woman's heart. "He wanted to marry you, didn't he?"

Two oversized tears appeared in Lorna's lovelorn brown eyes, answering Agnes's question.

"And they sent him away, those merciless hypocrites." Angry, earnest, she continued, "By the memory of Captain Dearsley, I hope they suffer as they're making you suffer! What right have they? And rights aside, how could anyone who calls himself a Christian turn away the father of his own grandchild?"

Lorna plunged against her aunt again, wrapping both arms around her spare frame. It felt so good to hear voiced the thoughts she herself had submerged all night, thinking them wicked each time they surfaced. During those silent minutes in her aunt's arms Lorna thought how sad that she could not approach her mother this way. It should have been Levinia in whose arms she poured out her most intimate feelings about the expected child, her love for Jens, and their future. But Levinia's arms had never been welcoming, nor her breast a comfort as Agnes's was.

"I spoke to your mother this morning," Aunt Agnes said. "I told her I know about your condition and asked her what's going on. She said it was none of my affair and admonished me to keep my lip buttoned, so I'm afraid, dear one, that I'm to be kept in the dark. Short of coming to console you, there's little I can do."

"Oh, Aunt Agnes, I love you."

"I love you, too, dear heart. You are so like me at your age."

"Thank you for coming. You *have* helped—more than you know."

Agnes stood back and smiled down. "He's a fine young man, your handsome Norwegian boatbuilder. There is something about the cut of his shoulder and the angle of his chin that reminds me of my own fine captain. Be assured, Lorna, that if there is anything I can do to see the two of you together, I shall do it. Anything at all."

Lorna rose and kissed her aunt on both cheeks. "You're the rose in all these thorns, dear Aunt Agnes. From you I learn the very best lessons, the ones I carry closest to my heart. But you must go now. No sense in getting Mother more upset if she finds you here."

Aunt Agnes's visit was the only contact Lorna had with anyone until late afternoon, when Ernesta came to her room carrying an empty trunk.

"Ernesta, what is it?"

"I've been ordered to help you pack, miss."

"Pack?"

"Yes, miss. Only one trunkful, the mistress said. She says you're going to college at last, and that your father's made special arrangements to get you in at the beginning of the second semester. Isn't *that* wonderful. I wish I could go to school. Only went through the sixth grade, but where I come from that was something. It got me this job, 'cause I could read my letters whereas some others I grew up with never learned that much. Now, what'll you be wanting to take? The mistress said to ask you what you'd like."

Woodenly, Lorna gave orders while inside she frantically wondered what was going to happen to her. When the packing was finished and Ernesta gone, Levinia came in, dressed in a traveling suit the color of a gun barrel. She stood the full width of the room from Lorna, with her fingers laced compactly at stomach level, her expression pinched and punitive. "Your father has made arrangements for you and me to take a trip. The train leaves at seven-fifteen. See that you're dressed properly and ready to leave the house at a quarter to."

"Where are we going?"

"Where this disgrace can be handled in a discreet manner."

"Mother, please . . . where?"

"There's no need for you to know. Just do as I say and be ready. Your sisters and brother will be in the library to bid you goodbye. They are to be given to understand that you're going off to school, and that your father pulled plenty of strings to get you there at this odd time of year, primarily as an assuagement for refusing to let you skip the boat in the regatta next summer. If you play your part convincingly, they'll believe it, especially after all the times you harangued your father to let you attend college. Just keep that maudlin look off your face and remember, you and your lax morals prompted these drastic measures; your father and I did not."

Saying goodbye to Jenny, Daphne and Theron proved excruciating: pasting a false smile on her lips while they studied her in bewilderment, disbelieving her story and wondering what was amiss. She kissed them all and said to Daphne, "I'll write." To Jenny, "I hope Taylor sits up and takes notice of you at last." And to Theron, "Do your studies and someday it'll be you going off to college." Gideon kissed her stiffly on the cheek. He said, "Goodbye," and she replied likewise, with little semblance of affection.

Steffens drove Levinia and Lorna to the Saint Paul depot, where Levinia purchased two tickets to Milwaukee and they boarded a private compartment in which the seats faced each other. Levinia closed the velvet privacy curtains on the door, removed her hat, stored it beneath her seat and perched herself like a stuffed owl. Lorna sat opposite, fixing her absent gaze on the window during the interminable minutes before the train began to roll.

Once it did, they watched the lights of the city dwindle into an indigo night studded by starlight and a one-quarter moon.

Finally Lorna turned to regard her mother. "Why are we going to Milwaukee?"

Levinia leveled her eyes on Lorna. Censure had settled in them and would remain—Lorna was certain—until either this child or Levinia herself was in the grave.

"You must understand something, Lorna. What you have done is not only a vile sin, it is in some states actually against the law. Anyone who even suspects your situation will judge you by it for the rest of your life. One does not live down bearing an illegitimate child. One survives it the best one can and hides the fact so as not to ruin the rest of one's life and the lives of one's family. Your sisters must be considered. Their reputations could suffer because of you, and if not their reputations, certainly their tender young sensibilities. Your father and I don't like sending you away, but we saw no other way. He has . . . acquaintances, shall we say, apart from our social circle, who put him in touch with the proper church authorities through whom he found a Catholic abbey of Benedictine nuns who'll—"

"Catholic?"

"Who'll take you in during the period of—"

"But, Mother—"

"Who'll take you in during the period of confinement. You'll have good care, and seclusion, and the help of the good nuns and of a doctor when the time comes."

"So I'm to be stuffed away in a stone turret and treated like a profligate, is that it?"

"You don't seem to understand, Lorna, your father paid dearly to get them to agree to this arrangement. He made a ridiculously large donation to a church that isn't even his, so I'll thank you not to take that tone with me! We needed somewhere to put you, and we needed it fast. And frankly, I don't think it'll do you a bit of harm to be sequestered with a group of God-serving women who value purity and have taken vows of chastity. If our own religion had any such group your father would have approached them. Since they don't, Saint Cecilia's will have to do."

"I'm to be sequestered?"

"How naive you are. Women who've gotten themselves in the family way outside the bonds of marriage simply do not parade themselves around in public. This is what happens to them; they are hidden away so that decent people need not face the embarrassment of confronting them out in polite society."

"And what about the baby? Will I be allowed to keep it?"

"Keep a bastard? And do what with it? Bring it home for your two young and impressionable sisters to learn about? For your little brother to explain away to his friends? Live with your father and me and raise it under our roof? You can't honestly expect us to put ourselves in such a position, Lorna."

They rode in silence for some time, Lorna staring into the dark, heartsick and afraid. Occasionally she'd wipe tears away to clear her vision. Levinia made no move to comfort her. Eventually the older woman spoke again.

"While you're with the nuns I'm sure you'll have plenty of time to realize it would be disastrous for everyone concerned if you kept it. The church knows good families who are looking for children to adopt. There is no other answer."

Lorna wiped her eyes again.

Outside, the nightscape sped by.

Milwaukee by moonlight lay beneath a haze of coal smoke. Ahead, the network of railroad tracks looked like shooting stars as the train slowed and rounded a curve. It traveled for some time within visible distance of Lake Michigan, where wharves and moored ships crippled the shoreline. Ribbons of fog drifted landward, and as the train nosed through them they eddied about the windows. The station itself was murky, nearly deserted, and smelled strongly of creosote. Descending the train steps, Lorna glanced uncertainly toward the depot. A brick apron stretched between her and it, the bricks sheeny with fog, caught in the beams of two lanterns whose topaz light was dulled by the weepy weather and the film of smoke on their glass globes.

"This way," Levinia said.

Following her mother, Lorna felt the chill air creep along her skin. What she was doing, where she was going seemed unbelievable, yet even the foreboding weather was in keeping with her situation: Following Levinia's briskly striding form through the dark, unknown city, shrouded by fog and secrecy, Lorna became duly convinced of the magnitude of her sin, and with that conviction came a heavy load of guilt.

Levinia tipped a porter to fetch Lorna's trunk and summon a coach. It arrived behind a horse whose hide gleamed wet and in whose mane sleet had begun to freeze. A side lantern swung on its bracket as the driver stepped down and opened the coach door.

"Evening, ladies. Nasty night to be out." His breath smelled of liquor as they stepped past him into the murky confines of the conveyance. The door closed behind them. The coach dipped and rocked as Lorna's trunk was loaded on the boot, then the driver reopened the door and thrust his face inside.

"Where to, mum?"

"Saint Cecilia's Abbey," Levinia answered.

"Right. Make use of that lap robe. You'll need it tonight."

The lap robe was heavy and scratchy as wet hay. Levinia and Lorna shared it, seated hip to hip on the musty leather seat while the horse stepped out and their heads jerked backward.

The air inside the coach became cloying and the windows clouded from their breath. Several times Lorna wiped hers off with the edge of a hand to see brick buildings sliding past, then houses and boulevard trees, and once a pair of bicycles leaning against a stone building.

They traveled for over an hour with the sleet continuously pecking at the roof and windows. Levinia fell into a doze, her head canted to one side, bobbing as if her neck were broken. Glancing at her occasionally, Lorna considered how the vulnerability of sleep had the ability to either endear or repel. When it had been Jens she'd watched in slumber, she had been bewitched by tender feelings at the sight of his unguarded face transformed by laxity. Watching her mother, however, Lorna found Levinia's open lips and sagging chins faintly repulsive.

Finally, the driver's voice came muffled from outside.

"We're just about there, ladies. About five minutes more."

Levinia's head snapped to. She smacked her lips, coming awake. Lorna cleared her window. Outside, the moon had disappeared and sleet had turned thicker, whiter. It seemed they were beyond the city, for the land rolled beneath barren fields, then became host to a barren woods. A stone wall appeared and when they'd traveled along it for perhaps a hundred yards, the coach turned right, crunched over coarser gravel for several more feet, then came to a stop.

The coach door opened. The driver's head appeared and his breath smelled ranker than before. "Anyone expectin' you?"

"Just ring the bell on the gate," Levinia replied.

The coach door closed and the horse shook its harness, then the driver cranked a thumb-bell that reported with so little resonance Lorna felt certain no one would answer. The bell rang three more times before a thick, waddling figure appeared on the opposite side of the gate, garbed in black, carrying an umbrella.

"Yes? What can I do for you?"

"Got two ladies here want to come inside," they heard the coach-man reply.

Levinia opened the door and stuck her head out. "I'm Mrs. Gideon Barnett. I believe you're expecting me."

"Ah." The nun withdrew a key from inside her robes and said to the coachman, "Drive them on up to the building at the far side of the courtyard."

He tipped his black hat and climbed aboard. First one gate squeaked long and lugubriously, then another sang the same song. The coach pulled through and stopped. "Won't you ride up, too, Sister?" came the cabbie's voice.

She replied in a heavy German accent, "Thank you, no. I'll follow. This snow smells fresh and the night air is very bracing."

Lorna glimpsed the nun as they pulled past her: a great round loaf of a woman with a black blanket folded over her head, anchored on her chest with one hand while she waddled up the ascending path beneath her black umbrella. Inside the stone wall a ring of evergreen trees seemed to hold the world at bay. The gravel drive was flanked by denuded hardwood trees and flower beds lain waste by winter. A building appeared: U-shaped, three-storied, made of dark stone, faced on the ground level by an arcaded gallery following the build-ing's contour. On the upper stories windows placed as regularly as pickets in a fence looked down darkly on the courtyard below.

At the central door the coach stopped and the driver went behind to get Lorna's trunk. Levinia stepped out. Lorna stepped out.

Levinia told the driver, "You'll wait, please. I'll return as quickly as I can."

They stood in the wet, falling snow while the fat nun labored up the drive beneath her umbrella, which was nearly the same circumference as her black, swaying robes. She was puffing as she reached them and ordered in the same guttural German accent as before, "Go . . . go . . . get out of the wet."

Together, the three of them entered beneath the hooded walkway and approached an immense arched door made of black wood with a leaded glass window shaped like a cross. Through its amber and red glass shone the faintest light, as if a single candle burned inside.

The nun led the way. "Come in," she said, her voice echoing from the high stone walls of a vaulted entry.

The sound of the closing door reverberated as if a dozen others had followed suit along the upper corridors that hung in shadow. The area held a line of ladder-back chairs pushed against one wall, a single huge obese-legged table holding three burning tapers in a brass candelabrum, and on one wall a wooden crucifix bearing a bronze image of the dead Christ. Stairs led off the entry to either side, and another stone archway fed into impenetrable shadows straight ahead.

"Mrs. Barnett, I'm Sister DePaul," the old nun said, letting the blanket slip from her head to her shoulders.

"Sister, it's very good to meet you."

"And you are Lorna." Her voice sounded as if she were gargling with stones in her throat. Her fleshy face pushed through her white wimple and drooped beyond its tight edges like bread dough over the edge of a crock. The simple gold ring on her left hand appeared to be cutting into her pudgy finger.

"Hello, Sister." Lorna offered no hand for shaking nor did the nun. The fat woman directed her words at Levinia.

"Father Guttmann let us know you were coming and arrangements are all made. She will have good care and good food and plenty of time to reflect. This will be good for her. Her room is all ready, but you must say your goodbyes here. Lorna, when you have bid goodbye to your mother I'll be waiting just there"—she pointed beyond the dark arch—"and we will get your trunk upstairs together."

"Thank you, Sister."

Left alone, Lorna and Levinia seemed unable to endure eye contact with each other. Lorna stared at her mother's left shoulder.

Levinia toyed with her pigskin gloves, stacking and restacking them as if they were twenty instead of two.

"Well," Levinia said at last. "You be obedient and don't give them any trouble. They're doing us a big favor, you know."

"When will I see you again?"

"After it's born." Levinia had always referred to the baby as "it," except for the one time she'd called it a bastard.

"Not until then? How about Father? Will . . . will he come and visit me?"

"I don't know. Your father is a busy man."

Lorna's gaze shifted to the crucifix. "Yes . . . of course . . . of course he is." Too busy to waste time on a pregnant daughter who was carefully hidden away and needed nothing more than creature comforts for the next six or seven months.

"When it's born, you can come back home, of course," Levinia said.

"Without it . . . of course."

To Lorna's rank amazement, Levinia's stern facade crumbled. Her lips—hard moments before—trembled, and her eyes filled with tears. "Dear God, Lorna," she whispered, "do you think this is easy for your father and me? We're trying to protect you, don't you understand? You're our daughter. . . . We want the best for you, but something like this follows you your whole life long. People can be cruel, more cruel than you can imagine. While you're blaming us and calling us heartless, stop to realize for just one minute that it is our grandchild you're carrying. We shall not come out of this without scars of our own."

Levinia's outburst revealed a vulnerability Lorna had never before seen. She had not suspected her mother's susceptibility to hurt over this impasse. Until now she had considered Levinia merely dictatorial and hard, separating her from Jens for selfish reasons. In that one moment, when tears appeared in Levinia's eyes, Lorna realized her mother had been harboring a welter of emotions she had carefully hidden until now.

"Mother . . . I . . . I'm sorry."

Levinia clutched Lorna to her breast and held her, struggling to compose her voice. "When a mother has a child, she imagines that child's future will be ideal. She never plans for catastrophes like this. So when they happen, we just . . . we just . . . struggle along the best we know how and we tell ourselves that one day our children will see that we made the decision we thought was best for everyone." She patted Lorna's shoulder blade. "Now, you take care of yourself, and tell the sisters the minute you go into labor. They'll telegraph your father and I'll come straightaway." She kissed the crest of Lorna's cheek—hard—and hurried out before her tears became a greater embarrassment.

When the door closed, Lorna found herself surprised by her mother's emotional display. Odd that the outburst should come as a shock, but it dawned on Lorna, standing beside the door through which Levinia had just left, that for some people it takes a cataclysmic event to loosen their heartstrings and allow them to manifest the love they otherwise hide.

Sister DePaul came laboring in and picked up the candelabrum. "I'll take you to your room." She grasped one handle of the trunk and Lorna the other. "Ooph! So heavy. You'll find you won't have use for so many clothes here. Here we live simple and quiet and spend time in prayer and contemplation."

"I'm not Catholic, Sister. Did anyone tell you that?"

"You don't have to be Catholic to pray and contemplate."

The upper hall stretched into blackness divided into increments by symmetrically placed doors. Halfway along, Sister DePaul opened one on the right. "This is yours."

Lorna entered and looked around. A bed, a table, a chair, a window, a crucifix, a prie-dieu: prayer and contemplation in a monastic cell of immaculate white, representing purity, she surmised.

They set down the trunk; the nun lit a candle on a square bedside table, then turned.

"We have Mass at six o'clock and breakfast at seven. You're welcome at Mass anytime you might want to go, but of course it's not required. After Mass tomorrow someone will come to show you the way to the refectory. Sleep well."

Minutes later, in total darkness, lying flat on her back on a hard cot no wider than a baby's crib, Lorna rested her hands on her stomach and attempted to believe there was a fetus within her that had prompted this galvanic change in her life. The sheets were coarse and smelled cleaner than rain, the blankets woolen and heavy. The bed-spread was stiff but textureless. The baby within all this covering, within her deceptively flat stomach, was no bigger than a teacup. Or was it there at all? How could it be when there was so little physical evidence of its existence? This entire day viewed in retrospect seemed like a drama being played out on a stage, with Lorna as its protagonist. She felt as if she could rise at will and leave this bed, this abbey, this stage, and end the scene whenever she chose. She could board the train and ride back to Jens and say, I took part in the strangest play—everyone was plotting to keep me away from you, and the baby away from us both. But I'm back, and I'm happy, and we can get married now.

Her mother's parting tears, however, struck fantasy from her mind and put reality firmly in place. Levinia's tears had made Lorna admit for the first time the very real stresses the conception of this child had brought to bear upon her parents. She considered all her mother had said about the eventual cruelty of people to a child born out of wedlock, and the stigma forever attached to the family of that child. Until now she had been idealizing, premeditating the day when she and Jens and their baby would be a family, as if social censure was of no importance. But it was. With one giant leap toward maturity, she realized she'd been denying it until now.

In the morning a soft-spoken, seraphic nun named Sister Marlene came to show her down to breakfast. Sister Marlene's lips tipped up at the corners in a permanently benevolent expression—not a smile, not a grin, more a radiance emanating contentment and inner peace. She walked, stood, waited with her wrists doubled upon each other inside the oversized black sleeves of her habit. She called Lorna "Dear Child."

"Dear Child," she said, "be not afraid. God will take care of you as he takes care of all his children." In the hall: "This way, Dear Child. You must be very hungry." And in the refectory: "Sit down, Dear Child, while Mother Superior says Grace."

Mother Superior had a face with more sags than a Monday wash hung out on a crowded clothesline. She was white as an altar cloth, bowing over her folded hands without once glancing at Lorna. She led the other women in the sign of the cross, and together they intoned a meal prayer that was strange to Lorna's ears. They were not singing, yet their voices blended as pleasingly as hymnsong. Everyone moved slowly here, holding back their ample sleeves to keep them from getting in the food when they reached beyond their plates. The food was simple: spicy links of wurst, pungent cheese, coarse white bread, saltless yellow butter, cold milk, hot coffee.

Sister Marlene made the necessary introduction. "Our young guest is Lorna. She came last night from Saint Paul, Minnesota, and will be with us until perhaps early summer. She is not Catholic, so our ways will seem strange to her. Sister Mary Margaret, when breakfast is done would you please show the Dear Child where the kitchen and the dairy are—she'll be wanting fresh milk often, I'm sure."

Though Sister Marlene spoke in perfect English, most of the others spoke with a German accent or, when conversing among themselves, in German itself. To Lorna's surprise, they laughed often, and occasionally appeared to be teasing one another. Each of them spoke to her at least once during the meal, giving her name and imparting a bit of information about life at the abbey, or what the cooks had planned for supper, or where and when Lorna should leave her dirty laundry. Nobody demanded she either attend Mass or pray with them when the meal ended. Nobody mentioned the expected child.

The abbey nestled among wooded hills with farms visible in the distance. Lorna's room faced opposite the central courtyard, looking west across a frozen stream and a landscape patched with forest and meadows that rose toward the horizon, where a pair of horses could occasionally be seen inside a split-rail fence. She spent many hours studying the scenery beyond her window, sitting on her hard ladder-back chair with her chin and forearms on the stone sill.

Saint Cecilia's Abbey, it turned out, was a place of prayerful and contemplative retreat for both retired nuns and nuns from the sur-rounding states on extended sabbaticals. Prayer and contemplation: Like the nuns, Lorna spent much time on both. It was a peaceful expanse without pressure. She was neither blamed nor chastised for her condition. She was merely accepted by the women, whose very serenity seemed to seep within herself the longer she was among them. Most of them were like Sister Marlene: They moved quietly and smiled as if with some inner tranquility, so different from Gideon and Levinia Barnett. They occupied themselves with the simplest activities—dipping candles, crocheting lace, making altar cloths, baking communion hosts. Their austere living conditions removed all sense of competition, which had been so strong a force among the circle in which Lorna had grown up. She found a great relief in simply *being*, without having to be what somebody else wanted: wittier, prettier, from the richer family, among the right class, wearing the prettiest dress, charming the most promising men.

At Saint Cecilia's Abbey she was simply Lorna Barnett, God's child.

November became December. In the common room, plaster statues of the infant Jesus, Mary and Joseph appeared on a bed of hay. The common room became her favorite place, with its diamond-paned windows overlooking the courtyard in one direction and the countryside in the other, and the infant Jesus smiling benevolently at anyone who entered. She studied him soulfully, asking him questions about the right thing to do. He returned no answers.

The common room held an ancient piano, set before the rear windows with their view of the snow-covered hills. Lorna played it often, its metallic scintillation sounding much less like a piano than a harpsichord. The nuns would enter and sit in silent appreciation, occasionally requesting a song. Sometimes one of them would fall asleep listening.

Sister Theresa taught her the care of houseplants.

Sister Martha let her knead bread.

Sister Mary Faith taught her to stitch.

December became January and Lorna's girth surpassed that of her clothing: She made two simple garments that looked little different from the nuns'—brown homespun dresses that hung from shoulder to ankle in a line broken only by the single hillock of her stomach.

January became February and the nuns skated on the frozen stream behind the compound. Their cow, a beautiful biscuit-brown creature named Prudence, gave birth to a beautiful biscuit-brown calf named Patience. Lorna often sat in the stable with the animals, the air warm and fecund, the structure crude, reminiscent of the boat shed where she and Jens had spent the summer with the *Lorna D.*

She had not written to him, for each week without fail her mother sent a letter admonishing her to give up the idea of seeing Jens Harken again, to accept the fact that she must give up the baby, to ask God's forgiveness for the shameful thing she'd done, and to pray that nobody they knew put two and two together when this was all over.

Lorna wrote to nobody except Aunt Agnes. To Aunt Agnes she poured out all her personal ache over the painful decision that lay ahead, and admitted that she'd avoided writing to Jens in order to give herself time to evaluate all that her mother had said and make the decision that would prove least painful for everyone concerned. She asked Aunt Agnes, *What have you heard of Jens?*

The reply said that he was using Tim's place for the winter and had built a boatworks nearby, where he had begun work on another boat, though she didn't know for whom.

Lorna read the words over and over again, sitting at her window staring at the linen landscape. In her throat a lump lodged. Upon the snow she saw his face. In the wind she heard his voice. In her imagination she saw their newborn child.

But one thought kept recurring and prevented her from contacting Jens.

Suppose my mother is right.

Chapter
FIFTEEN

After Lorna's banishment, an even greater strain than usual separated the master and mistress of the granite house on Summit Avenue. The children were asking a lot of questions about why Lorna was attending a *Catholic* college, and whenever Levinia tried to describe the abbey to Gideon, his mouth got small and he claimed he was busy.

One night shortly before Christmas, Levinia was waiting in the master bedroom when Gideon entered to prepare for bed. The city house, built well before the lake cottage, had no running water or bathroom facilities. She waited while he stepped behind the screen and used the toilet chair. The cover clacked shut and Gideon emerged with his suspenders drooping like overturned rainbows.

"I'd like to talk to you, Gideon," she said.

"About what?"

"Sit down, Gideon . . . please."

He stopped unbuttoning his shirt and came to sit opposite his wife on a small, uncomfortable chair beside the oval heater stove which had been installed in place of the fireplace grate.

"I thought you'd gone to bed already before I came up."

"No, I was waiting for you. We must talk about Lorna."

"Lorna's taken care of. What more is there to say?"

He moved to rise but she bent forward and stayed him with a

touch on his hand. "You feel guilty—I understand. But we did what we had to do."

"I don't feel guilty!"

"Yes, you do, Gideon, and so do I. Do you think I liked leaving her there? Do you think I don't worry that someone will find out about it in spite of all the precautions we took? We did it so her future wouldn't be ruined, and we must both remember that."

"All right! All right!" Gideon threw up his hands. "I agree, but I don't want to talk about it any more, Levinia."

"I know you don't, Gideon, but has it struck you that it's our grandchild she's carrying?"

"Levinia, goddammit, I said enough already!" He leaped from his chair and strode toward his humidor.

It took a lot to make Gideon Barnett curse.

It took even more to make his wife stand up to him.

"Come back here, Gideon! And please don't light one of those reprehensible things. I have something to say and I'm going to say it. Furthermore, I don't intend to do so to your back!"

Surprise turned him around. He glared at her as she sat stiff-backed in the small tufted chair, dressed in her voluminous cotton nightgown with her hair still pinned up in tight daytime sausages. Leaving the cigars in the humidor, he returned to the matching chair and sat.

"I think you'll agree that I rarely ask for much from you, Gideon, but I'm going to ask now, and before you vociferate I think you ought to give it some consideration. The child is a bastard, there's no disputing that, but he's a bastard from our blood lines. I shouldn't like to think there's a grandchild of ours living in some . . . some *hovel* somewhere, perhaps cold and hungry. Maybe even sick." She paused as if regrouping, then went on. "Now, I've thought it all over and I know of a way we can see that he's cared for, and nobody need ever know. I'd like your permission to speak to Mrs. Schmitt."

"Mrs. Schmitt?"

"She's been threatening to quit for years, using her poor ailing mother as an excuse. I think she could be trusted."

"To do what?"

"To raise the child."

Gideon jumped up. "Now wait a damned minute, Levinia!"

"It would cost you money, I know."

"It's *already* cost me money!"

"Of which you have plenty. I'm asking you to do this for me, Gid." She had not called him Gid since their salad days. It stopped him in his tracks and returned him to the chair, where he dropped with a sigh while she went on speaking with absolute conviction. "Nobody would suspect a thing if Mrs. Schmitt were to quit now. She would be gone from here for several months before Lorna returned, and since she's been so outspoken about her mother's ill health, it'll be understood that was the reason she left. In return for taking the child, we would of course make sure she and her mother were well provided for for the rest of their days."

Some pensive quiet passed. Gideon remained in his chair, Levinia in hers, while their thoughts ranged backward to Lorna's childhood, forward to that of their grandchild's. During those silent moments the grandparents grew despondent with the weight of unwanted responsibility and worry.

At length, Gideon asked, "How old is Mrs. Schmitt?"

"Fifty-three."

"That's old."

It was the first hint Gideon had given that he, too, had been concerned about the child's welfare.

"Do you have any better ideas?" Levinia inquired, with one eyebrow arched.

Elbows to knees, Gideon studied the floor and shook his head. Finally he raised his gaze to Levinia. "You'd be willing to give up Mrs. Schmitt after the way you fought to keep her last summer?"

"Yes," she answered simply. Her voice broke into a whisper as she reached out and gripped the back of his hand. "Oh, Gid . . . he'll be our grandchild. How do we know where he'll end up if we let him be given away for adoption?"

After years of near physical estrangement, he turned his hand over and clasped hers.

"You never intend to let Lorna know?" he asked.

"Absolutely not, nor anyone else in this household. And Mrs. Schmitt will be sworn to secrecy."

They sat on awhile, faintly uncomfortable with their hands joined and their purposes suddenly unified.

"One thing," he said. "The child must never know."

"Of course not. It's for our peace of mind and nothing more."

"Very well." Gideon released Levinia's hand. "But I'll tell you something, Levinia." He studied some distant point while his face hardened. "I'd like to kill that damned boatbuilder. I mean every word of it. I'd like to kill the sonofabitch."

In the days after Lorna disappeared, Jens thought he'd lose his mind. He felt helpless, godforsaken and afraid. Where had they sent her? Was she all right? Was the baby all right? Had they killed it? Would he ever see it? Had they convinced her never to see him again? Why didn't she write?

He went back to the Barnetts' Summit Avenue house several times, only to be turned away at the door.

Tim was gone and there was no one he could talk to. He didn't confide in Ben, because it would mean divulging the fact that Lorna was pregnant. When days went by and no word came from her his despondency redoubled.

He spent Christmas like any other day, working on his building, constructing stairs to a loft he wondered if Lorna would ever see.

January turned bitter. He wrote to his brother, baring his heart with the truth about the expected child and the disappearance of the woman he loved.

In February the boatworks was complete. He moved his mold over from Tim's cabin and began construction of a scow commissioned by Tim himself, to be christened *Manitou*. But somehow his heart wasn't in it.

In March, bitter blizzards blocked him in for days at a time. He walked to town several times but found nothing at the post office from Lorna.

In April, five months after her disappearance, he received a letter in a strange handwriting. He opened it on the sidewalk in front of the post office, unprepared for the news it brought.

Dear Mr. Harken,

Given a set of circumstances of which I'm fully aware, I thought it my beholden duty to inform you of the whereabouts of my niece Lorna Barnett. She has been sent by her parents to the Abbey of Saint Cecilia on the outskirts of Milwaukee, Wisconsin, where she is being cared for by nuns. You must understand that Lorna's parents have placed and continue to place upon her a great burden of guilt. Bear that in mind if you are tempted to judge her.

Kindest regards,
Agnes Barnett

Standing in the late morning sun with the letter quivering in his fingers, he reread it. His heart thundered. Hope sluiced through him. Love and longing came, too, those emotions he had schooled himself to submerge during the past few months. He lifted his face to the sun and concentrated on its redness behind closed eyes. Already its warmth felt warmer. The spring air seemed fresher. Life seemed fairer. He reread *the Abbey of Saint Cecilia on the outskirts of Milwaukee,* realizing with a leaping heart that his decision was already made.

At Saint Cecilia's Abbey spring had arrived. The northerly winds had shifted to the southwest, and the surrounding fields had emerged from their blanket of white. The smell of thawing earth lifted over the abbey walls, while out in the field to the west a foal appeared with the mare. In the courtyard tulips sprouted. The song of the chickadee changed from the whistle of winter to the salutation of spring.

On an afternoon in late April Lorna was in her room napping when Sister Marlene knocked on her door.

"You have a visitor," the nun said.

"Someone to see me? Here?" Lorna had not known visitors were allowed. "Who?"

"I didn't ask his name."

"A man?" She pushed herself up straighter and dropped her feet over the edge of the bed. The only men she'd ever seen here were Father Guttmann, who came daily to say Mass, and a country doctor named Enner, who called occasionally to examine her.

"He's waiting for you outside in the gallery."

The door closed silently behind Sister Marlene, leaving Lorna sitting with one hand pressed to her bulbous stomach, her emotions in turmoil. Her father or Jens? They were the only men who might come to see her here. Undoubtedly it would be Gideon, fulfilling his parental duty, for Jens had no idea where she was.

But suppose he'd found out. . . . Suppose . . .

She pushed herself off the cot with both hands and waddled across the room, poured water into a pitcher, washed her face and stood a moment with her wet palms covering her flushed cheeks, her heart racing crazily. The room held no mirror: She dampened the sides of her hair and combed it by feel, clubbing it back into a plain tail at the base of her neck as she'd been wearing it since she'd come here. She exchanged her wrinkled brown dress for another, equally as plain, equally as brown, equally as coarse, wishing for the first time that she had something more colorful. Opening her door, she moved awkwardly down the stairs, her locomotion a queer combination of the sedate slowness of the nuns combined with the awkward hitch of a pregnant woman whose feet are no longer visible from above.

The central hall was empty but the front door stood open with a bright cone of afternoon sun fanning across the speckly granite floor. All within Lorna seemed to well up and push against her thudding heart as she stepped outside into the arcaded gallery and looked to her right down its length.

Sister DePaul was out for her usual midafternoon prayer-stroll, reading from her German prayer book while navigating the perimeter of the courtyard gallery.

Lorna glanced the opposite way . . . and there was Jens, hat in hand, rising from a wooden bench in the shadow of the gallery roof.

Her heart felt as if it would leap from her body. Relief and love swooshed through her as she started moving toward him with knees that suddenly felt unstable. He was wearing his Sunday suit and his hair was freshly cut, a little too close to his head. His face looked afraid and uncertain as he watched her approach in her drab maternity dress with her belly leading the way. She moved toward him in a morass of emotion—the need for him doing moral warfare with the repeated denigrations and warnings of her mother.

"Hello, Jens," she whispered, reaching him.

He could tell by her utter calmness the nuns and her parents had conditioned her to their way of thinking. They had stripped her of her beauty. Hair, clothing, somberness—none seemed fitting for the Lorna Barnett he remembered. Her spirit was gone, and her glee at seeing him. In its place was an obeisance that terrified him.

"Hello, Lorna."

They stood a respectable distance apart, aware of Sister DePaul strolling prayerfully nearby.

"How did you find me?"

"Your aunt Agnes wrote to me and told me you were here."

"How did you get here?"

"I took the train."

"Oh, Jens . . ." Her expression held a fleeting moment of pained love. "All that way . . ." She paused, then said softer, "It's good to see you," in that trained, martyred way.

"It's good to—" He stopped. Swallowed. Unable to go on. He wanted to draw her into his arms and whisper against her hair, tell her how glad he was to see her, and how he'd imagined all kinds of things, and how lonely and awful the winter had been without her, and how relieved he was that she was still carrying his baby. Instead, he stood apart, distanced from her by a new shield of untouchability that surrounded her as surely as if she, too, wore a habit.

"Why didn't I hear from you?" he asked.

"I . . . I didn't know where to write."

"Where did you think I'd go with you in a family way? You could have found out if you'd wanted to. Didn't you stop to think how worried I'd be?"

"I'm sorry, Jens. There was nothing I could do. They made the plans in secret and Mother packed me off on the train. I didn't even know where I was going until we were under way."

"You've been here five months, Lorna. You could have at least let me know you were all right."

Sister DePaul turned a corner and encroached.

"It's cold under here," Lorna said. "Let's sit in the sun."

They walked, untouching, from the shadows beneath the arches to a wooden bench drenched in afternoon sunlight. There, at the edge of the courtyard, they sat.

"You've grown . . ." he remarked, laying his hat on the seat, letting his eyes pass down her roundness, which raised such an emotional response within him he was sure she could hear his heart clubbing.

"Yes," she replied.

"How do you feel?"

"Oh, I feel fine. I sleep a lot, but otherwise, just fine."

"Do they take good care of you here?"

"Oh yes. The nuns are kind and caring, and there's a doctor who stops by periodically. It's lonely but I've come to learn the value of isolation. I've had a lot of time to think."

"About me?"

"Certainly. And about myself, and the baby." Quieter, she added, "About our mistakes."

His growing trepidation took a swift turn to anger when he thought of how her parents had manipulated their lives. "That's exactly what they want you to do, think of this as a mistake. Can't you see that?"

"They did what they thought was best."

"Sure," he replied sardonically, letting his eyes wander away from her.

"They did, Jens," she appealed.

"I've been alone a lot, too, but I can't say I've found any value in it!" He shifted, as if at some painful memory. "Jesus, I thought I'd lose my mind when you disappeared."

"So did I," she whispered.

They were both close to tears, and tears would not do with Sister DePaul so near at hand. So they swallowed them and sat stiffly beside each other, locked in an impasse not of their making, miserable, in love, watched by the nun. After some moments of awful silence, Lorna tried to redeem the situation.

"What have you been doing?"

"I work a lot."

"Aunt Agnes told me you've started your own boatworks at last."

"Yes, with Tim Iversen's backing." His eyes returned to her but he withheld the warmth from them. "I'm building a boat for him that'll run in the regatta in June. Tim says if I finish it in time, I can skip it."

"Oh, Jens, I'm so happy for you." She touched his arm and they both thought about the *Lorna D,* unfinished in a shed on Manitou Island, and those carefree days while it was being built. "You'll win, Jens, I'm sure you will."

He nodded, withdrawing his arm under the guise of sitting up straighter. "That's what I came to tell you after they took you away—that Tim was going to back me and everything was going to be all right and we could get married right away. But they wouldn't let me in. They treated me like offal on their boots. Now . . ." He fixed his eyes on a rose bed still locked in winter barrenness. Old memories swept over him while he ached as if those thorny roses were wrapped around his very heart. "Damn them to hell."

A cloud passed before the sun, its shadow trailing over them, bringing a momentary chill before it sailed on, leaving them in warmth.

He wanted to turn her into his arms and beg her to leave this place with him. Instead, he sat his distance while Sister DePaul made another circuit inside the plaster arches, her lips moving in silent prayer.

"My parents want me to give up the baby for adoption."

"No!" he exploded, turning his tortured expression on her.

"They say the church knows childless couples who are looking for babies."

"No! No! Why do you let them put such ideas in your head?"

"But, Jens, what else can we do?"

"You can marry me, that's what!"

"They've made me see the price we'd pay if we did that. Not only us, but the baby, too."

"You're just like them! I thought you were different, but you're not. You've got these stupid rules you live by, and you put what other people think before what you feel!"

Her anger flared, too. "Well, maybe I've grown up a little since all this happened! Maybe I reasoned like a child then, thinking you and I could simply do whatever we wanted without a thought for the consequences."

"How can you talk to me about consequences! The consequences are a baby that's as much mine as it is yours, and I'm willing to take you out of here today, and marry you and give you a home, and to hell with what people say. But you're not, are you?"

Without a physical movement he sensed her withdrawing even further.

"What we did was a sin, Jens."

"And giving away a baby isn't?"

Tears came into her eyes and her mouth shrank as she looked away from him. She had been at peace before he came here. Like the nuns, she had learned acceptance and humility, and had spent time praying for forgiveness for what she and Jens had done. She had decided that giving up the baby was best for everyone. Now she was disturbed, distraught, questioning everything again.

Jens turned to her with love and hurt in his eyes. "Come with me," he urged. "Just walk out of here."

"I can't."

"Can't or won't? They can't keep you here against your will. You're not one of them."

"My father has paid a great deal of money to keep me here."

Jens jumped to his feet and towered over her. "Damn it! You are like him!"

Sister DePaul glanced at them and stopped walking.

"Jens, remember where you are!" Lorna whispered.

He lowered his voice and the nun resumed her prayers. "You care more about your reputation than about your own child."

"I haven't said I'm going to give it up."

"You don't have to. I can see you've fallen right into line with their way of thinking. Get rid of the kitchen handyman and get rid of his kid, then nobody has to know, isn't that right?"

"Jens, please . . . this hasn't been easy for me."

"Easy for you?" He had trouble holding his volume in check. "Have you given one moment's thought to what it's been like for me? Not knowing where you were, why you didn't meet me at that train, if they cut the baby out of you, if you were lying somewhere dying of fever from some butcher's knife? I'm here begging you to marry me and you're saying no, and you want me to cry because this hasn't been easy for you?"

He turned away, struggling to control his anger, struggling with the fact that he had no redress in the face of her refusal to go with him; hating her parents, and—fleetingly—her. He contended with his emotions for the better part of a minute, facing the cloistered world of Saint Cecilia's, taking in little of it—not the sprouting tulips, nor the barren rosebushes, nor the nun who created intermittent black flashes behind the arches. He labored in silence until he'd regained control and could speak more calmly.

"Do you want to know something funny?" he said, his back still to Lorna. "I still love you. There you are, sitting on that bench, saying you're going to stay here and let them take our baby instead of leaving with me and doing the right thing, and I still love you. But I'll tell you something, Lorna . . ." He turned back to face her, picked up his hat, put it on his head. "You give away our baby and I'll hate you till my dying day."

Torn, aching, trapped between two forces, she watched him walk away, into the stringy shadows of the bare elms by the gate, where his carriage waited. Sister DePaul had stopped praying and stood watching from the shadows of the gallery while the uncaring afternoon sun rained its warmth upon the sad creature Jens left behind.

"Goodbye, Jens," she whispered with tears in her eyes. "I love you, too."

Jens left the abbey hurt, so hurt.

Angry.

Frightened.

Searching for a vent for his roiling emotions.

By the time he reached the Milwaukee depot he'd made a decision: He might be nothing more than a kitchen handyman to the whole Barnett bunch, but he'd show them! And he'd do it where the whole damned world would find out.

Before boarding the train for home, he sent a telegram to his brother, Davin.

Come quick. I need you. Boatworks all ready.

Back in White Bear Lake everything seemed to happen at once. Spring turned unseasonably hot. The summer people returned to their cottages. Tim came home from his winter sojourns. The yacht club opened. Sailing resumed. Everywhere, every day, everyone spoke of the upcoming mid-June regatta: The obsession was revived.

Tim reported that Gideon Barnett had stubbornly refused to have the *Lorna D* completed, so Tim's *Manitou* would be the one all eyes would be watching. Jens worked like a dervish on the *Manitou*, toiling away his frustration and anger while Tim commenced picture-taking, as he'd done the previous summer, chronicling it all for the yacht club wall.

On a day in mid-May when the lilacs and plum trees were bloom-ing, and the town of White Bear was busy with commerce, and the trains once again were running every half hour, Jens went to meet the one bringing his brother, Davin.

He waited beside the tracks, studying the passing windows as the train pulled in, its steel drivers slowing, plumes of steam billowing aloft until it clanked to a final stop. The porter stepped out, followed by a woman carrying a basket, leading a boy by the hand. Then Davin himself . . . and Jens was running toward him with open arms. The two of them embraced with glad lumps in their throats, smack-ing each other's backs, smiling so hard their cheeks hurt, blinking against the sting in their eyes.

"You made it! You're here!"

"I'm here!"

They drew back, inspected each other and laughed with happi-ness.

"Ah, brother, look at you!" Jens clasped his younger brother by the muttonchops and wobbled his head around. Davin was blond, slightly shorter and slightly burlier than Jens. "You've finally got enough beard to shave, I see!"

"Well, I hope so. A married man with two babies—one you haven't even seen yet! Cara, come here!"

"Cara is here?" Surprised, Jens turned to find his sister-in-law waiting with a child in her arms, holding another by the hand. She was plump and smiling and wore her blond hair in a braided nest the way their mother always had. "Cara, darlin'!" He'd always liked her. They hugged as best they could with the one-year-old between them. "That big lummox never told me you were coming!"

"Jens . . . it's so good to see you."

Davin explained, "I just couldn't leave her behind."

"I'm glad you didn't! And who is this?" Jens reached for the towheaded baby who'd been balancing on his mother's arms. He lifted the toddler high overhead.

"This is little Roland," Davin answered proudly. "And that's Jeffrey. Jeffrey, you remember your uncle Jens, don't you?" Jeffrey smiled shyly and leaned his head against his mother's hip. Roland began to bawl and got returned to Cara. Jens gave his attention to Jeffrey, who'd been in diapers the last time he'd seen him.

"Jeffrey, that can't be you. Why, look how you've shot up!"

Family! Suddenly they were here, filling Jens's lonely world with a less lonely future. He and Davin exchanged some more affectionate whaps and bantering before Davin said, "I know you weren't expecting Cara and the boys, but we talked it over and decided where I go, she goes, no matter what uncertainties are waiting at the other end. We'll put up in a hotel until I can find us a place."

"Oh no you won't. I've got the loft, and it's big enough to hold us all."

"But that's your place, Jens."

"Do you think I'd let you out of my sight now that we're back together? We've got some catching up to do! There'll be time for you to look for a place after you've been here awhile."

Thus it happened suddenly—in the span of a week Jens's empty loft became a home. To his meager furnishings were added those Cara and Davin had brought, and to these more that the two brothers built or purchased. At breakfast there were hot biscuits and bacon, and one child in a high chair and another on a stool. While the brothers worked downstairs, there were footsteps overhead, and the sounds of the children's voices, and sometimes Cara's, singing to the boys, sometimes scolding. Between the trees around the building clotheslines appeared, and on them diapers blew in the summer breeze. In the heat of the day, while the young ones napped, Cara would come downstairs with iced coffee and lean against the workbench, visiting while the men drank, relishing the togetherness as much as the break.

Best of all, deep into the evenings there was a brother to talk to and plan with. That first night, after the babies and Cara were bedded down three abreast in Jens's own bed, he studied them, then said to Davin, "You're a lucky man."

The two were sitting on a pair of bent willow chairs with a kerosene lamp on the table at their elbow. Davin, too, studied his sleeping family, then shifted his regard to his brother.

"So what about this woman of yours? Where is she?"

When Jens had told him, Davin pondered long and silent before asking quietly, "What are you going to do?"

"What can I do? Wait and hope she comes to her senses."

"And marries you?"

When Jens made no reply, Davin reasoned, "It would be hard for her. She's high society. People would wag their tongues. They'd call the kid a bastard, and call her worse."

"Well, sure they would, but if it was Cara and you, she'd do it. Hell, look how she followed you out here, with no home to come to, no real assurance that this boatworks is going to pay off. That's how it ought to be when you love somebody."

"You say her parents live somewhere right across the lake?"

Jens blew out a breath of frustration and answered, "Yes, and I know what you're going to say next—they'd probably never speak to her again, right?"

Davin studied his brother, his face flat and thoughtful, offering little encouragement. He spoke, at length, as if he'd reached a dour conclusion.

"You should have taken her out of that convent."

"Yeah . . . how? Dragged her by the hair?"

"I don't know how, but if it was my baby I'd have put her in the carriage with me and gotten her out of there."

Jens sighed. "I know. But they've got her convicted and found guilty and they've convinced her that she's committed this unforgivable sin that will absolutely ruin her life if people find out about it, and she believes them. She doesn't sound or act anything like the girl I used to know. Hell, I don't even know if she loves me anymore."

Davin could do nothing but squeeze his brother's arm.

Jens sighed again and looked off toward the bed where Cara and the children were peacefully sleeping, wishing it were Lorna and two of their own. He told Davin, "This has been the best year of my life and the worst. Getting this at last . . ." He gestured to their surroundings. "And falling in love with her, and now the baby coming, and neither one of them mine . . ." He shook his head despondently, then said with much feeling, "What I do know is that I'm damned glad to have you here, Davin. I needed you for more than just helping me build a boat."

The two brothers worked on the *Manitou* eighteen hours a day. Jens told Davin right from the start, "You're sailing this thing with me."

"Are you sure they'll let me?"

"It's Tim Iversen's, and Tim is the lousiest sailor this yacht club's ever seen, but the rules allow him to hire his crew. We'll sail 'er together—you'll see."

The first day Tim came by to meet Jens's family, Cara talked the men into ending work early and invited Tim to supper. Before the meal ended, Tim cocked his head to one side—the better to give the stocky Norwegian a look-over with his one good eye—and said, "What do you know about sailing?"

Davin smiled, shot a grin toward his big brother and replied, "I taught him all he knows." It wasn't strictly true, but the two Harkens exchanged good-humored glances.

"Then you'll crew for Jens?" Tim inquired.

"I'd be proud to, sir." And the matter was settled.

Two alone, however, could not sail the *Manitou.*

"We'll need a crew of six, including the skipper," Jens said. "They'll act as ballast, you know."

"Six, eh?" Tim replied.

"And I think one of them should be you."

"Me!" Tim laughed and shook his head. "Thought you wanted to win."

"The name of this boat isn't the *May-B* anymore. Considering those tubs you've been sailing, it's no wonder you lost and got teased in the bargain. Stick with me and we'll change your reputation in a single race."

Tim scratched his head and looked sheepish. "Well, I can't say it doesn't sound tempting."

"I had in mind to let you fly the spinnaker."

Tim's real eye got bright and his cheeks pink at the thought of skimming across a finish line in the lead, with the giant sail bellied out full before him. "All right, you've twisted my arm."

"Good! Then I need to talk to you about the rest of the crew. With your permission I'd like to ask my friend Ben Jonson to be the pole setter and jiber, and one of Ben's friends, Edward Stout, to be the board man. They both know what they're doing and they're familiar with the boat design. And there's a young fellow I've had my eye on, tall, well-built kid who sails like he was born with a tiller in his hand. Mitch Armfield. I thought I'd ask him to tend the mainsheet."

"You're the skipper," Tim replied. "Whatever you say."

"It'll be a winning crew," Jens promised.

"Then get them together."

Cara went around the table filling coffee cups. Jens took a sip of his hot brew, then sat back with his gaze leveled on Tim. "One other thing . . . Do you have any objections to launching the *Manitou* at night?"

"Why?"

"Well, I'll tell you . . ." Jens glanced from Tim to Davin, then back to Tim. "I've got a plan, but to make it work, none of the other yacht club members can see the *Manitou* sail until the day of the race. We've got to take them completely by surprise."

"You're pretty sure of what she's going to do, aren't you?"

"Absolutely. So sure, in fact, that I'm willing to put money on it." Jens rose and went to the end of the loft near his own bed. He returned with a stack of money, which he placed on the table. "I have one last favor to ask of you, Tim. I'm not a member of the yacht club, so I can't place any bets. But I'm prepared to wager every penny I've saved—nearly two hundred dollars—that the *Manitou* will win. Will you place the bets for me?"

While Tim studied the money, Jens added, "I hear there are still those who think our boat will capsize and sink. The odds will be in our favor."

"Four to one right now," Tim added, "and probably going up once they see that flat little thing on the water."

"So you can understand why none of them must see her run before the first race."

"Perfectly."

"Will you do it?"

Tim covered the money with his hand. "Of course I will."

"And the first person I pay off when I win is you," Jens promised.

"It's a deal," Tim replied, as the two shook hands.

Jens had had many moments of misgiving about inviting young Mitch Armfield to crew for him. They all stemmed, however, from the boy's social class, not from his ability to sail.

The day Jens approached the Armfield house and knocked on the door with his hat in his hand, he hoped to high heaven he was doing the right thing.

A white-capped maid answered the door, bringing flashbacks of getting thrown out of the Barnett house. The woman was polite, however, and asked him to wait in a summery room with potted palms and rococo furnishings.

Young Armfield came jogging down the stairs less than a minute later and entered smiling. "Harken?"

"Yessir," Jens said, extending his hand toward Mitch's outstretched one. "Jens Harken."

"I remember—you used to work for the Barnetts."

"That's right."

"Lorna used to talk about you. And now you've got the boatworks."

"My brother and I—that's right. We're sailing Tim Iversen's boat, the *Manitou,* in the challenge cup against Minnetonka. You've probably heard about it."

"Heard about it! That's all everybody's been talking about around here."

"I came to ask if you'd crew for us."

Armfield's astonishment flashed across his face. "You mean it? Me?"

"I've been watching you. You've got good boat sense. You're quick and limber, and you love sailing as much as I do. Unless I'm mistaken, you've been doing it since you were a boy."

"Well, gosh, Mr. Harken . . ." Mitch ran a hand through his hair, surprised, delighted. "I'd be happy to. I'm just so surprised I don't know what to say."

"What you've just said is enough. You'll be tending the main-sheet."

"Yes sir."

"We plan to launch her at the end of next week. Think you could be at Tim's place Friday evening?"

"You bet!"

"Good. And one other thing—I know it's an odd request, but we don't want an audience when she sails the first time."

"Oh, absolutely, whatever you say." Armfield had heard Harken's detractors declaring the boat would turtle the first time the wind hit it. No wonder they didn't want an audience, just in case the boat went bottom up. "Friday evening."

The two shook hands and Jens left feeling he'd secured the best man for the job.

On the day of the launching, with one week to spare before the race, the crew of the *Manitou* assembled at Harken Boatworks. Tim took photographs of the craft from every angle, of its builders standing beside it, and—with Cara's help—of himself among the crew that would sail it for the first time. Together they guided the boat down the ways that had been laid of stripped logs, the double tracks leading straight from the wide doors of the boatworks down the incline to the shore.

When the *Manitou* took to the water and floated for the first time, they all cheered. Jens felt a pride unlike any he'd known before. Her fair lines were as gently curved as distant hills, her sheer line equally as pleasing, and she displaced so little water. Floating, she looked as pretty as a work by an old master.

On the dock, Cara, holding Jeffrey, said to her son, "Someday, when you're as old as your papa, even older, you'll be able to tell people that you watched him and your uncle launch the first flat-bottomed boat ever raced, and after people saw her sail the sport was never the same again."

Jens boarded, felt this work of his dreams buoy him up for the first time and knew a keen impatience to be under sail.

"Davin, you're tending the jib. Ben, you'll be setting and jibing the spinnaker pole. Edward, you understand how the sideboards work. Just listen for my orders, I'll tell you when to raise and lower them. Mitch, you've tended enough mainsheets to know what to do. Tim, just keep the lines untangled and fly that spinnaker when I tell you to."

Jens seated himself at the tiller.

At last—at long, long last—he gave the order he'd dreamed of giving since he was a boy of eighteen.

"Hoist the main." Up went the mainsail bearing the number W-30.

"Hoist the jib."

The sheets whirred through the blocks and the sails made sounds like quiet hiccups as the first puff of wind caught the canvas. The bow lifted. The boat came alive beneath their feet. No lag, no drag, no delay. She leaped to their command the way a well-trained dog obeys an order to fetch.

At the tiller Jens beamed and called, "Feel that!"

"I feel it, brother!" Davin rejoiced. "I feel it!"

"Glory be!" Tim exclaimed in disbelief. "I don't believe it!"

"Believe it!" Edward yelled.

"She flies!" Mitch put in, while Ben let out a whoop of excitement.

They skimmed over the water, exhilarated, joyous, laughing, fists in the air.

Trimming the jib, Davin called, "How does she feel on the helm?"

"Light as a feather and balancing out beautifully!" came Jens's reply.

Mitch asked his skipper, "How much do I dare trim the sail?"

"Let's find out. I'll point her up and all you guys hike out!" Jens steered the boat closer to the wind. "Okay . . . hike!" All five men leaned their bodies over the weather rail as the *Manitou* heeled higher. There they hung while the night wind freshened. The boat swept over the water and the dark waves whispered on the hull beneath them.

"We'll leave the rest of them floundering at the starting line!" predicted Mitch.

Indeed, it seemed so. The *Manitou* did precisely what Jens had said it would do. As he feathered the boat into the wind, she settled down;

as he bore off, the heel increased and she accelerated. She was the perfect blending of quickness and balance.

"She's unbelievable!" Jens rejoiced.

"Smooth as silk!" Davin called back.

"Try tacking 'er, Jens," Edward suggested.

"Coming about! Drop the sideboard!"

When Jens pushed the tiller, Edward worked the boards—dropping the port, raising the starboard—and the *Manitou* performed splendidly. Jens pointed her up and she swung through the wind and sailed off on a new tack. They flew through the night, the crew and the boat responding to the skipper's orders, getting the feel for one another and the immediacy of the craft itself. The moon rose and they left a silver wake spinning diamonds out of moonshine. They sailed to Wildwood Bay, where Tim hoisted the spinnaker and they ran with the wind home, exuberant, smiling, dampened by night-spray and loving the very feel of their wet shirts against their hides.

Back at the dock they furled the sails reluctantly and took their time drying down the deck. When there was nothing left to do but call it a night, they spoke to the boat in terms a lover might use.

"You're quite a lady."

"Good night, sweetheart."

"I'll be back and you be ready."

"Don't forget who stroked you best."

Amid a sense of ebullient camaraderie, the crew bid good night to one another. When the others had gone, leaving Jens with hearty claps on the back, he walked the length of the dock with one arm draped over Davin's shoulders.

"She'll shame everything else off the water," Davin said.

"There's not a doubt in my mind," replied Jens. "And we'll win that cup and the purse along with it."

Climbing the loft stairs toward their beds, they both knew they'd lie awake into the wee hours, their hearts going a little crazy with anticipation.

Jens had promised himself he wouldn't think of Lorna on the day of the regatta. But when he awakened at four A.M. her memory was strong and forceful. Since visiting the abbey he'd pushed her from his thoughts time after time. Today, however, her image would not be banished. She hailed him from times past, in poses that tore at his heart while he wondered why he put himself through this today of all days.

She was so much a part of this day, though, had been since the night she'd stepped into the kitchen and questioned him for the first time about his knowledge of boats and boatbuilding.

Had she had the baby? Where was she this morning? Was the baby still with her—either born or unborn?

He pictured her standing on the yacht club lawn with the baby on her arm when he sailed over the finish line victorious. He imagined her smile, her wave, her hair, her clothing, a tiny blond head near her own . . . a welcome . . .

When the ache got too immense to bear, he thrust back his bedcovers and rose, determined to make it through the next twelve hours without dwelling on her or the baby again.

The day dawned fair with the wind at eight to ten knots. Jens felt an undeniable clench of satisfaction at dressing for the first time in the uniform of the White Bear Yacht Club: white duck trousers and the official club sweater, blue with white letters.

As he stood with his hands on the initials across his chest he realized that within the hour he would confront Gideon Barnett, dressed the same as he. The thought brought a surge of bitter resentment, followed quickly by another of satisfaction. Barnett had entered his own boat, the *Tartar*, in today's A-class race and was skipping it himself. Given all that had passed between them, Jens would take immense satisfaction at whipping Barnett at his own game. The fact that he would do so in the uniform of Barnett's elite club would only make the win that much sweeter.

He combed his hair and left the loft with a word to Davin. "See you at the boat. Sail well."

Precisely one hour before race time Jens entered the White Bear clubhouse for the skippers' meeting. It was held on the second-floor porch overlooking the water. Though a number of skippers had gathered, Jens's attention was riveted on just one: Commodore Gideon Barnett, as walruslike as ever, speaking to the race judge in a grating voice, wearing his white commodore's cap with the gold braid above the visor.

At Jens's approach Barnett looked up and fell silent. His mouth thinned. His jaw set. Jens met the older man's cold regard with an inspection several degrees colder. Not so much as a nod tempered the enmity between the two.

"Skippers . . ." the race judge intoned, and Gideon looked away. "Today's course will be . . ."

Jens knew the course as well as he knew every plank in his boat. He felt an almost surreal detachedness as he stood among the skippers, getting his instructions for running the race, knowing them before they were spoken.

Barnett looked at him only once more, when the meeting ended and the skippers headed outside. His glare held unmitigated hatred while his eyes said, You may be wearing that sweater, kitchen boy, but you'll never be a member.

Outside, spectators had gathered in amazing numbers. There must have been a good two hundred people. Jens walked through them heading for the crew of the *Manitou* who had assembled, smiling and confident, on the yacht club lawn. They had sailed their boat five out of the past seven nights and as a team had become meshed and efficient.

On his way toward them Jens grinned in reply to the disparaging remarks thrown his way.

"You gonna sail that loaf of bread, Jens, or eat it?"

"Who stepped on your cigar, Harken?"

"Better to leave a skimming dish like that in the kitchen!"

Jens merely greeted his crew. "Good morning, men. Let's board and sail!"

The crowd was still snickering when the crew of the *Manitou* carried their spinnaker aboard.

Heading down the dock beside Tim Iversen, Jens asked quietly, "Did you place my bets?"

"Yours and a few of my own."

"At four to one?"

"Five to one."

He stepped onto the boat experiencing a blend of exhilaration and confidence. Let them snicker. In ten minutes his craft and crew would wipe the smiles from their faces.

He gave the order to hoist the main, and up it went, smaller than some of the others, but more effective, Jens knew. He sensed their snickers turning to murmurs when, with twenty boats jockeying for a place on the favored end of the starting line, the *Manitou* proved herself maneuverable beyond anything they'd ever seen. From clear out on the water the hue was audible, "Watch W-30, watch W-30!"

The five-minute gun sounded. The crew was tense with anticipation. Jens felt his pulse thrusting hard against his ribs. He steered the *Manitou* near the *Tartar* and caught a glimpse of Gideon Barnett's set face. He caught glimpses of skippers' faces from the Minnetonka club, too, the M's on their sails identifying their club. But none of them mattered—only Gideon Barnett, the man who'd done him out of a wife and child.

A minute to go, and Edward held his watch in his hand, counting down the seconds to the gun. "Five . . . four . . ." Hearts surged, and Jens experienced that single damned last-second doubt: What if something goes wrong and the *Manitou* fails us today?

"Three . . . two . . ."

The starting gun sounded.

Jens pushed the tiller and ordered, "Hike!"

The *Manitou* surged forth while her competition hunkered as if dead in the water.

They plowed.

She skimmed.

They lagged.

She flew.

On the shore, murmurs of astonishment lifted. In the boats left behind, curses sounded.

"Let's show 'em what she can do, boys!"

Jens's crew cantilevered their bodies over the purling water and gave the spectators a show they'd never forget.

The call "Hike! Hike!" drifted shoreward on the wind and the spectators began cheering. Before any of her deep-keeled competitors struggled its first boat length, the *Manitou* was a quarter of a leg ahead. She rounded the weather mark with the second-place boat so far behind, its sail numbers were unreadable. The entire crew of the *Manitou* laughed for sheer joy.

"Waa-hoo!" Mitch cheered.

"Yee-ha!" Edward Stout joined in.

"They'll talk about this day till kingdom come!" Davin rejoiced.

"Damned shame so many of them are going to lose their money," Jens remarked with a glint of victory in his eye.

"You boys better be ready to build boats," Tim told them, "because everybody in the country's going to want one like this."

"You ready for that, Davin?" Jens shouted to his brother.

"Damn right!"

Ben asked them both, "You ready for all those reporters when we get back to shore?"

"Been waiting my whole life for 'em," Jens replied.

By the time Tim hoisted the spinnaker their closest competitor was a dot on the horizon. On the last windward leg the *Manitou* met the second-place boat, number M-14, coming downwind with one whole lap to go, followed closely by Gideon Barnett's W-10.

When W-30 crossed the finish line the roar from the crowd drowned out the judge's gun.

The crew were regaled like heroes. Spectators on the dock jostled for elbowroom as the *Manitou* tied up. A man was knocked into the water. Women were holding on to their hats. Reporters were shouting questions.

"Is it true you built boats in New England?"

"Will you sail the same boat next year?"

"Will you build one of your own?"

"Is it true you're not members of this yacht club?"

"What's the official time on this race?"

"Mr. Harken, Mr. Harken . . ."

Jens replied, "If you don't mind, we're hungry, boys, and Mr. Iversen's offered to buy dinner for the whole crew."

On his way toward the clubhouse, still hounded by reporters, Jens remained the center of attention. He stalked along feeling as if his body possessed a spinnaker of its own that was filled and billowing! Everyone reached for him, touched him, patted his back, treated him like their hero.

Suddenly, through the crowd, he caught a glimpse of Levinia Barnett.

His stride faltered and his glory dimmed.

She was standing back with a group of family and friends. Her eyes were fixed upon him, steely, arctic. Her rigid jaw was held level with the earth. She stared at him for three hateful heartbeats, then turned her back.

The thought rushed in unbidden: Lorna should be here, and the two of them should be married, and the baby should be here, too, and his boat should have been the *Lorna D*. If it had been, and if he and Gideon Barnett had sailed on the same crew, and if Lorna had been waving from the shore with the baby on her arm, and her mother smiling beside her . . . Ah, what a soul-sweet day this would have been.

But Lorna had been banished in shame. His baby was being stolen from him. Gideon and Levinia Barnett had coldly snubbed him today. And the *Lorna D* sat moldering in a shed, the reminder of what could never be.

He turned from the ramrod set of Levinia Barnett's back and took his bitterness along as he headed toward the consolation prize of collecting his winnings and eating his first meal ever inside the White Bear Yacht Club.

Chapter
SIXTEEN

*T*wo days after the regatta, Lorna received a letter from Aunt Agnes with the news of Jens's illustrious victory. "He blew past everyone like a hurricane, leaving them gaping in disbelief, their crafts laboring as if sailing through mud, while his leaped forth as if upon a sea of mercury. He rounded the first buoy before the others had gotten halfway to it, and passed them all on his second way around the course. The cheers when he crossed the finish line were so uproarious they could be heard on the opposite shore. By the time the second-place boat crossed the same finish line, your Jens had tied up the *Manitou* and was in the clubhouse eating dinner with Mr. Iversen and being congratulated and interviewed by newspaper reporters from as far away as Rhode Island."

He's done it, Lorna thought, sitting in her room at the convent with the letter in her fist. Her face wore a wistful smile as she stared through her tears at the distant green hills and imagined blue water and white sails. How terribly she'd wanted to be there, to see his boat beat all the others, to watch that low, sleek courser distinguish Jens forever in the realm of yachting.

Her eyes returned to the letter.

"Your father, as commodore, was supposed to present the cups to the winners, but after the race he seemed to develop gastritis and turned the job over to the mayor."

So her father's pride was wounded. It somehow mattered so much less than Jens's victory.

She should have been there to see it. She'd had a hand in starting him out and had been through so much of it with him when he was designing the *Lorna D*. All those days of watching him work, of listening to his dreams, of encouraging them, falling in love. She should have been there.

Instead she was hidden inside this stone fortress, gravid with his child.

Outside, summer lay ripe upon the rolling hills and forests. In a crested field that sloped eastward, a crop of rye—blue-hued and shushing—undulated like the Caribbean before the hot summer wind. Staring out over it, longing, Lorna ran both hands over her distended belly ... lightly ... lightly ... grazing it as if the one inside could feel her external touch. Her burden had grown immense, thrusting down so firm and wide her knees pointed outward. How overwhelming to realize this was her child ... hers and Jens's ... striving toward life. The baby had become for Lorna much more real in the last month, with elbows and heels that thudded the walls of her womb, and occasional hiccups that brought a smile of love to her lips. Sometimes at night he rolled around in his liquid world and awakened her as if to make her question herself and the answer she had given Jens. She would lie with her hands upon the subtly shifting shape within and try to imagine giving this baby up once she'd held and kissed it.

And she knew, beyond a doubt, she could not do that to herself or to the child's father.

Aunt Agnes had called him *your Jens*. He was not her Jens, but she wanted him to be, wanted it yet as she'd wanted it in the days when their intimacy had first flowered. She carried her love for him like a great stone that lodged in her chest and made breathing, moving, living a constant toil.

From the moment he'd walked away angry, declaring he'd hate her, that stone had grown heavier. Give up his child? And him? How could she? He was right: To give away this child—one conceived in love—would be heinous and unforgivable. It had taken the threat of losing the man she loved to make her realize she could do no such heartless thing. She would keep the baby and would marry Jens Harken. If it meant giving up her family forever, that's what she'd do. She'd been a fool not to leave with him when he'd asked her.

Her labor began three nights later. Awakened by a cramp, she lay waiting it out, staring at the night outside to gauge the time, discovering the moon had already begun its descent. When the first pain eased she rose and stood at her window with a hand on the ledge, waiting for another of verification. It seemed to take an hour, but when it came it brought an unquestionable clench and warning. She bent forward and flattened her hands on the window ledge and rode it out, Jens's face in her imagination to help her through it.

Afterward, she donned a wrapper and went to Sister Marlene's room, knocked softly and waited. The door was opened by a stranger, a beautiful young woman with wavy dark hair flaring out from her cheeks and forehead, her face lanternlit to a luminous coral glow.

"Sister Marlene?"

The young nun smiled at her uncertainty. "Yes, Lorna?"

Lorna continued to stare, struck dumb.

"You've never seen me with my habit off—is that it?"

"You have hair!"

The nun smiled again, the same serene smile as that on the statue of the Virgin Mary in their chapel.

"Has your time come, Lorna?"

"Yes, I think so."

Sister Marlene moved calmly, turning back into her room to set the lantern down and free her hands to don a robe. "Have you been awake long?"

"An hour, maybe less."

"Is it getting close?"

"No, I think it's just started."

"Then we should have plenty of time. I'll awaken Mother Superior and tell her. When Father Guttmann comes for five-thirty Mass we'll tell him and he'll contact the doctor. Your mother asked to be telegrammed, too."

"Sister, I have to ask you something."

"Yes?"

"Did she talk to anyone here about my giving the baby away?"

"Yes, she spoke to Mother Superior."

"But I'm not giving it away. I've decided I'm going to keep it."

Sister Marlene came forward bearing the lantern. By its light she touched Lorna comfortingly on the cheek, as if bestowing a blessing. "God has his ways, and sometimes they're not easy, as this will not be for you. But I cannot believe a child would be better off without its mother. I believe he will bless you for this choice you've made."

The messages were sent with the good Father when he left the convent shortly after dawn. The day progressed with agonizing slowness, a full nine hours of Lorna resting in her room while desultory pains waned and ebbed with great irregularity. Not until three in the afternoon did her travail begin in earnest. Dr. Enner arrived, examined her and declared it would be some time yet.

"S . . . some time?" Lorna asked, breathless after a contraction.

"These first babies can be stubborn."

For another two hours the pains worsened. Each felt longer and closer to the last while Lorna lay on her narrow cot believing surely this was the moment of birth, wondering where Jens was, if he somehow knew this was happening today, if she'd live through this. Sister Marlene stayed at Lorna's side, ever serene, ever attentive. "Rest," she would murmur between pains, while during them she would wipe Lorna's brow or offer her hands for gripping. Once, when the pain grew grievous, the nun murmured, "Think of your favorite place," and Lorna thought of the lake with the sailboats out and the spray from the bow cool on her hands hanging over the coaming, and Jens at the tiller with the sun on his blond hair and neck, and Queen Anne's lace blooming along the shoreline and the willows trailing their boughs in the water. Another pain smote, and when Lorna opened her eyes Levinia was there, leaning above her.

"Mother?"

"Yes, Lorna, I'm here."

She smiled weakly. "How did you get here so fast?"

"There's nothing in America as dependable as a train. The doctor says it won't be long now."

"Mother, I'm so hot."

"Yes, yes of course you are, dear. The nuns will take good care of you and I'll be waiting outside."

When Levinia went away Lorna turned her weak smile on Sister

Marlene. "I really didn't think she'd come." An intense contraction clutched her and she moaned softly, lifting her knees and twisting to one side. The doctor tied leather straps to the footboard of her bed and threaded her legs through them, advising her it would soon be time to push. The nuns, she saw, had rolled back their ample sleeves to the elbow and had pinned their veils back with common pins, joining them between their shoulder blades. Their ears made white bumps within their pristine wimples, and she wondered foggily how they could hear with that starched cloth covering their ears so tightly. During the next quarter hour there were helping hands, and cool cloths, and gushes of liquid, and her own growl, and a great trembling over the entire length of her body, and muscles straining to the quivering point, and her head rising off the mattress, and her voice calling, "Jens, Jens, Jeeeeeeeeens!" A slithering forth, followed by some relief, and a gentle female voice saying, "He's here. It's a boy."

Then a respite and a warm, wet weight on Lorna's belly, and the corners of the ceiling slipping sideways into figure S's as her tears welled and dribbled in warm streams onto her earlobes. Her own hands, reaching downward, and someone supporting her head as she touched the slimy red creature whose spindly arms and legs were doubled over like carpenters' rules.

"Oh, look . . . look at him . . . what a miracle."

"It is a miracle, indeed," Sister Marlene pronounced softly at Lorna's ear before lowering her head to a pillow. "Now rest a minute. You deserve it."

Later, when the cord was cut and the afterbirth taken, and Lorna had heard her son squall for the first time, Sister Marlene placed the infant, wrapped in white flannel, in Lorna's arms.

"Oh, Sister . . ." Lorna's tears welled again as she saw his features for the first time, distorted from the rigors of birth beyond comparison to anyone. "Look at him. Oh, precious little thing, I don't even have a name for you." She kissed his bloody forehead and felt him wriggle in his wraps. "Whatever shall I call you?" She lifted her eyes to the nun's and whispered, her chin shaking, "Oh, Sister . . . his father should be here."

Sister Marlene only smiled and rubbed Lorna's hair back from her brow.

"I wanted to marry him, you know, and my parents wouldn't let me."

Lorna thought she saw a suspicious brightness in the corners of Sister's eyes, but her eternal tranquility remained, superseding any other emotions she might be feeling.

"Well, I'm going to," Lorna vowed. "I should have followed my heart to begin with, and Jens would be with me now. With us." She returned her attention to the baby, touching his chin with a fingertip, which he followed with his seeking mouth. "Has my mother asked to see him?"

"I don't believe so, but she's waiting to see you." The nun reached for the baby. "I'm sorry to take him, but I must give him a bath, and you, too."

Lorna was bathed, garbed in clean white and lying on fresh sheets when Levinia entered her room. The baby had been taken elsewhere for his bath, so the room was quiet and stark as a cell once more. Though Levinia closed the door silently, she need not have bothered, for Lorna was lying awake waiting.

"Did you see him, Mother?" she asked.

Levinia turned, startled by Lorna's lucidity.

"Lorna dear, how are you feeling?"

"Did you see him?"

"No, I didn't."

"Mother, how could you not want to? He's your grandson."

"No. Never. Not in the sense you imply."

"Yes. In every sense. He's your flesh and blood, *my* flesh and blood, and I cannot give him up."

"Lorna, we've been through all that."

"No, *you've* been through all that. You told me how it would be, but you never asked me how I wanted it to be. Mother, Jens was here. He came to see me."

"I don't want to speak of that man!"

"I'm going to marry him, Mother."

"After all that your father and I have done for you, and after he came to our house and threatened me, how dare you even suggest such a thing!"

"I'm going to marry him," Lorna repeated determinedly.

Levinia turned heliotrope and quelled her urge to shout. Quietly she remarked, "We shall see about that," and left Lorna alone.

Outside the office of the Mother Superior, Levinia took a moment to compose herself. She drew and exhaled two deep breaths, pressed her palms to her flushed face and adjusted the veil on her oversized gray silk hat. When she knocked and stepped inside, her heart was still jumping in outrage, but she hid it well.

"Mother Superior," she said coolly, advancing into the room.

"Ahh, Mrs. Barnett, how good to see you again. Please sit down."

Mother Superior was approaching eighty and had a huge face with two chins and a giant German nose. The wire bows of her spectacles seemed to have grown into her temples, like barbed wire into a tree. Her hands were fleshy and liver-spotted as she deposited a fountain pen in its holder and braced her knuckles on the blotter as if to push to her feet.

"Please don't get up," Levinia said, taking one of the two leather-seated chairs facing the old nun's desk. Seated, she rested a silk-covered pocketbook on her knees and withdrew from it a check made out in the amount of ten thousand dollars, consigned to Saint Cecilia's Abbey. She placed the check on the blotter before the nun.

"Reverend Mother, my husband and I are both very grateful for the gracious care you've given our daughter these past few months. Please accept this as a token of our gratitude. You cannot know how it has eased our minds to know that Lorna was in a place like this, where she could be at peace and heal from this . . . this unfortunate interruption in her life."

Mother Superior looked down at the check and hooked it off the blotter with short, blunt fingernails. "Bless you both," she said, holding the check in both hands, reading and rereading it. "This is most generous."

"Bless you too, Sister. You'll be happy to know we've found a good, God-fearing family to take the child and raise it."

Mother Superior's eyes flashed up to Levinia's in some surprise. "I hadn't heard that. We have families, too."

"Yes, I'm sure you have. But as I said, the arrangements are all made, so I'll be taking the infant with me today."

"Today? But so soon."

"The sooner the better, don't you agree? Before his mother grows attached to him. I've brought a wet nurse with me who is waiting at a hotel in Milwaukee, so there's no need to worry about his welfare in any regard whatsoever."

"Mrs. Barnett, forgive me, but Sister Marlene has given me to understand that your daughter hadn't decided whether to give the child up or not."

Levinia impaled the nun with unsmiling eyes. "A girl of her age, in her state, is incapable of making a rational decision about something as important as this, wouldn't you agree, Sister?" She let her gaze drop to the generous check. "I understand that the money will be used to build a new wing on a nearby orphanage. I must say I'm relieved to think that this baby need not ever live in a place like that."

The old nun laid the check down, knuckled the blotter and pushed to her feet. "I shall see that the infant is properly dressed for travel and brought to you here." In her aging rheumatic gait she left the room with her right shoe squeaking.

"No, Mother Superior, you must not do it!" Sister Marlene's face flared as brilliant red as a blood spill against her white wimple.

"Sister Marlene, you will follow orders!"

"But Lorna told me she wants to keep the baby and marry his father—the young man who came to visit her here; you remember, don't you?"

"The decision is made. The child goes with his grandmother."

"Not by my hand."

"Are you *defying* me?"

"I'm sorry, Mother Superior, but it would be the greatest sin of all."

"Enough, Sister!"

The younger nun clamped her lips shut and fixed her eyes on Mother Superior's flat, bound chest.

"Get the infant."

Softly, dropping her gaze to the floor, Sister Marlene replied, "I'm sorry, Sister, I cannot."

"Very well. Go to your room. I shall speak to you later."

*   *   *

In her monastic cell with its single cot, white bedspread, white walls and curtainless window, Sister Mary Marlene—née Mary Marlene Anderson of Eau Claire, Wisconsin, who at age seventeen had borne a bastard child and had it taken from her this same way, and had been sent by her parents to this convent to repent and had stayed to live out her life—removed the rosary from her waist, held it in her right hand and raised her eyes to the simple brown wood crucifix on the wall. "Lord, forgive them," she whispered with tears in her eyes, "for they know not what they do."

Penitently she dropped to her knees, then lay down flat on her face on the cold stone floor, her limbs extended, duplicating the shape of the crucifix. Lying so, she silently prayed for forgiveness, and transported herself to a sublime vale far beyond this earthly one with all its pain and suffering and sorrow.

She was still lying prone when Lorna's scream vaulted through the building. It echoed along the barren stone halls in tenfold those that had accompanied the birth of her child. It raked the ears of eighteen black-clad virgins who had never known either the joy or the woe of procreation, and of the one prone woman who remembered both.

"Nooooooooooooooooo!"

They let her scream, let her run from room to room, jerking doors open, slamming them, shrieking, "Where is he? Where is he?" over and over again. Terrified, they hunkered against the walls, gawping, these obedient nuns who had chosen a life of contemplative prayer and seclusion, who had just watched Mother Superior be struck down when Lorna had bounded from her bed, screaming.

Sister Mary Margaret and Sister Lawrence helped Mother Superior to her feet, mumbling in terrified voices, "Oh dear, oh dear . . . Sister, are you all right?" The old woman's glasses were broken and she could neither straighten fully nor readily draw breath.

"Stop her," Mother Superior whispered as they lowered her carefully to a chair.

No one stopped Lorna, however. Not until she reached Sister Marlene's room. She flung the door back, found the nun lying prone as a postulant, and screamed, "Where is my baby? Where is he, you wicked heathens?" She kicked Sister Marlene on her left hip and fell to her knees, pummeling the nun with both fists. "May God damn all of you, you pious hypocrites! Where!"

Sister Marlene rolled away, reared up and caught three cracks to the face before subduing Lorna with a cinch hug. "Stop it!" Lorna struggled to inflict more damage, flailing uselessly. "Stop it, Lorna, you're hurting yourself."

"You let my mother take him! Damn you all to hell!"

"Stop it, I said! You're bleeding!"

The younger woman suddenly collapsed in the nun's arms, weeping, drooping, her weight going slack. They knelt together, a tangle of black and white and the single, spreading, brilliant patch of scarlet seeping through Lorna's gown.

Lorna whimpered, "Why did you do it? Why?"

"You must go back to bed. You're bleeding badly."

"I don't care. I don't want to live."

"Yes you do. You will. Now come with me." Sister Marlene struggled to draw Lorna to her feet, to no avail. Lorna's body remained limp. Her coloring had grown waxy. Her gaze became bleary, fixed on Sister Marlene's face.

"Tell Jens . . ." she whispered weakly. "Tell him . . ." Her eyelids closed and her head sagged back against the nun's arm.

"Sister Devona, Sister Mary Margaret! Anyone! Come and help me!"

It took a minute before two nuns came to the doorway and peered timidly inside.

"She's unconscious. Help me get her back to bed."

"She knocked Mother Superior off her feet," Sister Devona whispered, still shocked.

"I told you, she's unconscious! Now, help me!"

Hesitantly, the pair entered the room to do as ordered.

Lorna emerged from a black well into the silver haze of a late afternoon. The day was bright and glittery, the sky white, not blue, as if in the aftermath of a hot summer rainstorm. A fly buzzed somewhere in the room, then landed and hushed. The air felt gummy and heavy upon her face, her blankets, her arms. Something bulky pressed against her genitals, which ached and felt sticky.

Suddenly she remembered.

I had the baby and they took him away.

Tears heated her eyes. She closed them and turned her face to the wall.

Someone braced a hand on the bed. She opened her eyes and turned to look. Sister Marlene, with her serenity returned, leaned over Lorna with one hand pressed to the mattress. On her face two bruises bulged like strawberries. Her black veil was perfectly ironed and draped symmetrically over her shoulder tips. A smell of cleanliness emanated from her, of clean laundry, and fresh air, and sinlessness.

"Lorna dear . . . ." she said. "You're back." Upon her delicate frame she made a sign of the cross.

"How long have I been asleep?"

"Since yesterday afternoon. Nearly twenty-four hours."

Lorna shifted her legs restlessly and Sister Marlene removed her hand from the bed.

"It hurts."

"Yes, I'm sure it does. You tore yourself when the baby was born, and afterwards, running. We were afraid you might bleed to death."

Lorna lifted the blankets from her hips. An earthy-bloody-herbacious smell drifted forth. "What's down there?"

"A comfrey poultice to help you heal. It will help your torn flesh bond faster."

Lorna lowered the covers and lifted apologetic eyes to Sister's. "I kicked you and hit you. I'm sorry."

Sister Marlene smiled benignly. "You're forgiven."

Lorna closed her eyes. The baby had been taken. Jens was not here. Her body ached. Her life seemed pointless.

The fly began buzzing again. No other sound intruded into the overwhelming convent quiet. Sister Marlene sat with the patience only a nun could muster . . . waiting . . . waiting . . . giving Lorna all the time she needed to acclimate to what had happened.

When finally Lorna opened her eyes, having swallowed repeatedly and mastered her urge to weep, Sister Marlene told her in a voice placid with acceptance, "I, too, gave birth to a child when I was seventeen years old. My parents were devout Catholics. They took it away and sent me here and I've been here ever since. So I understand."

Lorna slung an arm over her eyes and burst into noisy weeping. She felt Sister Marlene's hand take her own.

And squeeze.

And squeeze.

And go on squeezing.

She clung to it, weeping behind her arm, her chest heaving, her stomach bucking, until her keening seemed to rebound upon itself and detonate the viscous summer day.

"What will I do?" she wailed, drawing into a ball, covering her slimy face with one hand, feeling her flesh pull where it had begun healing. "Oh, Sister . . . What will I dooooooo?"

"You will go on living . . . and you will find reasons to persevere," the nun answered, petting Lorna's matted hair, remembering with great sadness the handsome young man who'd come here to find her, and her own young man those years ago.

Lorna left Saint Cecilia's eleven days after the birth of her son, garbed in one of three new gowns Levinia had left. Mother Superior gave her an envelope bearing a train ticket and enough additional cash for the carriage back to Milwaukee and dinner aboard the train. Also in the envelope was a note from Levinia.

Lorna, it said, *Steffens will be waiting at the station to drive you to the Summit Avenue house or Rose Point, whichever you prefer. The entire family will be at Rose Point, as usual at this time of year. Love, Mother.*

Lorna made the return trip in a state of malaise, focusing on little, assimilating none of what she saw and smelled and touched en route. Her body had healed sufficiently to make the ride reasonably comfortable. Occasionally, when the train rocked, she felt a twinge down low that revived memory more than pain. Sometimes, from her train window, she saw in fields mares with foals that called back the view from her room at Saint Cecilia's. Between Madison and Tomah a woman boarded with a little blond boy about three years old, who peeked at Lorna around his coach seat and smiled shyly, breaking her heart. The money for her meals went untouched. She sat through the dinner hour without noticing either hunger or thirst; indeed, she had grown accustomed to living without liquids during the awful days when her breasts filled with milk and were bound and dissuaded from producing it. They hung now, slightly larger than before, slightly less resilient, useless pendants used only to rest her wrists beneath. It was how she thought of her body, when she thought of it at all—a useless, emptied vessel.

At Saint Paul the porter had to rouse her from her reverie and remind her to disembark.

Steffens was waiting, doffing his hat, greeting her with a formal smile. "Welcome home, Miss Lorna."

"Thank you, Steffens," she replied woodenly, then stood waiting as if she had no idea where she was.

"How was school? And your trip to Chicago?"

It took her a while to absorb the lie her parents had disseminated about her whereabouts since the end of the school term.

"It was fine . . . just fine."

When he'd helped her board and loaded her trunk, he inquired, "Where to, Miss Barnett?"

She thought awhile and murmured to the middle distance, "I don't know."

Steffens turned in his seat and studied her curiously. "The family's all out at the lake, miss. You want I should take you there?"

"Yes, I guess so. . . . No! . . . Oh dear . . ." She touched her lips and felt her eyes fill with tears. "I don't know." Around them the bustle of the train depot created a din of voices, rumbling wheels, hissing steam and clanging bells. In the midst of it, Steffens awaited her bidding. When she continued silent and vacuous, he offered, "I guess I'll take you out to the lake, then. Your sisters and brother are out there, and your aunts, too."

Lorna at last snapped from her muzziness. "My aunts—yes. Do take me to the lake."

She arrived in the late afternoon, when a game of croquet was in progress. Daphne was on the court with a group of her friends. Levinia was sitting at an umbrella table with Mrs. Whiting, drinking lemonade and watching. The aunts were on a glider in the shade of an elm tree. Henrietta was fanning herself with a palmetto fan and Agnes was doing punchwork embroidery, stopping occasionally to fan herself with the hoop. Down by the dock Theron and a friend were scooping minnows with hand strainers.

Nothing had changed.

Everything had changed.

Henrietta noticed Lorna first and arched her back, waving with the fan high overhead. "Lorna! Hello! . . ." and to everyone at large, "Look, Lorna is back."

They all came, the croquet players dropping their mallets, Theron clanking a minnow bucket against his knee, Levinia bussing Lorna's cheek, Aunt Henrietta clucking and babbling, Mrs. Whiting hanging back smiling, Aunt Agnes squeezing Lorna the longest, with moist, tacit affection, while over her shoulder Lorna searched the Dellwood shoreline where Jens's boatworks must be, making out at this distance only an undulating line of trees.

Daphne exclaimed, "Oh, Lorna, you got to go to Chicago! Is your new frock from there?"

Lorna looked down at the dress about which she cared so little. "Yes . . . yes, it is." She hadn't the enthusiasm to add that she had two others.

"Oh, Lorna, you're so lucky!"

Theron said, "Gosh, we thought you'd never get back." He'd grown a good three inches during her absence.

The young people offered smiles and hellos and Levinia said, "There's cold lemonade."

Lorna asked, "Where's Jenny?" and Daphne answered, "Out sailing with Taylor."

So things *had* changed.

Certainly for Lorna they had. She declined the invitations to join the croquet game, and to dip for minnows with Theron and his friend, and to sit on the glider, and to drink lemonade. She was tired from the trip, she said, and thought she would go to her room for a little rest.

There, the windows were open, the curtains fluttering, and Aunt Agnes—sweet, thoughtful Aunt Agnes—had picked a bouquet of every variety in the garden and left it with a note written on blue deckle-edged paper: *Welcome home, dear. We missed you.*

Lorna dropped the note, removed her hat and laid it on the window seat. She sat beside it and stared out across the water, wondering where he was, if he sensed she was home, when she would see him, how she would tell him about the baby. Below, the girls' voices drifted up in arpeggios of laughter from the croquet court, and she thought, Yes, laugh while you may, while you're young and carefree and the world seems nothing but good, for all too soon your childhood fantasies end.

Gideon came home on the six o'clock train but stayed clear of Lorna.

Jenny returned from sailing and bounded straight into Lorna's room to hug her and exclaim that she was truly in love with Taylor, and Lorna didn't mind if she was being courted by him, did she?

Mother came along and tapped on the door, reminding, "Supper at eight o'clock, dear."

With great difficulty Lorna put in the expected appearance, encountering her father for the first time, garnering another stiff kiss on the cheek, fielding her siblings' questions about her nonexistent school and shopping trip, avoiding Aunt Henrietta's eagle eye that said very clearly *Lorna has changed!*, listening to Levinia prattle on and on about the diminished quality of the food since Mrs. Schmitt had retired, biting her tongue to keep from asking Aunt Agnes if she'd seen Jens, realizing she herself didn't belong here anymore but accepting that there was no place else for her to go.

In the evening, when the family had dispersed, Lorna cornered her mother and father in the morning room, entering it silently and standing between the open pocket doors for some time before speaking. Her father's face was hidden behind a newspaper. Her mother was sitting in a chair by the French doors, staring out at the lake. Lorna made her presence known by announcing, "If you don't want to risk the children hearing this, you'd better close those doors."

Levinia and Gideon started as if arrows had whizzed past their ears. They exchanged glances while Lorna rolled the pocket doors closed, then Gideon rose and shut the French doors and remained beside Levinia's chair. It struck Lorna they had probably been expecting her: On a balmy summer evening such as this, when they stayed home they usually sat on the veranda in the wicker.

"I thought I should tell you how I feel about you stealing my baby."

Levinia replied, "We did not steal your baby. We made arrangements for its adoption."

"By whom?"

"The church doesn't tell you that."

"You stole my baby without even asking me."

"Lorna, be sensible. What would you have done with it? How could we possibly have allowed you to bring it back here—can't you see how your sisters adore you? How they admire you and want to be like you?"

Lorna ignored the oft-repeated refrain. She told her parents with absolute dispassion, "I want you both to know that I have lost all feeling for you because of what you've done. I'll live here for now, because I've nowhere else to go. But I'll marry the first man who asks me in order to get away from you. I hope you're both very happy with the outcome of your malevolent deed."

Calmly, imitating Sister Marlene, Lorna left the room.

A different mood prevailed when Aunt Agnes slipped into Lorna's room near eleven o'clock that night. The two women clasped each other and struggled to calm their pitifully pounding hearts.

"It was a boy," Lorna managed in a ragged whisper. "They took it from me against my wishes. I never even saw him w . . . washed . . . only with blood on his little f . . . face. I don't even know what color his hair was."

"Oh, my precious, wounded child."

While Lorna cried against her shoulder, Aunt Agnes asked, "Does Jens know?"

"No. I have to tell him." Lorna pulled back, swabbing her eyes with a cotton hanky. "Have you seen him, Aunt Agnes?"

"No. I've spoken to Tim, though, and the business is flourishing. Since the regatta everyone wants a boat from Harken Boatworks. You know where it is, don't you?"

Lorna gazed toward the window. "Yes. I've spent many weeks imagining it there."

She went the next day, dressed in the blue-and-white-striped skirt she'd worn the very first time she'd shared a picnic with Jens. Solemn-faced, she put a pin through her straw hat, staring at her countenance in the mirror, finding a dour woman where a carefree girl had stood one year before. She took the catboat, asking no permission, unshakably certain that Gideon wouldn't have the gall to forbid her the "unladylike sport of sailing" after all she'd been through. The few lessons she'd sneaked from Mitch Armfield left her ill-prepared to handle the one-man boat. If she capsized and drowned, so be it: The possibility brought not the slightest quiver of dread, given the reaction she was expecting from Jens. Indeed, drowning would be preferable to being shunned by him.

She found his place with no trouble. It was visible from clear out in North Bay, its new wood still blond and bright against the green backdrop of shoreline. So big, she thought, approaching it, admiring its high roof and grand proportions. She had intended to remain as calm as Sister Marlene, but catching sight of Tim's boat, the *Manitou*, tied up to a startlingly long dock, and the boatworks itself with its loft windows open above, and its wide, west-facing crossbuck doors doubled back to the late morning light, and the ways stretching down from them straight to the water, Lorna felt a rush and race within. It was coupled with a keen longing to be living here with him, in this place they had both dreamed of. Oh, to watch their child steady himself against his father's leg, and learn to walk between those ways down to the water's edge, and to design and build and sail yachts the way Jens could teach him.

Lorna tied up to the dock and walked its length, eyeing the *Manitou* as she passed it, feeling a great surge of nostalgia because it looked so much like the *Lorna D.* Approaching the beach, she glanced up and realized, to her dismay, that there were diapers drying in the wind.

Dear lord, he's found the baby!

She paused, rooted, staring at them until common sense brought a more believable if shattering probability: He's married some widow.

She forced her feet to move . . . up the dock to the newly cleared beach, across the sand to the wooden skids, between the skids, closer and closer to the sound of sandpaper scuffing and the light tap of a hammer.

In the double doorway she stopped. The building was as high, wide and venerable as a church inside, with dappled light falling through open windows and doors, and the new wood of the building itself still as bright as ripe grain. It smelled the same—aromatic cedar, glue and sawdust.

Three men were working on a new boat—Jens, Ben Jonson and a square-built stranger.

The stranger noticed her first and quit sanding.

"Well, hello," he said, straightening.

"Hello," she replied.

Jens and Ben quit working and straightened, too.

"Can I help you?" the stranger asked.

Her eyes left him and found Jens while Jonson offered, "Hello, Miss Barnett."

Jens said nothing. He stared at her for five flinty seconds, then returned to his sanding. From upstairs came the smell of cooking and the sound of children's voices, magnifying Lorna's dread.

"You're Lorna," the stranger said, coming forward with his hand extended. "I'm Jens's brother, Davin."

"Oh, Davin," she said, relieved. "Well, my goodness, I didn't know you'd come. It's good to meet you."

"I imagine you've come to see Jens."

Jens went on sanding, ignoring her.

"Yes . . . yes, I have."

Davin let his glance dance back and forth between the two of them. "Well . . . listen . . . smells like Cara's got some dinner ready upstairs, and I for one could use a break. How about you, Ben?"

Ben set down his hammer and wiped his hands on his thighs. "Yeah, sure. Sounds good."

To Lorna, Davin said, "We've heard a lot about you. I'm sure Cara would like to meet you before you leave. Maybe you'd have time to go up and have a cup of coffee with her."

She gave him her best Sister Marlene smile, though everything inside her was jelling and quivering. "You're very kind," she said, and meant it, liking him on sight, this man who under happier circumstances might have become her brother-in-law.

"Well, let's go, Ben," he said, and the two clumped up a railed stairway to her left.

In their absence Lorna waited by the door for some acknowledgment from Jens. He continued sanding, presenting his back. The sight of it, so familiar and broad, rocking into his work, constricted her throat. She approached him timorously and stopped five paces behind him.

"Hello, Jens," she said plaintively.

Nothing.

The armpits of his blue chambray shirt were damp. His black suspenders were covered with sanding dust.

"Aren't you even going to say hello?"

Nothing.

She stood like a schoolgirl reciting a verse, feet primly planted, hands joined behind her back, aching with despair and mortification and the terrible need to have him turn to her and speak kindly.

"It's a grand building . . . everything you ever wanted. And your brother here working for you, and Ben, too. My goodness, you must be happy."

"Yeah, I'm real happy," he replied bitterly.

She swallowed the lump that rose into her throat and tried again. "I hear you won the regatta in grand fashion."

He straightened and turned, shoulders back and chest flared, slapping the sandpaper against his thigh to free it from dust.

"I'm a busy man, Lorna. What is it you want?"

"Oh, Jens . . ." she whispered, her voice breaking, "please don't . . ." Her chest hurt and tears rode the rims of her eyelids. "Because I don't think I can . . . oh, God . . . it's been so terrible these last few weeks." She closed her eyes and the tears spilled. She opened them and whispered, "I had a boy, Jens." The sandpaper stopped flapping. "I only saw him once before they took him away from me. My parents took him without asking me and gave him away."

From above came children's voices and the scrape of chairs.

Jens said, "I don't believe you. You gave him away."

"No, Jens, no . . . I didn't." Lorna's face contorted. "My mother came, and when she left, the nuns told me the baby was gone, too, and nobody will tell me where."

"You'd like me to believe that, wouldn't you!" He was so angry a white line appeared around his lips. His trunk jutted toward her and for a moment she thought he would strike her. "Well, I know better.

You had your mind made up when I came there to visit you. It was plain as the nose on your face that they'd talked you into it, and you could see that your life would be a whole lot simpler if you didn't have to explain away some bastard baby you'd have to bring home, so you just scuttled it, didn't you? Just . . . just sloughed it off on somebody else and the problem was taken care of! Well, listen to this, and listen good!" He grabbed her left forearm and doubled it hard against her breast. "The sorriest day of my life was the day I met you. It's brought me nothing but misery ever since. Little miss rich bitch, sniffing around the kitchen, sniffing around the boat shed, and sniffing around my bedroom, looking for some big damned stupid peckered-up fool to cure your itch. Well, I sure cured it, didn't I? But you've got enough money to fix even that, haven't you?" His face was thrust close, filled with disgust. "Aaah . . ." He gave her a sudden shove. "Get out of here. I've got nothing to say to you."

She landed with her hip against a stack of lumber. A shard of pain shot down her leg as she stared at his back through her tears. He spun away and fell to sanding again with fierce, vehement strokes.

She rubbed her bruised arm, repeated in her mind a dozen denials, knowing he would listen to none. He only sanded . . . and sanded . . . and sanded . . . trying to sand away his anger, his hurt, her. Every stroke seemed to wear away a thin layer of her heart until she felt its wall would burst. When she could bear his enmity no longer, she gathered herself away from the stacked lumber, whispered, "You're wrong," and fled.

When she was gone Jens gave up sanding and straightened his back, bone by bone. He listened to her footsteps run down the dock, watched her tiny sail carry her west, away from him. After several minutes his shoulders sagged and he sank back against the boat mold, letting his body double upon itself as he slid to the floor. There, gripping his head, with the sandpaper caught in his hair, Jens Harken wept.

Chapter
SEVENTEEN

OH, that bitter, doleful summer while Jens lived across the lake and Lorna seemed incapable of living at all. She existed, little more. She placed one foot before another and moved about when occasion demanded; placed food in her mouth when her body sent out warning signals; spent insomnious hours watching moonshadows from her bed and sunrises from her window seat; wrote countless pages in her journal; composed the beginnings of nearly one hundred poems, the ends of none. She declined all invitations.

Only one activity brought her a measure of peace.

Sailing.

She neither asked permission nor received admonition for using the catboat. Gideon grew conditioned to finding it gone at all hours of the day. The residents of the lake became accustomed to seeing her out in the pink mists of morning with her sail up before there appeared to be any wind; and in the hard white sun of midday with the catboat keeled up and her hanging over its side; and in the gentler breeze of evening—drifting, sail reefed, lying back staring at the sky so the craft appeared unmanned.

Levinia said, "You're growing thin as a rail and so appallingly tanned. Please stay out of that sun."

Theron said, "You never let anyone go out with you. Couldn't I go just once, pleeeeease?"

Phoebe Armfield said, "Lorna, I miss doing things with you."

Jenny said, "Is it because of Taylor that you're so blue? Do you still have feelings for him? If you still love him, you've got to tell me."

Gideon said, "No man will ever marry that girl. They think she's queer the way she sails around the lake mooning, day in and day out."

Aunt Agnes said, "Don't pay any mind to what anyone says. I acted the same way after Captain Dearsley died."

Lorna found solace in Aunt Agnes, who knew the details of her tragedy, and whose commiseration became balm to her wounded soul. They shared their innermost feelings, Lorna's recent heartbreak bringing forth Agnes's earlier one like pentimento upon an aged painting. The brushstrokes of Agnes's loss seemed to bleed through and superimpose themselves upon Lorna's present canvas, which was painted with loneliness and despair.

The two women went for long walks upon the beach and sat in the garden reading John Milton and William Blake. They took tea on rainy days in the gazebo, and on hot days picked switches of fresh lavender to fan away the flies while reciting poetry aloud to each other on the wickered veranda.

And so the summer passed.

Jens saw her often, recognized the little catboat when it came into the bay and sailed back to windward carrying her away once more. He would stand in the open door of the boatworks, tools forgotten in his hand, and watch her go, and wonder where his son was, what he looked like, what name he'd been given, and who was caring for him. He would think about any future children he might have and how they would never know their little brother existed somewhere in the world.

His son and Lorna Barnett.

His deepest despair and his utmost happiness forever embodied in the sight of a woman in a boat, skimming past, reminding him of what he wanted to forget.

Tim said, "Here, I thought you might like these," and gave Jens photographs of Lorna and himself documenting that idyllic, honeyed summer while the *Lorna D* was being built. He put them among his clothes, between his folded winter underwear in a trunk at the foot of his bed. Sometimes at night, lying with his hands doubled beneath his head, he would think of getting them out and looking at her, but remembrance brought bitterness and a wish for what could not be, so he'd focus his thoughts on other things and will her out of his memory.

He would succeed for a day or two at banishing her image, then he'd catch sight of her sail again, or hear her father's name, or glimpse one of the steam excursion crafts crossing the lake from the big hotels and wonder if she was aboard with the moneyed crowd whose laughter could be heard on the stillest of evenings as they headed toward the yacht club for dinner, or the Ramaley Pavilion for a play. Often music drifted from the water after dark, and the lanterns from some craft broadcast the ostentatious display of a dance in progress right out there in the middle of the water. Jens would stand on the end of his dock evaluating the chasm between himself and Lorna Barnett, and feel hurt well up at her unwillingness to challenge social pompousness when he'd asked her to marry him. *Dance then,* he thought bitterly, watching the lights on the water blink and bob. *Dance with your rich partners and forget you ever gave my baby away!*

The *Manitou* remained moored at his dock, bringing curious yachtsmen to view it almost daily. Often prospective customers would want to sail it, so Jens and Davin would get up a crew to take them out, coursing the length of the lake, passing the narrows off the east end of Manitou Island, where Rose Point Cottage gazed out over the water with its French doors thrown open and its emerald lawns spread like a velvet gown down to the water's edge. Once he passed a croquet game in progress, and another time what appeared to be a large-scale ladies' tea beneath a white gauze awning that had been erected on the lawn. Both times, after a single glance, he kept his eyes resolutely fixed upon his course, avoiding an inquisitive study of the girls with their long skirts trailing and their giant hats towering.

His business flourished. Orders came in for more yachts than he could build in a year, coupled with so many inquiries about boat repair that he hired Ben's friend Edward Stout to do repair work only. His second boat took to the water, christened *North Star,* commissioned by club member Nathan DuVal. It and the *Manitou* won every weekend race in which they took part. Reporters came from Chicago, Newport and New Jersey to interview Jens and write articles about his outlandish, unbeatable design and its impact upon the inland-lake racing scene. Quotes were printed and reprinted about the first race, when the crew of the *Manitou* were already in the yacht club having dinner before the second boat crossed the finish line.

A boatworks in Barnegat Bay, New Jersey, and another in South Carolina wrote and offered Jens jobs designing for them. He replied no to both but saved the letters, tucking them away in his trunk, using them as an excuse to cast a glance at the photographs of himself and Lorna Barnett.

Then one day Tim came over and said, "I've brought some news. Gideon Barnett is finishing the *Lorna D* and intends to put her in the water before the season is over. Speculation has it he's going to run her in next year's big regatta against Minnetonka."

Gideon Barnett had, indeed, hired a local man to finish the hardware and rigging of the *Lorna D*. When it was complete, he approached his daughter and told her, "I'm going to put the *Lorna D* in the water. Would you like to crew on her the first time she sails?"

Lorna was sitting on a chaise longue on the veranda desultorily buffing her nails. She paused and looked up at Gideon.

"No, thank you."

"But that's what you've always begged for, and you've been sailing the catboat all summer. Why not the *Lorna D*?"

"It's too late, Father."

Gideon's eyebrows beetled and his cheeks turned florid. "Lorna, when are you going to give up this infernal self-absorption you've been indulging in and join the human race again?"

"I don't know, Father."

Gideon wanted to shout that Levinia and he were getting mighty sick of her continuing this persecuted air and shutting them out of her life. Guilt sealed his lips. He turned and left her behind in the sultry air of late August.

It was inevitable the two boats would meet. It happened on a day in late September, when Jens and his crew had taken the *Manitou* out for a pleasure sail—a dark day with the wind up and the pebbled clouds lumped across the sky like scree. They met in the passage between the point and the peninsula, the *Manitou* sailing south, the *Lorna D* north. Approaching each other, the skippers of the two boats locked glances. They sat at the tillers of their respective yachts with eyes as turbulent and stormy as the clouds behind them, watching each other pass. Tim raised a hand in greeting but Gideon made no response, only glared from behind his great graying eyebrows, while Jens did the same. Had they been aboard warships, cannonballs would have flown. Lacking cannonballs they sent merely hate, and the certainty that the next time they met, their yachts would be going in the same direction.

In late October, the Barnett family closed up Rose Point and packed itself off to the city for the winter. Before leaving, Lorna stood a long time at the tip of the peninsula, looking northeasterly toward Jens's, wrapped in a winter coat with her arms crossed, her flossy hair fluttering loose from its twist and stinging her forehead. The wind slapped her coattails against her thighs and whipped the water's edge into creamy furrows. Out over the waves two gulls bucked a headwind and mewed at the gray billows below. Lorna thought of their child, four months old now, smiling and cooing for someone else.

"Goodbye, Jens," she said with tears in her eyes. "I miss you."

With winter just around the corner, the city house was as drear as the weather. Lorna's siblings were in school all day. Levinia worked diligently on benefits and balls, encouraging Lorna to get involved, receiving only refusals, though she volunteered some time at the lending library on Victoria Street. She loved the library work, which got her out of the house and put her in an environment of quiet and study, suiting her present mood. The holiday season brought a plethora of entertainment, which Lorna avoided whenever possible. Some houseguests came from the state of Washington, among them a thirty-one-year-old bachelor named Arnstadt, who showed overt interest in Lorna from the first moment he met her. He was involved with the railroads in some way, and her father did big lumber business with the railroads. It seemed Arnstadt was rich and available on the marriage market: She could perhaps fulfill her threat to marry the first man who asked her. But when he took her hand in the library one night, she yanked it back as if scorched, got tears in her eyes and hurriedly excused herself to run to her room and wonder if ever again in her life she could allow herself to be touched by any man besides Jens Harken. . . .

Phoebe came to visit over the Christmas holidays, wearing an engagement brooch from a man named Slatterleigh, who was a rising star in Mr. Armfield's business firm. In early January came the announcement of other upcoming nuptials: Taylor DuVal finally popped the question to Jenny, the wedding to take place the next summer. Levinia went into raptures planning the grandest social event of her matriarchal career.

Life flourished all around Lorna, while she lived in as insular a bubble as she could manage, shutting it all out and her pain all in.

Then one day in late February she returned from a stint at the lending library to find Aunt Agnes rushing toward her across the echoey front entry.

"Come upstairs quickly!" the old lady whispered urgently.

"What is it?"

Agnes crossed her lips with a finger and grabbed Lorna's hand, hauling her upstairs with her coat still on. In Agnes's own bedroom she closed the door and turned to her niece with eyes as bright as polished sapphires.

"I think I've found him."

"Who?"

"Your baby."

Lorna quit tugging at her scarf. "Oh, Aunt Agnes . . ." she whispered, while a thunderclap of hope slammed through her body.

"Come here." Agnes took her hand and toted her to a rosewood secretary between a pair of windows. She picked up a small white paper and thrust it into Lorna's hands. "I think he's been with Hulduh Schmitt all the time at this address."

Lorna read, *Hulduh Schmitt, 850 Hamburg Road, Minneapolis, Minnesota.*

She looked up sharply. "But why would she have him?"

"I don't know, but I suspect Levinia and Gideon had a fit of conscience after all and talked her into taking him to raise."

"But how did you find out? What makes you think—"

"I've been systematically ransacking your father's desk ever since they sent you away." Aunt Agnes looked bright-eyed and smug.

"You haven't!"

"I most certainly have. It took me some time to figure it out, though. You see, I was looking for the name of someone from some church or orphanage—some stranger's name, or some documents of adoption. Here I was, overlooking Mrs. Schmitt's name all these months until it finally hit me—he started paying her while you were gone, but he's still doing it! I asked myself why, when she's no longer employed here. It all adds up, Lorna, doesn't it?"

Lorna's heart was thudding so hard her face turned cherry. Still dressed in her coat, she gripped her aunt's hands. "Oh, Aunt Agnes, do you really think so?"

"Well, don't you?"

"It could be, couldn't it?" Lorna paced, excitedly. "Mother came there and the baby disappeared. While I was away, Mrs. Schmitt retired. It all makes sense."

"And who would have suspected anything after Mrs. Schmitt harped for years about quitting? Why, summer before last, when this whole affair between you and Jens started, half of White Bear Lake heard about the fuss Levinia put up in the midst of a dinner party over the idea of losing her cook. Everyone knew it would happen sooner or later. I say they paid her off to quit when she did, and she's got your little boy now."

"I've got to go find out." Lorna reread the address. "Immediately . . . tomorrow!" She lifted excited eyes to her aunt. "If it's true, I'll never be able to thank you enough."

"If it's true, that will be all the thanks I need."

They both smiled, imagining it, then Aunt Agnes sobered.

"If you find him, what will you do?"

A haunted look came into Lorna's eyes. "I don't know." She dropped onto the chair before the secretary, stared at a crystal pen holder and repeated, quieter, "I don't know."

If it was true, what could she do? Take the child? Raise him alone? Go to Jens and tell him? Every solution spawned a dozen more quandaries to which she truly had no answers. First she would find Hamburg Road and hope that Aunt Agnes's suspicions proved true.

* * *

She went by streetcar the following day, leaving her family believing she was volunteering at the lending library again. Changing cars twice, she traveled west toward Minneapolis, and through it to its far western reaches, disembarking at a place called Ridley Court, where she asked instructions in a chocolate shop, and once again from a man driving a Washburn and Crosby wagon loaded with flour barrels. Her walk terminated, after a good half hour, on a gravel road, where the houses were wideset and situated beside open country, with small barns and sheds in their backyards. Evidence of livestock wafted in the air, though she saw none. There were backyard pumps, and front yard pickets, and woodpiles stacked against sheds.

Number 850 was made of yellow brick, a modest house, narrow, with a deep overhanging roof supported by decorative white barge-boards that needed painting, just as the surrounding fence did. The gate squeaked as she opened it and navigated a plank walk between piles of snow. When she was midway up the walk a dog rose from a braided rug on the doorstep in the sun and barked at her twice. She paused and he came loping down the path, his tail wagging, to circle her and sniff at her rubber overshoes. He was shaggy and as yellow as the house, with a fluffy tail and a foxy face.

"Hello, boy," she said, offering her gloved hand for sniffing.

He looked up at her and wagged, and she proceeded toward the house with him accompanying.

At the door trepidation reared and sent her heartbeat thumping. If Aunt Agnes was right, the next few minutes could change her life forever. Poised to knock, she paused like a diver breathing deeply and measuring the distance down. Her throat felt constricted and the tops of her arms tingled as if her sleeves were too tight.

She knocked and waited.

The dog ambled to one side and ate a mouthful of snow. Drips fell from icicles on the eaves, drilling deep holes into the snow on either side of the door. Off in the unseen distance a crow scolded. An interior door opened and sucked the outer door against its frame. Through a thick lace curtain Lorna saw someone approach. Then the door opened and there stood Hulduh Schmitt, holding a dishtowel. When she saw Lorna her mouth and jowls went slack.

"Well . . . Miss Lorna."

"Hello, Mrs. Schmitt."

The dog went in but the two women remained motionless, Lorna in a red plaid coat with matching tam-o'-shanter, and Mrs. Schmitt in a great white starched apron just as she'd worn in the Barnett kitchens.

"May I come in?" Lorna inquired.

Mrs. Schmitt considered a moment, then seemed to resign herself, stepping back and waving Lorna inside with the dishtowel. "You might as well. You're here now."

Lorna stepped into an unheated entry no larger than a pantry.

"Go on inside," Mrs. Schmitt ordered, and followed her guest into the main body of the house, closing the door behind them. It was warm inside and smelled of freshly baked bread. Steep stairs climbed straight ahead against the right wall, and a stretch of hall separated the stairwell from two rooms on the left, the frontmost one a parlor visible through a wide archway.

An aged voice called from the room beyond it, in German.

In German, too, Mrs. Schmitt shouted a reply. "My mother," she explained to Lorna.

They could hear the old woman scolding the dog, probably for having wet feet. Lorna looked into the parlor, then back at Mrs. Schmitt.

"Is he here?" she asked simply.

"How did you find out?"

"Aunt Agnes figured it out."

"Your mother and father swore me to secrecy."

"Yes, I'm sure they did. Is he here?"

Hulduh thought about the generous monthly stipend that eased her retirement and provided for her mother. The fleeting thought brought not the slightest inclination to lie to Lorna Barnett about the child she'd brought into the world. Hulduh raised her hands in surrender and let them fall. "He's in the kitchen. This way."

The place was immaculately clean, filled with stolid old furniture and trimmed with crocheted doilies. The downstairs had only two rooms: the parlor at the front—it held an empty crib—connected by a doorway to the oversized kitchen at the back. In the latter, an ancient white-haired woman sat on a rocking chair shaking a homemade stocking doll before a beautiful blond baby. He sat suspended in a curious little hammocky seat which hung from a ring-shaped frame equipped with casters, his little feet—in booties—tiptoeing the floor. His hand was reaching toward the toy when Lorna entered the room—a chubby hand on a chubby arm with five perfect little outstretched fingers which closed upon the doll with the questionable coordination of an eight-month-old. At her appearance, he forgot the doll and looked toward the doorway: soft pale curls, eyes as blue as a Norse midnight, pudgy peachy face, and an innocent mouth as perfect and bowed as a cherub's. His perfection dulled all Lorna's surroundings. She moved toward him as if down a shaft of heavenly light.

"What's his name?"

"Daniel."

"Daniel . . ." she whispered, floating toward him.

"We call him Danny."

Lorna's eyes remained riveted on his fair little face as she dropped to her knees before his rolling chair, shy, yearning, uncertain. "Hello, Danny."

He stared at her, unblinking, his eyelashes curved and fine, a shade darker than his hair. He had so much of Jens in his features and so little of her.

She reached . . . took him slowly from the chair, his hand trailing the limp doll while he stared at her face and his legs and arms stuck out straight as a stuffed teddy bear's. "Oh, my beautiful one . . ." she whispered, as she brought his soft small body to her breast and placed her lips against his temple. ". . . I've found you at last."

She closed her eyes and held him, simply held him, allowing the moment to heal and hearten. He began babbling—"Mum-mum-mum"—and flailing the doll against her arm while she remained motionless, her eyes closed, transported to a plane of absolute maternal grace. He smelled milky and bready, like the room, and felt too soft for this world. She had not known love could feel this way, filling her so superabundantly that all the previous emotions of her life felt paltry by comparison. In that single moment of holding, feeling, smelling him, she was rendered complete.

She sat back on her haunches and stood him on her thighs, feeling her gaiety billow now that she knew he was here and really hers. He put a finger in one corner of his mouth, distorting it, showing two tiny bottom teeth, while continuing to flail the doll. Suddenly he seemed to realize he held it and grew animated, bobbing on his stubby legs and smacking her softly on the mouth with a wet hand. Laughing, she chased it with her lips, tipping her head back.

"He's so beautiful," she said to the two old women.

"And smart, too. He can say 'hot' already."

"Hot. Can you say 'hot,' Danny?"

His eyes got exuberant and he pointed a stubby finger at the big iron range. "Hottt."

"Yes, the stove's hot."

"Hottt," he said again, directly at Lorna's face.

"Smart boy! Is he good?" she asked.

"Oh yes, an angel. Sleeps all night long."

"And healthy?"

"Yes, that too, though he's been a little fretful lately 'cause he's teething."

"Are you teething? Getting pretty new teeth? Aw, mercy, but you're beautiful." She hugged him and swimbled left to right while joy sluiced in to replace her first awe. "Sweet, sweet boy!" And to the world at large, "I can't believe I'm holding him."

"He's drooling on your coat, Miss Lorna. Wouldn't you like to take it off?"

"Oh, I don't care! Let him drool! I'm just so happy!"

The dog, who'd been drinking across the room, gave himself an allover shake and came across the hardwood floor with clicking toenails and a friendly nose for the tot. Danny bounced and let out a shriek of welcome, lunging toward the animal.

"Oh, he loves old Summer. They're the best of pals."

The baby doubled over Lorna's arm and got the dog by the ruff, making burbling sounds, grabbing handfuls of hair.

"Noooo," Hulduh Schmitt warned, coming quickly to take the two chubby fists from the dog's fur. "Be nice to old Summer. Danny, be nice." He opened both fists and patted the dog clumsily, looking up at Hulduh for approval.

"That's a good boy."

They were simple displays—hot, nice—but to Lorna, prodigious, these first demonstrations of her baby's intelligence. During the while she remained she learned that Danny could stand on wobbly legs beside a chair while holding the seat, and point to his nose, and identify both Tante Hulduh and Grossmutter, and would point at them with a sausagey index finger when asked to.

Hulduh Schmitt said, "Mother and I were going to have our afternoon coffee, and there's fresh bread if you'd care to stay."

"Yes, please, I'd love it."

She set the table with well-used dishes designed with tulips and roses on an ivory background. Once long ago they'd been rimmed with gold but only faint chips of it remained. She apologized for not using a tablecloth. They were afraid, she explained, that the baby would accidentally pull it off someday and scald himself with their coffee. Indeed, while the women enjoyed their drinks and ate fresh bread and butter and peach sauce, Danny crawled around the claw-footed table, and played with wooden spoons on the floor, and pulled at the women's long skirts, and faked a little crying when he wanted to get up on a lap. The dog had retired to the back door rug and lay on his side, asleep. Once Danny crept over and poked at Summer's black lip and babbled. The dog raised its head, blinked once and went back to sleep. Hulduh got up and washed the baby's hands and put him in his rolling chair, where a circle of playthings were tied on with yarn.

The ancient woman spoke no English but smiled at the baby with her wrinkled eyes and wrinkled lips, and followed his every move, even over the rim of her coffee cup. Sometimes she'd bend over as best she could, to adjust his clothing, or give him the tiniest piece of soft buttery bread, or mutter something loving or instructive in her native tongue, and he'd go *whap! whap! whap!* with some toy against his chair, and the old grandmother would smile down at him, then at Lorna.

Once she asked Lorna a question; its meaning came through no matter the language barrier, as the old one pointed her gnarled finger first at Lorna, then at the child: "You are his *Mutter?*"

Lorna nodded and spread one hand on her stomach, the other on her heart, with a soulful expression on her face.

The baby grew tired of his rolling chair and was allowed to maneuver around on his own once more. He toppled over and clunked his head on the table foot and Lorna shot to rescue and embosom him. "Oh, noooo, don't cry . . . it's all right . . ." But he cried and strained toward Hulduh Schmitt, and the old woman took him on her ample lap, where he settled down and got his face wiped off, and received a sip of her creamy, sugary coffee off the end of a spoon. Then he rested his head against the starched white bib of her apron and stuck a thumb in his mouth and stared at the wainscot. "He's tired. He didn't nap long."

Lorna wondered how long a nap was required by an eight-month-old. And what one did if he fell down and *really* split his head open. And how a person learned everything she needed to know about mothering if her own mother chose to shun her.

Danny's eyelids began drooping and his lower lip lost its grip on his thumb. Mrs. Schmitt took him into the parlor and tucked him to sleep in his crib.

Returning, she refilled their cups and asked, "Now that you've found him, what do you intend to do?"

Lorna set down her cup very carefully and looked the old cook in the eye. "He's my son," she replied quietly.

"You want to take him, then."

"Yes . . . I do."

Hulduh Schmitt's face seemed to grow puffy and pale, perhaps even slightly afraid. She glanced at her mother, who was nodding off in the rocking chair.

"They'll stop the money if you do. My mother is old and I'm the only one she's got."

"Yes, I . . . I'm sorry, Mrs. Schmitt."

"And the baby is happy here with us."

"Oh, I can see that. I can!" Lorna laid a hand on her heart. "But he's my son. He was taken from me against my wishes."

The old cook's face registered shock. "Against your wishes?"

"Yes. My mother came when he was born, and they told me they were taking him away to have his first bath, only I never saw him again. When I asked to see him, he was gone and so was Mother. Now, that isn't right, Mrs. Schmitt, it just isn't right."

Mrs. Schmitt covered Lorna's hand on the table. "No, child, it isn't. Nor was I told the truth. They said you didn't want him."

"Oh, but I do. It's just that I must . . ." Lorna swallowed and glanced toward the parlor. "Well, I must find a place for him, and a way to take care of him. I must . . . I must speak to his father."

"You'll pardon me, miss, but I can't help asking—might that be young Jens?"

Lorna's expression grew sad. "Yes. And I love him very much, but they wouldn't hear of my marrying him." She ended bitterly, "His family doesn't have a summer place on the lake, you see."

Mrs. Schmitt studied the creamy skin on the surface of her coffee dregs. "Ah, life. It's so hard. So much sorrow. . . . So much."

They thought of it while the baby napped and the old woman quietly snored, her head bobbing and jerking occasionally.

"I can't take him with me today," Lorna said.

"Well then, that's something, anyway." Longing already showed in the old woman's eyes.

It was Lorna's turn to lay her hand on Mrs. Schmitt's. "When I get settled and have a place, you can come and see him as often as you wish."

But they both knew it was unlikely, considering Mrs. Schmitt's age, and the length of the walk and the streetcar rides, and the old woman who couldn't be left alone for long.

"When I take him . . ." Lorna hesitated, unable to brush aside the nagging sense of responsibility she felt for the two women's welfare. "Will you be able to make it all right without the extra money?"

Mrs. Schmitt pulled her chins in, her shoulders back and said to her coffee cup, "I've got a little put by."

When Lorna rose to leave, the grandmother awakened, dried the corners of her mouth and looked around as if wondering where she was. She saw Lorna and gave a sleepy smile, nodding goodbye.

"Goodbye," Lorna said.

On her way through the parlor she kissed the downy head of her son. "Bye-bye, dear one, I'll be back," she whispered, and quailed at the thought that she must once again visit his father.

Chapter
EIGHTEEN

THE next day dawned bitter cold and windy. Dressing for her trip to White Bear Lake, Lorna took extreme care, selecting far different clothing from the last time she went. Then, she had worn the girlish outfit meant to evoke nostalgia. Now she felt far from girlish, far from nostalgic. She had suffered, matured, learned. She would face Jens as a woman fighting for happiness at the most significant juncture of her life. She dressed in a somber wool suit covered by a heavy black sealskin coat with a matching muff and a plain wool bonnet.

The countryside from the train window looked indistinct, as if viewed through lace. Snow slanted across the landscape, dissecting it into blurred diagonals that shimmered and shifted as the train rumbled through it. Woods, fields, frozen streams—all appeared grayed and vague.

The railroad car was cold. Lorna crossed her legs, tucked her coat tightly around them and watched her breath rime the window. Projecting to her meeting with Jens, she wondered, *What will I say?* But one did not rehearse dialogue as grave as this. She was no longer the moony, lovestruck jo who had courted the kitchen helper and hauled picnic lunches off to forbidden peccadillos with him. She was a mother—foremost—and a wronged one at that.

Danny's precious face appeared in her memory with its wheat-white hair, watercolor-blue eyes and his father's features. Love rose in a remarkable swell that filled her eyes with tears and pushed fear through her veins at the thought of never having him.

At the station she rented a sleigh and driver to take her around the north shore of the lake to Dellwood. Tucked beneath a fur lap robe with the snow stinging her face, she scarcely heard the endless note played by the runners on the snow, nor the bells on the harness, nor the *whuf-whuf-whuf* of the horse's breath. Her senses were all turned inward to thoughts of Jens and Danny and herself.

She made out Jens's building as they approached it through the needles of white, a giant New England barn of a place, painted the same green as most yachts, with HARKEN BOATWORKS painted in white on its huge triangular side. Beneath the sign immense sliding doors hung on a metal track. To the left of these a smaller door held a sign, saying, "Open."

"Here you are, miss," the driver announced, pulling up.

"I'd like you to wait, please."

"Yes, ma'am. I'll just tie Ronnie up. Now, you take your time."

How many times since meeting Jens Harken had she approached a door with trepidation beating in her throat? The door of the servants' steps leading down to the kitchen. That of the shed where he'd built the *Lorna D*. The door of his own bedroom to which she'd sneaked in the dead of night to spend stolen hours in his bed. The open double doors on the opposite side of this very building last summer, when she'd had to tell him that Danny had been stolen. And yesterday, the door of that yellow brick house with the dog out front and the hope that she'd find their son inside.

Now she faced another, and the same apprehension she'd felt on all those occasions had multiplied a hundredfold, clubbing at her vitals, warning that if this failed, her life would ever after be shadowed by the loss of this man she loved.

She drew a deep breath, lifted the black metal latch and stepped inside.

As always the place in which Jens Harken worked beleaguered her with memories and brought the past sweeping back—damp fir, fresh planed cedar and burning wood. She saw a boat half finished and another that seemed to be under repair. At the far end of the cavernous building someone was whistling in a warbling fashion. Others were speaking and their voices carried as in a church. Jens's enterprise had grown: Six men toiled now over boats, molds, sails and rigging. One of them noticed her and said, "Someone to see you, Jens."

He was bending a rib with his brother, Davin, and looked over his shoulder to find her at the door.

As always, there passed that first impact of stunned motionlessness before he could mask his face with indifference.

"Take over here, Iver," he said to one of his workers, and left his station to come to her. He wore a red plaid flannel shirt, open at the throat, rolled up at the cuffs, showing the placket and sleeves of his winter underwear. His hair was longer than she'd ever seen it, curling away from a side part, whisking around his ears. His face was the mold from which their son's had been cast. He kept it devoid of all expression as he stopped before her.

"Hello, Jens."

"Lorna," he replied smilelessly, removing his wet leather gloves, letting his eyes scan her face for only the briefest second before dropping to the gloves.

"I wouldn't have come, but it's important."

"What?" The curt word left little chance of mistaking his enmity.

"Could we talk somewhere privately?"

"You've come to say something—say it."

"Very well. I've found our son."

For the space of a heartbeat he looked stupefied, but he recovered swiftly and donned his stoic face again. "So?"

"So? That's all you've got to say is so?"

"Well, what do you want me to say? You're the one who—"

The door opened and her driver came in, shimmying his shoulders from the cold, closing the door behind him.

"Afternoon," he greeted when he saw them nearby.

"Afternoon," replied Jens, tight-lipped and unbiddable.

"Bit nippy out there." The driver looked from one to the other, aware that he'd stepped into something tense. "You don't mind if I wait in here where it's warm, do you? I'm driving the lady."

Jens nodded sideways toward the stove. "There's coffee on the fender and mugs on the pegs. Help yourself."

The driver went away unwinding a plaid scarf from around his neck.

"Come on," Jens ordered, stalking away and leaving Lorna to follow. He led her into his office, a ten-by-ten cubicle jammed with sailing paraphernalia surrounding a messy desk. Slamming the door, he rounded on her.

"All right, so you found him. What do you want me to do about it?"

"For starters, you might ask about his welfare."

"His welfare! Ha! Now's a fine time for you to be lecturing me about his welfare, after you gave him away!"

"I did not give him away! They took him and hid him out with Hulduh Schmitt in the country on the other side of Minneapolis!"

"Hulduh Schmitt!" He glowered.

"She's had him all this time. My parents are paying her to keep him."

"So what do you want me to do, go to Hulduh's and steal him back for you? Go into town and beat up your daddy? I tried that once and I got put out on my ass!"

"I don't expect you to do anything! I just thought—"

He waited a beat before replying sardonically, "You just thought I might beg you to marry me again and we could go collect him and make a cozy little threesome, hiding from all your high society friends for the rest of our lives, is that it?" She blushed while he raged on. "Well, let me tell you something, Lorna Barnett. I don't want to be anybody's husband on suffrance. When I marry a woman she's got to accept me unconditionally. I'm not high society but I'm no lowlife, either. When I came to that abbey and asked you to marry me I came offering you a damned decent future, nothing you'd have to hang your head about. I expected you to fight for me, to tell your parents once and for all to go to the devil, and to stand up for your rights . . . for *our* rights! But no, you whimpered and curled up and decided you just couldn't face the names they might call you if you showed up at the altar pregnant with my baby. Well, so be it. You wouldn't have me then—I won't have you now."

"Oh, you think it's so easy, don't you!" she spit, lowering her head like a she-cat facing a tom. "Big, bullheaded Norwegian he-man with your pride all hurt and your chin jutting out! Well, you try living with parents like mine! You try getting them to give just one inch on anything! You try falling in love with the wrong man and ending up—"

"The wrong man! That's for sure!"

"*Yes, the wrong man!*" she yelled louder. "And ending up carrying his bastard, and being shipped off to Timbuktu and manipulated and lied to and told over and over and over again what hell your life will be if people find out about it. You try living in an abbey with a gaggle of neuter women, who pray for your salvation in whispers until you want to scream at them to go get a little lusty themselves and see how they handle it! You try having two younger sisters and being re-minded in every letter from your mother how you'll horrify them if word of your pregnancy leaks out, and how you'll ruin their chances of finding a decent husband because your shame will rub off on them. You try getting it through some man's thick Norwegian skull that at least *some* of this is not your fault, that you're human just like every-one else, and you fall in love and you make mistakes and you get hurt and you try your best to make things right, but you can't always do that so easily. You try it, Jens Harken!" Her insides were trembling by the time she finished.

He held up two fingers beneath her nose. "Twice I asked you to marry me—twice! But what did you say?"

She slapped his fingers away. "I said what the circumstances forced me to say!"

"You said no, because you were ashamed of me!"

"I was not! I was scared!"

"So was I." He tapped his chest. "But that didn't stop me from fighting for you! And that's some pretty damned flimsy excuse for how you acted!"

"Oh, you're so self-righteous you make me sick! I found Danny again, didn't I? I found him and I told Mrs. Schmitt I'm going to take him, and I will—with or without you I will, and I'll raise him if I have to do it by myself!"

"Oh, that's some big talk from a girl who's scared of her mommy and daddy's shadow. You told *me* you were going to raise him, too, but when it came right down to it you knuckled under to the Barnett commandment: Honor thy father and mother, even if they're wrong as hell and ruining your life!"

She stepped back, her mouth cinched. "I can see I made a mistake by coming here."

"You made the mistake when you decided not to meet that train. And a bigger one when you said no at the abbey. Now you can live with it."

She pulled decorum around herself like a fine fur stole and spoke levelly. "It strikes me, Jens, that I really never knew you. I knew one side of you, but it's more than that a wife's got to live with. You're more like my father than you can imagine, and that's the last sort of man I'd want to marry!"

She sallied out and slammed the door.

He stared at it through popping eyes for ten full seconds before dropping to his spring-mounted desk chair. First he glared at the cubbyholes before him, then gripped the top of his head with both hands and rammed the chair back as far as it would go, slurring her to the ceiling. He snorted aloud and let the chair spring forward, depositing him at the kneehole of the desk. A drawer was open to his right. He gave it a whack, attempting to slam it shut. It stuck. He whacked it again . . . harder! And harder still, hurting his hand! "Goddamn sonofabitch!" he railed, kicking the drawer so violently it countersank itself in its fitting.

Then he rocketed from the chair, rubbing his hands down his face while his turmoil fermented with anger, self-disgust, frustrated love and the heart-whumping news that his son's name was Danny and he could be reached in a couple of hours' ride.

He held out for three weeks, thinking, What good would it do to see the baby, he'd only want to take him, father him, never return him.

In the end paternal passion won out.

Mrs. Schmitt answered the door, not a hair different from when they'd worked together in the kitchen at Rose Point.

"Well . . ." she said, "I should have known you'd show up eventually."

"Been a long time, huh, Mrs. Schmitt?"

"You might as well come in, too. All the rest of his relatives have. It's beyond me why they thought I could keep him a secret."

He followed her inside and she awakened the baby from his nap. When Jens saw Danny the first time—oh, what a feeling! Stars seemed to be bursting and burning within him. Suns seemed to be glowing where once only his heart had been. He took the bleary-eyed child from Mrs. Schmitt's arms, held him high and kissed him, and soothed him when he cried, still shaky from sleep and discombobulated by his premature rousing. Jens held him on his arm—a warm little snail smelling of urine—and bounced him gently, strolled awhile, kissing his forehead and calming him in a remarkably short time.

He stayed the afternoon, meeting the old German woman who spent most of her time in the kitchen rocker; eating streusel, drinking coffee, acquainting with his son.

Hulduh Schmitt said, "His mother told you where he was, I suppose."

"Yes."

"Actually, I expected you sooner."

"I didn't know if I should come or not. Pretty hard to walk away from him."

"She says the same thing every time she leaves." Jens made no reply, only studied Hulduh Schmitt's droopy cheeks with a younger droop on his own.

"She comes every Thursday," Hulduh added.

"I was afraid she might have taken him already. She said she was going to."

"She wants to, but what's she going to do with him? A girl so young with no man to support her. The way I see it, that's your job. You ought to marry that girl, Jens Harken."

"Ehh . . . that wouldn't work out, her being the old man's daughter and me starting out as their kitchen help. We should have seen that right from the start."

Mrs. Schmitt nodded, though her expression remained dubious. "Well, he's a fine little boy, and I love him to high heaven. I'm not denying that the money I get from the Barnetts makes my life a lot easier, but as far as I'm concerned, it's a crime Danny ain't with his own mama and papa."

The following Thursday Mrs. Schmitt said, "Your man was here."

Lorna's head snapped up before she forced herself to show disdain. "Took him long enough."

"Left some money under his coffee cup. I told him your father pays me more than fair, but he left it anyway. I thought you should have it."

"No, he gave it to you."

"Your father pays me once. It wouldn't be fair to take money twice for the same job. Here . . ." She waggled her hand. "Take it."

Lorna looked balefully at the folded bills Mrs. Schmitt held out. Her anger smoldered. Damned bullheaded Norwegian ass! And that's where he could stuff it as far as she was concerned. It was nothing but conscience money, anyway.

In the end she snapped it out of Mrs. Schmitt's fingers and tucked it into her waistpocket.

"When was he here?"

"Tuesday."

"Is he coming back?"

"Next Tuesday, he said."

The following Tuesday Mrs. Schmitt said, "I gave the money to your woman."

"It was meant for the baby," Jens said.

"Oh, was it? Well, I didn't know. Miss Lorna took it anyhow."

When Jens left there were more folded bills beneath his coffee cup. Through the remainder of that late winter Mrs. Schmitt grew accustomed to seeing them on their chosen days—Tuesdays and Thursdays—and her heart went out to the two of them, who seemed unable to find a way to mend their differences and become a family.

April came and Lorna continued badgering everyone who would listen to open up a new paid position at the lending library which she hoped to fill, meanwhile squirreling away the money from Jens.

May knocked, and the cottage owners of White Bear prepared to estivate there once again. On the day before the Barnett family was to leave for the summer, adding all those additional miles to her trips to visit Danny, Lorna went to see him one last time.

By now she was accustomed to rapping on the door and letting herself in, which she did as usual that warm spring day, knocking first, then calling, "Hello, everyone!" as she went through the hall and front room. She could hear the hand agitator going on a washing machine and realized Hulduh had probably not heard her call.

She stepped into the kitchen and there stood Jens holding Danny while Hulduh washed clothes.

She came up short, her heart performing some wild dance in her breast.

"Oh," she said, blushing, "I didn't know you were here."

"I thought you always came on Thursdays."

"Well, I usually do, but my family is leaving for the lake tomorrow and I'm going along. Since it'll mean extra train time to see Danny after this . . . well . . ." Her explanation faded into silence.

He blushed, too. He did! Standing there holding their son on his muscular arm, the two of them as blond and alike as golden lab puppies in a litter, Jens Harken blushed.

The baby saw Lorna and got excited. "Mama, Mama!" he jabbered, bucking in his father's hold, reaching for her. She set down her package and rushed forward, smiling, taking him from Jens's arm for the first time ever.

"Hello, darling! Mmm . . ." She kissed his cheek and whirled once, devoting all her attention to him while the two old women looked on, Grossmutter from her rocker and Hulduh from her wooden washing machine, where she was working the agitator with a long wooden handle.

Hulduh said, "He missed you since you were here last time. He said Mama every day."

"Did you say Mama?"

"Mama," the baby repeated.

"I've brought you something wonderful. Look!" She sat down at the kitchen table with Danny in her lap and began untying the package. He lunged at the white paper circled with store string and slapped it a couple of times with his pudgy hands, burbling baby talk that made no sense. "Here, let me open it so you can see." She was struggling with the string and the rambunctious baby when Jens came to her rescue, saying, "Here, let me hold him while you do that."

As he plucked Danny off her lap Lorna looked up and her eyes met Jens's. The impact went through her like a wish. She was aware for that fleeting second of his freshly shaved face and his cedary smell, his crisply ironed shirt, blue blue eyes, his very beautiful mouth and the fact that they were sharing their baby for the first time ever. And on some existential level she was aware of the rhythm of the wooden agitator going *shup, shup, shup* somewhere in the room.

Softly, Jens told her, "Open it," and to their son, "Look, your mama's brought something for you."

His voice, calling her Mama, seemed to addle her hands. They grew clumsy while her face took color. She finally broke the string and produced a small white teddy bear with black button eyes, nappy fur and a real leather nose.

Danny reached for it eagerly as Jens returned him to Lorna's lap. The baby studied the toy, babbled, "Buh-duh," looked up at his mother for affirmation and claimed it for his own while his mother and father looked on.

"I bought it with your money," Lorna told Jens, keeping her eyes downcast. "I hope you don't mind."

"No, I don't."

"I've never bought him anything before."

"Neither have I."

She wanted to meet his eyes but was afraid. Her feelings were running very close to the surface and kept a faint blush on her cheek. They concentrated on the baby while Mrs. Schmitt gave up agitating for wringing, and wringing for rinsing, and finally Lorna had the sense to offer, "Oh, here, Mrs. Schmitt, let me help you!"

"Aw, no, you just play with the baby. You get little enough chance."

"Why, don't be silly! While you're washing his diapers? It's the least I can do." She gave the baby to Jens, removed her hat, rolled up her sleeves and helped Mrs. Schmitt slosh the batch of diapers up and down in a galvanized washtub, then guide them through a wringer while the older woman operated a hand crank. When the batch was done, lying like pressed snakes in the oval clothes basket, Lorna asked, "May I hang them?"

"Well, it don't seem right, you in your pretty dress. And look, you've got it all wet."

Lorna brushed at her skirts. "Oh, I don't mind—really, I don't. And I'd love to hang the diapers."

"Well, all right, if you really want to. Clothespins are in a bag on the end of the clothesline."

With the clothes basket on her left hip, Lorna escaped Jens's rattling presence and stepped out the back door into the warm spring sunshine of a cloudless blue day. There, she could breathe deeper and regain common sense. This was a chance meeting, not an assignation. She, Jens and Danny were sundered individuals, not a family. It was silly to pretend otherwise.

The yard spread out to the west, where a small red barn and privy divided it from some grassland beyond. Farther to the west a section of thick woods created a deeper line of green. The dog, Summer, was napping in the sun beside the stone foundation of the barn, lying in a sandy nest he'd scratched among some freshly sprouted irises. Between the house and the barn a dirt path was worn in the grass. To the right of it a garden patch was already tilled, giving off a faint tinge of manure. A wooden wheelbarrow stood beside it filled with seed potatoes. Against the barrow leaned a hoe and a hand cultivator. To the left of the path the clothesline stood halfway down the yard, nestled between two immense clumps of blooming lilac bushes.

Lorna set down the basket and picked up a diaper, flat and stiff from the wringer. Never in her life had she hung clothing on a line. Where she came from, servants did that. But she'd seen the maids hanging towels and did as they had: She found two corners and gave the first diaper a snap, hung it . . . and another . . . and found she enjoyed it immensely, the wind tugging at her hair and the damp gauze filling like a sail, lifting against her face, bringing the smell of fresh lye soap. There was a sense of peace in the scene—the dog asleep in the sun, the lilacs scenting the air, some sparrows fluttering into the lilac bushes to explore and Lorna . . . handling her son's diapers.

She was hanging the third one when Jens came out the back door and started down the path. At his approach, she turned her back and bent over the wicker basket to pick up another diaper. When she straightened, he was standing beneath the T-shaped clothespole, gripping it loosely above his head with both hands.

She snapped the diaper and hung it.

Finally he said, "So you come here every week."

"As Mrs. Schmitt informed you."

"I usually come on Tuesdays, but I have to go to Duluth this Tuesday." She made no reply. "Fellow up there is commissioning a boat." Still she made no reply.

She hung up another diaper while Jens tried to pretend he wasn't watching her. Finally he gave up the pretense and pinned his gaze on her profile as she raised her face and arms to place two clothespins above her head. Her breasts—fuller than before the baby's birth—showed distinctly against the backdrop of green field. The profile of her lips and mouth had become—if anything—prettier during the two years he'd known her. Her face was that of a mature woman now, not a girl. The wind had tugged a strand of her hair loose and fluttered it gently along her jaw. A diaper billowed toward her shoulder and she pushed it away absently while reaching for another. He thought about the child he'd left in the house, coming from within the two of them.

"He's the prettiest thing I've ever seen," Jens said sincerely, softened by the presence of the three of them together for the first time ever.

"He's going to look just like you."

"That'd be something, wouldn't it?"

"Probably be bullheaded just like you, too."

"Yeah, well, I'm Norwegian." He frowned at the distant woods for a long time. Finally he dropped his hands and dusted his palms together, searching for something to say. A good half minute passed without anything coming to mind. He shifted his feet and muttered, "Damn it, Lorna . . ."

She shot him a look. "Damn it, Lorna, what?" The crack of a diaper punctuated her words while the set of her jaw grew belligerent. "I suppose you're upset about me taking your money."

"No, it's not that!"

"Well, what then?"

"I don't know what." After some agitated silence he asked, "Do your folks know you come out here to see him?"

"No. They think I'm working in a lending library."

"You see? You still won't admit anything to them. You're still living under their thumb."

"Well, what do you expect me to do!"

"Nothing," he said, and started back toward the house. "Nothing."

She kicked the clothes basket out of her way and went after him. "Damn you, Jens Harken!" She clunked him between the shoulder blades with her fist. "Don't you turn away from me!"

He spun around in surprise. She was standing defiantly with both hands on her hips, a clothespin clenched in one, and tears in her stormy brown eyes. She had never looked more beautiful.

"Ask me!" she ordered. "Damn you, you bullheaded Norwegian, you ask me!"

But he would not. Not until she realized that she had still never put him first before her parents. She could love him as long as nobody else knew, but that wasn't enough for him.

"Not until you defy them."

"I can't afford to! Even the money from you isn't enough for Danny and me to live on!"

"Then make your peace with them."

"Never!"

"All right then, we're at a stalemate."

"You love me! Don't tell me you don't!"

"That was never the issue. The issue was did you love me?"

"Did I love you! Jens Harken, I was the one who did all the pursuing. Are you going to stand there and deny it? *I* came to the kitchen! *I* came to the boat shed! *I* came to your room!"

"Until you got pregnant, then you tried to hide it and me from everyone you knew. You're still trying to hide it. How do you think that makes me feel?"

"How do you think it makes me feel, having to sneak off into the country to see my own son because I haven't got a husband?"

"You still don't understand what it is you've got to do, do you?"

"Besides stand here and make a fool of myself? No . . . no, I don't!"

He couldn't help it: He grinned. The situation was pitiful but she looked splendid, standing there in the dirt path with her hair blowing and her temper fired. Sweet Jesus, how easy it would be to take three steps and grab her waist and plunk her right up against the front of himself, where she belonged, and kiss the daylights out of her and say, Let's take Danny and go.

And then what? Live a life of lies, maybe telling people the child was adopted—anything so she could save face?

He'd have her come public with the truth, or nothing.

So he stood there grinning, because she looked so fetching, and he wanted her so badly, and she'd just admitted she loved him and felt like a fool for it.

"What are you grinning at!"

"You."

"Well, stop it!"

"You said it, I didn't. If you're feeling like a fool maybe there's a good reason."

Without warning she fired a clothespin. It pinged off his forehead and landed in the grass.

"Ouch!" he yelped, lurching back, scowling. "What the hell was that for?" He nursed his forehead.

"I wouldn't marry you now if my parents asked me to!"

He backed up a step and dropped his hand. "And since we both know that will never happen, we're right back where we started before this argument began." He turned and headed back toward the house. Ten feet up the path, he paused and did an about-face. "I suggest you stick to Thursdays from now on."

She fired another clothespin. It flew past his shoulder and dropped harmlessly to the ground behind him. In the wake of her paltry effort to hurt him they stood for five terrible heartbeats, staring at each other defiantly.

"Grow up, Lorna," he said quietly, then turned and left her alone in the sunny yard.

When the kitchen door closed behind him it seemed to unleash her tears. She swiped them away with her sleeve and marched back to the clothesline to hang the last diaper. She plucked it from the basket, gave it a snap and was lifting her hands toward the clothesline when the torrent struck. It hit with the force of a spring flood—tears and sobs wrenching her entire body until she went as limp as the gauze in her hands. She let it happen, sorrow and self-pity spilling out and wallowing into the green and gold spring day. She dropped to both knees and doubled forward, knotting the cool damp diaper in her fists as she rocked mindlessly.

And cried . . . and cried . . . and cried . . .

And scared the sparrows away.

Chapter
NINETEEN

THE days following her encounter with Jens left Lorna truly
miserable. Seeing Danny at last with his father had left within her a
living picture of the three of them that she embroidered in her
imagination until it became more real than reality. In it, she, Jens and
Danny lived in the loft above the boatworks; the diapers on the line
were Danny's; at noon she cooked Jens dinner; in the evening the
three of them sailed; at night she and Jens slept together in a great
wooden bed.

Realizing this would probably never evolve, she cried often.

The next time she went to Mrs. Schmitt's, Jens was absent and her
reunion with Danny seemed lacking and sad. Her days had grown
empty and pointless and seemed to be leading into nothing but more
of the same.

Then one day she was in a mercantile store in White Bear Lake
and ran into Mitch Armfield.

"Lorna?"

At the sound of her name she turned and found him in the aisle
behind her.

"Mitch," she said, smiling. "My goodness, Mitch, is that you?"
He'd grown so much in the past two years. He was tall and strapping
and already wearing a summer tan, a handsome young adult where
a blushing boy had been before.

He grinned and spread his hands. "It's me."

"Where's the skinny young boy who used to want to teach me to sail?"

"Still sailing—how about you?"

"Still sailing, too, but mostly in the catboat alone."

"So we notice. Seems like you're never around anymore."

"I am. I just . . ." She let the thought trail, glancing aside and absently touching some fancy tea towels.

He waited politely, but when she remained silent, he spoke. "Everybody says where's Lorna when we go on the moonlight sails and over to the pavilion for concerts. Especially Phoebe."

Lorna looked up and asked wistfully, "How's Phoebe?"

"Phoebe's all right . . . but she misses you terribly."

"I miss her, too. We used to do so much together."

Mitchell's face became intent with thought before he inquired, "May I be honest, Lorna?"

"Why, of course."

"You broke Phoebe's heart. After you went away to school you never wrote to her, or called on her when you got back. She thought she must have done something to hurt you, but she didn't know what it was. Was she right?"

"No . . . oh no," Lorna replied heartfully, touching Mitch's sleeve. "She was my dearest friend."

"Then, what happened?"

Lorna could only stare at him and drop her hand from his arm. Time lengthened, and Mitchell pressed his point. "I know she missed you a lot when she became engaged and began making wedding plans. She said the two of you used to be the closest of confidantes about things like that. I know she'd love it if you could be again."

"So would I," Lorna whispered.

Sincerity shone from her face. Her eyes held a deep sadness that keyed in Mitchell a responsive sympathy. Whatever Lorna's reason for abandoning her friendship with Phoebe, it had hurt her as much as it had hurt his sister.

Mitchell extended his hand.

"Well . . . it was nice running into you. May I tell Phoebe I did?"

"Absolutely. And please give her my love."

He squeezed Lorna's hand affectionately. "I'll do that."

* * *

The conversation lingered on Lorna's mind for the remainder of the day. That night it stole her sleep and she arose from bed in the wee hours to sit on her window seat staring out across the dark water, analyzing why she'd cut herself off from Phoebe. It was senseless, really, to deny oneself the comfort of true friendship at a time in life when it was most needed. Was it shame that had held her aloof? Yes, she supposed it was. Her mother had said people would be shocked and horrified, and that she, Lorna, would be ostracized for bearing a baby out of wedlock. But would *Phoebe* be horrified? Would she cut off Lorna's friendship? The answer was no. Deep down in Lorna's heart she didn't believe her lifelong friend would act that way. Curiously enough, it was Lorna who'd done the ostracizing and she had no explanation why.

The following day Lorna awakened weary and puffy-eyed from lack of sleep. Inside, however, she was flustered with anticipation. Her decision had been made near four in the morning, and she rose hurrying, as if too long had been wasted already.

Anxious to see Phoebe once again, she declined breakfast, selected clothing, held a cold compress to her eyes, pouffed her hair up in a "Gibson girl" nest, dressed in a green-leafed skirt and a white shirt-waist, and at ten-thirty that morning presented herself at the door of the Armfield cottage. When Phoebe descended the stairs at the maid's summons and found Lorna waiting, her footsteps faltered. Her face withered as if she might break into tears, then she rushed down the last three steps into Lorna's arms.

"Oh, Lorna . . . Is it really you?"

"Phoebe, darling, yes, yes . . . I'm back."

They held each other and thrived for the moment on nostalgia. They grew misty-eyed, happy, and healed.

At last Phoebe drew back. "Mitch said he spoke to you, but I didn't dare hope."

"He certainly did, and made me see the light. We're overdue for a good long talk and I think it's time we had it."

The two went upstairs arm in arm, into Phoebe's room, where nothing had changed. The view out the turret was as splendid as ever, and the crocheted tester above Phoebe's bed the same one

Lorna had flopped back and studied during many confidential girl-hood exchanges.

"It's so good to be here again!" she exclaimed, walking to the window and looking out for a minute before turning to face the room and her friend. "I can't even remember the last time."

"Summer before last."

"Ah yes, summer before last, the year I first met Jens. So much has happened to me since then."

"Will you tell me?"

"Yes . . . everything."

"Come . . . sit." Phoebe stood her bedpillows up against the head-board and made herself a place at the foot of the bed. They both removed their slippers and sat cross-legged, facing each other.

Lorna smiled and said, "You first. I have a feeling your story is much happier than mine."

"All right. He's handsome and kind and outrageous and hard-working, and the first time I saw him I felt as if my guts got wrapped around my windpipe and choked me every time I tried to swallow."

Lorna laughed and said, "Your Mr. Slatterleigh."

"Dennis, yes."

"You're truly in love, then."

"So truly that I feel as if I'm dying every time he says good night and walks away."

"Oh, I'm so happy for you. When's the wedding?"

"Not soon enough. The last week in June. I wanted you to be one of my bridesmaids, but I was afraid to ask you. Then the time came for making plans and ordering gowns and you had become so with-drawn and stand-offish . . ."

"I know. And I'm so sorry for that, Phoebe. Mitch said you thought you'd done something to hurt my feelings but it wasn't that at all. It was me . . . just me . . . and my situation, that's all."

"What situation?"

Lorna's face took on a faraway expression. She gazed into the distance. "I've often wondered if you didn't figure it out—after all, you knew me so well." Her eyes returned to Phoebe. "We knew practically everything about each other's personal feelings."

"It was Jens Harken, the boatbuilder, of course."

"Yes . . . of course. We fell in love that summer he was building the *Lorna D.*"

"And?"

"And I had his baby."

Phoebe neither gasped nor cringed. She released a breath as if she'd been holding it in preparation for the revelation. Then she bent forward and offered both her hands for holding.

Lorna accepted them.

"So you weren't away at school."

"No, I was at an abbey near Milwaukee with a bunch of nuns." The whole story tumbled out with no detail omitted. Reaching the part about her painful meeting with Jens at Mrs. Schmitt's house the previous week, Lorna was trembling and battling tears. "And so . . ." she ended, ". . . he left me there in the yard."

Phoebe asked, "Did you mean it when you said you wouldn't marry him if your parents asked you to?"

"No," Lorna replied in a small voice. "I was upset so I blurted out the first thing that came into my mind. Marrying him is all I dream about."

She dreamed about it again for a passing moment while Phoebe watched the expression change in Lorna's eyes.

"I remember something you told me once, long ago, that first summer you met him. Remember the day we were sitting in the garden and you first confessed to me that you loved him? You were so sure of it, and your face became so serene when you told me. Then you said something that I never forgot. You said being with him made life suddenly feel more meaningful, and that when he left you it was the November of your heart."

"Did I say that?"

"Yes, you did, with such a beautiful and martyred look in your eyes. I was so sure that someday you'd find a way to be together with him, in spite of anything your parents might do or say. It seemed that you *should* be married to him. I've never stopped thinking so."

"Oh, Phoebe, I want to be . . . so much."

"Then do something about it."

"Do what? He's over there, and I'm over here and my parents haven't changed their stand one bit—"

"Of course they haven't. And if you wait around for them to do so, you'll wait your life away. Jens was right when he said that if you loved him enough you'd defy them. If it were me, I would."

"Defy your parents?"

"For the man I love? Absolutely."

"But, Phoebe, Jens said—"

"Yes, Jens said, then you said, then he said and you said, and you both were so upset and angry and stubborn that you weren't making sense. The fact remains that you love each other. You have a baby you want to call your own. Your parents have preached shame and fear and you fell for it, hook, line and sinker. Instead of telling *them* to go fly a kite, you told Jens to."

"I did not, Phoebe! How can you say that?"

"Well, it amounts to the same thing. You chose your parents over him, didn't you?"

"No I didn't!"

"Oh, Lorna, stop deluding yourself and listen to what Jens is saying. As long as you keep hiding the truth, and hiding the baby, and hiding your love for him, you're saying he's not good enough to meet your family's standards. If you want him, show him! Get Danny from Mrs. Schmitt's house and . . . and march up to your mother and father and say, 'Look, you can accept my baby, and accept my choice of a husband, or I'm walking out of your life forever.' "

"I did tell them that once."

"Yes, but did you follow it up or were you only blowing hot air? You're still living with them, aren't you? You haven't given them any ultimatums, have you? Well, if I were you, I'd do it! I'd . . . I'd . . ." Phoebe had grown more and more animated as she preached. She was on her feet, stirring the air with both hands and pacing beside the bed. "I'd take Danny out someplace in public where—"

"In public?"

"Yes, in public, like . . . like the regatta, maybe, and I'd—"

"The regatta?"

"—hold him on my arm and point to his father's boat—"

"Don't be silly."

"—and say, 'See your father sail? See the boat he built? He's the most famous boatbuilder in America, and I'm here to let the world know I've made my choice!' "

Silence fell in Phoebe's room. The idea was so outrageous it left both women breathless. They stared at each other, smitten by vivid images of Lorna doing such a brash thing.

Lorna whispered. "Would you really, Phoebe?"

"I don't know." Phoebe dropped to the bed. "I was just rambling, imagining . . . trying to find some answer for you."

"But *would* you?"

Phoebe gazed at Lorna. Lorna gazed back. Neither of them blinked.

Phoebe asked, almost secretively, "Gosh, Lorna, would *you?*"

It seemed too reckless to ponder, but ponder they did until their cheeks turned pink with excitement.

"It would be something, wouldn't it, Lorna? You, with Danny on your arm . . ."

"While my father skipped the *Lorna D* . . ."

"And your mother watched from the yacht club lawn . . ."

"And Jens skipped—what boat is he skipping this year?" Lorna's exhilaration was clear.

"The *Manitou.*"

"The *Manitou.*" After a beat of silence, Lorna asked, "Is he expected to win?"

"Nobody knows. Rumor has it there'll be ten flat-bottomed boats entered, including your father's. But rumor also has it that Jens has made some modifications to Tim's boat, only he's not saying what they are, and nobody else can even guess. Harken's the expert, everybody agrees."

"He'll win," Lorna said confidently. "I know he will. It's in his blood to win."

"And what about you?"

Lorna flopped to her back as she had so many times before, her wide eyes fixed on the tester.

"Jens wanted me to defy them. That would certainly do the trick, wouldn't it?"

Phoebe piled onto her knees, crawled over and looked directly down into Lorna's face. "You aren't seriously considering it, are you?"

"I don't know."

"Merciful heavens, you are!"

"You have to admit, the shock value would almost be worth the disgrace. And I have been spineless. And I do want to marry Jens Harken."

Phoebe flopped beside Lorna and for a full minute they lay in silence, staring upward, considering this outlandish idea.

At length Lorna mused, "I'd need one friend on my side. Would you stand beside me if I did it?"

Phoebe found Lorna's hand and squeezed it hard. "Of course I would." She considered a moment and gathered her courage before divulging, "I'm going to tell you something I haven't told another living soul." She turned her head, met Lorna's eyes and admitted, "The only difference between you and me is that you got caught and I haven't."

Perhaps it was Phoebe's admission that she, too, had lain with a lover, perhaps the fact that Lorna had been denied enough happiness that her time had come to claim it. Whatever the reason, within hours of her talk with Phoebe, she decided she would do this brash, unheard-of thing.

The regatta was only a week and a half away. She thought of little else, night and day from the time Phoebe put the idea into her head. She imagined herself with Jens and Danny, a mother and father and their child, a family at long last.

She imagined her own parents witnessing their reunion and her courage faltered.

She imagined living the rest of her life in this present limbo and her courage revived.

On her next visit to Mrs. Schmitt she took a package containing a little navy-blue-and-white sailor suit. When she laid it on the table the words were difficult to say.

"When I come next week, I'd like you to have Danny dressed in this. I'll be coming on Saturday, earlier than usual, and I'll be taking him with me."

"So the time has come."

Lorna covered Mrs. Schmitt's shiny, worn hand on the tabletop. "I'm sorry to take him away from you. I know you love him, too."

"So you don't plan to bring him back, then."

"No. Not if . . . well, if everything works out the way I hope."

"You and Harken."

"Yes. I hope so. He's a stubborn man but . . . we shall see."

Mrs. Schmitt removed her spectacles and cleaned them on her apron skirt. "Well, that's the way it ought to be, whether I'll miss the little one or not. The three of you being apart just ain't natural."

"I'll try to send you money when I can."

"Don't you worry about me. I've got a—"

". . . A little put by . . ." Lorna joined in. "Yes, I know. Still, I'll do what I can."

It was the first of many hurdles she would have to vault on her way to claiming happiness, but claim it she would, and with that goal in sight, she counted down the days.

The Saturday of the regatta had not yet dawned when Jens awoke, well before sunup. Carrying a mug of coffee, he left the sounds of somnolent breathing behind him in the loft and went outside into the rush of predawn wind and the sound of his own footsteps clunking on the dock.

The *Manitou* tossed restlessly on the water, giving an intermittent *thud-thud* that jarred the pilings and sent Jens's coffee swinging in his cup.

He sipped it down an inch and stepped aboard a deck that was sheeny with early morning dew, balancing, loose-kneed, shifting with the faint roll as the waves slapped the hull. He walked the length of the boat, touching things . . . wood, rope, canvas, metal . . . sipping his coffee. A sip . . . a touch . . . a sip . . . a touch . . . coffee and rigging . . . the wind already at ten knots and promising a good day for sailing. Only a thin pale line of clear sky showed above the eastern horizon, boding a stony-gray morning ahead. Between the hull ribs, collected water rocked with the rhythm of the swaying boat. He knelt to sponge it, then dried the dewy deck.

Times like this he felt close to his father, wishing the old man were here to see what he'd accomplished, to offer his deep, unruffled voice with its common sense and soothing tones.

Jens sent a thought to him: *Today's the day, Pa. Wish us luck.*

At dawn the sun poked through the narrow break between the clouds, beaming a false sunrise that gilded the tree-tips and mast-tips and the hair of Davin, who came ambling down the dock barefoot, carrying a coffee mug, too, with yesterday's wrinkled shirt thrown on over his trousers.

"You're up early," Davin greeted.

"Couldn't sleep."

"Yeah, I know what you mean. I didn't get to sleep myself till well after midnight. Just laid there thinking."

After a spell of silence Jens asked, "You think about Pa at all?"

"Yup."

"I wish he was here."

"Yup, me too."

"He taught us good, though, didn't he?"

"Sure did."

"Taught us to believe in ourselves. Win or lose today, we've got that."

"You want to win awfully bad, though, don't you?"

"Well, don't you?"

"Of course, but it's different for me. I haven't got Gideon Barnett trying to get even with me for getting his daughter pregnant."

"There's a lot riding on this race, that's for sure."

"Do you think there's any chance his boat can win?"

"Of course there is. I designed it, so it's going to be damned fast, and so is the *North Star,* but the moderations we made on the *Manitou* are going to make the difference." He had replaced the large single rudder with two smaller ones, which gave her quicker reaction on a turn.

"What about the Minnetonka club—you worried about any of their boats?"

"No, mainly the *Lorna D.*"

Davin clapped a hand on Jens's shoulder. "Well, tinkering around down here won't make the time go any faster. Come on upstairs and let's get Cara to make us some hot breakfast."

With race time set for noon, the morning seemed to crawl. Jens ate little but took time dressing, relishing as always the official yacht club sweater and vowing that one day he'd be more than an honorary member. Tim walked over from his cabin, all spiffed up in his whites, too, and grinning. "So, after today, can I take my boat home and keep it there?"

Jens had taken plenty of ribbing from the men about wanting the boat here the last few days "to make necessary modifications." Everyone knew there were no more to be made: They'd been done weeks before.

Davin had said, "If that boat was a woman she'd be hotter than Dutch love from all that stroking."

Ben had said, "We'll have to put a new coat of varnish on the splashboard if he polishes it any more."

Tim said, "Maybe I should offer to sell it back to him. Might make myself a pretty profit."

The rest of the crew arrived. Cara and the children boarded the *Manitou* for a ride over to the yacht club lawn, from where they'd watch the race. The ride over proved swift and wet, for the wind had increased to fifteen knots and threw spray over the bow.

When they arrived the B-class races were in progress. A crowd was already gathered on the lawn and milling along the dock, inspecting the boats tied there. When the spectators identified sail number W-30 approaching, a spate of applause went up. "Listen to that. They've got your number, Jens," Cara teased with a glint of pride in her eye.

Jens gave her a preoccupied smile that faded quickly as he scanned the other scows tied up at the dock. Immediately he picked out the *Lorna D* and Gideon Barnett among the crew, cleaning his deck and checking rigging. At the sound of the applause, Barnett straightened and peered out over the water to see who was approaching. Jens could tell the instant he read the sail number, for he spun away and became busy, giving some order to his crew.

The *Manitou* docked. Cara and the children alighted. Jens checked his watch—a quarter hour to go before the skippers' meeting and already there were chorus girls singing on the beach, and reporters and spectators galore. He checked the club flag fluttering from the tip of the cupola, gauging the wind and the scudding gray clouds to the south and west, the water surface, which was pilled and choppy. His crew hauled the spinnaker onto the lawn to fold and pack. Jens stayed behind to check the rigging, which he'd already done several times this morning. Still, it felt reassuring to be with the boat, keeping his hands busy.

Pins in the side stays.

Halyards untwisted.

Lines properly coiled.

He glanced up the lawn. Ladies with their petticoats luffing were holding their brightly colored hats on their heads. Children raced in and out, playing tag amid their mothers' skirts and eating lollipops. The chorus girls ended a song and a barber shop began one. He spied a contingent of spectators from Rose Point—Levinia Barnett and the two old aunts, Lorna's sisters and her brother (peering through a spyglass)—all of them milling among the society crowd who'd undoubtedly come to cheer for the *Lorna D.* Lorna herself was conspicuously absent.

Jens suppressed his disappointment and found things to keep himself preoccupied. He leaned over the stern to pull weeds from the rudders. He answered the questions of three young lads who stood on the dock with admiration in their eyes.

"You build this yourself, mister?"

"How long'd it take you?"

"My dad says I can have a boat someday."

Time for the skippers' meeting, and his crew came carrying the spinnaker aboard. He merely nodded to them—all the men tense now and introspective.

Approaching the Barnett group on his way toward the clubhouse, Jens felt their regard ricocheting his way but kept his eyes straight ahead, realizing that what he needed least during this final hour were distractions.

He had nearly reached the clubhouse when he caught a flash of something familiar at the edge of his peripheral vision. A color, an outline, a bearing—something made him turn to look.

And there stood Lorna.

With . . . with . . .

Dear God, she had Danny on her arm! Danny and Lorna were actually here at the regatta, where every person she knew would be watching!

For a frozen moment he stared. Then took a step toward them and halted while shock, euphoria and exultation exploded within him. His son and his woman, standing not twenty feet away, watching him! She was dressed in peach and Danny in a blue-and-white sailor suit, tugging fussily at a sailor hat that was tied under his chin.

Lorna pointed with an index finger and Jens read her lips.

There's Papa.

Danny quit fussing with the hat, focused on his father and beamed.

"Papa," he squealed, squirming as if to get down and run to Jens.

A lark in Jens's breast fluttered and sang. Never had he wanted to approach someone so badly in his life, but this was not the time. The seconds ticked away toward the scheduled skippers' meeting, and being late for it meant jeopardizing his chance to win if he missed the course instructions.

Someone came up the plank walk behind him. The footsteps halted and Lorna's face sobered. Jens looked around to find Gideon Barnett staring at his daughter and grandson. A murmur went through the crowd while Gideon's face turned gray as an old sail. Jens sensed when word reached Levinia, for a surge of motion parted the spectators. In that moment, while all factions recognized Lorna's presence and began counting back the months, it seemed the entire crowd held its breath.

Then a single young woman came forward with a smile.

"Lorna, hi! Where have you been? I've been looking for you." Phoebe Armfield stepped through the crowd, exuding an overt show of friendship. "Hi, Danny!" Not a soul would have known she'd never seen the baby before as she marched forward and kissed both him and his mother on the cheek.

Lorna's eyes reluctantly left Jens and he moved on toward the clubhouse with Gideon ten paces behind.

Inside, on the upper porch, it was hard to keep his mind on the race judge—a stern, officious man in white trousers, blue blazer and a tie, holding a blackboard in his hands.

"Skippers, welcome! Today's course will be a triangle, finishing to windward after two and one-third times around the course. We'll have a ten-minute assembly gun, a five-minute warning gun, and then the starting gun. Any premature starters will have to recross the starting line."

While the judge did his job, Jens felt Gideon Barnett's eyes skewering him from behind. Ten skippers were present, five from each yacht club, and all had entered scows. It would be a far different race from last year's.

The meeting ended. "Good sailing, gentlemen. Man your boats."

Amid skippers murmuring the standard refrain, "Sail well . . . sail well . . . ," Jens turned to find Barnett already stalking from the building ahead of him.

Outside, his eyes immediately veered to Lorna, seeking a cue—to go to her or directly to his boat, which did she want? Some friends of her age had gathered around her—he recognized faces from the yacht club crowd, plus one of the old-maid aunts, who was taking the baby from her arms. As Jens paused uncertainly with his crew waiting on board and his heart juddering, she left the others and came toward him.

He stood mute, quite nearly aching, waiting like some imbecile while she came straight on and stopped so close before him that her skirt blew across his ankles. She took his seasoned hand in her much softer one and said simply, "Sail well, Jens."

He squeezed her hand and felt as if his chest would explode.

"I will . . . for you and Danny," he managed.

Then he was stalking toward the *Manitou.* Surging! Sweeping! Ascending to some plane where only gods exist!

On board, he sensed his crew was fully aware of the human drama being contraposed with the nautical one soon to begin. They were soft-spoken, soft-smiling, non-questioning, taking their cue from his brother, Davin, who only said, "What do you say, skipper, shall we get this tub under sail?"

When Jens took his place at the tiller and gave the order to cast off, the crew of the *Manitou* understood they were racing under the orders of a skipper who had already won something far more important than an A-class race.

"Hoist the main! Hoist the jib!" There was a new note of alacrity in Jens's voice as he gave the command.

Mitch raised the mainsail, Davin the jib, and W-30 slid out among its competitors into the intermittently choppy waters of North Bay. They took her out toward the starting line on a broad reach, sailing leisurely downwind. Ten boats, sleek and speedy, cruised up and down, the sailors eyeing their competition and testing the wind in search of the favored end of the starting line. Every skipper cast his eye out for distant sails, gauging the wind shifts, checking the flag on the clubhouse roof and the telltales fluttering on their sails, looking for wind streaks on the water, anything to give him an edge at the moment the starting gun sounded.

The race officials manned a rowboat on either end of the starting line, surveying the milling fleet. Splotches of blue began appearing among the gray-bellied clouds, revealing even higher cirrocumulus clouds above.

"Looks like some mackerel sky showing up there," Jens remarked. "That could mean a high front, so watch for veering winds."

At the sound of the ten-minute warning gun, Jens ordered, "Edward, have your watch ready at the five-minute gun."

Edward got it out and stood ready.

Only necessary words were spoken after that as the crew of the *Manitou* continued reaching—sailing back and forth, back and forth—behind the starting line. Their shirts were already damp, their muscles tense, their gazes constantly scanning all the other boats, the *Lorna D* and the *North Star* among them.

The five-minute gun cracked. Edward checked his watch.

"Watch M-32," Davin said at the jib. "He's passing to leeward."

Jens steered the *Manitou* around the Minnetonka entrant and went on reaching. A moment later he picked his spot on the line and murmured to Davin, "We're going for the weather end. Trim! Let's get down there fast while the line is sagging." Then five of the others—six, seven—maneuvered in closer and closer, so close that their booms were swinging over their competitors' decks.

With one minute to go eight boats nosed toward the starting line separated by mere inches. Still Jens hung back, his sails luffing and the *Manitou* flat in the water. From his left he saw a boat heading up and heard the voice of Gideon Barnett shout, "Right of way! Right of way! Take it up and give me room!"

Recognizing the bluff, Jens held steady.

Fifteen seconds to go and chaos seemed to reign. Suddenly the wind freshened. Men shouted. Waves splashed. A Minnetonka skipper yelled, "We're going to be early! Ease the sails!"

Edward counted, ". . . Ten . . . nine . . ."

Amid the shrieking of wind through the rigging, boats heeled up and sails were trimmed. Bodies cantilevered over the weather rails as the boats gathered speed for the start.

Suddenly an opening cleared on the line.

"Trim in, Davin, there's a hole below me!"

". . . Eight . . . seven . . ."

"Trim! Trim!" Jens shouted.

Davin trimmed the jib. Mitch trimmed the main. The sails took full wind and Jens steered down as the boat picked up speed.

". . . Six . . . five . . ."

The *Manitou* heeled.

"Hike! Hike!"

". . . Four . . . three . . ."

The crew scrambled to the high side, angling their bodies so far over the water that their backs nearly touched the deck of the boat beside them.

". . . Three . . . two . . ."

The gun sounded as the *Manitou* leaped forward across the starting line.

"Keep 'er balanced!" Jens yelled, and they were under way, a nose ahead of the pack. A Minnetonka boat, M-9, dropped a length behind in the *Manitou's* wind shadow, followed closely by W-10, which tacked off for clear air. They sailed with the strategy of chess players, crossing each other all the way up the lake, using headers and lifts like pawns in a game.

Approaching the windward mark, Edward shouted, "W-10 has picked up a wind shift off of Peninsula Point. He's coming in on a full plane!"

From the *Lorna D* someone shouted, "Starboard!" asking for the right of way.

The *Lorna D* skimmed past and rounded the windward mark in first place with the *Manitou* inches behind her transom.

"Coming about, watch your heads!" Jens yelled. The boom swung as they cleared the mark. "Hoist the spinnaker!"

Ben set the pole, Tim hoisted, and a moment later their chute flew. With a smart crack the spinnaker filled and the boat leaped forward, chasing the *Lorna D.*

Ahead lay the turning mark, an orange buoy bobbing on the waves. Jens steered toward it with Barnett's boat close above him, and the picture of Lorna and Danny in his mind.

Mitch shouted, "There's a big puff astern!"

Jens swung around and saw busy black water. He turned down into it and felt the boat surge.

As he came abeam of the *Lorna D*, Jens yelled, "I need buoy room!"

Across ten feet of waves, he glimpsed Barnett's determined face, then the *Lorna D* dropped behind.

It was back and forth, back and forth for two more legs, one boat passing the other, calling for its rights and receiving them.

The *Manitou* led the race rounding the leeward mark, and the *Lorna D* led rounding the weather mark, with the *North Star* bringing up third place.

Off Peninsula Point bending wind shifts created tricky going as the land distorted the wind flow. Mitch continually played the mainsheet, and Davin the jib.

Approaching the leeward mark for the last time, faces were grave and wills determined. Jens and his crew were behind by a boat length. *For her, Barnett,* Jens thought, looking over the forward rail at Barnett's back. *For Lorna and the baby I'm going to win this race, then before you and society and God and the world I'm going to march up that yacht club lawn and claim them!*

"He's coming in wide. Let's dip inside!"

As the *Lorna D* took a wide swing around the buoy, Jens shouted, "Trim!" and ducked into the opening to round the mark first.

"Pull in the main! Hike for all you're worth!"

With the wind steady and strong off their bow, they headed upwind for the last time. Nose to nose they flew through the water. It was a game of inches. Laying the finish line, both skippers knew the race would be won by boat speed, not tactics or wind shifts.

"Hike for all you're worth! Hang by your toenails!" Jens hollered.

The crew hung so far over the weather rail that the waves were splashing over their throats. They tasted lake water on their lips and triumph close at hand as they pulled a length ahead. When they got close enough to see the cannon on the judge's deck, Jens shouted, "We're fetching the line! Hang on!"

Jens could hear the crowd cheering from shore. Could feel the power of the boat streaming up through the tiller. Could see the yacht club buoy beyond the line of hard, shivering bodies hanging over his weather rail and clinging to the lines. Water sprayed their faces as they looked over their shoulder at the *Lorna D* two full boat lengths behind. They headed straight for the flotilla of spectator boats dotting the water, saw the judge standing in his boat holding the string that would fire the cannon.

Teeth to the wind, they streamed across the finish line as the gun sounded.

"First place, W-30!" the judge shouted, drowned by the roar of the crowd. Though he called out the rest of the boat numbers as they came in, they were lost on the crew of the *Manitou*. Elation ruled them. Victory blotted out everything else.

They eased the sails . . . and their tense muscles . . . and let the rejoicing begin, meeting their skipper with open arms.

"We did it! We did it!"

"Nice job, Jens!"

A special hug from Davin. "You did it, big brother."

"We did it!"

And from Mitch Armfield, "Good job, skipper. Thanks for having me aboard."

"You're a hell of a sailor, Mitch. Couldn't have done it without you."

It seemed too immense to believe, now that it was all over. They had done this improbable thing that had started with a note in Gideon Barnett's ice cream dessert two years ago. It was over for the crew, who were only now realizing how tense, aching, wet and shivering they'd been; but for Jens there was so much more.

Under eased sail, he steered the boat toward a peach dress waiting on the shore. He picked her out with no trouble, partway up the grass, standing in full sunlight. She still held Danny on her arm, her free hand waving high above her head, and her friend Phoebe beside her.

Ah, that smile, that welcome—it was all that mattered. Not the trophies waiting on the cloth-covered table beneath an elm tree; not the crowd pressing to the water's edge and filling the dock with congratulations on their lips; not the photographers, or the brass band, or the rich club members waiting to order boats from him.

Only Lorna Barnett and the message she'd conveyed by bringing their child here today.

He kept them in his sights until his arrival at the dock forced his attention elsewhere. There were orders to be given, a boat to be secured, sails to be dried. During docking, spectators boarded and climbed all over the *Manitou,* asking questions, shaking the crew's hands, offering praise. Jens answered, complied, thanked, with Lorna ever on the edge of his vision and each moment tightening an emotional winch between them. The crew tied up the *Manitou* to the dock. Jens coiled the lines, got slapped on the back dozens of times, caught sight of the *Lorna D* tying up, its skipper and crew going through similar motions. The *North Star* arrived and the others continued straggling in. Two reporters vied for his attention.

"Mr. Harken, Mr. Harken . . ."

"Excuse me, gentlemen," he said, stepping around them, "there's someone I must see first."

She was standing uphill, her eyes the stars by which he navigated. He caught her gaze and held it, weaving through the throng while congratulations rained upon him, unheard now. He felt the beat of his own heart, like a sail filling and refilling, carrying him toward his heart's victory and the dark intensity of her unbroken regard as she watched him approach.

When he reached her the crowd receded into virtual unimportance. Among the hundreds of people beneath that June sun they recognized only each other.

His big hands closed around her arms just above the elbows and they beamed into each other's eyes.

"Oh Jens," she said, "you did it."

"I did it. . . ." He kissed her full on the mouth, one swift, hard, stamp of possession with Danny between them.

"Papa?" Danny was patting him on the cheek.

"And who's this? Why, it's Danny. Come here and give us a kiss."

Danny was too excited. "Ribe a boat?" He pointed toward the dock.

"He wants to ride the boat," Lorna interpreted.

"Y' darned right you'll ride a boat. We'll make you one that's just your size and we'll have you sailing it yourself as soon as you can swim."

Danny had quit staring at the boat in favor of staring at his father. Jens kissed Danny on his beautiful rosy mouth and rested his big, rough hand on the boy's blond head. "Lord, what a day," he murmured, and kissed him again on the hair, letting his eyes close.

Struggling to recover from a surfeit of emotions, he turned his attention once more on Lorna, who said, "You remember Phoebe, don't you?"

During Phoebe's congratulations someone said, "Two pretty women and where's mine?" It was Davin, arriving at the same moment as Cara and the children.

"She's right here, you big blond Viking. Oh, I'm so proud of you!" Cara gave her man a kiss. "And you, too." Another kiss for Jens as the round of celebration grew appropriately congested with baby Roland on his mother's arm, transferring to his father's, and Jeffrey pulling on his mother's skirt and Jens still holding Danny.

Finally Jens found time to say, "You've met my brother, Davin . . . and here's Cara . . . Cara, come here, darlin'." Jens put his arm around her shoulders while she smiled shyly. "This is Lorna . . ."

It went without saying: Their futures were inexorably entwined. The two women exchanged smiles and hellos rife with friendly curiosity. Then Davin and Lorna did the same while his big hand engulfed her much smaller one. He held it firmly, smiling into her eyes, and said, "Well this is some day. I'm not sure what I'm the happiest about."

Jeffrey was pulling on Jens's leg. "Lift me up! Lift me up!"

"Ho, it's Jeffrey!" Jens managed to pick him up. With a boy on each arm he said, "Look here now, this is your cousin, Danny. I wouldn't be surprised if the two of you sail in a race someday, just like your daddy and I. And you'll be winning, too, just like we did."

The round of babble and new faces suddenly became too much for Danny. His face crumpled and he began crying, reaching for his mother. The adults all laughed, relieving some of the tension.

A quavery female voice said, "I demand to be introduced to the winning skipper. I've waited long enough."

They all turned to find Aunt Agnes waiting, looking sprightly at Jens.

When she was holding Jens's hand, the pair created an endearing contrast, she no higher than his elbow, delicate, graying and somewhat bowed; he so tall, tan and strapping, robust with youth. Looking up into his windburned face, she said in her quaky voice, "I was not wrong—there is a striking resemblance to my own Captain Dearsley. I'm sure, young man, that this is the happiest day of your life. I want you to know it is also the happiest day of mine."

Lorna's sisters approached timidly, hanging back. Theron came with them, so fascinated by Danny that he went right to him, his eyes riveted on the baby. "Gosh, Lorna, am I really his uncle?"

"Yes, you are, Theron."

"What's his name?"

"Danny."

"Hi, Danny. Wanna come to your uncle Theron? I'll show you my spyglass."

The baby put out his arms and went to Theron as if he'd known him since birth. Theron threw a smile of pride around the group, while Jenny and Daphne inched forward.

Lorna, with a lump in her throat, said, "It's time you all met Jens."

The story would be told and retold for decades, about the day Jens Harken met Lorna Barnett's family, and she his, out on the yacht club lawn after he'd sailed his winning boat across the finish line to take the three-year White Bear/Minnetonka Challenge Cup. How she came there bringing his baby dressed in a little blue-and-white sailor suit, and how Jens and Lorna kissed in broad daylight before several hundred spectators. And how Gideon and Levinia Barnett watched from a distance just after Gid had lost the race in a boat named after his daughter. And how Jens Harken had at one time been kitchen help for the Barnett family. And how the day of the regatta began cloudy but ended up sunny, as if the couple's new life were being granted a heavenly blessing. And how Gideon Barnett, after stubbornly refusing to award Harken the cup the previous year, finally bent enough to do the honors.

* * *

The boats had all come in. The band had at last silenced. Shade dappled the single cup left standing on the white-draped table beneath the big elm.

Commodore Gideon Barnett placed it in Jens Harken's hands.

"Congratulations, Harken," Barnett said, offering his hand.

Jens took it. "Thank you, sir." It was a firm grip that lingered a beat longer than necessary, turning bitterness into doubt. Barnett's face was stern, Jens's wiped of all traces of vainglory. This man was his child's grandfather. Gideon's features and abilities and perhaps even his temperament would be passed down through their bloodlines for generations to come. Surely there was some way to resolve this bitter hatred.

The handshake ended.

"I'd like the cup to remain at the club, sir. That's where it belongs."

Barnett appeared momentarily nonplussed. He recovered quickly to reply, "The club accepts it. That's good of you, skipper."

"I'll keep it for today, though, if that's all right."

"Of course."

Jens turned and lifted the loving cup high above his head. The roar of applause seemed to ripple the curtain on the table behind him. He saw Lorna and Danny waiting . . . and Levinia Barnett standing off in the distance, looking very unsure of herself . . . and he sensed Gideon Barnett's rancor showing its first signs of cracking. There had been an undercurrent as the two of them shook hands and exchanged their first civil words in nearly two years. They had done it before a mob of people; surely they could do it again someday in private. It would take time, though, time and forgiveness and a swallowing of pride on both their parts.

Stepping from the dais, Jens put thoughts of Gideon and Levinia Barnett behind him as he headed for their daughter. But time was still not their own. Everyone had to touch the loving cup, then the crew had to drink champagne from it and have their pictures taken by Tim's big black-hooded camera with the cup held high above their heads. After that, Jens submitted to being interviewed by a circle of photographers, but throughout the questions and answers his eyes kept returning to Lorna. The baby had fallen asleep on her shoulder. Still on her feet, swaying with the slumbering child, her cheek against his golden hair, Lorna kept her eyes fervently pinned upon Jens.

He finally put an end to the hubbub. "Gentlemen, it's been a long day." He held up his hands, staving off more questions. "Now I've got some celebrating of my own to do. If you'll excuse me . . ." He said goodbye to his crew, shaking each man's hand, ending with Davin.

Quietly, Jens told him, "I may not be home tonight."

"Listen, Jens, Cara and I . . . well, we feel bad, taking up your house when you've got your own family to—"

"Don't say another word. There's time for that later. The woman hasn't even said she'll marry me yet. But if you'll let go of my hand, I intend to go ask her."

Davin squeezed Jens's knotty upper arm and said, "Go on, then."

At last Jens turned toward Lorna.

She was waiting for him, still swaying gently with Danny asleep on her shoulder. A wet spot had formed beneath the baby's open mouth on her peach-colored dress, turning the sateen to deep apricot. The wind, long since subsided, had loosened her auburn hair from its great drooping nest. The sun had burned her cheeks and forehead. Two years had turned her into his greatest reason for living.

"Let's get out of here," he said, reaching her. "Should I take him?"

"Oh, yes, please . . . he's gotten so heavy."

He handed her the loving cup and took the slumbering baby, whose eyes fluttered open briefly, then closed against Jens's shoulder.

"I left a bag of diapers over there under a tree."

They detoured to collect it, then walked—three at last—toward the gravel driveway with Jens's right hand resting on Lorna's shoulder.

"Where are we going?" Lorna asked.

"Somewhere alone."

"But where?"

He hailed a rig and driver, helped her board. "The Hotel Leip," he ordered, climbing in, then turned to question Lorna quietly, "All right?"

Her eyes answered before her lips. "Yes."

She set the loving cup on the floor between their knees. He settled the baby in the crook of his left arm and took her hand with his free one, studying it in his own—hers diminutive, slightly freckled from the summer sun; his wide and horny and red-burned from the wind.

Her fingers were slim as evening shadows while his were thick and coarse as rope. He lifted her hand to his lips and kissed the back of it, overcome at last, now that he could allow his emotions sway.

"My God," he whispered, letting his head fall back against the leather seat, his eyes closed. "I can't believe you're here." He rested so awhile, with her hand clasped tightly within his own, rubbing her soft skin with his thumb, listening to the *clip-clop* of the horse's hooves and the steady rasp of wheels on gravel. The air felt cool on his windburned face. The baby's wet diaper was soaking through his pants. He thought if he were asked to describe heaven he would ever after describe this moment. He opened his eyes. Lorna's face was turned sharply away with a handkerchief pressed to her mouth.

He lifted his head and cooed, "Hey, heeey . . . ," touching her far jaw to make her turn. "Are you crying?"

His words released one quiet sob and brought her coiling against him with her cheek on his sleeve. "I can't help it."

"The time for crying is over."

"Yes, I know. It's just that . . ." She had no reason. She sniffled again and dried her streaming eyes.

"I understand. I'm feeling the same way. We've been through so much hell it's hard to accept heaven."

"Something like that . . . yes."

They rode awhile in silence, passing under an arch of beech trees that threw green and gold streaks eastward as evening approached. They could smell the lake—wet rocks and weeds and water-cooled air mixed with a tincture of horse—and feel the warm sun on their left cheeks, the evening cool on their right. A rock flew up and hit the underside of the carriage. A meadowlark trilled from their right. A dog barked somewhere in the unseen distance. The metal of the loving cup had warmed against their knees.

In time Jens said, "Your father shook my hand, though," as if the subject of Gideon had been under earlier discussion.

"Yes, I saw."

"And he congratulated me . . . and you know what?" Jens looked down and Lorna looked up. "It's going to take some time, but I think we'll mend those fences. I could tell. Something was different. Something was . . ." He left the thought dangling.

"Something was making him question his own stubbornness."

"It seemed that way."

"That something was Danny," she said.

They both looked down at their sleeping son.

"Yes, probably so."

In time Jens asked, "Your father didn't say anything to you today?"

"No."

"Your mother either?"

"No."

He squeezed her hand and laid it against his heart.

"But it hurt them not to, I could tell. And the girls, and Theron, and your aunt Agnes . . . didn't they love Danny, though?"

"Yes, they certainly did."

He had no further consolations to offer.

At the Hotel Leip he said to the desk clerk, "We'll need two rooms."

"Two?" The young man with a protuberant Adam's apple and receding chin looked from the sleeping baby in Jens's arms to Lorna, then back to Jens.

"Yes, two, please."

"Very well, sir. Happy to oblige, especially with all the regatta guests leaving town again."

Jens signed the register first, then handed the pen to Lorna.

Lorna & Daniel Barnett, she signed.

The clerk plucked two keys from two hooks on the wall and came from behind his cubbyhole. "Bags, sir?"

Lorna handed him the cloth diaper bag with its looped handles. He looked down at its contents, easily visible within the open top, but led them without further questions to their rooms.

Lorna took Danny into the first. Jens went on to the second. Within a minute he returned to Lorna's, entering without knocking, closing the door with extreme care not to click the latch. She had laid Danny on the bed and was beginning to loosen his clothing.

"Wait a minute . . ." Jens whispered. "Don't wake him up yet."

She straightened and turned to face him. He dropped his keys on her dresser, then slowly crossed the room and stood before her. He took her head lightly in both hands, his thumbs lightly stroking the crests of her cheeks while their eyes partook of each other. Her lips were parted, her breath quick and reedy.

"Jens . . ." she whispered at the moment his head began tipping and his arms gathered her in.

At last, at last, the kiss they had so longed for. Since he'd seen her standing on the clubhouse lawn, since she'd seen him sail the *Manitou* to the yacht club dock, this moment had been glimmering like a promise on their horizon. They met in full length—mouths, breasts, hips seeking and finding mates. With hands and bodies and throaty murmurs they claimed what had been denied them so long. Their starved hearts pressed close. Her hands opened upon his back, rubbed his ribs, burrowed in his hair. He cupped her head, her disheveled knot filling his palm and falling further awry as their ardor brought the sweetest of swaying and refitting. Enough, enough—they could not get enough of this first taste and touch. To reclaim was not enough: The kiss became a struggle to achieve the impossible, to imbibe each other and so become a part of the other's heart and blood and muscle. They twined, curved one to the other, until like two meeting waves they seemed to lose distinction and become one.

He tore his mouth free, held her head in both hands and spoke into her open mouth.

"Will you marry me?"

"Yes."

"When?"

"Right now, tomorrow, as soon as the law will let us."

"Ah, Lorna, Lorna . . ." Squeezing his eyes shut he clasped her hard against him. "I love you so much."

"I love you, too, Jens, and I'm so sorry I hurt you. I've been just miserable without you." She drew back, took his face in her hands and touched her lips to his mouth, cheek, eye, mouth, speaking between strewn kisses. "So miserable . . . so wrong . . . so much in love that my life became meaningless without you . . . And then that day I saw you at Mrs. Schmitt's, saw Danny with you . . . Oh, dear, dear heart, I thought I should rather die than watch you walk away."

"Shh . . . later . . . we'll talk later. Come here." He scooped her up and sank into an upholstered chair with her across his lap. Their mouths were joined before their weight settled, and his hand made free swipes over her breast, hip, belly. Up to her throat and hair, where he began searching out what hairpins remained. It was clumsy going with his left arm pinned beneath her, so she reached up to help, dropping four pins onto the floor, shaking her head once till the hair fell free, then looping her arms around his neck and kissing him as if he were a peach that she had just peeled. In the midst of the kiss he tried opening the buttons up the back of her dress, which again proved awkward.

He ended the kiss impatiently. "Sit up. I can't reach."

She sat up and straddled his lap in a billow of peach-colored skirts, with her elbows on his shoulders and her fingertips in his hair. While he tended her buttons, she tended his mouth—full, beautiful, soft Norwegian mouth that had kissed her lips and breasts and stomach in those secret days of summer passion, and would kiss them again and again into the anniversaries of their years.

The buttons up her back were opened. He freed his mouth to say, "Your wrists." What exquisite torture to look into each other's eyes and bank fires while she sat erect and offered first one wrist, then the other for his chapped fingers to attend. She lifted her arms and he swept the dress away, working it over her breasts and making of her hair a galaxy of shooting stars.

"Your sweater," she whispered, when the dress had fallen. And he took a turn submitting to his lover's wishes.

When his sweater had joined her dress, he unbuttoned her chemise and bared her to the waist, then slid his hands beneath her armpits and tipped her forward to kiss her breasts—soft, pear-shaped, florid breasts that had been offered for kissing a dozen times before. He washed them with his tongue, and held them in his wide, rough hands, her chin tipping back, her eyes closing and her body beginning to rock to the primal rhythm set free within them both.

He stopped kissing her, still cupping her breasts. "These—what about these when they took the baby away? I've wondered so many times."

She drew her heavy head up and opened her eyes. "They bound them," she answered, "and after a few days the milk stopped coming."

"Then who fed Danny?"

"My mother brought a wet nurse."

In silence he absorbed her answer, his thumbs grazing her nipples, saddened by thoughts of that heartbroken, tormented time.

"That must have hurt."

"It doesn't matter anymore."

As if to wipe it from his mind, he growled deep in his throat and circled her ribs in a huge bear hug that buried the side of his face against her naked skin.

"Don't think about it tonight," she whispered, ringing his head with both arms and riffling her fingers along his scalp. "Not tonight, Jens."

"You're right. Not tonight. Tonight is just for us." He drew back, gripping her lightly, kneading the sides of her breasts with the butts of his hands. "So unbutton your petticoat," he whispered, "before our baby wakes up."

She followed orders and he rose, swinging her to the floor, her clothing collapsing like reefed sails till it caught on her hip. He brushed it down and it dropped to her ankles with a quiet swish.

"You're more beautiful than ever." There were changes—wider hips, a pouf to her stomach that had been absent before Danny's birth. He touched her there.

"No fair," she whispered. "I'm anxious, too."

Smiling, he worked off the remainder of his clothes, then took her down upon them, crushing her dress, his trousers, their underwear, caring little that they had no featherbed. Having each other was enough.

They touched, stroked, caressed, whispered endearments, made promises as eloquent and lasting as any they would speak in a marriage ceremony.

"I'll never let you get away again."

"I'll never go."

"And when our next baby is born I'll be beside you."

"And our next and our next."

"Oh, Lorna Barnett, how I love you."

"Jens Harken, my dearest, dearest one, I love you, too. I shall love you till my dying day and spend every day till then proving it."

When he placed his body within hers, he trembled and closed his eyes. She drew in a shaken breath and released it in a near sigh. They felt exalted as he beat a rhythm upon her, and smiles broke forth, quiet smiles of rightness as he folded his fingers tightly between hers and pressed the backs of her hands to the floor.

"Supposing you get pregnant tonight," he said.

"Then Danny will have a brother."

"Or a sister."

"A sister would be fine, too."

"Especially if she looked like you."

"Jens..." Her eyelids were closing. "Oh, Jens..." Her lips dropped open and he knew the time for talking was over. Time now to take their share of ecstasy, to store it up for the less than ecstatic times when babies were sick, or tempers short, or work hours long or loved ones troublesome—there would be those troubled times, they both knew. Yet they would take each other, in sickness and in health, in good times and bad, till death did they part, knowing that their bond of love would be strong enough to see them through. For ever waiting, beyond the troubled times, would be this, life's most wondrous recompense.

He shuddered, and groaned in broken syllables, spilling within her.

She arched and whimpered and cried out in repletion, and he muffled the sound with his mouth.

In the sweet reflux that followed, as he lowered his weight upon her and felt her arms loop loosely around him, he saw their life together spinning into the future of bright, shining hours undershadowed by occasions when tears would gather. He accepted both, knowing that's what true loving was about. He rolled to his side and held her close with one heel. He strummed her hair back from her face and touched her cheek lovingly.

"We're going to do just fine," he whispered.

She smiled, one arm folded beneath her ear. "I know we are."

"And we're going to try very hard with your mother and father."

"But if it doesn't work with them—"

He touched her lips to silence them. "It will."

She removed his finger. "But if it doesn't work we'll still be happy."

"I asked you to defy them for me and you did, but I'm not sure I should have asked such a thing of you. My mother and father are dead. Yours are the only ones we've got left—right or wrong, the only ones—and I want you to know that today or tomorrow or whenever we say our vows I'll be adding a silent one to you to do my best to win them over. Not for me, but for you . . . and for our children."

"Oh, Jens . . ." She captured him and drew him close. "You're such a good man. How can they help but see it?"

They rocked together on their lumpy bed until a sound came from up above: The first frightened whimper of a baby awakening alone in a strange place.

"Oh-oh," Jens whispered.

The whimper quickly turned to gusty bawling.

"Hey, Danny darling, Mommy's here!" There followed a less than graceful scuffle of lovers trying to disengage with the least amount of mess and the greatest amount of haste before their baby fell off the bed. "Look!" Lorna's head popped up as she made it to her knees. "Here's Mommy . . . and Daddy, too!" Jens popped up beside her, still tangled in clothing and struggling with things that made Lorna giggle.

Danny stopped crying and stared, his eyes still puffy from sleep, and a single tear caught on the lower lashes of each.

"Well, hi, darling boy. Did you think you were all alone? Oh, no, Mommy and Daddy would never leave you alone." Still kneeling, she leaned across the bed to kiss and comfort him. Danny, struggling to make sense of it, continued staring, first at her, then at Jens.

Jens leaned on his elbows and gave Danny's stockinged foot a kiss.

"Hello, little man," he said. "Sorry, but I was busy making you a brother."

Lorna whapped Jens on the arm. "Jens Harken!"

He raised his eyebrows and feigned innocence. "Well, I was, wasn't I?"

She laughed and told Danny, "You mustn't listen to everything your Daddy says. He's got an outrageous streak that'll do your tender ears little good."

Jens put one arm around Lorna's bare waist and slid her belly along the edge of the mattress till their bare hips bumped.

"Oh yeah? Who started this, you or me? You're the one who came courting. You're the one who wouldn't leave me alone. You're the one who showed up at the regatta today, bringing this child, and put him to sleep right on the bed, where he was bound to wake up and see what's been going on here on the floor."

She grinned smugly. "And you're mighty glad I did."

He returned her grin. "You bet I am."

For a moment they basked in happiness, then they each put an arm around their son's wet bottom and pulled him into their embrace.